THE
KNOWN WORLD
TRUSSAM
EMPIRE
NORTHERN
PROVINCE
LETHIARUM
SOUTHERN
PROVINCE

LEGEND
CAPITAL CITY
MINOR CITY
PORT CITY
NOTABLE LANDMARK
RAILWAY LINES
HEART FALLS
TARANOR
BELLS CROSSING
THE OBSIDIAN TOWER
SOLARIA
DRAGON RUINS

ISBN: 978-1-7387131-2-7

Cover design by: Sarah Benning
Chapter Heading and Section Breaks design by: Valerie Stokes
Map by: Racheal Ward of Cartographybird Maps
Font: Vollkorn Medium

Content Warnings

Parent Death
Death
War
Explicit Language
Witnessing Slavery
Non-Penetrative Sex Scene

This Book is written using Canadian/British English.

For those that need to be their own hero.

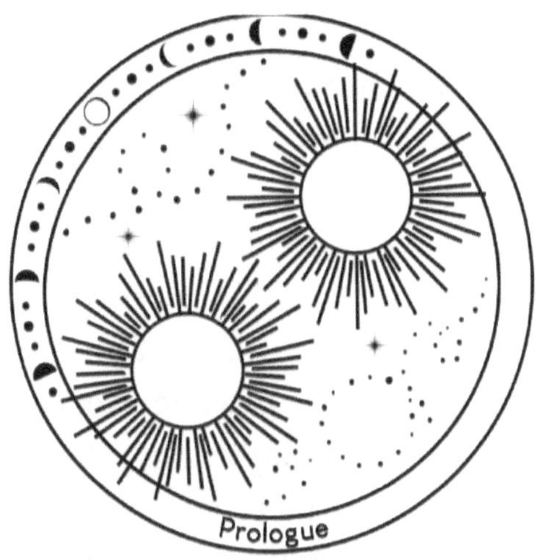

They were coming. *She* was coming.

Queen Serena ran through the Ivory Halls to the artifact room. Her most elite guards following her, keeping pace with her. She hadn't even had time to put on full armour, just a breast plate, and to change into enchanted leggings.

She had to stop them. If they took the Shard, everything would be over. The greatest weapon the world had kept separated and hidden would be one step closer to being put together.

Thank Arcanis Simon and Johanna had gone to the train crash. Thank Arcanis they weren't going to be here for this. They would be safe. It was bad enough Kira was upstairs. Kira, who she still hadn't found a cure for. Kira, who was still so young.

She slid to a halt in her silk slippers, right in front of the pedestal that held the shard. Her breaths even, but they felt jagged. It felt like she was inhaling glass.

Her gaze flew to the other set of doors that entered this space, as they burst open, broken. She had gotten here just in time. She took stance, a lifetime, however short it had been, of training her muscles to remember how to fight.

The figure prowled into the room, hood up and face shadowed.

Serena could see her eyes, one blue and cold like ice, and the other red and glinting. "Queen Serena…do you really think you can stop me where others have failed?" The voice was saccharine, sickly sweet.

Serena did not allow fear to take hold, she tilted her head at the figure instead. "I have to try." She replied, and with just the subtlest move of her body, her and all of her Elites charged.

It went quick, too quick. This intruder took each Elite out like they were nothing more than playthings. The laugh that emitted from the woman was awful. It chilled Serena right to the bone.

"Hand it over, and I'll let you live." The stranger said.

Serena knew it was a lie, that this being would not let anyone live in this room. "Never." She answered, and charged, sword raised.

She saw the black, corrupted blade protruding from her chest before she felt it. Before the rivers of blood started pouring out. Serena Maracroix, first of her name, staggered, fell to her knees, and then fell backwards. No, no no no no. She had failed.

She was never going to win. She had stood no chance. Her eyes started to fade in and out of darkness. She tracked the stranger walking to the pedestal with the shard, picking it up and joining it to the others. Her breathing was laboured, each breath felt like glass stabbing her in the chest.

With her last breath, her last thought, her last will, she sent a prayer to Arcanis, the Goddess of the Suns.

Arcanis, gift Johanna the strength to protect the world against the coming storms. Arcanis, let her know how much I loved her. Arcanis, tell them I'm sorry. Arcanis

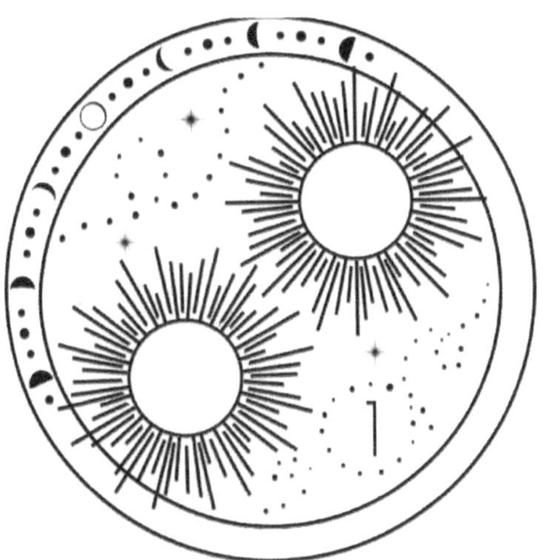

The Obsidian Tower of Solaria, the tallest structure in the world by far, a marvel of science and magic. Every other attempt to replicate it across the world had not come close or had catastrophically failed.

Built in the strangest of places, too. The centre of a vast desert, in the middle of the southern continent of Aethlier. Strange, to everyone who was not Solarian. Solarians knew that deep beneath the shifting sands there was water. So deep that it never reached the surface, but it could be accessed. Accessed, if you dug deep enough. Solarians knew that before the Fall of Dragons, the desert had been a jungle, a place teeming with life.

So, the Tower had been built here, in the epicenter of the once vibrant lands, to breathe life back where the lands had lost it. They had built here as a testament to their resilience. To show the rest of the world that against all odds, they would prevail.

I stood at the apex of this massive structure. The magical barrier that surrounded the platform slowed the freezing gale to barely a whisper. My bare feet trod along the rough stone to the edge, the railing stopping me from just walking off. It was still dark out, though to the horizon I could start to see the barest hints of light. The soft oranges and pinks of the rising suns. It was still cold up here, cold enough to raise bumps all along my arms and legs.

I had woken in a cold sweat almost an hour ago. Everyone was still asleep in the halls, even the servants. I also knew the only guards awake wouldn't be wandering inside the halls but posted at the only entrance. I had found myself once again climbing familiar cold metal steps and emerging through a door on the peak of the massive tower. The same thing I had done every day for the last 3 months. The same thing I would probably do every day for the rest of my life.

The ascension was tomorrow. No, not tomorrow, I recalled with a shiver not from cold but nerves, it was today. In less than 6 hours, I would be named Queen of Solaria. The recollection turned my stomach and left a bitter taste on my tongue. I had been raised for this moment from the day I had been born, just like Mother had been, and just like whatever children I eventually had would be. But that fact didn't change the reality.

My mother, Queen Serena. I could see her now, lying on the cold marble with the remnants of a black blade through her chest. It made me stagger, gripping the railing still moist with dew that felt too much like blood. It almost brought me to my knees. My mother, surrounded by a pool of her blood and lying in front of an empty pedestal that hadn't been empty before she had been murdered. It haunted me, haunted my dreams and thoughts, invading my mind at every turn. It kept me from sleeping, made me lose focus when I was in endless meeting after meeting about the state of the country, of details I would have to, need to remember. Names and people and policies and so much more. Things I needed to remember but would always forget.

I would never forget the feeling of blood under my shoes, the blood still wet in spots but half dried in others, so my shoes had stuck. I had already been dirty, bloody, from being down in the madness of the accident. But the blood from my mother had soaked through the leathers of my pants, making them cling to me all wrong. Blood on my hands I skidded on the tiles, collapsing beside her. Blood. So much blood. How her face had looked so wrong, her deep brown eyes open and lifeless, her mouth relaxed with no emotion, which wasn't like her at all. Mother had always been so full of life, of laughter and kindness and wit and determination. There had been the six bodies of her guards scattered around her, positioned almost in a circle, to protect her.

They had died for it. Their names were burned in my memory, too. Not because they failed, but because they shouldn't have died that night, either.

It was at that soul altering moment 3 months ago that I had gone from Princess to Queen. It was at that moment that I had lost my mother, my guiding light, my compass. It was that moment I had in all rights, become numb to the world around me. Nothing would be the same. The walls of my home would never have the sound of her laughter, would never feel her touch, for she often would run a hand along the wall, feeling the beating heart of the Tower below us. Never again would I hear the sound of her laughter. Her wisdom. Never again would I feel her touch. The crater left inside me was too large to bear, too deep to fill and hide. It sat there, impossible to ignore.

So, I became focused on only one thing - how to find and stop those who had killed not just my mom, but everyone that had died at their hand. So many had died at their hand. Not just Solarian's, but across the world. Lives snuffed out like small flames, many before they had really lived.

As the colours of the rising suns shot across the sky, I managed to bring myself back from the memories that plagued my mind. Managed to find things around me to ground my consciousness into the present. No matter how daunting and utterly impossible it felt.

My thick curly hair was wrapped in fine silk, and aside from that, I was almost invisible in the darkness up here, wrapped in a black cotton robe and my black nightdress underneath. The silk was the only thing that would stand out with a brightly coloured floral pattern. The same silk scarf Mother had worn to bed, just as I now did. Small, tiny things to keep her with me. It still smelled like her, though that was fading every day. I reached out, through the magical barrier that stopped the gale-force winds and relished, for a moment, that the stinging pain was present. This had become a routine now, waking up and climbing to the top of the tower, and shoving my hands out as far as I could into the winds. It was the only moment I felt human, that I really felt anything at all besides deep, burning anger and sorrow. The barrier prevented whole bodies going through - no one could jump from up here. But fingers? With enough fortitude, I could get them through.

I lost myself in thought again, that aching crater demanding attention. Demanding something to fill it, but I had nothing to offer it. Nothing. How had everything come to be? As the wind stung my fingers, making them so cold it almost burned, I was able to focus. Focus on what had all happened. Putting the pieces together, one by one, of a puzzle still incomplete and I had no idea how to finish. In one moment, the world had been in a relatively peaceful state. No open wars, though the countries and states continued to bicker, but trade progressed as normal. Sure, there had been small signals of what was to come, signals no one had seen until it had all started. A group calling themselves Nox had arrived, claiming the world was a scorn and it needed to be purged and cleansed. They had attacked various cities all over the world, killing thousands on the way. They traveled faster than seemingly possible, and the countries were struggling to keep up and catch them. Everywhere they touched, people died. Flames snuffed out.

Solaria had stood watching, the three giant, slightly oddly shaped pentagon black obsidian towers that slowly leaned into each other and then joined together as one near the top as a symbol of strength and unity, not prepared to aid in case we were the next target. Still a relatively small country, we needed to be sure we could protect ourselves before helping others. It wasn't like the other countries were doing differently - they were all scrambling to protect their own.

The prayers of being skipped over had been unheard. A normal day turned into disaster; one of Solaria's massive freight trains crashed, barreling right past the end of the line at the very centre of the city, and into the many buildings and people around it. That alone could have crippled my small country, but then the group had come for an artifact deep within the Ivory Halls. As my father, the King, and I had rushed down to aid those injured from the destruction, Mother and Sister had to stay with her guards in the Halls. It was too dangerous for three of the four royal family to be down below. It was dangerous for even my father and I to go down - but we had to respond. We had to help.

We had been sorting through the wreckage, directing the rescue effort and even pulling our people from the rubble. I remember the smell, the smell of burning wood and hot stone and burning flesh. The screams. Screams of pain, screams of sorrow, screams of grief.

All the while, a lone attacker had made their way up to the halls through back halls and staircases, killing everyone in their wake. Mother had heard of those falling to this intruder through the complex short-range radio the guards with her had, and she had gone running. Not away, but towards. To defend her home, defend the Halls, defend her youngest daughter, my sister, Princes Kira. She, with her guards, had done their best to defend against the attacker sent up to obtain an ancient artifact, completely unknown to her husband and eldest daughter. The Queen and her most loyal guards had ultimately lost.

Word of Queen Serena's death wouldn't reach Father and me for hours.

The country had been in mourning ever since, the King Consort had done his best to usher in my rightful position as Queen, while also having to bury his wife and keep the country moving forward.

Now it was my turn, and the only real emotion I could feel was rage and with it, the intense need for revenge. Revenge I could only take when I had been declared Queen, because I was still only a Princess, and everyone, for 6 more hours, still answered to Father. Resources I had been denied, over and over again, despite me demanding them until it felt like my throat was going to give out.

I was so tired of being told no. Of Father and the countless advisers and the General of the Army I was to lead telling me that chasing after those that had attacked our country, killed my citizens and my mother, their queen, was a fool's errand. That they would not strike twice, that Solaria had nothing left for them, and it was not Solaria's problem alone. That another country, a bigger one, could deal with it. Fools, I thought. They were all arrogant, placating fools and cowards.

I was no fool, and I was no coward. If Nox was promising destruction, after everything they had done so far? More was to come, for everyone. They would come back, and the next time even more would die. I knew it.

6 more hours, and I could finally, finally demand they listen to me.

I stood and watched the competing suns rise, far down below the industrial machines and trains moved like tiny ants, all wonders of technology but too far away for me to hear. Solaria, my country, the most advanced country in the world. Nearly every advancement had come from here - from trains and vehicles to the radio. Solaria always striving to become better, more efficient - qualities not every country was so quick to adapt to. Only two other countries had moved forward with rail construction. More had adopted Radio, if only out of desire to obtain information faster, and only the long-range radio, not the short-range communication that was networked into every part of the Tower and through Solaria.

I could barely see the speck of one train approaching from Solaria's Northern Neighbor, Taranor, and I knew another from the southern part of the country was mirroring it, probably full of people that would watch my ascension to the throne. None of that mattered at this moment, I could feel the warmth on my skin, and my eyes closed as I allowed myself to run through my plan again, and again, and again. I don't know how much time passed. All I allowed myself to feel was the warmth from the suns. I was startled when a familiar voice behind me spoke, dragging me back to the harsh reality that was my current life.

"Your Highness. I'm sorry to disturb you. It is time to start getting ready." It was one of my personal servants, Pendra. He had served each Monarch for generations, a drake familiar summoned a long time ago by one of my ancestors, Queen or King I could not remember, he was bound to the current or upcoming Monarch of the Maracroix family. While he could take the form of a Drake, most of the time he remained in a simple humanesque form, though he had a 4-foot tail that trailed behind him, and his blue-tinted skin made sure he stood out.

I sighed and nodded with a resigned look that his sharp gaze didn't miss. My staying up here would only delay the inevitable. My birthright, the throne. One that I desperately did not want, not right now. If I could pick, I would choose to have Mother back at every chance. I would trade my life for hers in every instant. She had been Queen for longer, sure, but she had been a natural at it. Natural in ways I would never be. I would never enjoy the meetings. I would never enjoy the snarky lords and ladies, always wanting more more more more, while people under them starved. Mother might not have enjoyed it, but she always knew how to pacify them, how to make those lords and ladies happy in ways I never would.

"Yes, very well." I agreed numbly, my tongue feeling thick in my mouth, and I followed him down the many steps back into the white marble-lined halls, improperly named the 'Ivory Halls' by the rest of the world, though the name had stuck. We headed to my room, still large, but not the standard Monarch Quarters. No, I had refused those, with vehemence, insisting that is where Father would remain until he chose to move out of the Halls. If he chose to move out of the halls at all.

Pendra assisted in getting my hair ready over any of my other hand maidens, refining each natural tight curl, and attaching very thin, fine strands of gold and platinum, some with small, coloured gems attached to different curls throughout my hair. This was a Solarian custom; the status of the person could be told by these strands of metal and gems weaved finely in their hair. Gold, Platinum, and rare gems such as diamonds, rubies, and emeralds were reserved for the Royal family. The more common the metal and gem, the lower class they were. Until then they wore nothing in their hair at all.

I wore no other jewelry and donned a floor-length dress in a rich purple, the silk bodice hugging my curves while the skirt fluffed out into gossamers and chiffon just above the hips. More gold and platinum were placed strategically along the bodice, providing extra support and highlighting the exquisite construction of the gown. It was exquisite, the design had been in the works since the week following Mother's death. Dozens of iterations, dozens of fittings and changes until finally it was this.

Personally, I hated wearing anything with a skirt. Pants were more my style - it made it easier to move in. I had tripped on too many skirts in my youth to appreciate them now. Now that I was Queen, I would have to wear a damn dress every day for the rest of my life. I was expected to. So many expectations, so many of them pointless. That was the first part of the plan, remove the expectations.

At least, until I abdicated at 60, the standard age for the Reigning Monarch to retire from the throne and let the next in line take over. It was even the standard for the Lords and Ladies. The elderly were not fit to rule - to set in their ways.

Innovation did not happen with old ideals.

I stood, staring at myself in the mirror. My perfectly done hair, the fine metal strands catching the light, my face covered with product, to hide a blemish that had appeared on my chin and to make my eyes seem bigger, to add a flush of colour to my cheeks, and to make my lips look fuller. Normally, I found herself just 'pretty', I did not think I was beautiful. Not like Mother had been. Mother, who barely needed kohl to line her eyes or a colour on her lips. With all the powders and creme's covering my face, I felt like a fraud, barely recognizing myself in the face staring back at me.

My fingers felt the soft, smooth fabric and I watched my reflection intently. "Now it just feels like she's really gone." I could not stop how solemn my voice sounded as it echoed through the room, and Pendra turned from tidying up the vanity. I observed him through the reflection of the mirror, noticing how sad and solemn he was as well.

"She would be very proud of you, Princess. She was always so very proud of you." He offered, his face kind. He didn't move closer to me, standing where he was. Through his years with the family, he had seen dozens of Monarchs pass, mostly to illness or old age, but only 3 had he seen die protecting the country. Queen Serena, King Malik and his eldest daughter, Queen Priscilla. Malik and Priscilla had both died during the war with Taranor over 300 years ago.

I straightened more, pulling my shoulders back and tilting my chin higher, fingers continued to glide across the material, "Well. I guess it is time to make my Country proud now, isn't it?" My voice was almost impossible to decipher, a cold mix of dread and sarcasm.

The throne room was 15 meters tall floor to ceiling, bordered with huge half pillars that were the same dark obsidian that the towers were made from. The rest was the clean, smooth white marble that gave the Ivory Halls their name.

There were only three steps up to the throne, which was carved from soft sandstone that had blue labradorite inlays that mimicked rivers and streams. A Solarian knew those labradorite inlays were a map of all the underground waterways that hid in the desert. It was well worn, from the many Kings and Queens that had previously sat on it. Two great black cats lifted their heads as the doors creaked open and I walked through. They weighed close to 90 kilograms each, their bodies sleek and muscular despite their lavish lifestyle. It was quiet in the room for now.

Hundreds would be packed into the Throne room within the hour to watch me say the same words as all the Monarchs before me, vowing to protect the land and people within it and all the inane formal things, and would congratulate me. Countries, Empires, and Monarchies from all over the world would be represented here. Great and Mighty Families would be in attendance, vying for favour from the new Queen of Solaria. Thousands of citizens would be waiting for the ceremony to start and finish, all the way down on the ground floor in the main square, for them to see their new Queen for the first time. A platform had been constructed along the track the elevator ran up, and I would take the elevator to it and step out and greet my country as their Queen.

Though, none of it mattered if the group that had led to my mother's demise was not stopped and destroyed. I was unable to do that until I had been named Queen.

I moved alone through the hall toward the throne, my feet felt unsteady beneath me. I felt like the whole world was shifting under me. Seeing that throne empty again, seeing it and knowing my mother was never going to sit there again? That gaping crater fissured into a chasm in my chest. The bright yellow-green eyes of the cats followed my every move, though not in a malicious or dangerous way. They rose, showing how lethal they truly were, ears going into sharp points, and both stretched, yawning at the same time before finally meeting me and pushing themselves up against me, a deep purr emerged from both. It grounded me, allowed me to focus not on what could have been but instead on what was.

The cats had been gifts when the Trussam Empire had allied with Solaria at the very beginning when both fledgling countries were finding their way in the world. Solaria's gift to the Empire had been a princess, to be married to their heir. Ever since the Trussam Empire and Solaria had been closely knit, their histories interweaving together so tightly it would be impossible to break. They were not, of course, the same cats that had been gifted centuries ago. But they were related.

The current Empress Yeska was my godmother and had been best friends with Mother. The moment the news had traveled to her of mothers' death, she had pledged 500 elite fighters to Solaria, to aid in the protection of the city, the Monarchy, and to find the group that had done the crime. And she had traveled for both the burial, and again for today, the Coronation of her goddaughter, of me.

I crouched in the damned dress, stroking the cat's heads, pressing my forehead to their own when they insisted on it. "Godmother, you cannot fool me. I know Tyshi is in my room, I left her there on the way down." I spoke quietly, but there was the unmistakable air of pride around me for sniffing out the ruse.

Suddenly the cat to the right shifted and changed to a tall and beautiful woman, with thick pitch-black hair and perfectly smooth olive skin. Despite her perfect appearance, I saw the wear of running an entire Empire on Yeska's face, the same intense pressure that I would soon face. As Yeska changed forms, I rose to a stand. As soon as she was back in her true form, I was enveloped in a hug that made my soul sing.

It felt like a hug my mother would have given me.

"I should know by now, shouldn't I? How smart you have always been. I've only managed to fool you twice." Yeska smiled, stepping back and holding me at arm's length, scanning me up and down with a faux critical eye. "You are so beautiful. You will be fighting off even more suitors, now that you are Queen." The smile was warm, kind and matronly, and for a moment I forgot about the brewing rage deep inside me at the bottom of that chasm. For a moment, I felt the same warmth I had always felt when my mother had smiled at me.

I took a deep breath, feigning a smile I had gotten very good at doing. "Well, I have no interest in taking a husband right now. I have a country to protect, and a war to fight, don't I?"

Yeska's hand cupped my cheek, thumb brushing the skin gently. "A heavy burden, for one so young. I am sorry you are faced with these troubles, dearest." She leaned forward, kissing my forehead before stepping back. She had watched me grow, through infrequent visits and more frequent letters and stories.

I had always loved her visits; she brought me gifts and trinkets and candies from her Empire. Her letters were always full of stories - of how beautiful her home was, of the birds and animals and people. She always wove the most intricate, wonderful tales for me, more like a fairytale than something that had actually happened.

She had been at mothers' side during mine and Katia's birth and had been one of the first to hold us. I wondered, for a second, if it was hard to see me now, fully grown and so full of grief and anger. If it was, she didn't show it.

"You will do well today and every day after. I know that. Now go along to your chamber, and soon you will ascend. The reason for you being Queen so quickly is sad indeed, but today is a day of happiness and celebration. Let's treat it so, before the hard work begins, yes?"

I nodded, that fake smile still on my face. I placed a kiss on Yeska's cheek, quickly, before hurrying off to the back chamber where I had to wait for the ceremony to start.

I stepped into the room, which was a simple long rectangle. It was bare of most furniture, with a simple set of plush chairs and a couch. It was the walls that were the most interesting, the last 20 Monarchs were shown in oil paintings, and at the very end wall normally the current Monarch was hung. Today, and every day since Mother had passed, it was empty. Sitting beside it, covered with a gold silk sheet, was a new painting that would be hung after the Coronation.

Slowly I moved back and forth, zigzagging across the room, saying hello to the Monarchs that had come and gone before me.

I meticulously greeted each one by name and said a small prayer to the God of Light, Arcanis. Eventually, I reached the oil painting of my mother. She looked radiant in the painting, dark curly hair cascading down over her shoulders, and flecks of real gold and platinum were scattered through the painting to give the illusion of the fine metal strands that adorned the Royal Family's hair. She had a smile on her face, which extended up to her rich brown eyes. Serena had always been so happy to be Queen - a stark contrast from me, her eldest daughter, whose oil painting held an unsmiling face, nearly a scowl.

The painter had pressed and pressed and pressed for a smile, but I had remained unsmiling and staring. I would not have my smiling face up on this wall, like taking the throne at my age was an accomplishment and not a tragedy.

For a long time, I didn't move from the spot in front of the painting. I reached out and brushed my fingers tenderly over the paint, trying to imagine the brush stroke texture was bringing Mother back to life. "Hi, Mom." I said softly, sadly. My voice almost cracked, and I willed it to stay even. "I wish you were still here. I don't know if I can be as brave as you were. You were always so strong in the face of adversity. Especially with Kira...She's gotten worse since you died. The doctors and scientists are furthering your work, but she's not responding to treatments as well." There was a long pause, and I wiped some tears from the corner of my eyes, fighting back all the bottled, pent-up anguish I had felt every day for three months. The looming fear that I might lose my little sister within a year of her mother, the fear I refused to acknowledge, but it lurked behind me. A shadow of death, waiting. "I have a war to fight, and I have to save her, too. But I...I don't know how Mom."

"You are stronger than you know. Find your strength in your family, both given and chosen. With them, you will not falter, you will not fail." A wise, feminine voice seemed to echo through the room, through my head. I startled, rising to a stand and swinging around to look behind me. Had I missed someone coming in? The stone normally echoed footsteps, but I hadn't heard anyone.

No, the room was still empty. I shook my head, dismissing it as the lack of sleep. That was the only logical conclusion. I did hear Pendra approaching, and I quickly dried my tears and smoothed my dress before he could see.

"Princess, it is time," Pendra said, holding his arm out to me and guiding me towards the front entrance of the Throne room which was now packed. I could hear them, even though the thick stone walls, the buzz of activity and murmured conversation. All these people, waiting to see me, Solaria's next Queen.

The next minutes were a blur as I walked up the long room to the stairs in front of the throne. The priest of the Temple to Arcanis was standing there in his full vestments and the 2-meter-tall staff where the top was a pair of blazing suns that even glowed due to clever enchantments folded into the metal when it was shaped.

Thankfully, the priest did not drone on and instead started the ceremony immediately. For that, at least, I was thankful.

"We are here today to watch Princess Johanna Maracroix, first of her name, ascend the throne of Solaria and be named Queen. Is there any in this room who have objections to her taking her rightful spot?"

Silence. Not even the whisper of fabric rustling could be heard.

The priest waited only a few breaths, which felt like a lifetime, before he nodded and continued, "Do you, Princess Johanna Maracroix, the first of her name, pledge under Arcanis's Suns and Osian's Moon that you will protect Solaria and all of its people to the best of your ability?" My gaze stayed on his, his pale blue eyes and wrinkled skin. He probably had been here; he had probably done the same thing with my mother.

"I do." The chasm inside my chest spread open, hungry.

"Do you pledge to uphold honour and graciousness when you represent Solaria and its people?"

"I do." I fought to keep my hands still, folded neatly in front of me. I wondered if I was clutching them too tightly, if my knuckles were going white. I couldn't look down to see. I focused on the pale blue eyes with wrinkled skin.

"And do you pledge to be fair and just in any matters that require your judgment?"

"I do." I didn't dare breathe. I knew what was coming next, the words that I had been dreading, hating, cursing for the past 3 months.

"Then with the power vested in me as a servant of Arcanis, I hail thee, Queen Johanna, first of her name."

I lowered onto one knee to allow the staff to be gently pressed against each of my shoulders. He placed a delicate circlet on my brow, defining me as the Queen and not just a member of the royal family. When I rose and turned around to the room full of people, I was Queen Johanna. Like a wave, they all knelt to show their respect to me. Respect given, not earned.

I would earn it. I would show them that despite them losing my Mother, I would make my country, my people, proud. I knew I had no other choice.

I slowly walked down the aisle, past all of those kneeling to me, and out, my gaze steeled ahead of me and only focusing on the wooden doors. Pendra swept me away as soon as I stepped through.

"Wonderful, Your Grace. You did perfectly." Pendra praised, but I could barely hear him over my thundering heart.

"Thank you, Pendra." I replied, looking up at him. "To the Gala, then?" A Gala, all the government leaders, the local lords and ladies, and various others that were invited will be there, all vying for my attention now. Frivolous, in my mind. I wanted to get straight to work. I would have rathered a meeting with the General right now to discuss what information had been gathered about the group that had attacked my city, my home, and solidify my plan for the future.

"Yes, Your Grace. They are all eager to meet the new Queen. Such is your future now, Your Grace." Pendra said, holding his arm out for me to take. The smile tugging at the corners of his lips was one of pride. "Let us go get you changed to something far grander, hmm?"

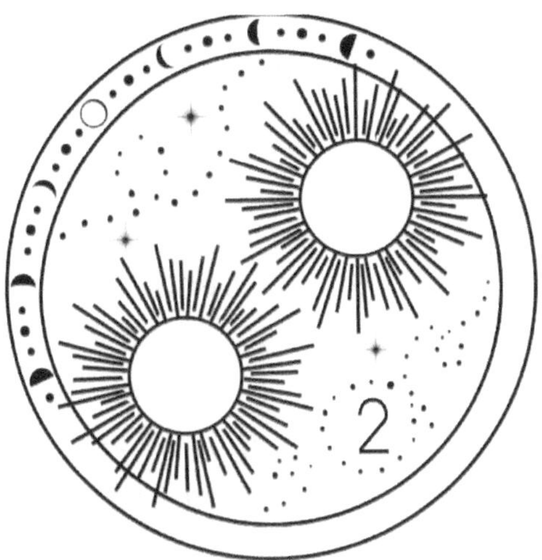

"Announcing Queen Johanna, first of her name!" The doors opened, revealing the full ballroom with the soaring ceilings, enchanted lights, and candles that floated through the room.

My gaze wandered around, I allowed myself to marvel a bit. Truthfully, I hadn't seen the grand ballroom like this, fully decorated and full of people and music and even the smell of food. All the previous functions we had had in the Halls were in the smaller rooms. Not this one.

My hands remained folded in front of me as I walked around. Keeping them this way prevented me from fidgeting with my skirt. Pendra always stayed a few feet behind me, moving with me through the crowd like a shadow, leaning forward to whisper names and facts into my ear as needed. Hands were shaken, polite smiles exchanged, and pleasantries said.

But it was the sight of a face I hadn't seen in so long that made me stop, inhaling sharply in surprise. I moved forward like I was dreaming and instead of a handshake, I was enveloped in a hug. "Oh, Veronica." I murmured to the older woman, and I knew my voice had cracked.

The hug broke too soon. I wish it had lasted longer. The ivory-skinned woman with her pitch-black hair that was pulled back into a neat bun looked me over. "Hello, Your Grace." She replied gently with a sad smile that extended up to her blue eyes. "I'm so sorry we couldn't make it to your mother's funeral."

Veronica Heart, Matriarch to the Heart Family outside of the country directly to the north, Taranor. She had been close friends with Serena, and I had spent a year living with her to learn Taranor politics and laws for me to be better versed with dealing with Taranor. Like Yeska, she was family.

"We? Is..." My hopeful words trailed off and her question was answered by the next person who spoke.

"Hey Queen Johanna." It was almost mocking, and I felt myself genuinely smile for the first time since my mother had died, turning and pulling the other young woman in.

"Dedria!" I exclaimed, my voice cracking in emotion again, and the empty ache in my chest dulled. "Oh, you made it?!" I didn't want to let go, worried that if I did, Dedria would disappear. I hadn't heard from Dedria since before the attack, all the letters I had sent had been unanswered. The past four months had been so isolating, but Dedria being here right now made me forget about that. Dedria, my best friend, who knew me almost as well as I knew myself. We had grown up together, letters sent back and forth, political functions attended together, and while I had spent a year in Taranor with the Hearts, the year before Dedria had been a ward in Solaria under the monarchy.

"Arcanis above and Osian below, let me go!" Dedria laughed, and it was the most magical sound as she pushed me off. She was practically a clone of her mother, just younger. The same pale skin, black hair and vibrant blue eyes. They were even dressed similarly - both had opted out of a formal gown, and instead Veronica was wearing her military dress from Taranor. Even though she hadn't served since her husband had died. Dedria was in pressed black pants and a beautiful silk blouse. Not nearly as dressy as everyone else in this room, but that was Dedria's style. "Yeah yeah, I'm here. Obviously." She visibly rolled her eyes, a smile on her lips.

Laughter bubbled through me, and even Pendra couldn't mask his shock at the sound. It was so bright, full of joy for the first time in months. I didn't know when I would feel this again, so I didn't stop it. I relented my grip, letting Dedria go. "This made the whole day so, so much better." I admitted.

Veronica chuckled, "I am glad." She said, "I hate to speak business today, but I have a feeling I know your next steps, and with that I know you will need continued combat training to be prepared for the trials ahead of you. As such, I would like to volunteer the combat instructor that has been teaching Dedria. However, Dedria needs continued training as well. Would she be able to stay in the Ivory Halls as your ward?" Veronica's tone was thinly veiled amusement, trying to disguise it with a tone of not wanting to impose. I knew both were fake, Veronica was just trying to bring my best friend back to me in a time when I so desperately needed her.

"You know me too well, Auntie. Of course, she can stay here. Thank you for your generosity of offering the instructor." I replied, and I felt more of the weight that had been on my heart lift away. I knew it was temporary, but I relished the feeling. In the feeling of the unending grief disappear.

Dedria winked to her mother, "I told you it wouldn't be a problem." she teased.

"You know I have to follow the rules and procedures, Dedria." The older woman replied, and then clapped her hands. "Very well! I will arrange for Dedria's things to be sent down, there is no point for her to return home with me."

Pendra nodded, "Of course, Lady Heart. I will arrange for her room to be prepared." He chimed in, "Ah, Your Grace, Lord Gustaf is approaching with his eldest son, Sir Delain. I believe from the look on Delain's face, he will want a dance."

I gave a bit of a pained sigh, nodding reluctantly. I didn't want to leave Veronica or Dedria so soon. Functions like these, so full of people, I probably wouldn't get a chance to speak with them again. But I made a promise anyways, "I will catch up with both of you later." I squeezed Veronica and Dedria's hands and turned to deal with the Lord of one of the southern territories of Solaria. I knew his territory, and his manse well. Delain was close to my age, so just like Dedria, we saw each other frequently.

"Lord Gustaf, so nice to see you again. And you as well, Sir Delain." I said with that perfect feigned smile that never reached my eyes, shaking their hands.

Delain was two years my senior and was taller than me by a head at least. His dark hair had thin strands of gold and silver that matched what his father had, which were appropriate for their political standing. His hazel eyes took in the sight of me, and I couldn't help but straighten more under the weight of his gaze. He smiled, unlike mine his was genuine, a few of his teeth were crooked but that didn't detract from his looks. If anything, it gave him a more rugged, handsome appearance. He held his hand out with a bow, "May I be honoured with a dance, Your Grace?" He asked - his voice was smooth and quite pleasant to listen to, I had always thought so.

"You would like to have the honour of joining me for my very first dance as Queen?" I countered with one corner of my mouth curling up in a smirk, one brow raising as I waited for his response.

He smiled fully at that, "Only if she finds me worthy." To his, and everyone else's, surprise, I took his hand and looked to the dance floor.

"Let us go, then."

We were no strangers to each other; we had been at Galas and functions multiple times together over the years. Flirtatious words, sly smiles, and many dances exchanged, most had been sure that the two of us would have started officially courting within the year if the attack hadn't happened. So many had whispered that we made quite a beautiful couple.

As we started to dance, all eyes on us, he spoke quietly to me. "I'm sorry about your mom." He said, I had heard it at my mother's funeral, too.

"I'm going to find the people that did it. I'm going to bring them to justice." I replied, and my tone was full of fire and determination. It was not a matter of if to me, it was a matter of when. A promise for the future.

"I know, and I do not pity those that did it. You are not one to be messed with, remember when I accidentally took the last slice of your favourite cake at the wedding in the Crossing? Baron Tetbald? The look you gave me, you were furious. I thought you were going to light me on fire." He said with that charming smile, and without knowing it, he eased me out of that tunnel vision of rage he knew I had entered, "You know I'm here to help if you need me."

"I was very cross; you knew it was my favourite type and you still took it...and I know you're here to help. I just don't know how you can yet." I was avoiding looking up to him, something about Delain made me feel soft and weak. I hated feeling soft and weak, especially for the past few months.

"Maybe I took the slice of cake because I wanted your attention, Your Grace." He mused now and he winked down to me. "That's all I've ever wanted, really."

My heart started to race, and I swore to myself as my palms started to sweat. At the same time, the chasm in my chest fractured in a whole different direction. My mother dying didn't just mean grieving her - it meant grieving a future I would never have. I had accepted that, come to terms with it even if I hated that reality too. But that wound was still fresh, so easy to reopen. It was made worse when Delain did it so easily, when I had sent him a letter about how the expected courtship would have to be delayed. How I would not be able to focus on it, on him. Not with everything that had happened, not with my grief, not with having to be Queen now. My gaze flicked up to his face with unmasked confusion that I knew was clear to him. "Delain, don't. I just ascended the throne...We're not kids anymore. I have a country full of people that I need to protect. I have told you this..."

Others had started to join in around us, but Delain continued to guide us around the floor effortlessly. "That letter you sent me...I know we're not kids anymore. That's the point. But would

[32]

it be so bad, the two of us?"

"In a different time? No. But right now, yes. I need to run this country, find the people that murdered my mother during the attack, and throw in courting at the same time? Absolutely not." I tried to remain calm, keeping my voice soft, my lips barely moving to ensure the many eyes on us didn't see my distress. I knew Delain could see it.

"I could be your King. I could help you, Johanna. Let me carry some of your burden." I noted how soft, desperate he sounded. I hated it. Hated how it made him sound weak, when he was trying to convince me that he was strong.

"If you have any respect for me at all...If you like me at all, you will drop this discussion right now." My voice wasn't firm, it was pleading. I hated that, too. Then, by the grace of Arcanis, the song ended, and we separated, Delain bowing, and I gave a slight curtsy as the crowd clapped for us.

I had a feeling this conversation was not done, and Delain looked to ask me for another dance. Arcanis seemed to smile on me, as my father approached next. Or maybe it was just my father's intuition. The Dowager King had married my mother, the then Princess and next in line to the Solarian throne. King Simon, beloved by all but none more so than me and my sister. "May I have a dance with my daughter?" He asked Delain, but the way he said it made it clear it was not a question. Even if Delain had wanted to deny him, denying the Dowager King a dance with his daughter? Social taboo, I knew it, my father knew it, and everyone around us knew it. He was forced to nod and step away. I felt my body release some tension I didn't know I had been holding.

"Hi, Dad." I said gently, and he took my hand and started to guide me into a dance. Relief flooded me, so grateful for my father in this moment.

"Hey, kiddo. I'm sorry I haven't spoken to you today. Kira has been trying to get into everything." He replied with a smile, "You are doing wonderful. I'm so proud."

"Where is Kira now?" I inquired, glancing around a bit as we continued to dance.

"I left her with her handmaiden, Nova." Replied Simon, nodding a bit towards where Nova and the little Princess were. Nova had the same dark skin as most citizens of Solaria, with her black hair in dozens of tiny braids which were pulled back out of the way. She seemed to be trying to convince Kira of something or other.

Kira Maracroix looked sickly even from so far away, with dark bags under her eyes and an almost grey tinge to her skin. She was supporting herself with her cane as well, but the smile on her face and the playful look in her eye made most forget how sick she truly was. They called what affected the little Princess 'The Rot', a terrible illness that first destroyed the immune system, and then started to attack organs. Before the mother had died, she had been furiously researching a cure for Kira and every other sufferer of it. The doctors were sure that was the only reason Kira had survived to see her 10th birthday.

Now it was up to those same doctors and researchers to continue that work and save the little Princess from a long and painful death, under my guidance. Add that to the ongoing list of things I could not fail at.

"She looks happy today." I finally said, breaking the solemn silence between us.

"Her big sister has ascended the throne and the biggest ball she has ever seen within these halls is happening. Of course, she's happy."

Kira's bright, rich laugh resonated through the room. It seemed to cut through the buzz of the crowd right to me. It had been a long time since I had heard my little sister laugh like that. I had lost sight of Kira, so I had no idea what was causing the sound. I wish I did, so maybe I could recreate it in the quiet moment we had together, even if those would be fleetingly short moving forward.

However, it didn't take me long to find out the source. Kira scaled the steps of the platform where the orchestra was, looking out over the crowd of people. "I would like to make an announcement!" Came her voice, amplified by the enchantment on the stage meant to make the instruments more easily heard.

"Oh no." Dad and I said together, both stopping and looking at the Princess in a state of shock. The rest of the room quieted quickly, giving Kira the respect she deserved.

"I just," Kira paused, coughing into a handkerchief before she could continue, "Sorry! Sorry sorry! Excuse me. I just want to say that my big sister Johanna is gonna be the bestest Queen of Solaria. I know my Momma was super-duper amazing, but I know Johanna is gonna do the best job ever." She had that same big grin on her face. "Okay, that's all! Thank you, bye-bye!" She said, moving far faster than anyone would have thought possible with a cane as she darted off the stage and away from Nova who had finally caught up to her.

Dad's face was a slight grimace through Kira's speech, trying to be that figure of imposing sternness, but he finally broke, smiling and laughing. "She's always been one to forge her own path, your sister." He told me, and I couldn't help but smile and chuckle along. He gave me a bow before moving to help handle the little Princess, and the crowd parted for him. He didn't have to nudge anyone aside where he went.

Before anyone else could get a dance in with me, Pendra moved up behind me now as silent as a shadow. "Your Grace," He said quietly, "I'm so sorry, but...there is a sudden visitor, and they are insisting on seeing you..."

I turned to him, a slight tilt to my head. "I don't understand. Isn't everyone of importance here?"

"Well...technically no. The Spirit-Bonded people initially declined, and the King of Lethiarum declined as well. Among several other Dukes, Duchesses, Princes and Princesses of other countries." He looked like he was about to list them off, but I lifted my hand to stop him.

"Okay. I get it." I replied, a sigh on my lips, "Let us go then." Quickly, the two of us headed off back to the throne room. Wherever I went, people parted for me, too.

I ran my hand over the throne, the soft sandstone warm to the touch even if the room felt chilled. Sitting down on it and looking to the door, I gave a subtle nod to the guards to allow the guest in.

The large double doors swung open, and it was not just one person, but a dozen. My curiosity spiked, I couldn't help it, and with that I sat a little straighter. Though the one walking in front of them all was not a person I ever thought I would meet. Nine huge, fluffy black and white tails flared out behind her, with two large, fluffy and sharply pointed ears on the top of her head that were also black and white. She was not adorned in fine silk or chiffon, but vibrant, colourful cotton and wool. Her skin reminded me more of the sun shining through tree leaves, with pale skin spots of all shapes and sizes contrasting the dark, olive tanned skin on every visible part of her body. She was strong, there was no mistake about that. Her hands were used to build, hunt, fight and protect. She barely gave a bow once she reached a spot about 10 feet from the steps leading to the Throne. "Queen Johanna." She said, and that is where I stopped understanding her. She continued in her native tongue for quite some time, and then one of the others, one who had a long feline tail and cat ears, spoke. Her accent was thick, but I still understood her with a little effort.

"I am Setsuna of the Plains, Alpha of the...ah, the best words I have for in your tongue is the Bright Moon Tribe. Too long my people have been ignored on a global scale and I have had enough. No longer will the Spirit Ascended be brushed off like we are nothing. I understand we declined your invitation for your ascension to the throne, but I believe that to have been a grave mistake of the Alpha's of the other tribes. I present myself and my nine finest warriors to you, as a representation of my people."

I listened quietly, still marveling that this group had traveled such a far distance for me. Over two seas and another continent. Such an incredible distance, and incredibly dangerous. I took stock of each person with her, besides Setsuna, and her translator, 10 others were with her. 9 obvious warriors, hunters just like Setsuna. Men and women, it didn't seem to matter. All strong, muscles well defined, all so serious looking. There was one smaller, slightly mouse-y looking one, who was carrying some parchment and was using magic to record things.

"Setsuna of the Plains, I thank you for your journey here." I said, confident the confusion that was running through me wasn't in my tone, "it is my utmost pleasure to meet you, and your warriors. May I ask, what can Solaria do for you?"

It took a moment for my words to be translated, and then Setsuna's response to be translated back. "I would like to request that three of my people stay here to represent us in all global matters and trade. If you agree, I will also stay to teach you how to Water Dance as I was taught by my mother, Kayori Ten-Tails." I paid close attention to their native tongue, how different reflections in my own words were used, and how Setsuna's tone sounded.

Kayori Ten-Tails, a Kitsune woman who had barricaded herself and her children away from the world on a small island that was called 'The Grotto'. Instead of the nine tails that Kitsune's were known for, she had ten. Nine were perfectly snow-white, and one that was black as the night. To date, no one had lived to meet her - except for Setsuna who had left the island many years ago and had found the lands of the Spirit Ascended people. Rumour was, she was a half breed, not a true Kitsune, and not a Spirit Ascended. But she would never confirm that if asked.

Kitsune's were different from the Spirit Ascended entirely, though incredibly rare. Kayori and her Grotto were the only really known location of a group of Kitsune's, the few others scattered through the world. Much like the Ascended, they had a secondary form, but they preferred their humanoid one, much like Setsuna was in. So little was known about Kitsune's, so little was known about Kayori, outside of her legendary fighting style that many heroes of old had known because Kayori had taught them, before she had closed that island and killed anyone who tried to go there.

I couldn't help but pause, scanning this woman over intently. What she was offering? It hadn't been offered in a century. Maybe more. Once someone had learned the Dance, they were forbidden from teaching it to anyone else without Kayori's approval.

What Setsuna was offering was going against her own mother.

I kept my voice measured when I spoke, "And why would you do that?"

One of Setsuna's ears flicked a bit before panning to her right, where the translator was. "Because the people that attacked your country have kidnapped my Mate. And I need you to help me get him back.

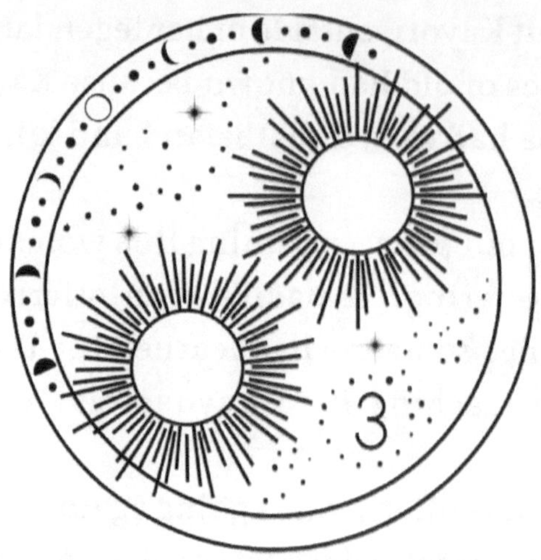

3

The training hall rang with the sound of metal on metal, and the occasional grunt of pain if the practice blade struck.

"Stop." Setsuna snapped out in her accented, sharp tone. Her tails were coiled all together as one. The translator continued, her voice layering over Setsuna's in a way I had come accustomed to hearing. "Queen Johanna, you are too defensive. Dedria you are too offensive. Both have their faults. Dedria, you defend. Queen Johanna, attack." Setsuna was circling around us as Dedria, and I sparred.

I heaved a sigh, just nodding and lifting my practice sword and moving forward to attack Dedria now. It was harder than I thought it would be - Setsuna would have had us practice 12 hours a day if she had her way. Even so, we were still practicing 6 to 8 hours a day, oftentimes starting before dawn and finishing long after the suns had set. The breaks between were just filled with royal duties. Setsuna had only been here for a week, and it was thoroughly exhausting. I had trained every day for years, for at least two hours at a time. But that felt so easy compared to this; I went to bed every night sore and for the first time since

Mom had passed, I slept soundly with no dreams. Dad had joked, more than once, that my bones were tired.

As Dedria brought down her practice blade towards my shoulder, an ethereal, but familiar voice sounded in my head, "Bring your blade up." Then it was like my arm moved of its own free will, blocking the blade easily. The voice was clear, confident, and feminine. "Forward, push her back." Feet moved forward, pushing Dedria back a few steps. "And...twist..." In a flourish, Dedria's blade went scattering across the floor. I stared, alarmed at what I had just done. I had not felt in control then, at all. It was unnerving, near scary, to lose total control of your muscles but to keep moving.

"Wow! Uh, that was cool, Johanna." Dedria said with a bit of a laugh, going to grab the blade. Completely oblivious to my panic.

"...Did anyone else hear that?" I asked as I looked around anxiously.

"Hear what?" Dedria inquired, going to grab a much-needed drink of water in the quick break.

I kept looking around, trying to find the source of that voice. I had heard it the day of my ascension to the throne. "That voice. That was telling me what to do."

"...Uh, there was no voice..." Dedria frowned. "You okay? Not sleeping well? Do you need a break?"

"Yeah...uh. A break sounds good." I reluctantly agreed, stepping away to have a moment to myself. My mind was going a mile a minute; who was that? What was that voice? I shook my head, taking a drink of water before heading back. I shoved what I had heard aside, it had to just be my mind playing tricks on me again. Sure, I had gotten better sleep the past week, but that didn't make up for the months of wretched sleep I had lived through since Mom had died. Sure, I had heard that voice before, the day of my ascension to the throne, but not since. Was I really sleeping as well as I thought? I'd have to ask Pendra to post a guard outside my bedroom, to ensure I wasn't sleepwalking or something foolish like that. "Okay, sorry, we can continue."

The translator, who I had come to know as Tianie, listened to Setsuna before nodding and looking at Dedria and me. "We move to magic now." She said, "She would like the two of you across from each other and exchange concussive wind spells to start."

Dedria looked over to me, one corner of her mouth lifting in a smirk, "That's like, first-grader stuff..." She muttered so only I could hear.

"Yeah, but do you want to tell her that? I don't." I replied just as quietly, like we were back in Heart Falls with a private teacher, and we were whispering childish things to each other. A pang in my chest, at the memories I was flooded with. I was overwhelmed with gratitude that I had Dedria here now. A sense of familiarity in so much unknown.

I to one side of the room as Dedria relented and moved to the other.

I harnessed some magic, just enough to create a swirling and concentrated sphere of pure wind before throwing it at Dedria, who then cast her own magic out like a net, catching the sphere and throwing it back like a ball. It was very basic, something young children learned very early on in their magical training. It taught control, discipline, and precision. After air came light, and then various defensive spells. At least, until their Magical

Aspect formed. If their Aspect formed.

There were a handful of major Aspects where the demand for Magical Guilds had been high enough to teach the users. The most notable were Enchanters, who strictly focused on adding enhancements to rooms or inanimate objects. Without enchanters, the Obsidian Tower wouldn't exist today. They were the reason it stood. The Enchanter's Guild was across the sea to the west, in a small but centrally located country called Triskal.

Summoners were next, they used complex symbols they drew with their magic to summon various beasts and creatures. Often these things could only be summoned once, but if they were exceptionally skilled, they could create a pact with one of these things and it allowed them to keep them summoned almost all the time. Pendra had been such a summon, at least, we think. His binding just shifted to the next Monarch.

After that, it was more job-specific guilds, Healers and Doctors, Builders, Law and Combat, Teachers. These guilds not only trained their students the magic specific to that career, while also giving them the necessary education to succeed as well. Most countries had their own set of career guilds, ensuring the citizens never had to leave to receive education.

Then, there were the rarer Aspects. Telepaths, who did not have that inner source of mana to draw from. They were unable to cast traditional spells that required mana. Instead, they were able to alter objects around them with their mind, able to read minds, cast their thoughts to all beings around them, and alter a person's body with just a finger. Out of all the aspects, Telepaths were arguably the most dangerous. Only a Telepath could truly fight another Telepath, as all a well-trained Telepath had to do was look at someone and they could break bones and stop hearts. They were also the most unheard of - if they existed, other countries kept them hidden and protected, seeking to use them more as a weapon than anything else.

Greenseers were after, magi with innate abilities to work with all types of flora and were able to craft something so poisonous it could take out a whole platoon of soldiers from a mere flower. One of the Tower's researchers was named Tyne, and she was a Greenseer. Mom had sought her out to help with the cure for Kira and had given the brilliant scientist more responsibility as time had gone on. Now she was one of the top researcher and development leaders, all while continuing work on the Cure.

Then came the Shifters, like the Trussams, with the ability to shift their physical form any way, even to take the form of something else if they knew the physiology well enough.

Finally, Chronomancers, most famously from the Heart line, including Veronica and Dedria. They were able to manipulate time and space, to an extent. They also had exceptionally long-life spans - up to a thousand years, though most never made it past two hundred for various reasons.

These rarer Aspect holders were considered highly dangerous in most other countries, where they were carefully monitored by the government or even forced to wear mana suppressors that prevented them from using magic, or worse, they were heavily drugged to complacency. Solaria was not such a country - it had been founded on magical freedom. As such, it had become a sort of 'magical haven' for people with these rarer aspects.

Time droned on as Dedria and I kept tossing this wind sphere back and forth. "Stop," Setsuna called out, switching back to her native tongue. Then, Tianie spoke after Setsuna had stopped. "She wants you to start hand-to-hand combat but using spells with each blow. Only wind or light for now."

I shrugged, grabbing some sparring gloves and tossing a pair to Dedria before she moved forward to be about five feet from me. "Let's do this then?" I said with a smile that I hoped looked genuine. As we started to exchange blows, the sound of padded leather on their training outfits starting to fill the room. Dedria cast a light spell, aiming her fist toward my side, that strange, ethereal voice triggered again. "Back!"

But this time, instead of stepping back or to the side to avoid it, I suddenly found myself 10 feet away, and Dedria stared at me with a slack jaw, and a concerned look in her eyes. I didn't like that look; Dedria never looked that concerned.

"Wh...what happened?" I asked, thoroughly confused as I looked from my friend to Setsuna and Tianie and back again. The Kitsune and Ascended both just stared at me as they leaned towards each other, muttering. Their lips barely moving, but I noticed them all the same. Unease was building in my gut. Something was wrong.

"You just used Chronomancy, Johanna," Dedria replied, her tone very concerned now. "Did you know that you were a Chronomancer?" I didn't believe her, I wasn't a Chronomancer. I was well past the age where Aspects normally presented. Normally. Outliers, was I an outlier?

"What? No. Of course I didn't know. How would I know? Solaria does not do the testing like Taranor does. We wait until the Aspects shows itself here." My tone was sharper than I intended, because I didn't believe her.

"Hm...I forgot about that...Fuck you, by the way. I knew I had

Chronomancy at ten. Mom started training me the moment..." Dedria trailed off at the absolutely unimpressed expression I was giving her, and she waved her hand. "Whatever! Anyways..." She frowned, clicking her tongue, "I will have to send a message to Mother about this, though we still don't have radio in the Falls...whatever. We'll figure that out. I can teach you, but she should really know. She is more qualified than I am in that department."

"Hold on, how can you be sure I am one?" I pressed now, looking a bit more frantic. "Maybe you just hit me really hard? Or maybe you used Chronomancy to jump back from me."

Dedria sighed; her concern being replaced by annoyance. "Setsuna, Tianie, what did you see?"

Tianie didn't even give Setsuna a chance to speak, answering herself. "The Queen moved from in front of you, to right there. I did not see anything else, she just...moved."

"Mhm. Thank you, Tianie. See, Johanna?" She sounded so self satisfying, I almost wanted to slap her. "You can't do that unless you're a Chronomancer. You must have felt threatened or something, and your instincts made you create a jump, allowing you to step back to where you are now. Basically...a tunnel from point A to point B, but it's incredibly short. So, you can move from spot to spot very quickly...Watch me." Dedria then demonstrated, and in a blink of an eye had moved from where she had been, to 5 feet to my immediate right. I was used to those things from my year in Heart Falls, but it didn't annoy me any less.

"I just don't understand...how could I be a Chronomancer? It's mostly genetic, and that's why only your family were

Chronomancers."

"C'mon, use that brilliant brain of yours. Anyone can be a Chronomancer, just like anyone could be a telepath or shifter or enchanter or whatever. You know this. It just depends on what their aspect develops into. You just won the lottery, so to speak."

As much as it annoyed me, her talking to me like a child, I knew she was right. Still, it didn't make it any easier. Hadn't I faced enough life changing things recently? Why did my aspect have to develop now?

I begrudgingly recalled several statistics Solaria had about how most aspects developed when the person was under duress. Something about how a stressful event would trigger the aspect to manifest as a defense mechanism. Was that really what had happened to me? I hadn't been in any actual danger - I was wearing enchanted Wyvern leathers that meant any hit I barely felt, forget about doing any damage.

I felt unstable on my own legs as I remembered exactly how it had happened, Dedria's fist going right for my ribs, and that voice screaming in my mind, 'Back!'

I didn't let the panic manifest on my features, even if my blood thrummed with it. I instinctively went to problem solving mode, it was what I had been trained for years to do. "What now?"

"You start to train. And think of it this way, Johanna...Whoever killed your mom? They probably aren't Chronomancers. I mean, statistically, the chance of them being Chronomancers would be..." She trailed off as I stared at her blankly again, and she shot me the biggest shit eating grin. "Gotcha. Anyways, there's a reason Taranor has a long and dirty history with Chronomancers, and the guild was disbanded. After they used the Chronomancers in the Long War against

Solaria, forcing them to be nothing more than killing machines, going as far as emotionally, mentally, and physically abusing each Chronomancer to get their way. Erasing their empathy and moral compass through the disgusting training habits so they would execute orders no questions asked? Yeah. You being a Chronomancer lets you fight these people way better than before. But you must train and master your skills first. It's not gonna be easy. I'm not even a Master, and I've been working on it for like 9 years, y'know?"

I did know. Dedria had shared so much of the training she had gone through with Veronica. Mostly about how brutal and unforgiving it was, and how Veronica always drilled into my best friend that anything less than perfection could mean Dedria's execution.

Taranor was unforgiving when it came to powerful magic wielders and believing them to be threats.

Tianie was talking with Setsuna again, the two of them talking quickly back and forth in more hushed tones. Despite being focused on Dedria, I knew they were talking. Finally, the cat-eared woman spoke up, "Setsuna says we will break for the day. She needs to reformulate her training plan going forward, as your new powers complicate things."

Dedria and I nodded in unison, and part of me wondered if we looked like two different sides of the same coin. Dedria couldn't look happier - her best friend, me, was a Chronomancer, exactly like her? Me, meanwhile, well I just hoped that my frustration and annoyance over this development wasn't showing. I was hoping that my years of training to be perfectly calm and collected in pressure was pulling off.

"Very well." I relented, "C'mon Dee, let's go." I didn't hesitate to start straight to the changing room to shower and get changed.

Dedria practically flounced behind me as she caught up. "Hey! C'mon lady, you seem so down over this. What's wrong?" She sounded so happy, and I was trying to figure out why.

"I spent a whole year living with you and your Mom. I haven't the slightest clue about Chronomancy. I barely even know it's history...not to mention everything else about it." A minor lie - I knew enough about the Chronomancer history and how it led to the massive mana crystals outside of the tower. Crystals so potent in mana that it was toxic without the right protections. Toxic enough to kill.

Truthfully didn't want to talk about the voice in my head, I knew Dedria would believe me, she always did. But she would mock me for hearing voices first, and besides, it would make this all so much more complicated. I decided I just wasn't sleeping enough. That's all. I refused to accept any other option.

Realistically, I also didn't want the Council to hear I was hallucinating voices, it would give them reason to remove me from the throne and put my father back there until, if a small part of me whispered, Kira became of age.

"Well, duh. You can't know the technicalities of it if it didn't manifest as your Aspect until now. None of it would make sense."

"I guess. I just wish I knew more; you know? I'm not the type that gets thrown into things totally blindsided, but this seems to be happening more often lately..."

"Oh, Johanna..." Her voice was one of pity, and I pushed down the instinctive reaction of anger over it. "I get it. It's been a tough couple of months. But it's only up from here, promise. We're gonna get you trained up, and we're going to find these terrorists and show them what it means when you mess with the Maracroix and Heart families." Dedria's elbow nudged my side encouragingly, and she smiled over to me.

I nodded a bit, that fire starting to rage inside again. "Yeah! Yeah, you're right. This is a gift; I'm going to do great things with it." I agreed forcefully, standing a bit taller. I had to fake it, had to fake the confidence and courage until I really found it. I didn't know if Dedria would buy it, but I didn't give her an opportunity to question me. "Well, let's go get that message written to your mom. I'll arrange for one of the fastest couriers based in Taranor's capital to bring it to her and bring her response back."

As the two of us walked through the halls and headed to my main office, Pendra joined us, bowing to me. "Hello, Your Grace. Lady Heart." He said, "Are you done with your training session early today?"

"If by 'done', you mean it was canceled because it turns out I'm a Chronomancer, then yes" I explained, reigning in a defeated sigh before it escaped my chest, "We're taking a break for the rest of the day to work out training going forward."

"Oh! Your Grace, your aspect has manifested! That is cause for celebration, truly. To ascend the throne and manifest your aspect within the same month, that is a blessing of Arcanis." Pendra smiled to me, and I had a feeling he was trying to do what Dedria had done - give me something to feel good about. Even if I didn't feel good about it. "If that's the case, I do hate to be the bearer of bad news, but if you are now free, you have some Royal Duties you can attend to today earlier. If you finish them ahead of schedule, you could have the evening off."

I suppress a groan. Of course he knew to bribe me with an evening off. Pendra was practically an Army General when it came to making sure I stayed on task and on schedule. That was part of his duty as a summon. That didn't mean I had to like it. "It is...something, yes. For right now, Pendra, can you arrange for our fastest courier in Nerath to report to the Radio Station there? Dedria is going to write a message to her mother about my newfound powers. We will need it delivered as quickly as possible, and they will need to wait in Heart Falls until Veronica has written a response and bring it back to the station to send it over."

"Of course, your Majesty. I will do that at once." Pendra confirmed, darting off to do just that. He was so damn fast, unnaturally so. Another summon benefit.

Dedria headed to the desk, "Cool if I sit in your spot?" She asked me, though she didn't wait for my response. She sat down, grabbing some of the royal Parchment and grabbing a pen and the bottle of ink. She quickly started writing, the pen moving across the paper seemingly faster than possible. After only two minutes, Dedria rolled it up, melting some of the black wax onto the seam and then pressing the Solaria Royal Seal into it. Beside it, she signed it with her name. "Done! You know, I bet she's going to be so delighted over this. Seriously, she considers you one of her own kids you know. Jessica and I get sooo bored with it. It's always 'Johanna this' and 'Johanna that'."

"I bet your sister doesn't take that well." I frowned. Jessica was a Mute - or someone who was born without any magical powers. They were very rare, and even rarer coming from a family with strong magical affinity like the Hearts.

"Eh, Jess is priming to take over the Enterprise in the next 5 years. Besides, she loves you, pretty sure she'd have Mom disown me if it meant getting you as her sister." Dedria laughed, moving to the couch and flopping down on it. She was so unbothered by it, by Veronica loving me like her own, by Jessica's sisterly affection. There was an ache in my chest, from missing them, too. My days in Heart Falls with them had been one full of laughter and joy. I was never going to have something like that ever again. "I asked Mom to send some of the Heart History books and Chronomancy books down too for you to study from. I know you do better with book learning anyways."

I paused, assessing her quickly, and I couldn't help but smile earnestly at that. "Thanks, Dee..." I said, hoping I sounded thoroughly grateful. "Did you want lunch? I can get the Kitchen Staff to deliver us an early lunch."

"Uh, yeah?! That sounds amazing." Dedria grinned, "So, I haven't had a chance to talk about your first dance as Queen...With Delain..."

I opened the door, talking to a Guard in Solarian quickly, basically just asking him to go to the kitchens and get some lunch brought to us. I make sure to thank him for it. Normally a task like this would fall to Pendra, or one of the other servants. Not a guard. Still, he nodded and headed off to the Kitchens. I turned back to Dedria, sitting down in one of the chairs across from her. I leaned back in the chair; grateful I wasn't in a dress right now as I stretched. "Ughh...I don't even want to talk about it..."

"Truly? When you stayed in Heart Falls you wrote to him almost weekly. It was so gross." Dedria giggled, winking to me.

"Yeah, but that was then...It's infinitely more complicated now. I wasn't Queen then...the country wasn't fighting some sort of racialist group then." I reminded, sitting up once I felt my muscles had gotten a good stretch.

"Well, yeah...but he's pretty cute. Okay, more than cute. Drop dead, I think. Tall, great smile, brown hair, blue eyes. Strong arms, great dancer...I bet he even looks amazing with his shirt off."

"You are absolutely insufferable. Yeah, he's handsome. But maybe in a different timeline. It's too complicated right now. I have too much on my plate, the country, combat training, now chronomancy training, figuring out the source of the attack, getting reports about Kira's treatments and hopeful cure..." I sighed, slumping in my spot. It was hard not to with everything that was weighing me down. "I can't court at the same time, Dee. I can't..."

Dedria waved her hand, but I could feel her eyes on me, concerned. "Fine, fine...But if you don't pounce on him, I will." She said with a coy smile.

A knock on the door, and then Pendra stepped in. "The Courier is going to be in Nerath in about 15 minutes, Your Grace. Lady Heart, I can take your letter." He said, giving a bow before taking the rolled parchment and disappearing again.

"Well, what now?" Dedria asked, looking over to me.

"After lunch, I guess I have Queenly Duties I have to attend to..."

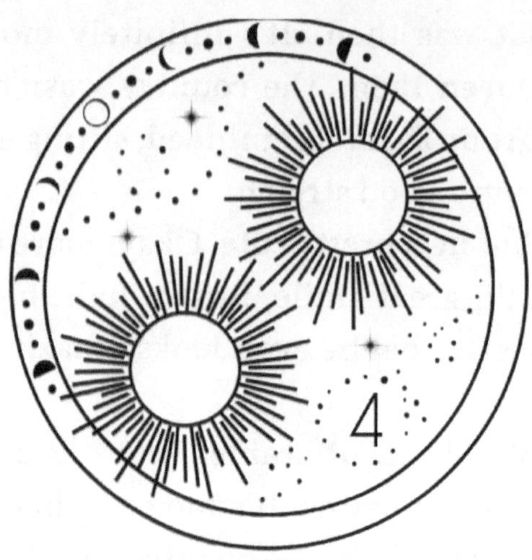

I sat on the throne, my hands folded neatly in my lap. Sitting on the throne still felt strange, and I wanted to fidget with my dress but keeping my hands in my lap prevented that. There was a long string of people seeking my counsel, favour, or guidance on matters. I couldn't figure out why anyone would want my counsel, I was 20. It was my first day handling an open court, after my parents had been crowned Queen and King, Dad had handled court. He had always been a natural at it. Even now, he was standing just behind me, listening quietly and there to offer his advice if I sought it. I was determined to not seek his advice though and hadn't faltered on that yet.

A younger man in a nicer-looking shirt and pants approached, bowing deeply at the waist. "Your Grace, may Arcanis shine upon you." He spoke. "My name is Castian Wesner. I am a historian and archaeologist. I have been doing some research in the southern mountains of Solaria. Primarily with ancient artifacts and ruins from the Age of Dragons."

I nodded slowly, "Okay, thank you for your work. How may I help you, Castian?"

"I have located a ruin in the Priscelet Range," The mountain range, that separated the vast Solarian desert from our southern provinces, "and my initial dating puts it at about 3900 years old. It is the oldest ruin to be discovered to date. I am seeking a team of dedicated archaeologists and historians that can aid me in cataloging, documenting, and studying the significance of this ruin." I had to admire him for a moment, he was so animated and excited over this discovery. It was a nice refresher from all the other petty problems I had listened to today. In another life, I may have asked my parents to let me go with him to learn. It was a significant discovery, who knows what treasures he could uncover.

"How many are you seeking for this team?" I inquired, even leaning forward a bit. I couldn't help it.

"Well, the more the better, Your Grace! A team of 5 would be the bare minimum, but ideally, a team of 30 would be even better. A team of 5 I project to take us at minimum one year to complete the research we need to just on this ruin. A team of thirty would cut that down to just a few months."

I nodded again, "Very well. I will grant you thirty of Solaria's best archaeologists and historians, but I do request the Crown receive all reports of this discovery first."

"Absolutely, Your Grace. I will personally write every update that will be sent to you." Castian promised, the smile on his face was so broad, for a moment I wondered if it hurt. It had to, I decided silently.

"Pendra, arrange a team of 30 to assist Castian with this research, courtesy of the Solarian Crown," I said, looking over to him.

"Absolutely, Your Grace." The Drake familiar nodded, making notes on the paper.

Castian was moved off, information to be collected from someone else.

Then the hours dragged on, lovers quarreling, families bickering, rivals squabbling, really mind-numbing things. I couldn't help but feel it was all petty and pointless. However, I knew that all of these matters, from a wife being angry her husband kept going out for drinks after work instead of seeing his children, or a business owner feeling resentful that their landlord was trying to increase their rent unfairly or even a farmer from the south asking for blessing over his crops for the harvest, were important to them. They did not have the worries of a racialist or a missing relic to worry about. They worried of their children, of putting a roof over their head and food on their table. They trusted me to keep them safe.

Finally, the doors closed at the end of the Throne Room, and I leaned back on the throne. I was sore, everywhere. Even training hadn't left me like this. "Oh, gods above and below it's over…" I murmured to myself.

My father laughed gently, moving and giving my shoulder a reassuring squeeze. "Your first of many, Your Grace." He said. "You handled it beautifully. I quite admired your terse 'If the two of you do not stop bickering, I will give the horse to my third Handmaid's Cousin's In-law's Brother. I don't even have a third handmaid, but I will hire one just to take that horse from you.'" He said, mimicking my exhausted, no-nonsense tone quite wonderfully, a larger smile on his face and he winked down to me. He took my hand, helping me to a stand and offering his arm to escort me out of the Throne Room and back into the private living quarters. As we walked, he kept talking, "That even got the guards to smile. That was always my goal, it got me through the day. If I could make them all smile over some wit or joke, I had won. If I got them to chuckle or even openly laugh, I treated myself to extra dessert that night."

"Father!" I said astonished, shaking my head. "Oh! Did Mother know?"

"Know?! It was her that got me onto it. She told me about it a month into me handling the Court." He nudged me gently, stepping into the elevator and nodding to the attendant.

Astonishment was on my face, staring up at Dad with wide eyes. "No! Mother would have never done such a thing."

"According to her, your Great-Gran Queen Cordelia told her about it. I only got to meet her once, Cordelia. She was something else, truly. I brought her a gift, you know, something that was the custom at the time, and she harassed me for 20 minutes over it. She said what good was I as a suitor for her Granddaughter if my ideals were so stuck in the past. That I needed to forge an innovative path forward if I was going to succeed with your Mom and be King." His chest had puffed out, and I imagined he was mimicking how my Great Grandmother Cordelia had looked like.

"I never heard that story before..." I said, frowning. "What did Mom say?"

"Oh, absolutely no one messed with Queen Mother Cordelia. She was wry and witty and simply brilliant. She could talk a con artist into a con. You wouldn't believe it. You know, I see a lot of her in you, just like I see a lot of your Mom in you, too."

I couldn't fathom how my father saw someone so sharp minded in me. Queen Cordelia was known in the books to be ruthless, especially when it came to policy and trade. Instead, I smiled, soft and sad as I instead focused on the part about Mom. "I miss her." I said, voice so soft it was almost impossible to hear over the gears and chains lifting the elevator up along the slanted edge of the northern side of the tower. Each side had an elevator going up, but only one led directly to the Ivory Halls. "It's hard…I'm barely 20. I wasn't supposed to take the throne so soon. We were supposed to have more time…I was supposed to have more time."

I found myself enveloped in a hug just as the elevator door opened. "I know, Johanna…I know." He stroked my back, pressing a kiss to my forehead. I closed my eyes and inhaled a shaky breath.

Pendra was waiting outside of the elevator when the hug finally broke, and I nearly jumped out of my skin, "I thought you were still down in the Throne Room."

"No, Your Grace. I slipped out of the back while you and the Dowager King were talking." He replied, bowing his head. "One of the Greenseers working on your mother's project for the little Princess Kira believes she has reached a breakthrough. Would you like to go speak with her?"

A breakthrough!? My heart started to pound in my chest, the sound overwhelming in my ears. "Yes. At once." Motioning for Pendra to get into the Elevator, a new sense of urgency to me.

"Down to Basement Level 38 please," Pendra told the attendant.

The Obsidian Tower reached high into the sky, over 1500 metres, a feat only possible with heavy enchantments and engineering marvels. From the very centre column to the tip of one of the triangle pillars it expanded two kilometers, meaning along each side of the tower structure was four kilometers long. And it hadn't stopped there, extending into the earth were sprawling hydroponic farms and even animal stock. Expanding out on the sand wasn't practical, not with the Wyrms. Our enchantments and magic could keep them out underground, but in those early years I had read that we had tried to expand beyond the base of the tower on the sands and the Wyrms would just dig under whatever barriers we put in place and dig up. But with the tower expanding down, not out, we could put barriers on the side and underneath effectively.

The entirety of the Obsidian Tower had been designed with a future war on the horizon. It wasn't until the 18th King that the construction of the top of the leaning elongated pentagons had started, what would then become the Ivory Halls. With the farms and animal stock under the earth, and each tower meeting along one side, the gates in walls 100 feet tall, that made the Obsidian Tower an impenetrable force.

It had only been possible after Ground Zero, the massive toxic crystal structure outside the tower, had formed, where Queen Maria, first of her name, had given her life to protect Solaria against Taranor forces - specifically a woman called Rozalin Heart, a Chronomancer who was revered as ruthless, cold-blooded, and absolutely fearless. The fatal clash that had taken both of their lives had led to Taranor retreating, and the giant crystal structure forming, with so much pure magical energy radiating from it that it had killed anyone who got too close. Before that, the sheer power of enchantments needed to keep the tower standing wasn't possible. They had been able to harness that magical energy to strengthen the tower and keep it standing. Of course, not without some losses. But progress meant risks, and those at the time had risked it to see it happen.

Basement level 38 was highly classified, only those directly employed by the Ivory Halls and the Crown were permitted on that floor. It was on this floor that studies of Ground Zero crystals were conducted, and the research into the cure of The Rot.

I stepped out of the elevator, looking around and surveying everything before briskly heading towards the laboratory where the cure was being researched. Even before Mom had died, I had come here often.

Inside was a smaller, pale-skinned woman, turned away from me and bent some sort of sample on the table. I was nearly a head taller than her. "Professor Tyne." I greeted, and I tried to keep the eagerness out of my tone.

Tyne turned around a headband magnifier on her head. She flipped it up, "Your Grace." She smiled, "Hello." Her voice was oddly calm and even, even if her smile implied, she was full of joy. It was always so at contrast, I had never seen her happy, I had rarely seen her happy, but no matter what her emotion, she always sounded calm. Like everything around her was just as she wanted it.

"I see Pendra passed along my report. Excellent, yes." She stepped to the left, just slightly. "I was reading some of late Queen Serena's research on the Southern Isle's burnberry bush, a very fascinating plant, truly. The seed pods must smolder in coals for 127 days for the seeds to release and start to grow. Completely impractical, but truly a marvel of nature. Anyways, sorry Your Grace, I'm getting off subject. Her notes explained how the residents of those islands do not seem to be afflicted by

The Rot and how they drink Burnberry Bloom Tea...I was able to get some significant samples of it brought here, and I convinced it to root and bloom, and ground that bloom up and steeped it for Princess Kira. I took a blood sample 30 minutes before and 2 hours after. Of course, it could be just a good day for her, and the bloom tea and the lack of The Rot on the islands is a coincidence. But! Her initial blood work indicated some unusual activity and possible improvement I had never seen before. With your permission, I would like to continue this line of discovery."

I had to take it all in, the small woman was a flurry and zipped through point A to Z that even I had a hard time catching up. But I latched on to what she had said in the last part. "Wait, you said unusual activity and improvement? What does that mean?"

"Ah, well, it's a bit complicated, Your Grace. Basically, the Rot eats the white blood cells, meaning Kira is susceptible to infection, illness...a myriad of things, really. As it progresses, it eventually attacks the organs causing total body failure. So, instead of declining white blood cells, or even the stagnant numbers that we have seen for the past year, it improved. Only by point three eight...but it improved Your Grace." The look Tyne gave me, it looked almost like this woman was about to cry with excitement herself. She had dedicated so much of her life to this.

I moved forward, taking Tyne's hands and squeezing them. "Then keep going. Whatever you need, you let Pendra know. Please, save my sister."

"Of course, Your Grace. For now, I have enough Burnberry Bushes to bloom three times a day. I have instructed Princess Kira to drink the tea twice a day at least, and I will keep investigating more concentrated avenues of these properties."

"You are brilliant, absolutely brilliant. I will let my father know and he will help make sure she drinks it. Thank you, Tyne. You have given me the best news I've received in 3 months." Now I felt like crying, but I held it together. I had to.

"It is my pleasure, Your Grace." Tyne moved to lower her headband magnifier again and turned back to the table.

I took Pendra's arm as we moved to leave. "...Kira may live to see her 11th birthday, Pendra..." In private with him, I felt my lower lip wobble, the emotion overcoming me before I was able to compose myself.

"Indeed, Your Grace. It sounds like that will be the case." He gave my hand a reassuring squeeze and smiled down to me.

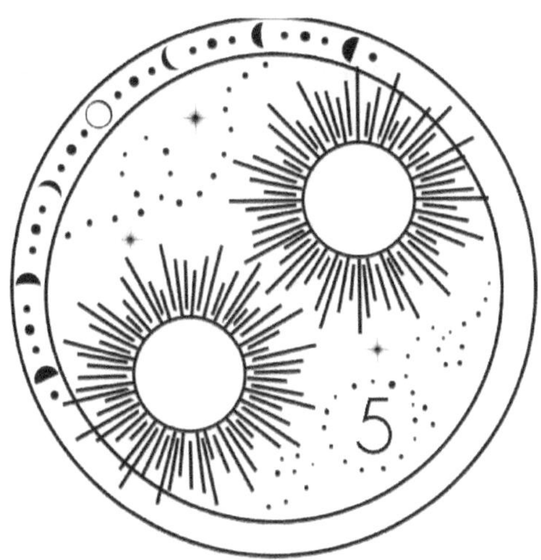

The Ivory Halls was split into 3 major parts between the thirty floors. The first was the top four levels, floors twenty-seven to thirty, as the living quarters of the Crown. The second was floors ten to twenty-six was everything to make the monarchy and country run, offices, meeting rooms, servant quarters, library, the kitchens to serve it all. It also included military operations and the training halls for both guards and The Crown. The third and final part was floors one through nine, which included the Throne Room, the three Ball Rooms, the Art and History halls, and the radio broadcasting center.

Currently, was in the Military Operations Center. Dozens of different military officers were moving around the different rooms, but I was in the main room, where most of the activity was. Close to twenty different officers were at different workstations, most connected to different radios as they kept up with all different types of chatter.

I stood overseeing all of it from a platform about 10 feet above, my Military General standing beside me with his hands at his sides. "Most recent Intel suggests that the relic that was stolen from the Ivory Halls was a piece of something called The Ember. From records that I can find, The Ember was once a sphere, dating before the Age of Dragons. It may have been a weapon at some point, but I can't confirm that Your Grace." He explained, his voice was gruff, and he was battle-worn, a scar going across his face. I know how he got that scar, defending my grandfather while he had been on a trip to Taranor.

"What do you mean, piece?" I asked, looking over at him. He already knew I was annoyed, the moment I found out we didn't have an accurate detailed list of all the relics in the hall my mother had died in, it had taken everything in me to keep from lashing out. I had immediately instructed for every single item in the halls to be recorded, their known history added and any magical significance to them noted as well.

"Well, from our limited records on it, it was split into eight pieces. Solaria, Taranor, the Trussam Empire, the Northern Spirit-Ascended Tribes, Lethiarum, Yonshia, and Kunshu all received pieces...The last one is lost at least to our knowledge." He further explained, "Setsuna of the Plains, her Mate that was kidnapped. He originated from the Northern Spirit-Ascended Tribes. I can wager a good bet that he was kidnapped for knowing where the piece of this...Ember is within his homelands."

The Spirit-Ascended people had two regions they roamed on a continent. Separated by the Lethiarum kingdom, the Northern Tribes lived in very cold, hostile environments. Whereas the Southern Tribes roamed vast plains and savannah. Occasionally, a southerner got sick of the heat and traveled to join their Northern counterparts and vice versa.

"...That complicates things," I glanced over to him as I spoke. It was hard to look away from all of the activity down below. "If that is the case, how fast could I possibly travel there with Setsuna, Dedria, and a group of soldiers?"

"Your Grace, I can not in good conscience advise such a thing. You should stay here in Solaria, where it is safe." He protested, shaking his head firmly.

My face turned to steel as I faced him full on, and even if he was taller than me, I did my best to look at him like he was nothing but an inconvenience. Which, he was. "You misunderstand, General. I am not asking for advice. I am asking as an order. Arrange it, I want fifty soldiers ready to leave by dawn tomorrow. I am tired of sitting around waiting for answers. It's time for me to start going and getting answers. Setsuna will obviously come with us; it is her Mate on the line. It's why she's here to begin with." I turned away from him, "Get it done, General." I added before walking off.

I finally saw an opportunity to catch up to this group and maybe even enact my revenge. Besides, I knew realistically the trip back to the Northern Tribe lands was going to take close to a month and a half. Most of that would be on a train or boat, so there would be lots of time to build my skills.

I found Dedria first, my friend was going through the package Veronica had sent back with the courier which had been put on the first train to Solaria. "Oh, the things came. That's good." I nodded, but I didn't really care about that... "The General found out what the Relic that was stolen was and put together why they kidnapped Setsuna's partner. We are going to track them down." I explained, "you will have to pack. We leave at dawn tomorrow."

"Whoa whoa whoa, hold on. Slow down. What do you mean we

are going to track them down?! Johanna, these people killed your Mom sure, but we aren't ready for that." Dedria replied, launching up to stand in front of me.

"Dedria, this is the first lead we've gotten on this group. I can't just sit by and not do something, especially considering they have Setsuna's Mate, and the whole reason she is here is because they took him. Dad can handle the throne. We are going. It's not a discussion." I stood there as tall as could be. I was in a dress for once, having to do some of my duties earlier in the day. But despite that, I knew looked fierce and ready to fight.

Dedria heaved a sigh, "well thank Arcanis I haven't unpacked fully yet..." she said with a faint smile.

"I am going to go talk to Setsuna now, do you want to join me?"

"Absolutely not. She's going to con us into training, and I want nothing to do with that right now."

I just shrugged and turned, walking away and finding Tianie and Setsuna in the dining room of their guest quarters. "I want to let you know we believe we know why your...Mate...was kidnapped."

That got Setsuna's attention, her ears moving from pointing at Tianie to me in a split second. "Why?" She asked in my native tongue, the first time I had heard her speak Solarian since she had shown up the night of my Ascension. It was heavily accented, but I still understood her perfectly.

"The relic that my mother died trying to protect was a piece of something called The Ember." I said, and it dawned on me that Tianie hadn't translated what I had said when I had come in. I wondered if Setsuna knew more Solarian or common then she let on. She had to. "The Northern Tribes were given a piece to protect when it was broken...did he ever tell you about this?"

Setsuna frowned, thinking for a moment. As she thought, her tails danced behind her idly before curling all together into one. She spoke, the words now being Translated as she went. "No, I don't recall him ever mentioning it."

I paused and nodded quickly. "The original item was broken into eight pieces, but we only know the locations of seven of them. We are more focused on stopping them with what they are doing now...Which means finding them, and your Mate."

Setsuna then smiled, and she looked relieved and elated at finally being able to finally, finally go find Karne. Tianie spoke for her; "Frankly, it is about time."

I reached out, offering my hand, "Thank you, Setsuna."

The Kitsune woman gave me a wink, and even if I did not understand her as she spoke, I knew she was being a hard ass. It was only confirmed when Tianie spoke for her, "Do not think this gets you out of your training. Far from, now we only train harder."

"I am aware," I nodded again, my chest getting tight with anticipation. Setsuna and I both had a reason to be motivated for this trip. "We leave at dawn tomorrow, on Solaria's fastest Military train to the harbour city." With that, I had turned and was leaving quickly, needing to get my affairs in order. First, Dad. Letting him know what was going on and that he would need to manage the country once again.

He worried and fretted over me, of course. Concerned that I was making a rash decision, worried that sending me out into the world so soon was going to mean he would lose me, too. I spent the most time with him, reassuring him that I needed to do this. I needed to go find this group because if I didn't the country would be in further danger. He didn't believe me at first, but I was always the more stubborn one.

"I'll be okay, Dad. I've got 50 of our best coming with me, I have Dedria and Setsuna. I can't sit here in this tower, protected and hiding after what they did. They didn't just kill Mom that day. They killed 3285 civilians, too. Those lives mattered. Their families would be furious if I sat and did nothing if I was presented with an opportunity to do bring justice for those this country lost." I didn't say revenge, even if I wanted to. But I wasn't lying, either. My first act as Queen had been putting in place a memorial construction for the lives that had been lost that day. It would not be about my mother - Mom's name wouldn't be anywhere on it. It would be for all the other lives lost that day. From the guards to civilians. A massive gear and clock display that counted the days of the year, with all of the names engraved into the structure. Personally, there was more I wish I could do. But outside of paying families for those lost - something the monarchy had already done, a monument to remember them was the next best thing.

Simon sighed, reaching over to me with both of his hands and cupping my cheeks. His touch was always so warm and affectionate, and even though I was 20, I still leaned into it like a child. "I know nothing I say will change your mind. So, may Arcanis shine upon you and bring you home safe." He said, kissing my forehead.

I leaned into him for a hug, for just a moment, closing my eyes. "Thanks, Dad." I said softly, "I'll be home as soon as I can, okay?" Reluctantly I pulled away and reached up, taking his hands in mine. I gave them a reassuring squeeze as I took a step back from

[68]

him. "We'll have radio wherever we go, hopefully...We'll touch in whenever we can. Keep me up to date on things, okay? Especially with Kira..."

"Of course, kiddo. I'll make sure we keep you up to date." He said, "Maybe by the time you get back, she'll be cured."

"Wouldn't that be nice?" I asked as I stepped away from him some more. I wouldn't hold onto that hope. "I need to pack. Oh, can I bring Pendra?"

"What? Of course, you can bring him. He's the Monarch's familiar, Johanna. And you are the Monarch." His gaze was one of worry, and I don't think that would ever go away.

"Oh, right...Yeah, I guess so." I chuckled awkwardly, a fact that I was still getting used too, and then I was gone. I let muscle memory guide me back to my living quarters where Pendra joined me. "Pendra, you're coming with us."

"Well, I'm not a fighter, Your Grace. Planning, organizing, order. That's more of my thing..." Pendra replied, looking a bit unsure of himself. It was not a look he had often, that was for sure. It almost unsettled me, but I wouldn't let it. No, I buried that feeling with all the others.

"I know you're not a fighter. I need someone who can plan and organize and add structure to things. It will be significantly easier on me if you come with us."

He sighed as he rubbed the back of his neck, looking contemplative, "Yes, You're Grace. As you wish." He relented. "Let me help you pack."

"I don't need dresses or skirts. Pants, long shirts. Practical attire. Training outfits, armour. The family sword." I explained, "And we need to pack as light as possible, too. We'll be on our feet a lot once we get to the Northern Tribe lands."

"Of course, You're Grace." He said as he headed into my closet. "I do have a summoning spell I can use for these situations. We can pack as much as you need, and I can hide it away in a sort of...pocket dimension of sorts."

I deadpanned over to him, "You should have said that earlier." I muttered, and I silently chastised him for wanting to not come with me. Power like that? He was invaluable. That and well, Pendra couldn't really die. But that was a technicality. "Very well. We leave in less than twelve hours."

Pendra had started to carry various clothes out from my closet, laying them on my bed in neat piles. He started to fold each item, and once it was folded his aura flared and the item disappeared. "Should I get some warm jackets for you out of your travel wardrobe?" He inquired.

"That's a brilliant idea, Pendra." I agreed, a smile on my lips. I was grabbing various books, empty journals, spare ink bottles, fountain pens, and parchment, stacking them up together on my bed for him to vanish as well. "Am I able to use a spell like that?"

"Well, yes, probably. With much training and practice. I would not recommend trying such a thing with items you are attached to." He chuckled, his tone shifting to one of reminiscing, "When I was first summoned, the Princess at the time, Princess Ashira, wanted me to hide a certain stuffed animal from the Prince. I did, but I was unable to retrieve it until near 60 years later. She was 70 by then, but she did find great humour when I presented it to her."

"Perhaps you can teach me on our journey, then," I said hopefully as I glanced over to him from what I was doing.

"It would be an honour, your Grace." He said, giving me a slight bow of his head and a kind smile.

The two of us continued to prepare for the next four hours, steadily finding more and more that needed to go with us. Some things ended up in chests and travel cases, but most ended up in Pendra's pocket dimension.

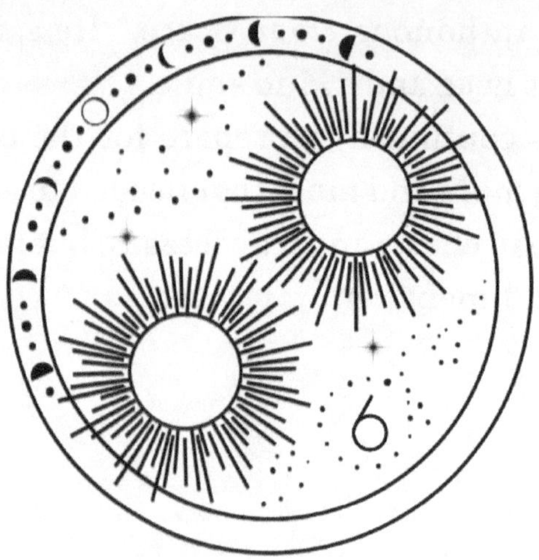

"Again," Dedria said, we were on the train, and Dedria was putting me through Chronomancy training drills.

I groaned, walking back to my starting point. There was an 'X' marked on the floor in the centre of the exceptionally large train car, specifically designed for combat training. Military trains were larger than passenger trains - the cars longer and without the need for windows in most of the cars, the walls could be thinner allowing for more floor space. About 15 feet from me, there was a circle painted on the floor about two feet in diameter. I was practicing my 'jumping', trying to get into the circle. For the past two hours that I had been at this, I had fallen short two dozen times, had missed to the left or right about a dozen times, and had overshot over three dozen times. I stood on the X, staring at the circle. Right now, I was feeling particularly murderous towards it. Not that I could murder a circle marked on a steel floor. Destroy it, maybe.

"Visualize the tunnel in front of you. Channel your magic, create the tunnel, and step in and to the spot." Dedria instructed, standing off to the side with her arms crossed. She made it sound so fucking easy. It wasn't, clearly. I had been at this for two hours and hadn't even gotten inside the circle once.

I ground my teeth together and heaved a sigh, focusing a moment and creating the tunnel, and stepping off the X. I did not, in fact, hit the circle and instead hit the steel wall that was 10 feet past the circle. I collided with it face first. I fell backward, flat on her rear, holding my nose and groaning. "Arcanis above…" I did a quick check, it wasn't broken. But I could feel some blood coming from one of the nostrils.

Dedria couldn't help but huff a laugh, moving over and helping me to a stand. "If it makes you feel better, when I first came into my powers, Jessica scared me, and I jumped straight into a glass table and shattered it. It took three healers and several hours for them to get all the pieces of glass out of me without creating any scars." She chuckled, checking over my face. "Nose isn't broken, but you will probably have a black eye tomorrow."

I glanced up to my friend, "Only moderately." I replied, taking the hand and getting up, moving back to the mark to try again.

"Did you want to take a break?" Dedria asked, only for me to shake my head in response. I needed to get this right. I needed to do it once, to know I could.

"I need to get this down." I told her, and I attempted it again. The voice that I hadn't heard since my training session in the tower, in a soothing, confident tone, said, "You can do this." This time I ignored it.

As the tunnel formed and I moved through, I landed in the circle, my left foot just barely going over the line. "Ah! I DID IT." I exclaimed, turning to Dedria with a triumphant look. I wanted to dance, but my nose was still aching so bad it put a damper on some of my elation.

"Yeah! You did," Dedria praised, a wide smile on my face. She winked as she said, "But can you do it again?"

I proved that I could, repeating my success six more times until Dedria nodded with approval. "Very good! Now we have to focus on decreasing and increasing the time flow around you. Increasing is trickier than decreasing. But if you get advanced enough with it, you could slow time around you to an absolute crawl and read a book that would normally take you 8 hours, but only ten or fifteen minutes would pass in reality." She explained.

"Have I told you Chronomancy makes absolutely no sense?" I said as I chuckled. "Seriously." But I couldn't deny the usefulness of such skill, especially being a Queen. I could fit in so much more work in such a small amount of time.

"Yeah, tell me about it. It is what it is. One thing, increasing and decreasing the time around you takes an immense amount of power. As you get older and your power grows, it'll be easier. But right now, you'll be lucky to slow ten minutes to five." Dedria explained, moving over beside me. "Watch my aura, watch how I manipulate it." She explained, and she picked up a rubber ball, manipulating her aura and throwing the ball across the car.

As soon as it got five feet from Dedria, it slowed. It was obviously still moving, but it was moving significantly slower than it had or should. I watched in fascination; I couldn't help but take a step closer to inspect it. "So, everything around you will slow down when you decrease the time flow. You won't, you will be able to move as normal. But people, things, whatever, will slow. Mom is so good that things almost look like they've stopped they move so slow. It's wicked cool."

"Yeah, but your Mom is effectively Grand Master level," I argued. A 'Grand Master' was a term normally used in Guilds. They were so experienced and skilled that they were considered not just a master, but a master of a high enough caliber no other Master's could challenge them easily and win a fight. They usually led the Guilds, teaching others and making sure everyone stayed in line and followed the rules. It kept things in check.

"Yeah, if a Chronomancy guild existed and she wanted to teach in it she would be. But it doesn't and she wouldn't. So, it doesn't really matter what she is in terms of skill." Dedria released her aura, and the ball continued flying to its destination, hitting the side of the car and bouncing back towards us. "Okay. Go pick it up and you try." She said.

I nodded, moving over to grab the ball and going back to Dedria. "Okay, so..." I released my aura, harnessing its power. It felt vaster than before, more like a large lake instead of a small pond. Only days had passed since my Chronomancy had manifested, and I already felt so much more powerful. I manipulated it in the way I had felt Dedria do, throwing the ball. So colour my surprise when, as the ball got 5 feet from me, it slowed to a near stop. "...What?"

Dedria paused, the shock clear on her face. She moved to inspect the ball while staying in the radius of me and my magic. "Huh. I mean...Alright. Whatever, you prodigy." She scoffed, moving back to stand beside me. "Well since you seem to have no problem with this, we can move to combat using Chronomancy." She suggested.

"Combat using Chronomancy? Are you sure?" I asked,

furrowing my brows. "Shouldn't I practice this more?"

"Johanna, you just slowed the ball to basically a stop, just like my mother does. So no, I don't think we need to practice this more. If the combat turns out to be too much then we can revisit this anyways."

"If you're sure." I nodded, she was following the lesson plan Veronica had sent us, and I couldn't lie, Dedria *was* a good teacher. The first three days on the train, she had guided me through understanding how to manipulate my magic to do the various aspects of Chronomancy, the most complex being the 'jump'. It had taken me until today to even get to forming the tunnel to jump through. She had never gotten impatient or annoyed, and had just dutifully guided me through each step, correcting my mistakes.

Dedria stretched, "Let's take a break though, I'm famished."

The two of us exited the training car. The train was 20 cars long, the engine, then cars one through six were reserved for me, Dedria, Pendra, Setsuna, and Tianie. It included a food car, training car, sleeping cabins, the make-shift library, and the multi-use room which was mostly used for socialization and winding down at the end of the day. The rest were for the military that was travelling with them. The training car was car six, so we had to go up through the library and multi-use car to get to the dining car.

Pendra was be in the dining car, cooking away in the kitchen that was set up. "Oh! Your Grace, Lady Heart. Welcome, did your morning training session go well?" He asked, a smile on his lips. Despite being away from the Tower, Pendra was proving to be invaluable. He kept us on track, made food every day for us, communicated with the soldiers that were with us, covered radio communications and made sure we stayed on time. If anything, we were ahead of schedule.

The train had to travel from the Tower to the east, to the eastern port city. From there we would board one of the military ships and go across the sea to a neighboring country. It would be train again to cross their lands, then boat to Lethiarum. Their city - the only city, really, was a port city as well. They made most of their money from mining valuable metals and gems.

"Oh yeah, Johanna's just a show-off and prodigy as usual." Dedria teased, winking to me as she sat down at one of the tables.

Pendra smiled at that, quickly bringing a platter of cut fruit, cheese, crackers, and smoked meats and placing it down before heading back to the kitchen. "I am making stuffed meat pastries for lunch. They will be another forty minutes, but the two of you can snack off of that while we wait." He explained.

I sat down in my seat, trying to be graceful as always. It was a little harder with my all over ache. Now that my nose wasn't throbbing as much, the rest of my body was making it apparent that I had run straight into the steel wall. "Thank you, Pendra." I said, starting to help myself to the snacking platter. "We haven't had any issues with Wyrms on our trip?"

"No, Your Grace. The Sand Wyrms have not bothered the train. The sonic device is working exceptionally." Pendra explained. Sand Wyrms were huge, adults being over 100 meters long and 10 meters wide. Their maws were full of razor-sharp teeth, and they did not hesitate to attack strong sources of Magic. Trains were a common target, a steel can of dozens of mages that were a delightful snack for the beasts. The Obsidian Tower was only safe because of the Obsidian the tower was built from. For some reason, the Wyrms hated it. Fifteen years ago, it had been discovered that they also hated a certain sonic radio frequency when they had been installed in the trains to have them communicate with different stations and each other. The attacks had been sporadic as the country had finessed the devices and had increased the strength of the devices, honing them to exactly what the Wyrms seemed to hate.

Ever since the technology had been refined and amplified on the trains in Solaria, and now Wyrm attacks on trains were almost completely unheard of. As such, Solaria's tourism had increased ten-fold. No longer did visitors need to worry about if they could even survive the train journey in the country. It also meant immigration was up.

"Good. And the Military Officers with us, they don't want for anything?" I asked, watching him closely.

Pendra shook his head, "I had a meeting with Major Lionel this morning. She says that everyone is quite happy, and the food offered is better than what they normally get."

My face twisted, the idea that my military officers weren't getting good food bothered me in ways I couldn't quite place. Another thing to handle when I got back to the Tower. "Well, that's good." I nodded, "If they need anything please make sure they get it though." I added. "We will be in the port city in two days. We can radio ahead and make sure any supplies we need will be ready when we arrive."

"Of course, Your Grace," Pendra said with a bow. "I need to go get Setsuna and Tianie, let them know lunch will be ready soon." He added, walking off when I nodded permission that he could leave.

"What was that sour look on your face about?" Dedria asked the moment the door shut behind Pendra.

"What sour look?" I asked, nibbling at one of the crackers that I had put some cheese on.

"The look you had just then. When Pendra said the officers said the food is better than they normally get. Don't pretend we didn't see it." Dedria pressed, she looked annoyed. I didn't know why.

"Well, the food on the train shouldn't be better than they normally get. I'm going to have to revisit the Military Budget and find out why they don't get excellent food." I explained, trying to keep my tone even. I was feeling so angry lately, it took so much effort to keep it tampered down. "They are serving Solaria. They deserve proper food while they are."

"I mean, at least they get free food." Dedria offered with a reassuring smile.

I rolled her eyes, "Oh don't give me that. It isn't an 'at least' situation. They are serving Solaria and the Crown and the People. They deserve proper food and shelter and pay. If those are not being offered, I have to deal with that once I return."

Dedria shook her head, "Yeah, yeah. You sure have high expectations for this stuff, you know that?"

I ignored her, opting to not respond to something so silly. Of course, I had high expectations, the military kept my country and my people safe. They put themselves in danger for it, sacrificing time with their families and friends for it. Sacrificed their lives for it. Of course that mattered, why wouldn't it? "I was hoping to study from some of those chronomancy books after lunch." I deflected.

Dedria shrugged, "Sure, alright. If that's what you wanna do. I thought we were going to do combat training, but if you'd rather read books, fine." It didn't sound fine, and that was annoying.

"I would just like to read some of the material on my powers before we jump into more training, okay?" I said, unable to keep my voice from being terse and annoyed.

"Jeeze, yeah. Okay, whatever." Dedria shook her head, making a little sandwich with some crackers, cheese, and meat and shoving it into her mouth. I caught her rolling her eyes, and I bristled.

Just as the tension was starting to rise in the air between us, Pendra, Setsuna and Tianie walked back in. Tianie waved over to us happily, sitting at the table. "Hello Your Grace, Dedria." She said, bowing her head. "How was your morning training?" She was oblivious to the tension, or maybe she wasn't, and she was just ignoring it.

"It was fine, thank you Tianie." I replied, looking over to the feline bonded woman. Her ears were curious, not quite like one of the Big Cats that were located in the Southern Spirit-Ascended lands, but not like one of the smaller, more domesticated cats found in other parts of the world. "Tianie, is it an offense if I ask what you are bonded with?"

Tianie smiled at that, her deep brown eyes were always kind, and she had dark skin like most Solarian's. "Of course not, Your Grace. I am bonded with a celestial feline called a Prowler. They are medium-sized cats, but very rare in the Spirit Realm. When I was approaching my bonding age, I meditated into the Spirit Realm, and one was sitting in front of me when I arrived there. She claimed me as her bonded. They have an affinity for sneaking and darkness. I can virtually turn invisible in shadows in shadows using the abilities she gifted me with."

"Gifted you with?" I asked, "I'm sorry, I do not know much about your people or culture." Another failure I intended to correct. Having Tianie and Setsuna here meant I could do that. To learn.

"That is okay, Your Grace. That is why Setsuna wanted to leave representatives in Solaria to help educate more on our culture and traditions and people." Tianie explained, reaching out to take some fruit. She never sounded angry at my questions, though I hadn't had much of a chance to ask them. She was so patient, and kind. Never did she make me feel like I was a child for asking. "So, before a young child becomes ascended, they do not have many magical powers. They can do basic things, but they mostly rely on their physical capabilities. From the ages of 14 to 16 they train to meditate into the Spirit Realm where they meet the spirit they wish to bond with. Some know what they want beforehand, and they will find a spirit that will accept them, some do not. I did not know what I wanted, I was willing to let a spirit, any spirit, choose me. When they turn 16, they go through the Ascension ceremony that is guided by at least one elder. The stronger the spirit, the harder the ceremony is. The Elder or Elders must pull the Realm close enough to the physical world, as the one ascending links to it and convinces their spirit to proceed with the bonding.

"Some spirits may agree before the ascension, and then resist once the ceremony begins. If they resist, the Elders have a harder time keeping the Realm pulled close to the physical world, and the spirit may even lash out at them as well. As such, there is a chance of failure. The one ascending may end up with a completely different spirit or failing to bond at all. If successful, the spirit may gift their bonded with unique magical powers or skills. Someone bonded with a bird of prey may benefit from exceptional vision. Someone bonded with a cat will be more agile. Someone bonded with a bear more physically strong. Things like that."

I nodded as she listened carefully as I always did. Committing this to memory. "I will admit, that is much more complicated and dangerous than I ever thought…What happens to someone who failed their bonding, or bonded with something they didn't intend?" I watched her so closely.

"Sometimes they die in the process." Tianie replied, her voice and expression were somber, "if they live but don't have a bonded spirit, they often leave the tribe. It can be hard, being around your people but never fitting in, never having a Bonded of your own. Isolating. Often coming to places like Taranor or Solaria, or other stationary cultures. Or maybe they die on the journey. Even if it is unfortunate, it is the reality of our people."

I frowned at that, "I am sorry. That must be hard." I tried my best to sound sympathetic. I was so grateful to learn, I always was. Dedria always teased me for being a book worm, but I loved learning. I loved reading. Before Mom died, I was in the Royal Library almost every waking moment where I had free time. "Thank you. We don't have any books on your people in the library in the Halls. I've never been able to learn."

"Of course, Your Grace! Thank you for asking. You knowing this only furthers our mission in education and building relations." Tianie smiled, grabbing some more fruit. "Inara above, this fruit is some of the best I've ever had."

"Inara?" Dedria asked, furrowing her brow.

"The Goddess of our people. You do not think everyone believes in your gods Arcanis and Osian, do you?" Tianie laughed, it was bright and full of life.

"Well, kind of..." Dedria replied dejectedly as she frowned.

"That's the most stationary civilization thing I've ever heard." Tianie laughed.

I watched the exchange, trying to decide what I thought of this. Arcanis and Osian were the gods of Solaria, and Taranor. Most countries, really. Arcanis, the goddess of the Suns. She gave us life, while also representing justice and loyalty. Osian was the god of the Moon. He was the Shepard of Death, but also was mischievous and chaotic.

"Tianie, you've said stationary culture or civilization a few times since we've met...what do you mean?" I had an idea, but I wanted to be sure.

Tianie paused, thinking, "Oh, I suppose I have. The Tribes roam and wander the lands. We follow the herds and hunting. We don't tend to be stationary. But your culture, and many of the countries and cultures, are, well, stationary..." She got distracted as Setsuna talked to her about something, only continuing when Setsuna stopped. "Setsuna says she would like to one day have our Tribe settle in a spot, so we too can have radio and much of the technology she has seen in Solaria, but it is dependent on her finding the right land. For now, the tribe wanders."

I found that very interesting, but I knew that about the Spirit-Ascended. I just had never heard of other countries and cultures being referred to as 'Stationary'. Still, it made sense in the context Tianie spoke about. It wasn't like I could never just up and move the Obsidian Tower. As I continued to pick at the snack platter, Dedria, Tianie, and Setsuna all talked to each other about various things. I had tuned them out, thinking to myself. About the things I had learned from Tianie, but also about training this morning.

I remembered quite suddenly that the voice had triggered again earlier, and I found myself fixating on this. 'Why do I keep hearing that weird voice?' I thought, 'It isn't my voice or the voice I hear when I think to myself...What does it mean?' I lost myself in those thoughts, circling over these questions over and over again. I closed my eyes a moment, just a split second.

But when I opened them, I found myself in a black void of space, standing on what felt like solid ground but it was completely black. I couldn't tell, "What? Where am I?"

A figure materialized in front of me, a moderately tall woman with dark brown skin, hair in tight coils with glimpses of gold and platinum, rubies and diamonds. Her nose had a slight bump in the ridge, and her full lips were curling up into a smile. I knew this face; I had seen it on countless of paintings in the Ivory Halls.

She spoke, her voice was inexplicably the one I had heard in my mind before. "Hello, Johanna. It's wonderful to finally meet you. My name is Maria Maracroix, and I am your Archon."

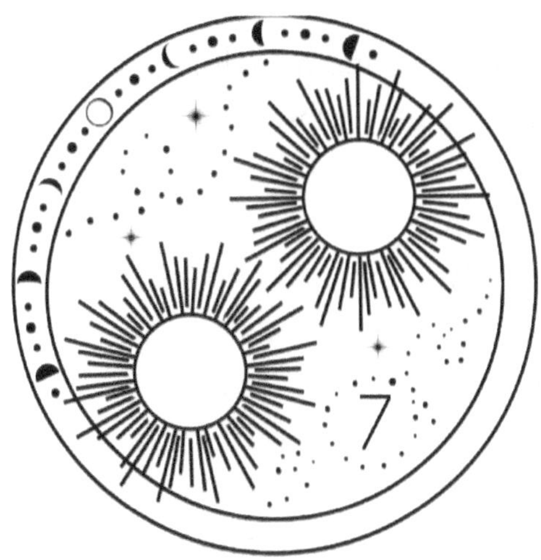

I stared at this figure, Maria, jaw slack and I was at a total loss for words.

Maria was in her battle armour, the same armour she had worn when she marched out to face Rozalin Heart. The crest of Solaria, which was the top-down shape of the future Obsidian Tower, was engraved onto the metal breastplate. "You are confused, I can see that." She said, her voice was kinder than I had imagined it. "Many, many thousands of years ago, during the birth of our realm, a prophecy was predicted. It foresaw a day when the power of Arcanis would be gifted to a human, and in doing so, they would be gifted with the powers of four Archons. Those Archons are hand chosen by Arcanis herself to aid this human. The human would be named the Ash Queen...or King. They would rise from the ashes of the world and bring true peace and prosperity."

I felt myself sit down on the hard, black surface. I didn't register doing it, but I went from standing to sitting. I truthfully felt like I should be falling for eternity here. I didn't understand how I was standing on anything solid in what felt like a void. "I...what?"

Maria smiled and laughed a little, moving to sit across from me. She was graceful, her movements so fluid. She didn't even have to try. "I know it's confusing...Before now you were not strong enough to be pulled into your mindscape and speak with me." She said, reaching forward and taking my hand. It felt real, solid. Add that to the other confusing things with this space.

"I don't understand. What do you mean Ash Queen? What do you mean Archons and Arcanis? I thought that was all just religious nonsense." I frowned. For my bookish, logical brain, accepting that two gods existed, and one of them had given me these...Archons...it was extremely hard to rationalize. Sure, people believed in the gods, like they believed that the realm was flat. That didn't mean either were right.

"Arcanis is real. But she is weak and in hiding. But she is real as anything...and I am Maria, or...her soul, I suppose. When I died, my soul did not move on. Arcanis brought me to where she is and told me I would be needed. There are three others, but you aren't strong enough to meet them yet. In time you will." Maria was so calm and confident in how she spoke. "As you get stronger you will be able to use all our powers and memories. For now, I can guide you through combat. If you put your trust in me, I can guide your body like I did the first day you heard me."

I paused, registering what she was saying. "That...that was you." I said, and I felt numb. "That...makes some sense...I guess..."

Maria nodded, squeezing my hand before letting go. "I will guide you through your training, teaching you what I know, and make you stronger as we go. Unfortunately, I can not help with your...Chronomancer thing. Unfortunately, a Chronomancer was the one thing that killed me." She had a wry smile on her lips, finding humor with it. I didn't know how. "But you and I together will still be an iron force until the other Archons can be brought forward too."

"Yup, sure, that sounds totally good." I rubbed my face, flustered and confused still and I knew my tone was sarcastic. "Sorry, normally I am much better with words."

"I know." Maria winked, and she chuckled softly. "You should go back to your friends; it has only been a few seconds out there, but they will get suspicious. I will always be with you." She said. Just as fast as they had appeared, Maria and the black void was replaced by the dim light shining through my eyelids, the voices of Tianie, Dedria, and Setsuna returned in an onslaught of unexpected senses.

"...ever met the Malbora family?" Dedria asked as I started to tune back in.

"The...Malbora Family?" Tianie asked, glancing at Setsuna and translating quickly. The Kitsune woman nodded, speaking quickly to Tianie in response. "She said once, she met a Shae Malbora a long time ago when she first travelled to the Southern Lands. She said she was a spitfire and annoying as hell. After that, she does not know what came of her."

Dedria bit her bottom lip in that way she did when she was deep in thought, "Well, Shae was Professor Suki's mother, from what I know. Professor Suki has been living in Taranor forever. She married an Archmage named Jamal. He's going after the Grand-Archmage position next Election. That's how my Mom knows her and got her to teach me history. She's a nasty thing. Bonded with a rabbit, believe it or not. But she's MEAN. And she's a Summoner, she can summon this giant semi-sentient armour to fight for her. One time, at school, some kid nailed her right in the forehead with a spitball. She summoned the armour and made it grab him by his foot and marched him to the office like that, dangling."

Tianie listened, visibly paling as Dedria talked. "She sounds quite unpleasant." She admitted.

Dedria nodded, "She has twins, a daughter named Isabella and a son named Vincent. They're 25 now but have the rabbit ears and tail that Suki has." She explained, "Isabella's been an actress for the local theatre for some time. I don't know if she is going to bond with something else? We don't have a lot of Spirit Ascended in Taranor."

Tianie whispered to Setsuna about this, and Setsuna made an unhappy face, her lip curling up unpleasantly before she replied. "Setsuna said thank you for informing her of this...she will find 10 Ascended to send to Taranor, with at least two elders, to help these young ones achieve their bonding."

Dedria stammered, "O-Oh! Oh, uh, that wasn't my intention." She said with an awkward laugh, "please don't tell them it was me..."

The cat bonded woman laughed, her tail dancing behind her in amusement. "Oh, never. I promise I would hate for this Suki to hear you had a role in this." She giggled. "Don't worry, Lady Heart. You will be absolved of any association with this. But for Spirit-Ascended youth to not have a proper chance at an ascension ceremony? That is a crime in our culture."

"Well...thank you. I am glad Isabella and Vincent get a chance to...ascend. Isabella is friends with my sister, she seems like a nice person." Dedria shrugged, glancing at me. "Well, did you want to head to the library?" Her tone wasn't the most welcoming, but there wasn't the obvious disapproval as before.

By this point, Pendra's stuffed pastries had been handed out and devoured between the five of them. I nodded, cleaning my hands off with a spell and taking another sip of water. "Sure, yeah." I replied, rising to a stand. "Let's go." I added, nodding to Setsuna and Tianie before turning and heading back two cars to the Library car.

I grabbed two of the chronomancy books that Veronica had sent to Dedria, settling down in one of the oversized, overstuffed chairs. "Hey, Dee, have you ever heard of the...uh...Ash Queen prophecy?"

Dedria glanced at me in confusion, grabbing a few books herself and settling down in the chair across from me. "What prophecy?" She asked.

"The Ash Queen prophecy," I repeated, trying to be nonchalant, opening the first book.

My friend thought for a while, the anticipation was grinding at my frayed nerves slowly. "I think Suki mentioned it once. Something about Arcanis and Archons and someone who will rise from the Ash and make the world all hunky-dory, right?"

"Yeah, something like that," I replied with a nod. "Did...she think anything of it?"

"Nah, she said it was some ancient prophecy and that prophecies that old are...well. Unreliable at best. False at worst. Anyways. She said if they haven't come true after that long, they aren't going to come true."

"Right, sure." I nodded again, slowly scanning the page. It was just about the technical side of Chronomancy, instructions on how to manipulate your aura to control the powers.

"Why do you ask, Johanna?" Dedria asked, grabbing her book which was about some military strategies or training.

"I just read something about it when I couldn't sleep last night. I wanted to see if it was taught in Taranor or not, that's all."

"Ah, well. Sort of. I mean, I don't think most professors would talk about it. But Suki is something special, super thorough about stuff, you know? So she goes into things that seem pointless. But she had us do a historical religion paper last year, which is why it was brought up in class."

"Ah, that makes sense." I nodded, my voice becoming a bit quieter as I processed this. "Well, thanks Dedria." I added, giving her one of my perfected feigned smiles.

Dedria cast a critical look, her eyes narrowing into a squint as she suspiciously took me in. "You're being weird." She decided, "I'm getting Pendra to make us some hot cocoa and bring us cookies!" She got up and disappeared. This time, I would be able to see the faint trace of a time jump as Dedria left.

I perused through the book, which gave written and illustrated instructions on various beginner Chronomancy. The illustrations were the difficult part to understand. Some books did it, where they illustrated an aura and try to show how to manipulate it to do what you wanted. It was more like a very complicated mathematic equation, some people got it but most didn't. Still, the illustrations did work well in combination with the written instructions. Though every Aura was uniquely different, every single one did follow a set of rules.

According to the book, the space or time 'jump' was one of the fundamental basics that every Chronomancer should learn.

From there, slowing and increasing time around you was next. Just like Dedria was teaching. Then there was the combat that combined the first two fundamentals. There were a few other, more hypothetical skills that only certain Chronomancers could do.

The first was something called a 'blink', where a Chronomancer could disappear from one spot and appear in another without using a space or time jump. It was wildly rare, and even though the book was written five hundred years prior, said there were only two documented cases of this ability. It probably hadn't increased much since then.

The second was the ability to create those same space jump tunnels, but instead of for yourself, for other people or objects. It explained how a Chronomancer that was able to do this would be able to move objects to totally different locations without doing anything but manipulating their aura. Of course, the size of the object - or being -, plus the distance to move it, all affected its success rate of it. It further detailed how a Chronomancer with this power had tried to help move a herd of 1000 livestock, only for the spell to falter part way through and 60 of the animals had been cleaved clean in half when the spell broke.

The last was healing, some Chronomancers were able to use targeted increased time flow to help with faster, more efficient healing. Though, it went on to say that using such methods was also incredibly painful and should only be used for short amounts of real-time.

The book was at least interesting as I went through it, being able to learn more about the lengths Chronomancy could be used, not just in a combat scenario but in day-to-day life. I continued to read, getting engrossed in the studies that I didn't even notice I had subconsciously slowed the time around me to that near standstill until I closed the book and time resumed as normal. The only way I realized was by wondering why Dedria wasn't back yet, only to catch sight of the clock on the wall and see that time had barely passed - maybe five or ten minutes. Instead of the hours it should have taken me to read that text.

Dedria returned after five minutes, carrying a platter full of cookies and a large carafe of steaming hot cocoa with two mugs and a smaller plate of marshmallows. "Ta-Da! Hot Cocoa and cookies. The perfect pick-me-up for you." She smiled, placed the platter down on the table between us, and sat down. "You are in a funk, and we need to get you out of that funk."

I rolled my eyes, "I am not in a funk, Dedria. I've just got a lot going on right now. We have a lot going on right now." I corrected, grabbing one of the cookies anyways. Pendra's cookies were always amazing, and these still felt warm.

"Yeah yeah, I know. You didn't choose to be a Queen at 20, you didn't anticipate the whole world order to go to shit. But that's what it is. You finally have a lead on finding the people that attacked Solaria and killed your Mom and we are on our way to try and find them. It's a bad situation, I get that. But we need to make our best with whatever soup we've been given. And that starts with cookies, hot cocoa, and marshmallows, okay?" Dedria pressed; blue eyes intense on me. I knew she wasn't going to back down from this, she was as stubborn as I was. Worse, even. "I'm not saying it's going to be better overnight. It won't. You have a lot of work in front of you to even begin mastering Chronomancy. But if anyone can do it, it's you. You don't mess around and when you put your mind to it, I bet you could move the Obsidian Tower itself. So c'mon, just…try, alright?" Her tone at the end was more pleading, just wanting me, her best friend to be more like myself, and not the tense ball of stress that I knew I had turned into.

I sighed as I pinched the bridge of my nose as I thought to myself for several minutes. It was hard, moving my mental state from everything being wrong, mourning everything I had lost, to knowing I could get through it. I knew I could get through it; I didn't have a choice. There was a sliver of me, deep down, that liked being stuck in the negative cycle I had been in.

"Okay." I finally said, offering Dedria a half-smile. Besides the ball, I had barely smiled in even her presence. "I'm sorry. It's just been a lot happening and I don't know how to process it. So, I've just been…bottling it up."

"Yeah, I know." Dedria nodded, pouring some hot cocoa into one of the mugs, tossing a few marshmallows in and passing it to me. "You can tell me everything, you know that, right?"

I thought about that, wondering if I could tell Dedria everything. Would my best friend be so accepting of the whole, 'Hey Arcanis blessed me with these things called Archons and I can use their powers?' thing? For a moment, I wasn't sure. I really wasn't, which said more about me than it did Dedria. I took a resolving breath; I did have to try and open up. This was the first step, even if it was borderline terrifying.

"You're going to think I'm crazy," I admitted, voice barely a whisper as I sipped at the drink. "You won't believe me."

"Try me." Dedria challenged, pouring herself drink and nibbling at a cookie as well.

I took another deep breath, "The day I came into my Chronomancy…I heard a voice in my head. It's how I disarmed you…I heard a voice and my body moved on its own." I started, not looking at her. I couldn't look and see her staring at me like I had lost my mind. "I hadn't heard it since. I wrote it off as being tired, not sleeping enough. Until today. When I finally hit that mark, I had heard it again. It told me I could do it. When we sat down for lunch, I zoned out…and I ended up in a totally black void place. And…Maria Maracroix was in front of me. She said she's an Archon. One of four. And I…am the Ash Queen…whatever that means…"

Dedria paused mid-sip, some of the hot cocoa dribbling out past the cup and down her chin onto her shirt. She stared at me critically, not sure what to make of what I was saying. "…You aren't one to lie about something like that…" She said slowly, lowering the cup and grabbing a napkin to try and clean herself up. "Uh. I don't know how to take that, Johanna. Going to be honest with you. How am I supposed to take that? Like, yeah, that is pretty crazy. Seriously? The Ash Queen? So, what, Arcanis…handpicked you to save the world or something?"

"I…don't know. I don't know what it means. All I know is that I've…got a connection to the soul of Maria Maracroix and she can guide me and help me learn combat and stuff. The others I'll connect with as I get stronger. Apparently." I admitted, picking apart a cookie but not eating it. "I'm just as confused as you, Dee. Seriously. I don't know what any of it means."

Dedria sighed, dabbing at the spot on her shirt with a frustrated look. "Well, we're going to have to figure it out together, right?" She asked, and she shot me a reassuring smile.

Relief flooded my whole being, and I cracked a smile, "…Yeah, yeah we will." I replied. At least I would always have Dedria by me. That was a reassuring thought, wasn't it? "Thanks, Dee." I said, shuffling a bit in my chair. I bit my bottom lip, worrying on it before I spoke next, "Do you really think I should let Delain court me?"

"Girl, if you don't get it, I will." Dedria laughed, "He is a tall glass of cold water on a hot Solarian day. Seriously."

I smiled, nibbling at the cookie I had practically disassembled. I missed the warm feeling I got when I looked at him, I hadn't felt it at the ball. Just dread. "Okay. When we get back to Solaria...after all this...I'll let him know. Provided he hasn't started courting someone else."

"That's the spirit!" Dedria laughed and winked at me, taking a drink of her hot cocoa again. "And if he has started courting someone else, I'll castrate him for you."

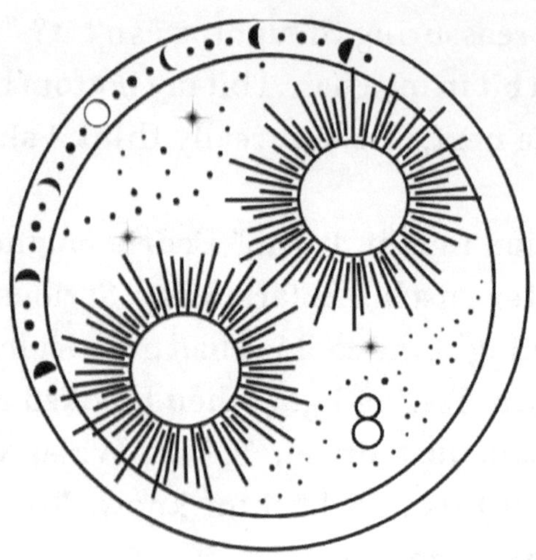

Weeks passed, and each day I got stronger, faster, more precise with my magic and my combat. Each day I fell asleep bone tired, only to get up and do it again. Training had slowed, if only moderately, on the ships. They didn't travel as smooth as rail, after all.

I stepped off the boat at the port city in Lethiarum, and I stared up at the cliff-side city. The port was in a smaller, calmer cove, and there was low ground for about a hundred, maybe two hundred metres and then the mountains started, sharp and steep. The stories were Dragons had built homes in these cliffs, and when the Dragons had become extinct, humans had moved into the extensive tunnel network.

"We don't have mountains like this back home..." I murmured in absolute marvel.

Dedria smiled, "Same. But how do we get past them to where we are going?" She asked, glancing at Tianie and Setsuna.

Tianie seemed annoyed, her tail flicking at the very end. "We have to travel through. There is one passage that leads through the mountain and out the other side." She explained, "Wretched dark thing. But we can walk it in a day. We should go now."

I looked over, "So soon?" I asked and frowned at the tension radiating off of the Ascended. By now I knew the girl well enough and could tell by looking at her she was agitated. I didn't hesitate, "Of course, we leave now." I turned to the Major standing just behind and to my right. "We are to move on immediately."

The Major saluted her, "Yes, Your Grace! I will make sure we unload quickly."

Pendra looked around, his long tail moving behind him as well. "I believe we should check in with the King before we leave. It will give time for the troop to unload our gear, and we will be able to secure a set of wagons and horses." He explained, "He will be slighted if we do not visit him." He added whenI looked hesitant.

Tianie spoke up now, "Setsuna and I will stay here. We will do better being here." Her tail still twitched around in annoyance, every muscle on her body tense. Setsuna didn't radiate the same tension, but I noticed she kept looking around with a narrowed gaze.

I just sighed, "Fine, fine. We will go say hello to the King." I relented to Pendra. "Let's go then." This was the last thing I wanted to do, when the two women I had started to consider friends were so uneasy. I started along the road heading straight to the mountain, "He didn't make it to my Throne Ascension, but I'm expected to go out of my way to see him?"

"It is only courtesy, Your Grace. It shows that you care about the relations with this country moving forward. Even if they are so far away." Pendra was always so diplomatic, "do try to be polite and courteous when you meet him."

Dedria laughed, "Johanna? Courteous to some other silver

spoon-fed royal? This is Johanna we are talking about."

"I should have dumped you in the ocean three weeks ago," I said with a warning glare. "After you switched out my sugar for salt for my tea."

Dedria giggled, grinning widely at the memory, "Oh, I thought that was hilarious. It even got Setsuna to smile."

I grumbled to myself, still slighted over the prank, "I'll show you hilarious."

"Grumbling is not very regal, Your Grace." Pendra chided firmly, "Please do be on your best behaviour when you meet the king. It's very important."

As we walked along the road and found themselves in the vast tunnel and cave network, we found it easier than expected to navigate up to the 'Palace'. I was fascinated by the people bustling everywhere and quickly noticed that it seemed one in four seemed to be Spirit-Ascended people. The mountain city was warm, and I was glad that Pendra had forced her to bring a silk dress to wear. He had probably foreseen this scenario and had packed accordingly, which is exactly why I had wanted him with me.

On the uppermost cave system, it had a large set of wood and steel gates that stopped anyone from getting through. Four Guards were posted outside the gates when we arrived.

"Hello, we are seeking an audience with King Agustus," Pendra said to one of the Guards, using his best Common.

"The King isn't seein' no one today." Said one of the guards, "Come back next week, ey."

Pendra puffed up, his tail flicking in annoyance, "Queen Johanna of Solaria, first of her name is seeking an audience with

King Agustus." He said now, his tone showed his annoyance and displeasure at being brushed off. His gaze narrowed on the guard.

"Don't matter, he isn't seein' no one. Come back next week." The Guard said, resting his hand on the pommel of his sword, glaring at Pendra. Pendra bared his teeth in a silent snarl, he was not a fighter, but he did not like the unsaid threat, and I knew it.

I reached up, touching Pendra on the arm and presenting myself from behind him. "My name is Queen Johanna of Solaria. I understand that King Agustus is not seeing anyone, but I would appreciate it if you would notify him of our presence and let him decide if our surprise arrival is worth his time?" I said as sweetly as I could muster, offering a smile. I didn't like the silent threat of that pommel touch either, but I couldn't be cutting down another country's guards.

Others told me I was beautiful, but I didn't care about those things. Pendra made sure I was well-groomed and dressed, something suitable for my station. He always said I would blend in with peasants if he let me. Today, however, I knew I looked like I fit my station, the long blue silk dress reaching her leather boots, and the gold, platinum, ruby and emeralds scattered through my hair shone in the never-dying mana lights in the cave system.

One of the Guards grumbled to one of the others before he finally turned, knocked three times on the gates and it swung in, and he disappeared. Forty minutes passed before a mousy woman with pale skin and big frizzy hair stepped out when the gates opened again. "Hello, the guard said you are Princess Johanna of Solaria?"

"Queen." Pendra corrected, his voice bordering a snarl he was so angry. "Queen Johanna."

The woman recoiled, taking a step back "R-Right! Queen, yes. My apologies. If you would follow me, I will bring you into the palace."

I patted Pendra on the arm again, "It is okay, Pendra." I said, "Let's go." I stepped forward, with Dedria and Pendra joining me.

"Oh, sorry, just you, Your Royal Highness. No one else may come with you." The woman said, shaking her head at Pendra and Dedria.

Pendra let out a growl this time, very animal in nature and not like himself at all. "Not likely! Queen Johanna goes nowhere without me!"

I sighed, "Pendra, it's okay." I tried, using my best placating tone for him.

"It absolutely is not okay! You may be in danger in there, and I will not be able to get to you!" Pendra insisted, his tail thrashing behind him.

I pinched the bridge of my nose, "Pendra, I will be okay. I promise. And if I'm not, then they will face the full force of Solaria and the Trussam Empire." I explained with what I hoped was a reassuring smile.

The woman stammered at that, "Oh, oh, oh, no! No, nothing will happen to Her Majesty the Queen. I-I will make sure of it."

Pendra turned to squint at the woman, and he leaned down and forward towards her until they were almost nose to nose. "And why should I trust your word?" He asked, his eyes narrowing into slits.

"Pendra, enough," I said, my tone authoritative and firm. I was tempted to flick him right on his nose for being so insufferable. So much for being on 'best behaviour'. "I will be going in with her. You and Dedria stay here."

Pendra stayed where he was for another 30 seconds before he finally rose to his full height again and stepped back. "If you are not back in two hours, I am coming in for you." He told me, and I knew he would do just that.

"I would expect nothing less." I turned to the woman, "lead the way."

The small woman nodded, turning and heading back in through the gates with me following. "I am sorry your slaves couldn't come with you. But only the King's slaves are allowed in the palace." She explained.

I gave her a strange, dumbstruck look, "Slave? They are not my slaves. Pendra is a familiar servant and Dedria Heart is my friend. Solaria does not practice slavery. It is barbaric, and against our values as a country."

The woman went beet red at that, "Oh, uh, well." She stammered, "Still, His Grace would not like anyone but you coming to see him."

"And why is that? Why is he so secretive, anyways? He didn't make it to my ascension of the throne." I inquired now, looking around the cave walls. Many were covered in intricate, beautiful carvings. Some had paint to add colour, but most weren't. Some were of our best idea of what Dragon's looked like. Some were wars of old. Though more than enough depicted what I could piece together a slave uprising that had failed.

The servant tittered at that, unsure of what to say. She was anxious, wringing her hands together. "Well. His Royal Highness has been quite ill. Him travelling outside of the palace isn't reasonable right now." She explained finally.

I squinted at that, pulling as many facts as possible about Lethiarum and it's Monarch from the deep corners of my memory forward. "Isn't he unmarried without any heirs?" I inquired now.

The frizzy hair bobbed up and down as she nodded frantically, "Yes, Your Grace. Which is why we must keep him safe until he gets well again." She paused outside of an ornately carved wooden door. "His Grace is inside." She said, knocking twice before opening the door. "Your Majesty? Queen Johanna of Solaria."

The voice that responded was raspy and weak, barely audible from the entrance. "Bring her in."

I stepped in, greeted with a large room full of plush warm furniture and a large four-poster bed. The man lying in the bed was covered with even more blankets and propped up to a sit with pillows behind him. I instantly knew what was afflicting him - The Rot. The same disease that affected my little sister.

I gave a slight bow. "Good Day, Your Majesty." I said respectfully.

He could barely lift his hand, and he made a dismissive motion, but it was more like a twitch. "Enough with formalities. You can call me Ravan. I am sorry for missing your ascension to the throne, and for your mother's passing."

"Then you may call me Johanna and thank you. I...understand now." I moved closer to the bed to get a better look at him. He had dark hair and a tanned complexion, but the black veins from the Rot affliction were creeping up his neck. His eyes had looked to be dark with shadow, but were actually rimmed with the black veins, his hands weak, frail. His hair was falling out in spots. He was much further along than Kira was. Kira had never gotten to be this bad. "How long have you been afflicted?"

"Long enough that it has scared off any potential wives." He said with a hoarse laugh that just devolved into a coughing fit, picking up a handkerchief to cover his mouth and catch the blood.

I frowned; I was seeing Kira in the same situation if our mother hadn't worked on finding a cure. "Solaria is researching a cure." I said, "I will radio the Tower and instruct them to send their information here. But it is the blooms of the Burnberry Bush off the Southern Isle's that seem to be the key. It must be brewed down into a tea. Given your country's location, it will be easy for you to get there. You must drink the tea three times a day. From my memory, it is recommended to do two full flower blooms per cup."

The king watched me intently now, though I couldn't parse what he was feeling, "I did not agree to see you in hopes of that information." He said, but he looked over to the mousy woman who was standing quietly by the door. "You heard her. Get on it! Find those blooms!"

She squeaked, almost jumping a foot in the air at the fright and she quickly left.

I cleared my throat, deeply uncomfortable by that. "My sister suffers from the ailment. My mother started searching for a cure, and it is continued by scientists and researchers who aided her in her quest," I explained, folding my hands delicately in front of me. "Why did you agree to see me?"

He looked back to me now, "Because I am wondering why the Queen of Solaria is in my country and didn't give advanced notice."

"Ah." I nodded, reasonable enough, "We are seeing the people who attacked Solaria and killed my mother. We have on good authority they are in the lands to the north."

"And why would they be there?" His tone was suspicious suddenly, and I felt suddenly on edge from it.

I considered my next response and took a measured breath, "I am afraid I can't share that with you. All I can say is that we have a solid lead on the criminals."

Ravan's eyes narrowed a bit, watching me with great scrutiny before he nodded. "Very well." He relented, "Is there anything I can provide you to aid your journey? In exchange for the information about the Bloom?"

I nodded, though I still didn't like how he looked at me like I was a mouse, and he was the cat. "Yes, actually. Three wagons, two covered and one open, to help carry my officers and supplies. And twenty horses, four per wagon and the rest that we can ride, so full tack as well." I started, listing off things Pendra had said we would need to procure. He had originally wanted me to get recommendations on the best vendors - but getting them for free would be better. "And any fresh and non-perishable food that your country can spare, enough for a few weeks for 60 bodies. Just until we get our bearings in the Northern lands when it comes to hunting and foraging as we go."

He sighed, "A big ask." He noted, grudgingly, "but given that you may have provided me with a source to cure my ailment, I will grant it to you." He reached over to the side of his bed where a long rope hung with a tassel, and he pulled it. Not a minute later, a Spirit Ascended man stepped in, keeping his head bowed. I noted the fox-like ears and tail he had with a frown.

"Yes, Your Majesty?" He asked.

"Arrange for three wagons, twenty horses, tack for 8, five crates full of flour, oats, rice and spices, three crates of cured meat and fish, six crates of vegetables and one crate of apples to be delivered to the Northern Passage as quickly as possible." He said, and despite his illness, he managed to cast a spell. Parchment, ink and quill would float up from the desk along one of the walls, and writing appeared on the parchment using the quill and ink. Once it was done, the parchment rolled itself up and it was magically sealed with his royal crest. The Ascended man bowed and took the parchment and left the room.

"There, it is done." He used the same spell on another piece of parchment, and it floated over to me where I was able to reach out and take it. "That will tell the Guard at the front gates to escort you and your company to the Northern Passageway." He explained.

It did not need to be said that I was dismissed, and I bowed deeply, "Thank you, King Ravan." I said and I quickly left the room, finding my way back through the maze to the front gate where Pendra and Dedria waited. I handed the rolled parchment to a guard, who just grunted when he read it and passed it to his colleague. They looked at each other and then the one on the left, a slightly shorter man with pale skin and blonde hair. "Very well, I will take you." He said and he started along.

"Come on," I told Dedria and Pendra in Solarian, "I secured us three wagons, over a dozen crates of food and twenty horses." I explained as they caught up.

Pendra beamed in pride, absolutely bursting at the seams,

"Brilliant, Your Grace! That is quite astounding! That means we do not have to use our gold for those things."

"Yes, well, I had to trade knowledge of our continued study of a cure for the Rot." I said, before switching to the common tongue, "Sorry, Guard, I didn't catch your name."

The Guard looked back to me, "Dal, Your Majesty. Can I do something for you?"

"I need to use a radio, to let Solaria know we have arrived safely. May you bring us to one first?"

He looked reluctant, but when I pulled two golden coins from a hidden pocket in my dress, he nodded. "Very well. We have to go to the top of the mountain for that." He said, starting up another path.

Finally, after twenty minutes of walking up steeper and steeper paths and stairs, we emerged at the top of the cliff and were able to breathe fresh air again. I didn't know how stifling being underground could be, it never felt like that in the Tower. He continued to walk along a worn path, to a tall radio tower with a hut below it. "In there. It isn't used much, just tell the person inside what ya need to do."

I nodded in thanks, heading over to the hut and knocking on the door before I stepped inside. "Oh, hello." I greeted, coming almost nose to nose with a wiry woman almost my height, with a large pair of spectacles on.

"Who're you?" The woman asked, eyes narrowing suspiciously.

"I'm Queen Johanna of Solaria." I replied, forcing a polite smile. "May I know your name?"

"Sophie." She said, "Er, Y'ur Grace."

I chuckled, unable to help it at the hasty add-on of hers, and I held out another two golden coins. "May I use your Radio privately for ten minutes, Sophie?"

Sophie snatched the coins out of my hand lightning fast, "Shure," She said and grabbed a small fabric sack on the table, "Time fer my lunch anyhow." She added as she left.

I shrugged to myself, moving up to the radio and nimbly and deftly tuning it to Solaria's Ivory Halls frequency. "Hello, is anyone there? This is Queen Johanna." It felt nice speaking Solarian again.

It crackled and static answered for several long moments, and then a voice responded, "This is the Ivory Halls of Solaria, we hear you loud and clear, Your Majesty!"

I smiled, feeling a rush of relief. "Oh, it is so nice to hear a friendly voice again. Please inform my father that we arrived safely in Lethiarum, and I met King Ravan. He said his apologies for not attending my ascension to the throne."

Again, crackling and static for long minutes before the voice returned, "I will pass that message on, Your Majesty. We are all very relieved to hear you are safe."

"Thank you, and this next part is confidential. It is of utmost importance for it to remain that way." I paused, taking a deep breath before continuing, "I need all research of the cure of the Rot to be sent to Lethiarum immediately and of utmost haste. Please have Tyne package up 400 blooms of the Burnberry bush, as well as 15 specimens that are to be kept alive on the journey."

Silence followed, even after I suspected they should have responded. "Yes, Your Royal Highness," came the final voice, one deeper and far more serious. They had done a change of recipient, as I had suspected they would have. Someone with the clearance to know about the cure. "I will personally see to it at once."

"Thank you, again." I breathed a sigh of relief. "Please ensure the country knows I am alive and well, and we are all working hard to catch these people to bring them back to Solaria and put them on trial for their crimes."

"It will be done, Your Grace."

"Goodbye, Ivory Halls. May the Suns bless you."

"Farewell, Your Majesty. May the Suns guide you."

I adjusted the dials and knobs to remove the frequency - it was classified to only those who served in the Ivory Halls. I left the hut with a broad smile on my face, one of relief. I felt as light as air. "Let us go down to the Passage then, Sir Dal." I told the guard.

As we wound back down through the maze of a city, I couldn't help but notice more and more Spirit Ascended people with collars or shackles on their wrists or ankles than I had on our way up to see the King. It sent a chill down my spine and realization swept through me on why Tianie and Setsuna were so hesitant to come with us. Why would they want to see their kin as slaves? Perhaps they even knew some of these people. The unsettled feeling started to be overcome with rage, it coursed through my veins as easily as I could breathe. Solaria did not practice slavery; it had been abolished a century before I had been born. Sure, there were still problems when it came to divides in social and economic status, but that was inevitable. Even Solaria could not escape that despite its progressive stance.

However, I knew I could not save these people. It was not my place or my country or people. Still, I silently vowed to myself to form an Alliance with Setsuna and anyone who follow her, and if they sought to overthrow the slavers taking and controlling their people, then Solaria's military force would back them if the time came of it. When the time came of it. I would not, could not stand by and let this continue.

I mindlessly followed the guard, contemplating how many soldiers Solaria could give, weapons, food, provisions. I had not been paying much mind to the world around me, but a sharp, childish cry cut through my thoughts like a dagger. We were outside now, making our way towards the ship, still being unloaded. My gaze flew towards the source, a small child who couldn't be more than Kira's age, pale skin and dirty blonde hair. They were curled up into a ball, scrawny arms and boney hands covering their head, protecting it from a whip that was coming down on them again. It felt like everywhere I looked, their skin was covered in welts, old and new.

I saw red, magic flaring and as the whip was pulled back. I acted before I knew what I was doing, using chronomancy to get between the child and the man who wielded the whip. The two and a half months of boat and train travel had given me plenty of time to train with Dedria and I was getting better by the day. I held my arm up, the whip coming down on it and wrapping around. I ignored the sting as it bit into my flesh, instead twisting my arm, catching the whip in my hand and yanking it out of the man's grip. "What? You lack so much confidence in keeping your position of power you seek to beat a child?!" My voice was wrath as my aura flared again.

The man's upper lip raised in anger, "Who do ya think ya are?! She's a damn slave and I can beat 'er if I like. She's not even worth a single copper piece, no one wants 'er."

My aura flared up again like a flame being fanned, and I barely noticed the man having to take a step back from me. An exceptionally strong aura, not controlled by its wielder, could practically suffocate people around it. That's what was happening now, and my aura was starting to get so relentless it was making the air feel heavy in his lungs. Good, the moments this took to be sorted was worth it - he deserved to feel an ounce of the discomfort he had given this girl, given all the slaves who had ever had *him* as their master. "Pendra!"

Pendra was by my side in an instant, giving a deep bow, "Yes, Your Grace?" I watched as the slaver stammered, confused at the royal address. That brought me a deep-seated joy I did not express outwardly.

"Give the man a single copper piece for this child. Free her of her signs of slavery. Send one of the officers with five gold, enough to find her some proper clothes. She will travel with us until we go home to Solaria." I said, not caring to be quiet. I took notice of all the onlookers staring at us, whispering to each other. Good, let them watch.

Pendra nodded, producing a single copper piece out of his money pouch and passing it to the slaver, taking the key and turning to the child, helping her to a stand and getting her collar and shackles off. "You can go over to her," He said, pointing over to Tianie. "She'll keep you safe, okay?"

The man was stammering, his whole face red in anger. "You can't do that!"

I advanced forward like a predator stalking prey, my gaze burning in the wrath I swore would consume me. "I can, and I will. You said she wasn't worth one copper piece, so I gave you one copper piece. That's how slavery works, right? I pay you for her life. I paid you. And be lucky I didn't put my sword through your heart instead."

Only those around me saw it, though it wouldn't be until later that day for Dedria to tell me about the ethereal set of nine tails had formed at my back, and a matching kitsune-shaped helm even with a snout coming from my face. All in an eerie glow of red and orange like shifting flame itself. I was oblivious to all of it, the rage that had been building inside of me since my mother had died was seeping out of the seams now and it was taking me everything to contain it and not burst. I mustn't burst; if I burst here, over a tiny slave child, I had failed Mother, Father, Kira, and my country.

The man ran, convinced I was going to gut him right then, and as he disappeared, a voice rang in my head. It was deep, powerful and full of the same rage I had. "Show them who you are."

I turned to look at the crowd that had formed, knowing what to say like it was in my very blood. "I am Queen Johanna of Solaria, first of her name, and the Ash Queen of Arcanis." As I spoke, new ethereal armor shimmered over me, like I was covered in diamonds. My voice carried, winding through the caves and tunnels for all in the city to hear my claim. For all of them to tell them what could come for the slavers here - the justice of Arcanis.

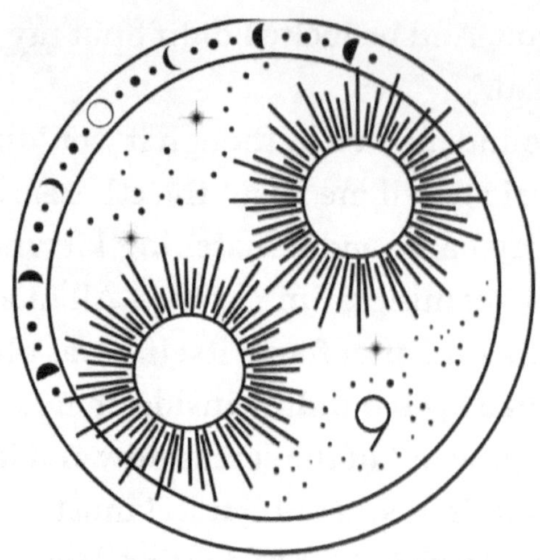

It took us two days to travel through the mountain passage, our pace impeded by a few random boulders that had fallen recently that we needed to break up and get out of the way to make way for the wagons. It was a quiet journey; the only sounds were those of the horse's hoofs on the granite and the creaking of the wagon wheels. I led the way on my horse, a blue roan stallion that was a bit flighty at times but was growing to trust me. Even if it took more treats than I liked to admit.

Dedria nudged her horse to catch up to me as they finally reached the end of the passage and the gates opened for them.

In the Tower, I never felt like I was underground, or without natural light. Our lights and the translucent obsidian pieces that made up the windows meant I never felt trapped. Even the lower levels, which didn't have the windows and were just the kilometers winding back and forth upward over each other, with the cleverly enchanted ceiling to match the weather, never felt suffocating. Being in the tunnel the past two days? I had wanted to rip my skin off with how uncomfortable I was. There was no air flow, just stagnant air that smelled of mildew and dust.

Past the gates was a sprawling forest, with a well-worn road cut into it. "Are we going to talk about what happened in the city?" Dedria asked with a hushed and concerned tone.

I looked over to her, trying to puzzle out her tone. "What do you mean?" I inquired.

"Oh, don't play dumb. You know what I mean." She sounded exasperated and annoyed, and her look was scathing.

I heaved a sigh, nudging my horse off the trail to make sure the others on horseback and the wagons got out of the passage, slowing to a stop. "I...connected with another Archon. Briefly. I haven't connected with him since. Being there, seeing that little girl getting beaten? Seeing the other slaves everywhere...It made me so angry. All I wanted to do was gut that slaver. The next thing I knew, this voice rang in my head and told me to show them who I am. So...I did what came naturally to me." I kept my tone hushed, not wanting anyone to overhear so I even went as far to speak in Taranorian. My accent in it was rough, and I knew it, the language felt sloppy on my tongue since I didn't use it as often as I should.

Dedria sighed, frowning as she listened, "Even I didn't know what to make of it. You told me about the whole...Archon thing but I didn't think that meant you'd get some ethereal armour or whatever." She admitted, waving her left hand a little in a dramatic show. "I'm just worried about you, Johanna."

"There's nothing to be worried about." I pressed, almost annoyed, my tone insistent. "I am fine, I feel a bit better now. Like...a weight is off of me."

Dedria mulled over that, rolling her lips together as she contemplated. "I only hope that these people we are chasing don't catch wind of your new powers before we catch them." She sighed, "last thing we need is them preparing for it."

I nodded in agreement. I give myself two breaths to accept that possibility, to know I may have made an error in judgment with my display. Then I let it go, and seeing the last wagon emerge from the mountain tunnel and I turned my horse towards the front, nudging him into a quick canter to get back ahead. Dedria followed quickly behind me, her voice carrying as she nearly shouted, "You can't just run away from this. Come on, Johanna."

"I'm not running away from 'this'. I just don't think there's anything else to be discussed. It happened, maybe it was an error in my judgment, but it happened. I very well can't go back and change that or hope for something we don't know will happen or not. All I can do is continue training and continue chasing this group." I replied, my tone exasperated and tired. Sometimes, just sometimes, I wished Dedria would stop being such a mother hen over me. "You are wanting something out of me that you can't have. So yes, can we drop this?"

Dedria just heaved a sigh, "You are impossible sometimes..." She muttered, only for Tianie to catch up to us on her horse.

"Setsuna says there is a permanent camp about 15 kilometers from the gate. Tribes use it when they want to make camp close to the city to bring in trade items without having to have the whole tribe go into the city." She explained. "Given the time we should make camp there."

I glanced to the sky and didn't like how the suns were already sinking to the horizon. Getting set up would take time, we were still working out the kinks of the process. I wanted to keep going, but I knew us setting up in the dark, even with summoned light, would mean a later meal and less rest. Still, I couldn't help but ask, "She's sure we can't make it further?"

"She said attempting to go further would be a mistake and our best option is to make camp and she can discuss with you the different directions we can go," Tianie replied with a tight nod.

I relented with a nod, "Fine. Dedria, can you spread the word we will be stopping at the camp for the night then?"

Dedria just rolled her eyes, "Of course, Your Grace." She said, tone mocking as she turned her horse around to trot along the group to let them know.

Fifteen kilometers passed quickly, much quicker than going through the solid rock tunnel where we had markers of how fast we were moving now. Being able to see the sky and flora and fauna was a much-needed change for all of us, as well as being on horseback over being on a train or a boat. It finally felt that we were making tangible progress to our goal, that they could finally stop the people who killed my mother, and all the citizens Solaria and many other countries had lost in the string of attacks.

Once the camp had been made and food had been eaten, I met with Dedria, Pendra, Setsuna and Tianie in the largest tent. The General was sorting out watch schedules and had said she didn't need to be present for this meeting - that she and the soldiers would follow me wherever I went.

Setsuna spoke to Tianie for a moment before Tianie nodded. "Setsuna wants to know what this…Ember…does."

I frowned, looking to Pendra. "I don't really know. It's been broken for hundreds and hundreds of years. We barely had anything recorded on it in the Tower."

Pendra paused, "Wait, that is what we are looking for? A piece of The Ember?" He asked and he looked stressed. Seeing him stressed, lips pursed into a grimace and eyebrows pinched, made the air go cold around me.

"Yes, Pendra. Get with the program." Dedria snickered with a smile.

"Oh...that is...bad," Pendra muttered, and he sat down to gather his thoughts. "The Ember is a weapon. Or was a weapon. Rumoured to have come from Hel itself. Stories said it could destroy whole cities, or even open gates to Hel itself to let Helspawn through. If that is what this group is piecing together, we are in grave danger. Even them wielding part of it is catastrophic. No wonder your mother gave her life to try and keep it out of their hands."

My heart stopped at the mention of my mother, what she gave her life to try and protect. What it meant, if Pendra was telling the truth. "Pendra, why didn't you tell us sooner?" I asked, and I tried to keep my voice free of the hurt I was feeling.

"Frankly, You're Grace, why didn't you tell me what the relic we are hunting for was?" Pendra countered sharply, daring to glare at me. It was rare he ever lost his temper like that; I don't think I had ever seen him look so angry and hurt. I had to remember he had watched my mother grow up too, just like me. That he had known the moment she had died, because his tether to this world would have transferred to me. That he had never shown his sorrow at her death, had always been supportive and present for me as I navigated the crippling grief. Guided me.

My eyes started to burn with tears as I watched him, the two of us staring at each other, tension thick between us.

"Enough squabbling. We should head for the Ancestral Lake. There is almost always a Tribe there, they go there when a member is of bonding age. Many Elders live there year-round, it is tradition for a Tribe to bring plenty of food and supplies with them for the Elders to live off. I believe if Karne's people would keep anything of that importance, it would be there." Tianie translated for Setsuna, but her voice was not stern or sharp, but soft.

I tore my gaze from Pendra first as I nodded, "Okay." I conceded, "Pendra, Dedria, can you leave me with Setsuna and Tianie for a moment?"

Dedria and Pendra exchanged glances, but they left quickly.

"Yes, Your Grace?" Tianie asked.

I thought to myself for a minute before I spoke, trying to find the right words. "What...we saw, in Dragons Gift...I wish you had told me ahead of time. I'm sorry. I would have never had the boat go there had I known."

"Do not apologize, Your Grace. We knew you wouldn't have gone, and we also knew and understood we needed supplies from the city for our journey. So, it's best that we went. Even if it was hard." Tianie spoke softly, the pain was there. I wondered if she had seen someone she knew, bound in chains. Unable to do anything to help them. My soul ached for her, for both of them.

"Right," I frowned, "Even so...Please do not keep those things from me again. We could have stocked up on more supplies when we first boarded that ship and made sure we had been equipped for this journey without stopping there. Regardless. I want to tell you both...Solaria doesn't practice slavery. We haven't in a very long time. It's a criminal offense to own, buy, sell or trade slaves. I want to tell you how disgusted I am by it. And, if your people choose to liberate your own, Solaria's army will be yours to aid you in that. Once all this is over. I give you my word, and I have written this for you if anything happens to me." I passed them a folded parchment with my royal seal on it. "I know it doesn't mean much. But I hope it means something. Your people deserve to be free."

Tianie paused, looking at the folded parchment and passing it to Setsuna. "Honestly, Your Grace, that is more than any country has offered us." She replied, her voice still quiet. "I do not speak on behalf of Setsuna...but thank you. My sister was taken by slavers when I was little. I wonder often if she is still alive. And what it would be like to meet her."

I nodded, reaching forward and showing a moment of softness, and squeezed Tianie's hand. "If it means making an enemy, I don't care. No one that allows slavery in their halls is a true friend of mine."

Tianie's eyes welled up with tears, and she fought them back, her hands aggressively wiped her eyes. "Thank you, again." She said, her nose sniffled a few times.

Setsuna moved forward, placing her hand on my shoulder and her tails unfurled, flitting over me in an affectionate gesture. "You are good people, Johanna Maracroix." She said in common, accent so thick my name sounded more like 'Jo-nna Mar-crok'.

I laughed and smiled unable to help it, putting my alternating hand on Setsuna's shoulder. "Thank you, Setsuna of the Plains."

We stepped apart at the same time, nodding in respect. "I will see you both on the morrow." I said, "May we all rest well for the long journey ahead." With that I turned to leave, heading out of the tent to another smaller tent where Dedria and I would be sleeping.

I crouched into the tent, blurting out, "I told Setsuna and

Tianie that Solaria would provide their army if they wanted to liberate their people that have been taken as slaves."

"You what," Dedria exclaimed, jolting to a sit from her roll on the floor, eyes wide with astonishment at me.

I sighed, "You heard me." I said while giving her an indignant look.

"Yeah, but why? Solaria needs its army to fight against this group." Dedria protested.

"Yeah, but this isn't a...I'm commanding the army to come to assist them right this second. In the future. When this is all over and things have calmed down again." I sighed, pinching the bridge of my nose. "It's important to me, and I do not need to be lectured for it, Dedria. I'm the one that has trained my whole life to be a Queen, remember?"

"Oh, so that makes you immune to making mistakes now? Why would you offer your army to a cause like that?" Dedria pressed.

"A cause like what?! Freeing slaves? Are you saying they deserve to be slaves, Dedria? That they asked for it?" I snapped, slamming my hand down on the ground in frustration. Small stones and dirt dug into my palm, but I didn't care. I relished that sting. "Slavery is archaic and barbaric and cruel. No country could partake in it, and if I must lend Solaria's army to fix it, then I will."

Dedria visibly winced, "I just meant that doesn't Solaria matter? What if this group isn't the last of it?"

"Then I have bigger problems on my hands, don't I? I will just have to make Solaria's army bigger then. But right now, all I can think about is all those slaves in that city, and how the only thing I can do is pledge my army to the people who can help them. And

I would appreciate your support on the matter." I was seething now, and I laid down facing away from Dedria. "Good night, Dee." I practically spat the words out, the taste of them sours on my tongue.

Dedria frowned to herself as she laid back down. "I just don't want to lose you like my mom lost your mom…" She said softly, and she sounded sad. "You mattered more; your grief mattered more. But Mom cried for weeks when she got the news that your mom had died. They were best friends, like us. Against all odds. And I want our kids to be best friends, and our grandkids and great grandkids. I don't want to lose you, Johanna…"

My own grief was becoming more tolerable, so without me being stuck in the cloud of it, I was seeing more and more how many lives my mother had touched. Truly touched - and how terribly she was missed, not just by me, or my father and sister. By everyone.

I gritted my teeth, trying to hold onto that anger but I felt it starting to melt away. How couldn't it? I wanted those things too. I wanted my children to be best friends with Dedria's eventual children. For our kids to have a relationship like we had, right now. Reluctantly, I rolled over to face Dedria. "You aren't going to lose me. Don't be silly like that. Nothing is going to happen to me, Dedria."

Dedria sighed; I could barely make out her shape in the dark so I couldn't see her expression. "You don't know that."

"I do. Arcanis and the Archons wouldn't let anything happen to me if they can help it. I'm part of some…bigger picture now. I don't know what that bigger is, but it's bigger. It's bigger than even this. I can feel it." I insisted, and I hope I sounded confident and sure. I didn't totally believe what I was saying, but there was a tiny voice in my gut telling me it was true.

"Do you really think so?" Dedria asked as she sat up and cast a soft light to get a better look at me. Her expression told me she didn't believe me, not for a second.

I nodded and sat up myself, shifting to face her fully, crossing my legs. "Yeah." I replied, "I can't explain it. But it's this…tug on my soul. I don't know what it means outside of I'm meant for something bigger. Maybe that's stupid, and I'm going to suffer for that arrogance. But for now, I just have to trust it."

Dedria scrunched her face up and she nodded, "Okay." She replied. "I trust you. And I have your back, okay?"

I smiled at that, open and honest, "I know." I said.

Just then, Maria's voice spoke in my mind. I don't think I'd ever get used to that feeling, the feeling of someone's voice all around me but not. "She is your Shadow, and she is just as important to your success as us."

I put my hand on my forehead a moment, "Guh. Never going to get used to that I think…" I voiced aloud, "Maria…she says that you are my 'shadow', whatever that means…"

Dedria leaned forward, almost eagerly, "She's talking to you right now?" She was absolutely eager; her tone was like a child being promised sugar.

"Your Shadow is the one being who moves with you in battle as effortlessly and seamlessly as your own shadow. She will protect you and guide you where it matters most." Maria sounded in my mind.

I nodded, still holding my forehead. "Mhm." Once Maria was done speaking, I repeated it word for word to Dedria.

Dedria pondered on this for several moments of quiet between them. Outside the tent, the sounds of the officers and guards were milling about, working out watch schedules and making sure there was no spot someone could slip through. "So basically, she's saying we're stuck together till the end huh?" She finally said as she cracked a smile.

I couldn't help but give a broken laugh at that, "Yeah, I guess so." I nodded, "not that that's anything new." I added with a smirk.

"Obviously not. She's clearly late to that news." Dedria winked, "I'm sorry for my pestering. I should know by now that you know what you're doing."

I adjusted my legs, fixing the light blanket over myself. "I'm trying really hard here. I need to bring the people that killed Mother to justice and everything else that has to do with it. It's not easy. The only things I've known for sure are this trip, chasing these people, and promising Solaria's army to Setsuna to free her people."

Dedria frowned and nodded, "Yeah, I know. I need to support you with that. I'm sorry for doubting you. I am." She was just wanting what was best for me, I knew that, but some hidden protectiveness in her had made her question my abilities. Even knowing that, it hadn't made it hurt any less.

"I know, Dee. Thank you." I said with a slight, hopefully reassuring smile. "We should really try and sleep. The boat and train journeys felt long, but the next leg is going to be grueling." I laid back down, and Dedria put the light spell out. "Goodnight, Dedria." I said softly.

"Goodnight, Johanna."

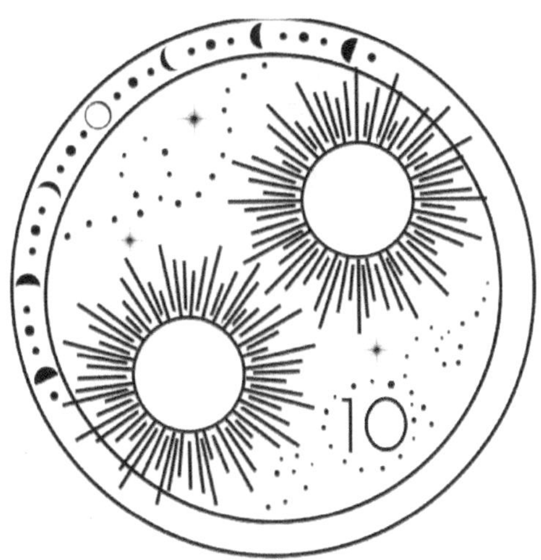

The Ancestral Lake was nestled at a high altitude where two mountains met. It took two and a half weeks to get to the base of the southern mountain. After that, the path was not well worn, and after three days of trying to clear the way for the wagons and making half a day's progress in that time, I reluctantly made the call that the wagons had to be left. We packed and saved what we could, Pendra stashing as much non-perishable items into his little pocket dimension and tossed what we couldn't to wildlife to devour. From there it was still slow going, but mostly because we were relying on Setsuna on guiding us, and she had only been to the Lake once before, not long after her mate claimed her.

On the fourth night, making camp as well as we could in the thick brush, everyone sleeping wherever there was uncovered ground, I sat across from Setsuna and Tianie at one of the small fires. Pendra was cooking a few rabbits that had been caught on the way. Questions about the Jinn were nagging me, and I was trying to come up with a way to ask. Finally, I broke the silence between us, "Tianie, can you explain what claiming a mate is?" I turned my gaze up from the fire to the other woman. "I have heard you say it a few times, but I don't know what you mean."

Tianie paused, she was roasting a few foraged vegetables on a stick, "It is...hm...complicated. There are many ways. An Ascended may lay claim to another by challenging them to combat. If they succeed, they get to mark the other. A mark is a bite on the shoulder, deep enough to scar. An easily visible way for anyone else to see that they are claimed." Her voice was calm and instructive as it always was, though she glanced up to me as she spoke. I could tell, even in the low light, that she was gauging my reaction.

Though, I hoped to Tianie's surprise, this just peaked my curiousity and desire to learn. My head tilted, and my gaze remained calm and nonjudgmental. "So, what happens if they don't want to be together anymore?"

Tianie was quiet for long moments, I could tell she was thinking of her next response, the best way to word it in the common tongue, "It depends on if they are Soul Mates or just Mates. If they are just Mates, yes...the one that was claimed can leave if they want, but having a strong Alpha is ideal. The Alpha cares for you, they provide you with food, shelter, and protection. The best Alpha's also make sure their mates are happy, in every sense of the term. In return, you tend to their needs. You cook, clean, make and mend clothes, make and break camp, and yes, have sex with them. But you always have an Alpha to care for you...I suppose Alpha is a broad term. Setsuna is the Alpha of our tribe, but she is not the Alpha mate to all within the tribe. She is the one that makes the choices for all. An Alpha Mate only has to concern themselves with the well-being of their mates and taking orders from the Tribe Alpha." She was careful with her wording, wanting to be sure nothing was lost in translation, and because of that she paused frequently. The hissing and sizzling of the fire hung in the silence.

I nodded a bit, contemplating. "Okay." I said, thoughtfully. "So...Let's say you are someone's Mate. What if someone else wanted you?"

Tianie smiled, and I didn't miss the way she seemed to admire me. Was it so strange for non-Ascended want to learn this way? Who was I to judge their culture? I knew things that Solarian's did made no sense to them, but they did not villainize me for it. "They would challenge my current Alpha for me." She explained, "If they win, then yes, they would win me if I consented. A Mate always has a choice. Even if they have not been claimed before. The combat is just a show of strength - that they are strong enough to care for you, better than you may care for yourself, or your current Alpha does if you have one. If they lose, then my current Alpha does not lose me."

I leaned forward and gently laid another piece of wood on the fire. "So, if you are claimed by five mates over your life, you would have 5 bite marks on your shoulder?"

Her and Setsuna chuckled, and Tianie nodded, a wry smile on her face, "Yes. But that is very rare, almost unheard of. Most Ascended only have maybe two or three mates in their whole life, with one of those tending to be a Soul Mate. Most only ever have one Alpha before finding what they would call their Soul Mate."

"What is a Soul Mate?" I asked finally, noticing Dedria, Setsuna, Pendra and even a few of the officers in the area around us listening intently too. A warmth bloomed in my chest at that, that these things which could be so easily misunderstood could be explained in a trustworthy space.

"A Soul Mate is the mate meant to make your soul feel whole. Beyond just a mutual contract. You do not seek to be with anyone else." Tianie said with a soft smile on her lips. From that, I couldn't help but wonder if Tianie was thinking of someone when she spoke of Soul Mates. I also knew that I would probably never know. "Karne is Setsuna's Soul Mate. Her Mate Mark is on her left shoulder, not her right."

I pieced together what was being said to me, like a small puzzle, "So an Alpha Mate would mark a non-soul mate on their right shoulder?"

Tianie smiled and nodded, "Yes, Your Grace. Just so." She pulled the collar on her long-sleeved shirt down across her right shoulder which showed a scarred bite mark. It was older, not the puckered pink of a newer wound, but pale against her dark brown skin.

I smiled, wondering if Tianie missed her Alpha, if her Alpha missed her. "Okay. Is...there anything else I should know?" I asked, "If we are going to be around Elders of your race and possibly a tribe, I want to understand your customs and not offend."

"An Alpha mate can have as many mates as they like. Excellent hunters have between five and seven. Man or woman, it does not matter to us. The act of sex and physical affection is not taboo in our culture. On the Solstice, when the Spirit Realm is the closest to ours, we celebrate by drinking strong liquor, singing, dancing and having sex openly with others."

Dedria was drinking some water just then and she choked on the liquid, having to cover her mouth and turn away as she coughed. She waved her hand, frantically encouraging them to ignore her. I had no issue doing such a thing, though I hid a smile in my hands, and I knew my cheeks were flushed. Multiple mates, not only openly discussing sex, but even having sex in front of others. It certainly made indecent thoughts come to surface that I had to tamp down.

"Multiple?" I asked and felt even more flushed at how high pitched my voice was. "Heh, and where I am from such a thing would be seen as immoral." I lifted her hand when Tianie went to speak, those gentle features starting to contort with anger. "That does not mean I view it as immoral. Just like with what I offered before; it is not my place. I do not expect you to tell me what is right or wrong with Solarians, so I would never tell you or your people what is right or wrong."

Her anger melted away just as quick as it had started to take hold, "Sorry, Your Grace...I am afraid we are very used to judgment and shame when it comes to our culture and way of life. It is why a place like Lethiarum views us as lesser and enslaves us."

I waved my hand dismissively, "I understand." I offered, "Tianie, thank you for taking the time to educate me through this trip." I offered a slight smile, it felt earnest and kind, though I wasn't sure it didn't come across that way.

The rest of the night went on mostly quietly, and the next day Setsuna announced that we would be cresting the highest point of the journey and after that, it should be easier going.

As we reached the peak of the walk, Setsuna rode beside me, with Tianie on the other side of her. The Kitsune woman's ears panned around, and her gaze shifted up towards the sky. She inhaled deeply and then frowned, "Something is wrong." She said in common, and then she was kicking her horse into a gallop down the gentle slope through the dense forest.

Panic shot through me, and I kicked my horse to follow with Tianie, Dedria and Pendra following behind. "Pendra!" I shouted over my shoulder, using magic to amplify my voice. I knew my voice lilted with the panic I was feeling. "Change forms! Get to the sky, now. Fly ahead!"

Seconds or maybe minutes later for how long it felt it took, the shadow of Pendra's drake form hid the suns as he raced ahead. Time felt strange, not strange like it did when I used chronomancy, but strange like when things were wrong, and adrenaline was pumping. My legs strained in the saddle as I leaned over the horse's neck. Even from here, below all the trees, I could catch glimpses of his blue scales and how his wings seemed almost translucent with the Suns shining through them. Drakes were not like Dragons of old, they only got to be a certain size, never bigger, and their bodies were longer, almost snake-like. I couldn't keep my eyes on him though, it took all of my attention to keep my horse chasing after Setsuna and not hitting the trees and bushes on the way. More than once I had to duck down super close to my horse just to avoid a wayward branch or use a spell to knock it out of the way.

Finally, I could see the break in the trees into the valley, the shimmer of water on the lake glistening. It was the smell that overtook me just before my horse broke through the trees.

I had the overwhelming sensation that I had been transported back to Solaria on the day Mom died, on the ground in the destruction of the train explosion. Burning wood, gas and oil, but the most pungent of all was burning flesh. Spread out in front of me were dead Ascended, cabins and tents collapsed and smoldering, the flames long burned off but the coals still hot. It took all my strength to pull the horse to a stop, the animal's eyes showing white from the terror of what lay in front of them.

My stomach churned with nausea, with panic, from the flashbacks that were slamming into me over and over again. I had to breathe through my mouth, though that almost was worse. I grabbed a silk scarf from my saddle bag, meant to tie around my hair but I tied it around my face instead.

Tianie and Dedria had stopped at the edge of the trees, both frozen and unsure of what to do. Their horses were stamping their feet and dancing back and forth, even they wanted to run. I could hardly blame the beasts.

Setsuna was already off her horse and running to each body, checking for life before moving to the next one. She was sobbing openly, heaving for breaths as she moved frantically with no real direction. I knew the sights and smells I was experiencing right now would follow me through the rest of my life.

My horse reared up suddenly, tossing me off. I barely landed in a crouch, having to use Chronomancy to fix my body so I didn't end up on my back. By now, the sounds of the soldiers who were crashing through the forest started to be heard, the wave of shouting of confusion and urgency hitting. I stood up, not letting my legs give out like they so wanted to, and I used the same amplification spell on my voice to call out orders - find anyone living, put the fires out, start collecting the dead.

I barely remember moving through what could be called a village, checking each body for signs of life, getting Pendra, still in his drake form, to help move rubble from the structures. Some bodies were cut clean in half, some stabbed with fatal wounds. Most I noticed, had been killed from behind. Like they had been running away.

I stayed in a state of disassociation, not processing the horrors I was seeing, not truly. If I took a moment to process it, I would vomit. I would cry. I would break.

Hours passed, the Suns had set, and the moon had risen. Pendra lifted one beam off a particularly large, half-collapsed and burned structure where I had seen movement.

"Here!" I called out, and suddenly five, ten, twenty others were around me, all starting to haul the debris carefully off the only living soul we had found so far. It was a man, huge in stature, over six and a half feet tall, with wolf-like grey and white ears and intense yellow eyes. He was barely alive, his eyes fluttering as he seemed confused at the Solarian soldiers and their Queen digging him from the rubble of the building. I heaved a piece of lumber off his legs. He was still half buried, but he was alive. Thank Arcanis, he was alive.

"Karne!" Setsuna screamed, her voice cut through all other sounds, full of anguish and despair. She had to be physically held back by Dedria and Tianie and even then, the two of them could barely restrain her. I knew all too well what she must be feeling, I had felt similar things when I saw my mother dead. That had just been Mom, not even someone I could say made my soul feel whole, as a Soul Mate did.

Finally, after what felt like hours but was only minutes, he was freed. It took six soldiers to move Karne from the rubble to a flat patch of ground. Thankfully, two of them were trained in healing, and they got to work. They moved seamlessly with each other, passing things back and forth, talking quietly in Solarian to each other only when absolutely needed.

I moved over to Setsuna, who was kneeling on the ground, still sobbing though it didn't wrack her whole body like before. No, now it was a soft sob that was all consuming. My heart broke as I observed her, her tails, which normally were up and shifting idly, were flat on the ground, lifeless. I knelt in front of her and pulled her into a fierce hug. A gesture of warmth that I had never displayed to her before, and even I couldn't stop my own tears from forming in the corners of my eyes. They burned, making it hard to see.

I finally let her go and sat beside Setsuna now and holding her hands tightly as we watched. Both of us feeling utterly, completely useless. The other soldiers, knowing they couldn't help here more, had resumed their work, putting out the smoldering coals and trying to find anyone else alive, moving every body respectfully so they were all together.

"Tianie?" I asked, my voice barely a whisper, after two hours of watching the healers continued to work. I only knew that much time had passed because of the moon that hung in the sky, full and bright. Too bright for a night like this, I decided. A new moon, or a waxing crescent. That would have been more suitable, though I didn't know why I felt like this.

Tianie jumped, not expecting to be called on. She had just been standing there, fretting and watching, gaze full of worry. "Yes, Your Grace?" Her voice was barely more than a croak from crying herself hoarse. How could she not, seeing her Alpha so low? Seeing her Alpha's mate like this?

"Please...instruct the General and soldiers on the way to handle the dead," I said, looking up at her. "So we can let their souls and spirits move on once more."

Tianie started to cry again silently as tears started to fall down her cheeks. "Of…course Your Grace." Her voice wavered, and she turned to do just that. She stood straighter, shoulders pushing back and chin lifting as she moved with a renewed purpose. She was no help just standing there, and even she knew that.

The healers finally moved away from Karne, looking to Setsuna and me. "He will live…we think." One said, "We have put him in a deep mana sleep. If he survives this, he will wake by the morning." They got up together and headed off to help the effort. Even though the healers were Solarians, I couldn't remember their faces. I couldn't place their names, or their rankings.

I squeezed Setsuna's hand, in my slivers of free time, I had been having Tianie teach me some words in their native tongue. Now seemed like a perfect time to use those new skills. "He will be okay." I told Setsuna now, sure my accent was awful, but I did my best, and the woman looked startled at familiar words coming from my mouth. "They put him in a mana sleep, he should wake by morning." I added, trying my hardest to be reassuring and comforting. Things I was not used to being, not lately.

Setsuna nodded, moving over to Karne and sitting behind him, lifting his head gently as she shuffled her lap under him. She stared down at his face, her hands shaking as she brushed soot and dirt from his dark skin. She started to cry again, though it was silent as tears fell from her cheeks onto his face. Relief, I noticed. Tears of relief.

At least there was this - at least Setsuna still had Karne. Even if so, many others had died, at least Karne was still alive. I chose to hold onto that fact.

I rose to a stand, my muscles stiff from sitting in the same spot for so long, trudging off to help the others. I was no longer needed there, providing support to Setsuna. I had to continue moving forward, and as the moon continued to rise and then start to fall in the sky, with the dead collected, the fires put out, and three more living had been found. Smaller children, who had no real auras yet and had escaped into the forest and hid until the commotion of the Solarian soldiers, and the familiar tongue of Tianie giving instruction, had caused them to be spotted. It had taken two hours of Tianie convincing them that they weren't going to be harmed for them to finally come out.

The eldest of the children, a boy who called himself Peyton, explained to Tianie that the group had come in the dead of night when almost everyone in the village had been sleeping. That he and his sisters had been with their parents in one of the furthest tents from where they had come, and that was the only way they had escaped. The three bickered for 5 minutes between them when asked how many, and they finally decided that it had been at least twenty-five, though it could have been forty or even fifty. I only picked up some of the words they said, my gaze darting between each one as they fought.

"They mo-moved so f-fast." The smallest stuttered and started to sob.

"What do you mean?" Tianie asked, she was sitting on the ground and had them all piled into her lap, her hands caressing and soothing them.

"I-I would b-blink and the-they would be in a d-diff..." She hiccupped between her sobs, "different spot. T-The ad-adults didn't stand...stand...stand...a chance."

Dedria frowned as she heard this, leaning into me and whispering, "Chronomancers..."

I nodded with realization, frowning deeply as I thought about this. Did that explain why this group was able to travel so fast? How they had gotten into the Ivory halls? How they had managed to beat the elite Guards that had been assigned with my mother to protect the shard of the Ember and the other relics? That was the only explanation, it felt clear as day now that it had been spelled out to me. I also felt like a fool, for not considering the possibility sooner. Which also meant that this group was far more dangerous than any of us had been preparing for.

As I listened to the children describe that night, the screams and how one figure had moved through the chaos, dragging the hulking mass of Karne with her like he was no more than a ragdoll, going straight to the longhouse that Karne had been found in. How they had emerged holding a strange, multi-pointed object that they described looking like a smouldering ember in one hand, and a flat, matte piece in another hand until they floated it into the air and said an enchantment in a strange language that made them feel ice cold. How the two objects had fused after that, spinning in the air and how they said it looked like part of it was missing still.

Still, the figure had used this relic to start lighting the building on fire all around them, summoning lightning straight from the clear sky.

"The Ember." Tianie offered in common, looking up to them. "It has to be..."

I nodded, "Thank you." I said, kneeling in front of the children and offering my hand to them, palm up. I felt the Archon that had made itself known not so long ago in Lethiarum push their way forward into her conscious, he was so full of rage. It bubbled inside of me, an angry tempest wanting to bring ruin to those who had done this. Ignoring it was like trying to swallow a huge rock, impossible. I knew I was just along for the ride at this point. As the children touched my hand, my aura flared and I heard as they all gasped, and Tianie started to sob again.

Confusion etched through my being until I looked beside me. A Kitsune in their true form had materialized there, he was huge, his shoulder while standing was where my shoulder was when I was standing. He bent his head low, to be even with me and the children and Tianie. His nine great, fluffy tails danced beside him, and he was black as the night but was also freckled with white like the stars. His eyes were blue, piecing into the very soul of whoever he looked at. He leaned forward, pressing his snout into the chest of each child. Just as he had appeared, he disappeared. I felt him speak into my mind now, "You need to go to Kayori. Setsuna needs to bring you."

I winced, not used to the voices ringing in my head that was not my own. They felt alien and strange still. "...He says that we need to go to Kayori, Setsuna..."

Setsuna had torn herself away from Karne at the sight of the Kitsune manifesting beside me, and she swallowed visibly, her eyes wide, "I can't go back there." She said, shaking her head. "I will not go back there."

En-Kai growled, and it was enough to make my hair stand on end, "She must. It is her true calling. To make Kayori see what her inaction has caused. Make her see that she must help. The world will fall without her help."

"He says we have to." I offered, gently as I could.

"No. She will kill me and everyone else here if we show up on her beach." Setsuna protested, and she was convinced of that. It came clear with her next words, "She's already tried."

"Not if I am there with you." I felt him shake his great head in my own mind, which felt like I had shaken my head too hard and mow my mind ached from it, "my daughter knows better than to defy me."

"He...says that she won't, because...he is her father..."

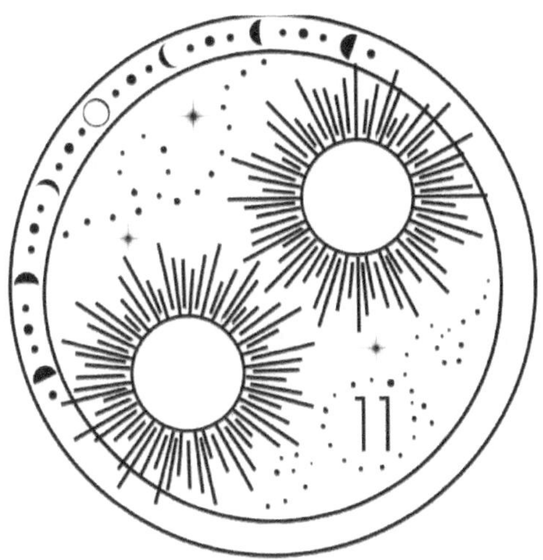

The boat was 500 metre's off of the shore of the white sand beach of The Grotto. Home of Kayori Ten-Tails and her many children. I stood at the edge, holding the rail, Setsuna to the left of me, Dedria on the right. Karne was on the other side of Setsuna, with Tianie tucked behind them both to translate as needed. Though as I had been getting more and more fluent it was needed less and less.

"We need to go to land," I said finally, breaking the silence. I hated how I didn't sound sure though. Setsuna had said enough about how her mother would receive us to warrant it, but I didn't like it any better. "Us hiding on this boat won't make it better."

Setsuna sighed audibly and glanced over to me. "She already knows we're here." She said, "She's going to kill anyone who steps foot on that beach." It wasn't like she hadn't said that at least once a day on the three-week journey here. Three weeks, we couldn't delay any longer. I had been away from Solaria for too long - been away from my people, my home.

I pinched the bridge of my nose, not letting the irritation flood through me, "So you've said." I pointed out, grinding my teeth together before I continued, "But we need to try. She has the last

Shard of Ember, and we need to make sure it stays safe, and out of this group's hands."

"No, you have to do that. I brought you here. I will see you to that shore, and then Karne and I are going home." Setsuna was annoyed and stressed. I didn't blame her. She didn't go into why she had left this island, but I knew it didn't hold good memories. That her relationship with her mother was not one of love. Not like mine had been. Especially given Setsuna was sure Kayori would kill her for coming back.

I nodded tightly, "Yes, of course. I told you the boat will bring you to your lands."

Karne growled to himself, looking down at me. He still didn't trust me, that much was obvious. But his mate seemed to, so he tolerated my existence. "She will not bring ya to shore." That seemed to be where he drew the line. I wasn't ready to argue with him, honestly. Even recovering from his injuries, he was still a beast of a man. He was over 2 meters tall, muscle rippling on his arms, legs and across his chest and abdomen. He could probably throw me and Dedria 20 feet if he really wanted. His eyes were yellow, flecked with green, and it added to the unsettling nature of him.

Setsuna looked up to him, "Karne, I will keep my word." She said now, firmly. I knew she would not tolerate him telling her she could not do something, just from knowing her the short time I had. Setsuna never let anyone tell her to do anything.

"I do not care. Ya will not bring 'em to tha' shore. You're not going to risk yer life for some stationary civilization's foolish affairs." Karne snarled down to her, his accent thick and hard for me to understand.

I bristled at hearing 'foolish affairs', but I shoved those feelings down, "It is fine, Setsuna. Dedria and I will proceed to shore alone." I was dismissive, looking back towards the beach.

Dedria sighed, rolling her eyes, "well, it's a straight line. We can jump there." She pointed out, "It will be a bit tricky because it's over water, but if we move fast enough, we can make it."

My expression was carefully blank as I looked at her, but my emotions were far from. "You want me to jump over water?"

"What, are you saying you can't?" Dedria asked, a smug smirk on her face. A challenge. One she knew I wouldn't turn down.

"...You are impossible," I muttered, and let my magic start to course through me, to build in the air around me like static. "Fine, let's go." I didn't hesitate as I climbed up onto the railing of the boat, my aura flaring as I channelled that tunnel through time and space to the beach.

I hadn't tried jumping across anything but solid ground before, so at first, I fumbled and had to catch myself on one of the ropes hanging from the side of the ship to be able to lower myself to the surface of the water and start again. I could already spot Dedria, halfway to the beach now, and I knew I would have to sprint hard to catch up. The water felt strange to run on, it threatened to break under each step, but my magic kept it solid enough. Finally, I reached the soft sand instead, and I slid to a stop with a pant. "I've never run so hard in my life." I told Dedria, putting my hands on my thighs as I glanced up to her.

Dedria's expression was unreadable, her eyes were on the tree line, "Yeah, well I don't think it will be the last time you've run that hard."

As I looked to the trees, I saw things I hadn't seen on the ship. Pairs of eyes, of all colours, piercing yellow, greens, blues and browns that blended into the shadows, peering out at them. Dozens and dozens. I felt my heart stutter, I swallowed hard, and my aura rippled out, confirming what I was seeing. Four dozen beings, all standing in the tree line. All watching Dedria and I, and the ship behind it. But it was one, right in the centre that I narrowed to having piercing yellow eyes, with the strongest aura of them all. I knew immediately who that was - Kayori. It could be no one else, not with magic that felt that strong, that potent. That ancient.

My aura flared up without my consent, and that ethereal form of the great Kitsune En-Kai appeared in front of me like a personal guard. I knew he probably couldn't stop anything from hitting me, I could walk right through him if I wanted. It was the symbol of him.

He spoke through me, me own voice mixing with a deep masculine voice that sounded strange to my own ears. "Kayori, daughter, it is time for you to come out of hiding and start helping the world as you were meant to be."

A snarl came from the brush, and instead of a Kitsune in true form, the lithe form of a dark-skinned woman appeared, nine white tails perfectly spread out behind her, with one extra as dark as the night that stood out like a sore thumb. "How dare you use the image of my father to try and trick me!" She snapped, her gaze and tone full of rage. She carried a blade in one hand, it hung limp at her side, but I knew she was coiled and ready to strike me down with it.

"Trick?!" That strange voice came from me again, this time it was a shout, and it was so, so full of anger. My whole body was flooded with anger. "You call me a trick?! I am En-Kai, Archon of Arcanis and the Ash Queen, and Shepard to the Ascended!"

Kayori visibly faltered at the end of the words; she had not heard that name in quite some time. "T-That's not possible..." She stammered now. "Leave the island! At once!"

"We will do no such thing!" Roared the voice, and the form stamped his foot into the ground. "How dare you, humiliate yourself, and me? Hiding from the world like a coward, like the matters of the other countries aren't important enough for you?!"

Kayori flared up, angry at the accusation. "You died! You and Mother and everyone else. You were stolen from me. I had to find my way, and how dare you suggest how I did it wrong?"

En-Kai stepped forward towards her, "I did not raise you to hide and cower. I raised you to fight against those that held the world down by the throat, who threatened to upset the greater good."

Kayori threw out a spell, which Dedria was able to deflect. I was locked in my own body, helpless to intervene. "Where were they?! Where were they for me? When slavers came and tried to take my children and raped me?! They didn't care!"

I pushed against En-Kai's hold on me. It felt like pushing against a wall in my own mind. "I...would have cared..." I was gasping for my words, my voice a rasp, "my mother would have cared." My vision was flickering, dark spots appearing, it was so hard to focus on what was going on. There was shouting, panic, but I couldn't understand the words. The world started to tilt, I knew I was falling but could do nothing to stop it, just as I heard Setsuna's voice. When had Setsuna gotten there?

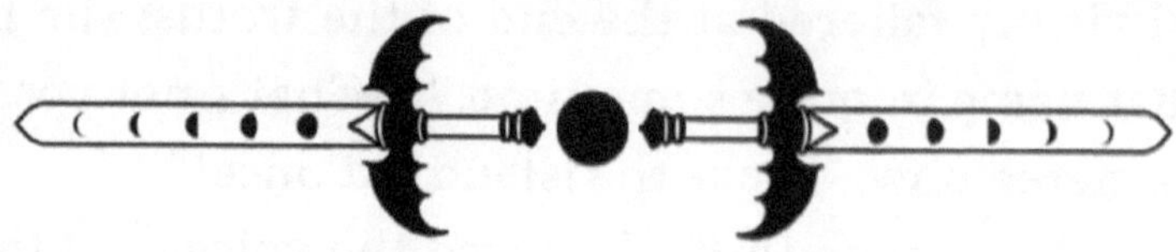

I finally woke up on a firm mat that was on a wooden floor, a fire crackling close to me, keeping me warm. I shot up to a sit, "Dedria?! Pendra?!" I called; voice frantic. I couldn't prevent that. "Setsuna? Tianie…?" With each name, my confidence was falling, my voice shrinking, as I noticed no one was with me. Where were my friends?

"Get out of my way!" Snapped Dedria's voice from outside of the room, and she shoved past two strange Kitsune's and into the room. "Oh, thank Arcanis above you are awake. You collapsed on the beach just as Setsuna got there. The fool swam from the boat after us because she was mad Karne told her she wasn't allowed to do something, and we took off without her."

"She followed us?" I asked, eyes widening, that's when my head throbbed, it felt like it had been slammed several times into a solid wall. "I don't…understand…How long was I out?"

"Three days," Dedria replied, sitting down. "We were really worried. By we, I mean me and Setsuna and Tianie and the soldiers. Kayori said you were in a mana coma but none of us believed her. You didn't use that much magic jumping from the boat, it didn't make sense."

I visibly winced at hearing how long I had been out, looking around the room. A fire in the center of the room, the roof partially open and slanted to guide the smoke up and out. Thin wooden walls. There was a low table, with cushions around it to sit on. "Water?" I said hopefully, my throat itchy. Dedria didn't hesitate, grabbing the pitcher of water and a cup, pouring the water and passing it to me. I took the clay cup that was handed to me, and I swallowed almost all of it at once. I drank three more before my stomach started to hurt. Add that to the list of aches. "The last thing I remember was hearing her voice, and then I blacked out."

Dedria nodded, sitting down beside me. Her face was near unreadable as she started to talk. "When she got to the beach, En-Kai disappeared, and you collapsed. It dissolved into chaos for a bit, Setsuna started accusing Kayori that she had done it, then Pendra showed up in his Drake form and threatened to eat Kayori whole. Then all of Setsuna's siblings came from the tree line, and Kayori started shouting at them to get back in the trees. When Pendra took off from the ship, the soldiers did as well because they knew something was wrong then. Setsuna was still shouting at Kayori; I couldn't understand a lick of it anymore because she started speaking Kayori's native tongue. It almost started a whole-blown battle, until I got between Kayori and Setsuna and shouted at Kayori that a group was going to come for the piece of the Ember she had and would destroy the world with it and that there was no point in making their job easier with all of us fighting. That shut everyone up pretty quick. She grudgingly agreed to host us and brought everyone to the village they have." Dedria took a breath; she had raced through that, and it took me a moment to catch up.

I frowned deeply, looking down at my hands. "I'm sorry. I don't know what happened." I admitted, feeling ashamed. "No one was hurt?"

"Hurt? No. Though Pendra has seen no peace from Setsuna's sisters pestering him. Same with the Soldiers. Man and

Woman." Dedria snickered, winking at me, "The woman has forty-five daughters. No sons. I don't know how; it seems bloody impossible to me."

"Truly? Forty-five? Statistically that is quite impossible." I agreed, but I couldn't smile at it. I sat up more, "everything hurts. What sort of bed is this?"

"It's not a bed." snorted Dedria, "It's a hard mat on the floor. Come on, let's get you up and outside. Everyone will be relieved you are awake." She got up, helping me to a stand.

I was wobbly on my feet at first, leaning on Dedria for support. "Thanks..." I muttered, slowly stretching each limb out to get better blood flow. After five or so minutes I wasbe able to stand and move on my own and followed Dedria out of the house, the sliding wood and opaque almost paper-like panel moving to one side and revealing lush green grass and at least 10 more houses, quite similar to the one I was in. The almost courtyard was full of activity, soldiers practicing against Kitsune in their humanesque form. Every pair I looked at, one of the Soldiers was being put in the dirt. Some of Solaria's best soldiers, being bested left and right. Still, I found myself smiling, it was a sight I never thought I'd see, ever. My gaze found Kayori, the woman standing and watching all the sparring and shouting instructions in near perfect common, and I walked over to the woman. "Kayori." I said, and I bowed at the waist in respect, even if I was still sore.

I noticed how critical Kayori's gaze was as she scanned me over, her yellow eyes narrowing. "Queen Johanna, is it?" She asked, voice terse. She didn't want me here, she had allowed us here because of the threat to the Ember, no other reason.

[144]

I nodded, slowly straightening, "Yes, but you may call me Johanna. It's okay." I replied, "I...want to thank you for letting us be here." I looked around again, admiring all of it. How could I not? "I understand that must be very hard for you...Taking a risk on us like that. I meant it. What I said before I passed out. I would have cared about what happened to you. And my mother would have too. If she had known...she would have helped you bring justice to those that hurt you, and your family."

The Kitsune scanned me very intently, lips pursed into tight lines, trying to decide if there was any hint of a lie to my words and I knew she would not find one. "Your friend, Dedria, she said that there is a group hunting the Ember pieces?" She finally asked.

I nodded, my expression turning grave, "May I sit?" I asked, motioning to the log bench a few paces away, and when Kayori nodded, I sat down. "Eight months ago, Solaria was attacked. A supply train barreled through the end of the line and exploded. It killed almost five thousand citizens. While we were panicking about that and the chaos, a group got into the Ivory Halls and killed my mother and 10 guards to steal a relic...At the time, we didn't know it was the Ember." I frowned, burying the pain of talking about it. Had I talked about it so openly before? "From our intel, we've understood that they have attacked every country that held a known piece of the Ember...Except we did not know one was here. We only knew that from Setsuna." I glanced over to Setsuna, who was walking through the sparring groups and giving instructions to the Solarian soldiers.

Kayori considered this, the silence hung between us, barely overshadowing the sounds of the sparring. "They will find out eventually where the last piece is." She said finally, "You and your group will stay here as long as you are able. You will train and get better. Once I've deemed you good enough, you will take the last piece and return to your home."

I frowned, thinking about this. More time away from Solaria. More time away from my people, my country, my family. Did I have a choice though? I didn't see another path. "Are you sure?" I asked, then visibly shrunk at the scathing look I received. "Then we will help earn our keep. We will help cook, clean, hunt, farm, everything." I said quickly.

Kayori nodded, "Very good." She said, "If keeping you and your lot here will keep the Ember shard away from the people you speak of, then I suppose it will be worth it."

I gave a faint smile, forcing it to look as genuine as possible, "Thank you…" I murmured.

"The vision of my father. Was that real? You didn't make it to trick me?" Kayori asked now. Her suspicion obvious.

I nodded, "He's real," I reached up and tapped my head, "I hear him occasionally. And another. There's supposed to be two more, but I haven't…er, well, I haven't met them yet."

Kayori nodded sagely, closing her eyes as she thought of her next words. "Very well. We will work on that as well. If you are to face these people, you need to be at your strongest. And that means having all of the Archons at your disposal."

I wanted to reach my hand out to give Kayori's a squeeze, but I resisted. Still, the relief on my face was palatable. "Thank you, Kayori." I replied gratefully, "Honestly, I mean it. Thank you."

"Don't be fooled, Johanna, Queen of Solaria, I am not your ally yet. But I will also not be your enemy while there is a greater threat on the horizon," said Kayori now, and she looked at me with a very serious gaze. "Tomorrow we start training at dawn."

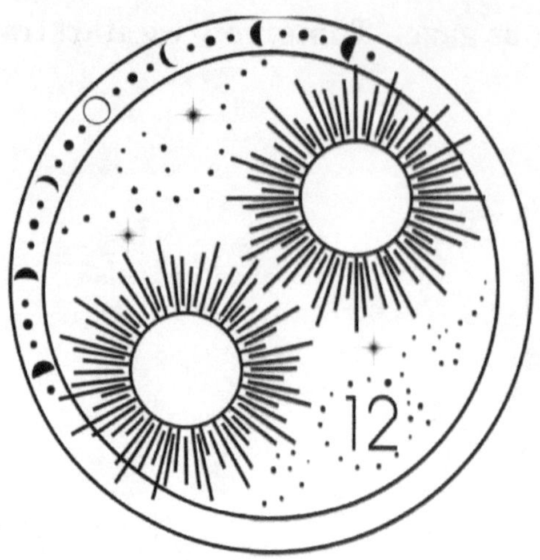

From a dead sleep, I jolted up and almost instinctively summoned a concussive blast at the gong that sounded outside before I remembered where I was. I was safe. It was okay. I was safe.

My heart was thundering so loud I could hear it and feel it in my throat. I had been running from a shadowed figure, carrying what I was sure was the Ember, as the mystery figure behind me cackled maniacally, summoning lightning down onto me, around me. The Obsidian Tower was falling all around me. My senses had been overwhelmed with the sounds of screaming, the smell of burning oil and wood and flesh. The air had tasted acrid. I had only been able to see a few feet in front of me the whole time. A stark difference from the absolute quiet I was now surrounded with, the fresh air of dew and salt water and soil.

I clutched my chest and realised just how hard I was breathing, and that sweat was collected on my forehead, in my hair, my clothes were sticky from it.

The spell dissipated in my hand, glad I hadn't set it off into the wall and destroyed it, and I got out of the bed. Grabbing my training gear and getting changed quickly, getting Pendra's help to put my hair back up into a tight bun before I headed out to the courtyard. Kayori was already there, all ten tails curled into one mass which idly swayed behind me. "You wake slowly." Was all she said, there was a hint of judgement in her tone.

I swallowed, my throat still dry, "Bad dream." I admitted and looked around. It was already full of life, Kitsunes and Solarian soldiers were up and moving around, getting breakfast ready, getting ready to spar, clean, whatever was needed.

"A premonition of what will come if you fail." Corrected Kayori, who looked at me with a stern expression. "So, we must make sure you do not fail."

I faltered at that, had it been a premonition? If the people who killed my mother succeeded? I supposed it was possible, my mind coming up with the worst possible scenario - they had said the world order needed a reset. A cleansing. If the Ember was able to connect with Hel itself, then that would surely do it, right?

The Obsidian Tower was built to be quite indestructible. At least, against the current technologies. Even Wyrms avoided it. But if this Ember could bring it down, then nothing was safe, was it? No one would be safe. "I guess you're right," I admitted, and I didn't hide the concern I felt.

"Hey Johanna." Dedria practically flounced up to us, sounding chipper as anything.

Before I had a chance to question why Dedria was so happy, Kayori nodded. "We won't practice here. Too much commotion." She motioned for us to follow her, and she started walking along a pebble path to the north. She guided us for almost half an hour, to a clearing with a pond and stream. It was well shaded, warm but not so warm we were sweating. "You will follow my movements exactly." She instructed firmly, and Dedria and I both knew better than to question it.

We formed a triangle, Kayori facing North with me behind and to the right, with Dedria to the left. Kayori started to guide us through a variety of strange stretches and poses, the two of us giving each other strange looks occasionally. Wondering what the purpose of any of this was. I had to trust Kayori, I didn't have much of a choice, but that didn't mean I couldn't question why we were doing this.

After about twenty more minutes of this, Kayori moved to a cross-legged sit. She stared at us unblinking until we sat down as well. "Close your eyes." She instructed.

Then, she continued to speak. "Breathe in. Focus on your mana. It's an old friend to you at this point, you know it, you know how to manipulate it to do what you need it to do. Be it light, air, water or controlling time and space itself. Dig into that. Let your consciousness float along its surface. Breathe out. Dive into it. It's thicker than water, resistant at first. It wants you to keep floating there. Keep going, it will succumb to you. Breathe in. Keep pushing against it. It's an orb, swim towards the centre of it. Even if your mind starts to hurt from the strain, keep going. You need to reach the centre. Now, do you see it? It's small, but it glows. The source of all your power, it radiates out, creating that thick liquid you are now swimming in." Dedria murmured in agreement, confirming she did see it. I didn't say anything, just gave a slight tilt of my head as confirmation. "Good. Breath out. Push through, you're almost there. And touch it."

It was strange, feeling the source of my power like this. It flowed through me, I felt it vibrating my blood, my being. Eager for release. I had to hold it in, contain it. I kept pushing down into the source, finding that orb. It was impossible to miss.

In my mind, it was no bigger than a marble but shone as bright as one of the suns. I inhaled sharply when I finally touched this little glowing ball. It felt like my whole body was on fire, full of electricity and it almost hurt.

What didn't hurt was the next voice that rang in my mind so clearly, "Excellent! You've done it!" Masculine, not like En-Kai's. It was new, but it felt so familiar.

"Haha! I told you she would!" Another new voice, feminine this time.

"Who are you?" I interrupted now mentally.

The masculine voice spoke first. "My name is Liang Trussam. The first shapeshifter who took the form of a dragon and ended the 20-year civil war."

"And I am Rachael Heart. Daughter of Victoria Heart, the first known Chronomancer." The feminine voice said next.

I found herself smiling, "It's nice to finally meet you both." The last two Archons, and with their appearance it felt like I was reunited with old friends. A strange feeling, but I accepted the warmth it gave me.

"Not nearly as nice as it is to finally meet you, trust me." Said Liang, and he laughed. His voice was so bright, happy and confident. With it, I felt like I could tackle the whole world.

"Oh, stop being such a suck-up, Liang." Rachael scoffed, but she laughed too. "You didn't even think she would be able to connect with us!"

Before they could dissolve into bickering, Kayori's voice cut through them both. "Now that you've connected with your inner mana, it's time to harness it." I snapped open my eyes and watched as Kayori walked over to a tree. She pushed against it, showing it was firm and real. "With practice, you will be able to do this." And she steeled for a moment, her aura barely even flared as she threw her first into the tree, the wood shattering and splintering before the tree fell.

"Oooh, I like her!" Rachael laughed, gleeful as a child. "En-Kai was so right, coming here was brilliant!"

Dedria scrambled to a stand, moving over to inspect the tree. "Whoa, that is badass." She marveled. "You are brilliant!"

There was a shadow of a smile that appeared on Kayori's lips, "I haven't heard anyone tell me that in...a very long time." She admitted, then gestured to the fallen tree and shattered stump, "doing something like this is going to take a lot of practice. You will have to channel your mana into your actual body, making you stronger, faster than you already are."

I got up myself now, "I've never seen or heard of anything like this." I murmured, more to myself, but Kayori still heard me. "I want to learn. No matter how long it takes, I will learn." Where I had sounded unsure at the start of the sentence, pure ferocity was showing at the end. Something like this, something so secret, hidden, unknown? Not only did I want to learn it so I could say I had, but it could also help even more in the battle against this group. It could be the key to my victory.

Kayori turned to me with a critical gaze, taking in the sight of the young Solarian Queen who was standing there with a determined look on my face. It was unmistakable, and Kayori nodded. "I have a feeling you could learn anything once you set your mind to it." She replied, "If you are serious about training with me, then it is time you learn my story, and how I came to this island. A student must know their instructor as well as the instructor knows the student." She motioned for both of us to follow her, starting back to the main living area, going to her home where she lived alone - all the other Kitsune's shared the other 10 homes. Once inside she used the small fire pit to start heating water for some sort of herbal tea. I watched her curiously, but cautiously.

"You already know my father is En-Kai. Hundreds of years ago, when he was still alive, the Ascended did not travel and roam as they do now. They were settled, in one great city. Because of him. He got them to join and live at peace together. Kitsune and Ascended, living as one." She sounded sad, and Dedria and I both sat quietly to listen, not daring to interrupt. This was more than I had ever read regarding Kitsune and the Ascended. This history was secret, unspoken. It did not get passed down from generation to generation from word of mouth.

"My family consisted of my parents and my 10 siblings and obviously me. Not every tribe was happy with all the Ascended living as one. There were fights often daily between different Alphas. Most were petty disagreements, and they just required a mediator. They were not the simple Mate disagreements, but disagreements about food, hunting responsibilities and housing. Eventually, my siblings and I oversaw whatever law enforcement was required. One day I was handling such a disagreement between two alphas' when one of them charged me, unhappy that I was not ruling in his favour immediately. He was well respected, but young. Strong headed and rash. I..." She trailed off, contemplating a moment before she continued. "I killed him. I did not intend to, not really, but he had tried to kill me first." As she was speaking, her voice was quiet and reflecting, I could tell, it had been the first time she had told this story in a long time.

Kayori added the dried leaves to the water, stirring them in with a wooden spoon as she then took the tea pot from the fire. "It caused a rift in the city. Some were angry I had killed the alpha, and others defended me because he had attacked me first. It was a messy affair, but of all of them, the one that was the angriest was his sister. While he was rash, he looked like a well-behaved pup compared to her." I could tell Kayori was chewing the inside of her cheek from how it puckered in on one side.

"She went blind with rage; she was furious at me for killing her brother. Furious at my family for allowing it to slide. Her bonded was a Wyvern. Not exactly known for their cheery attitude. None of us knew how far her anger went. One night, maybe a month after, my family and I were enjoying dinner all together. You have to understand, by that point, it was rare we all got together. Most of us had mates, and two of my brothers were expecting kits so they spent more time with them, understandably…So us getting all together, in one spot at the same time? It never happened anymore. She showed up, carrying some…wretched weapon that smelled wrong." Kayori's nose twisted, like she was smelling it all over again. Her eyes were focused on the tea, not looking up at us. I wondered if she reflected on this night often. If it plagued her, like the loss of my mother plagued me.

"I don't truly know how to describe how it smelled wrong, but it was like rotting flesh that had been baking under the summer sun." She had gathered small snacks, fresh fruit and vegetables and cured fish, and would lay the platter down in front of us before grabbing the teapot, pouring the still steaming liquid into small wooden cups that she handed to Dedria and me.

"She used magic I had never seen before; it was ancient and powerful and captured all of us in our home, and she made me watch as she killed every member of my family. My parents first, and then my sisters, and then my brothers. With the last being my best friend, my twin, Kytal. And then she killed herself, so I couldn't even get the satisfying feeling of killing her for what she had done."

Silence hung in the air, heavy and almost suffocating. I looked to Dedria, seeing a mirror of how I felt - sadness, sorrow, sympathy, before looking back to Kayori. "I'm sorry," I said finally. "I'm sorry that happened to you. I'm sorry you experienced that."

Kayori just shook her head, "I have had many hundreds of years to think about it, come to peace with it." She replied, "In my youth, my father had told me of a story about a myth called the Soul Forge...A weapon forge built into a mountain somewhere that the gods themselves had built, and it would use a fragment of a soul from a willing participant to create a weapon for that person. Perfectly balanced for them, perfect for their fighting style and their whole being. To be summoned and unsummoned at will, always sharp. Tethered to them for as long as they live. I spent a hundred and fifty years searching, and I found it. On this little island. And then I got to work learning how to use it. I needed to find it, to master it, to remember him. As a way to carry his memory into the world. To make him proud."

Just as she finished speaking, she summoned a sword that looked like crystal, its hilt fit perfectly in her hand, and she laid it down on the low table they were sitting around. Up close, the bladed edge had tiny, razor-sharp serrations, the hilt was intricate and beautifully crafted. "If you prove yourselves to me, I will make you each a weapon in the Soul Forge."

Dedria and I looked at each other, full of mixed emotions. We had both just heard a terribly sad story, and then been presented with an opportunity that we didn't even know had existed before. That no one else in the whole world would have besides Kayori and her children - to own a Soul Forge weapon.

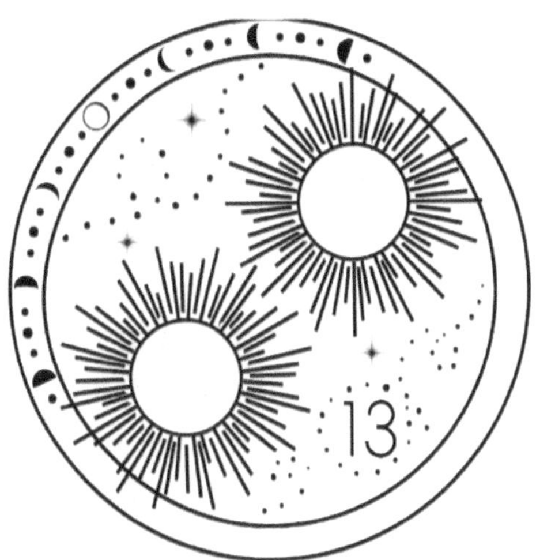

"Again!" Kayori's voice called out from the sidelines, and my chest ached from how fast I was breathing, Dedria leaning against me breathing just as hard. We were back-to-back as we defended against wave after wave of Kayori's daughters, all supremely skilled fighters in their own rights. Two full months had passed, quiet and peaceful outside of the intense training from dawn to dusk.

Occasionally the ship, which had docked in a more hidden cove, got incoming radio from Solaria and the other countries. They didn't have much information about the state of the world, besides the fact that the group had named themselves Nox and was continuing to travel the world, bringing destruction and death wherever they went. It pained me to stay where they were, hiding and just training. As each missive came in that detailed more attacks with death tolls, I started carrying those, too. I argued daily that the longer they hid, the longer Nox had a chance to get ahead, to train better, to know more about me, about my powers.

"If you can't harness the powers of the Archons willingly, then you will not win." Came the voice of the old Kitsune again, reminding me that to date, I had never been able to unlock the powers of the Archons on my own. Reminding me of my failure.

"I need a break." I protested, not daring to look in Kayori's direction. I knew if I looked that way, I'd end up on the ground for the dozenth time today. "Just five minutes, please."

"You think Nox will give you a break in a fight? No. They will take any weakness you have and exploit it against you. You don't get a break until you can show us you have the power of the Archons at your disposal." Retorted Kayori, she was circling the courtyard watching us intently. The past three days had been like this - unyielding and relentless.

I groaned, deflecting a series of attacks from one of the daughters - Sasori, I think her name was, and managing to harness the mana-enforced strength for a split second to toss her aside, only to end up face to face with another, Etsuko, I could tell it was her because she had a scar on her right cheek. This training was so much harder than what Setsuna had put us through. I dug deep, trying to harness that tiny but powerful bit of mana that was hidden within myself, while continuing to defend. This is what I had been training to do - it was easy now to find this source of power when I was meditating. It was significantly, almost infinitesimally harder when I was in combat. It kept slipping between my fingers, every time I thought I was close it moved further away when my concentration turned to defend myself.

I knew in meditation I could use that power to transform the power of the Archons to be at my disposal. I had practically mastered that. For the past two and a half weeks, I had been doing the current drills from the moment both suns rose until both suns set. The only meaningful break Dedria and I got during this time was to eat a simple lunch.

I deflected more blows, grunting as one hit me hard in the side. I ducked another series of punches, swinging my leg out to trip my assailant, only to rise back up and have to catch a punch that almost got me right in the nose. Letting out a hoarse shout of frustration, and there was a flicker of my aura that made the air crackle with electricity. Tossing that Kitsune to the side I moved on the offense now, taking a step forward and Dedria took a step back, mirroring me instinctively.

Dedria surprised all of us with how she moved with me in a fight - how she covered me, moved with me. Maria had not lied - she was my Shadow.

I met the oncoming blows fluidly and swiftly, my aura still flickering with that same electricity. I had to take a step back to avoid a strike to my head, throwing a fist to counter. Why did this feel so endless? So pointless?

"It's not pointless." Came Maria's voice in my mind, a soft reassurance that the Archons were always there, just waiting for me to unlock my full potential. They couldn't guide me with this, they had said that over and over. It was up to me to find my way. "You can do this. You must believe in yourself; you still doubt your ability in the face of adversity."

I grunted as a punch landed in my side, the pain radiating up my ribs. I deflected the second blow that was aimed at my shoulder. Mentally, I snagged that source of power. I could feel it slipping away again, like water in a hand, and I let out a primal scream, gripping it harder. Trying to keep it in my grasp.

I barely registered the small gasps floated through the crowd of Kitsune's, and the ethereal armour of Solaria that formed body, the helm with visor closed on my head. I found herself holding a sword that felt real in every way, and I started using that to deflect the blows, the Kitsune's not stopping. I was careful, only ever using the flat side of the blade. I didn't know how sharp it is, it looked plenty sharp on the quick inspection I was able to get, and I did not want to actually hurt anyone.

It went on for another twenty minutes before Kayori let out a whistle to signal the stop. "That's it!" She said, moving towards Dedria and I now. "You did it." It was praise, but it sounded hollow. Disbelieving, almost.

My chest heaved for breath. Would I ever breathe normally again? I refused to let go of that power just yet. "I did..." I managed out, and Dedria and I leaned back into each other fully, sliding down to the ground together. "Arcanis above everything hurts."

Dedria was breathing just as heavily, slowly lying down completely beside me. "If...we have to do that again today I might die." A gross exaggeration, but even I could agree with that. It sure felt like I was going to die.

"Kayori please don't make us train more today...we're exhausted." I pleaded now, not caring how whining I sounded. Lying down as well and finally cracking an eye to look at Kayori who was standing over both of us.

"No, we are done with the hard part today." Kayori agreed, "You will need to show you can repeat this and do it faster. But we can do that tomorrow." She had a wry smile on her face like she was enjoying seeing the two of us in their current state. Sadistic. "Up. If you keep lying down your muscles will ache more. Up." She motioned for a few of her daughters to help us to a stand, and to bring them some cold tea to drink.

"Now that you have proven you have the strength and resolve, it's time for you to see the Soul Forge. I have only crafted myself a weapon, and it took me some time. I don't know how long it will take me to craft one for each of you."

I and Dedria groaned while still leaning on each other and nursing a cup of tea each. "Now?" Dedria protested, eying Kayori suspiciously.

"You get thirty minutes, to eat, drink and stretch. Then we will make the hike." Kayori replied firmly, and she turned and walked off, talking to some of her daughters in their native tongue.

The moment she was more than 4 metres away, Dedria and I sunk back down to the ground, still sipping tea. Though the two of us grudgingly started to stretch our aching muscles while we sat, wincing and grumbling profanities under our breath as we did.

I sat up straighter, stretching my arms out now, they felt like lead. The little girl I had freed back in Lethiarum walked up to me now, holding a tray of food and more tea. Her name had turned out to be Bevy, and Pendra had taken her under his wing, so to speak, and was teaching her every possible skill he could that she showed any amount of interest in. "Oh, Bevy. Thank you." I said, helping put the tray on the ground.

Bevy's hair had turned out to be quite matted and unkempt, so we had been forced to cut it into a short style that made her look more like a boy than a girl. "Oh, you, you are very, very, very welcome, Your Grace." She stammered when she spoke, and Pendra had said he was sure it was nerves. I wasn't so sure, but I didn't pay it any mind.

"Sit with us, please?" I asked, motioning for the girl to sit. "I've been so busy training and everything I haven't had much time to talk to you." I offered a sincere smile that I hoped read as reassuring to her, "Pendra tells me you are very bright and have already learned to read!"

Bevy sat, brushing her pant legs off and nodding eagerly, "Mhm! Yes! Reading has been very fun. I can learn so much, much, much with books! Ma'am Kayori has, has a book on healing herbs and, and plants. I have been enjoying that." She didn't look at me, just kept her eyes on the ground, or her hands. I wondered how long it would take her to unlearn that.

I watched her curiously, "You know, if you are interested in learning about healing and medicine when we get back to Solaria, I will put you with the tutors needed so you can specialise in those things when you are old enough. Solaria has one of the finest schools of healers in the world." I offered, "Pendra has told you that you will remain in the Ivory Halls until you have come of age and have obtained the skills you need to thrive in life, right?"

Bevy nodded again, though her pale cheeks flushed bright pink. "Yes yes, Your Grace! It is ever, ever, ever so, ever so kind of you."

I just smiled again; it was hard not to with Bevy. "I freed you from slavery. I would never dream of putting you in a position where you end up back in it. As far as I can see, you are my responsibility. So, you will be a ward of the Monarchy of Solaria."

The young girl giggled, a bit nervously. "Thank, thank you, Your Grace." She squeaked, and we both heard Pendra calling

Bevy's name. "Oh, Sir Pendra is calling me. I better, better go to him. Yes yes." She scrambled up, giving me a half bow and curtsey and then turned and ran off to where Pendra was.

I watched her go, catching Dedria's strange look. "What?" I asked.

"You are basically adopting her." shrugged Dedria now, "Bit young to have a daughter your sister's age, don't you think?"

I rolled my eyes, "You are so dramatic. She is a ward of the Monarchy and my responsibility. Me freeing her means nothing if I do not provide her with a better life than she had when she was in slavery. It is only reasonable for me to do what I can for her."

Dedria giggled, nudging my shoulder with her own. "Yeah, obviously. But you're a big softie. Talking about getting her tutors and everything so she can be some nurse or doctor."

"Well, if she's as bright as Pendra says, then she could very well be a doctor." I scoffed, crossing my arms. It was hard to not to feel criticized right now. "Honestly, what is wrong with what I'm doing?"

Dedria laughed some more and shook her head. "Nothing is wrong. I'm just giving you a hard time, Johanna. I think it's nice what you've done and are doing for her. Truly. But I wouldn't be your best friend if I didn't give you a hard time now and again."

"Sometimes I feel that's all that you do." I muttered, finally pushing up to a stand. I regretted it almost instantly but hid the pain I was feeling. "Time is almost up. You know how Kayori likes us to be prompt."

Dedria made a disgruntled face, "Seriously?" Though at the glare I gave her she sighed and stood up, brushing herself off. "Fine, fine." She muttered, starting off along the path that

Kayori had gone. We caught up with her easily enough, sit was sitting on a small log waiting for us, and the Kitsune nodded to them.

"Good, you were early." She praised, "The hike there is nearly an hour. It will be good for your muscles after the training this morning." She started off along a path that headed towards the mountain of the island.

Along the way, we caught sight of various wildlife, from exotic birds to small mammals. The sounds of the forest and all the life living in it seemed to envelop the trio, and I couldn't help but smile. "I'd never hear things like this in Solaria..." I said softly, not wanting to speak so loudly to disturb the fauna. "Well, maybe in the south, where the mountain and forests are...but not in the Tower."

Kayori peered over her shoulder to me, I was sure I looked like I was in a state of bliss. "We have catalogued over 100 unique species of birds, 150 mammals of all sorts, 80 different reptiles and amphibians, and we stopped counting after the 500th insect." She chuckled.

I marvelled at that, "Just on this island alone?" I asked, and when Kayori gave a nod, I couldn't help but continue, "That's...that's amazing! And those are probably all unique to this place, not found anywhere else. Would it bother you if we were able to bring those catalogues back to Solaria with us?"

"Well, they aren't copied, and they are in our writing. I doubt anyone in your country would understand it." Kayori said, "One of my daughters is fluent in common...I guess I could request her to start translating them, but it may not be done before you leave."

I hid my disappointment, thinking about this. "That is fine. If it is not done, then…we will bring what has been completed. But I would greatly appreciate it, Kayori. Solaria could benefit so much from this new information. New species, never seen before."

Kayori thought to herself, "Hm, well I can arrange for it. But I need your word that no one will come to this island and try and exploit the animals that live here. It is my duty to protect them - those attempts would be met with death."

I instinctively paled at that, looking startled that I would even suggest that I would allow that to happen. "No, never! Some may request to visit to catalogue themselves, but I would never allow that without permission from you first."

The path was getting steeper as we climbed, my whole body aching with each step, but Kayori seemed to guide them effortlessly along the path of least resistance, "Very well, I will trust you with that then." She offered. "Have you decided who would like to have a weapon forged first?"

"Dedria." I said before she had a chance to speak. "Dedria should do it first. I have the power of the Archons. She deserves a soul forge weapon first."

"Johanna, no." Dedria protested, and I didn't have to look at her to know she was irritated. "It should be you. You're the whole Saviour of the world or whatever."

"Dee, I'm not discussing this further. It should be you. You're my Shadow. You need this." I countered, and I gave Dedria an almost scathing look that very much said that I was not going to budge on this.

Dedria sighed, pinching the bridge of her nose. "You are impossible…" She muttered, "Fine. Fine, I'll go first."

"Good." Kayori nodded, "we are almost there, just over this small ridge." She walked up over the ridge first, moving aside enough for the two of us behind her to follow though she turned. There was a break in the trees and brush so we could see out over the island now.

I turned with Dedria once we got up, and gasped. It was breathtaking - the expansive forest cascading down the mountainside, which faded into the grassy areas dotted with the tall trees where the houses stood could barely be seen. Then the expansive soft sandy beaches, and then the ocean. "Oh, wow." I breathed out. "I could stand here forever and never get bored of this view…"

Kayori smiled, "We are very lucky to call this island home." She nodded and turned. It was a cave entrance, and she headed inside, casting a spell to light the way.

I hated to turn away, but I forced myself to follow with Kayori and Dedria, having to almost jog to catch up.

The cave went into the mountain, the sides dotted with moss and lichen, and a few different reptiles hidden inside that were seeking shelter from the midday sun skittered out of our way. It had a few different turns, but Kayori walked the path with confidence. She knew this path like the back of her own hand, and I knew they would not be lost as long as they stayed with her. As we walked, the inside of the cave grew warmer and more humid, and I hated to think what it was doing to my hair. Pendra would probably be furious. The glow from Kayori's spell slowly faded as the stones themselves seemed start to radiate with light, and the dark stone started to transition to a soft white crystal that shone on its own.

Finally, we stepped into the main chamber, and I was once again struck with awe. It was lined with crystals, and it seemed to radiate the soft glow of sunlight at dawn or dusk. At the centre was a huge basin, full of hot lava that never seemed to cool. Kayori had worked hard to outfit it with everything she needed - anvils, smithing tools, various leather aprons and gloves.

"Welcome to the Crystal Forge." Kayori said, and her voice didn't even echo here.

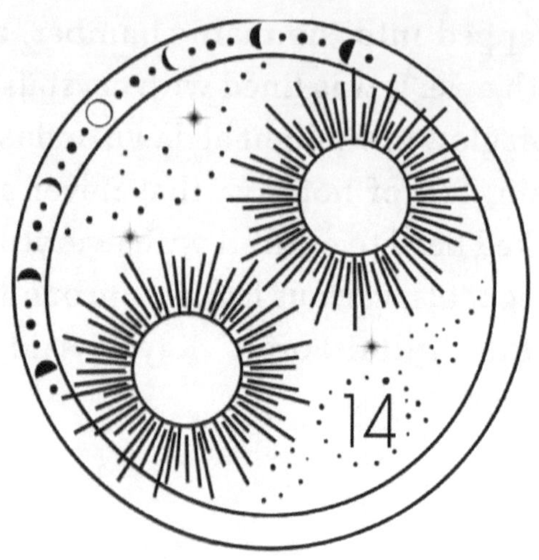

Kayori moved around the Crystal Forge silently, her leather shoes making no sound on the smooth floor. She collected her apron, and a pair of gloves, and moved to the basin. It was so hot the air pushed her hair away from her face. "Come here, Dedria." She said firmly. My muscles were tight in anticipation and anxiety. It took everything in me to calm them down.

Dedria just swallowed hard and nodded, moving forward. "Right then…What now? Do you need my blood or something? A finger? I'd rather you not take a finger. A toe maybe, I could probably live without a toe."

"You sure crack a lot of bad jokes when you're nervous." Kayori observed with a slight scoff, "No, I do not need your blood or finger or toe. Just your participation in this ritual. I will guide you through it." Once Dedria was beside the Basin, she was using her magic to draw runes around Dedria. I felt helpless as I stood back and watched. "I am encircling you in protective enchantments. Once I am done with this, we will start the ritual. You might feel very cold for part of it. You need to be fully willing through this whole thing, if you are not, it will fail, or the weapon will become corrupt."

"I thought you said you'd never done this before," said Dedria, with a bit of a worried look now. "So how do you know that?"

"It did not come with a full manual, but there were a few books in this room. I just was not able to discern most of the words because they were in ancient script, but I was able to get the general idea from the drawings inside." Kayori answered, her tone anything but reassuring.

"Sure. Cool, cool, cool, cool." Dedria nodded, standing patiently until Kayori finished the enchantments. I could tell Dedria was as tense as I felt.

Kayori nodded, "Alright. Remember, leave yourself open and willing. You are going to need to open your aura fully." Dedria nodded and did just that, releasing her full aura. "It's going to be uncomfortable," Kayori continued, "I am going to have to grab a part of your aura and remove it. You will instinctively pull back; you won't want me to do that. But you need to fight that instinct and let me." Dedria looked startled at that, but nodded weakly in response, not having any words.

Kayori focused before she started, channelling her own aura. She grabbed a few of her tools, aligning them on the edge of the basin and she reached up with one of her hands, and she murmured something in an ancient tongue before closing her hand. Except it didn't fully close, it was like she was grabbing an invisible force.

Dedria did recoil, but she forced herself to stay where she was, even if her eyes opened wide with the initial wave of fear.

My foot shuffled forward, but I forced it back, forced myself to stay where I was. I wanted to keep Dedria safe, and I had never seen her look so afraid before.

Kayori nodded in approval, "Very good." She praised before she continued her ancient chant, picking up a pair of very large iron shears and started to cut away at the invisible force. The force shimmered, and Dedria let out a pained cry that made me step forward fully now. "No!" Kayori snapped, "You stay over there. You must not interfere. Dedria, focus!" She continued what she was doing, and as she snipped away the force, whatever she held in her hand started to turn solid. It looked almost like glass, with liquid moving inside.

The process from start to finish took less than a minute but must have felt it felt like hours for Dedria. She was having a part of her very essence being ripped from her, I could tell from the tears flowing openly down her cheeks that it must hurt more than anything she had ever experienced. It was not physical pain, not truly, but that didn't matter. Kayori nodded and, in her hand, she held a sphere no bigger than a large apple, but it shimmered and swirled beautifully. "You did well." She told Dedria, turning to the basin, taking the sphere in another iron tool and pushing it into the roiling lava.

I finally rushed over, helping Dedria away from the basin and helping her to the floor. I crouched in front of her, wiping away her tears, cupping her cheeks. My gaze scanned her face. "It's okay, it's okay. I'm here." I whispered urgently. "It's over."

Dedria was stifling sobs and gasping for breath as she reached up and clung to my arms, desperate for familiarity, desperate for something she knew.

The only thing I could do was kneel and pull Dedria into a firm hug, continuing to whisper reassurances to her. "I got you. I got you, I'm right here."

[170]

The sound of Kayori working was emerging behind us, and the old Kitsune's gaze turned to us. "When she has recovered more you can go back to the houses. This will take me time to forge. There is no point in the two of you sitting here waiting."

I just nodded stiffly, helped Dedria up into a stand, "Come on. Let's get you back down the mountain and we'll get you something to eat. Maybe a bath in the hot springs?" I offered.

Dedria nodded numbly, looking like she was in a trance now as she stumbled along with me, holding onto my arm and waist tightly as we walked down the path back towards the houses.

We took our time, and despite going downhill, it took twice as long to get back as it had taken to first get up to the Forge, Dedria needed frequent breaks to recover some of her energy. I was patient, passing Dedria her water container at each rest, even if she didn't need it. "We're almost there, Dee."

Dedria nodded and just mumbled a confirmation of that, still leaning on me as we walked. Finally, we got to the houses and murmuring spread through the area quickly, a few soldiers rushing over to help Dedria instead, one even just scooping her up and carrying her into the house that Dedria, Pendra, Bevy and I were staying in.

Pendra rushed over when he saw Dedria's state, "What happened?" He asked me, voice laced with concern and confusion.

"Kayori...cut off part of her aura," I said quietly, sitting down beside Dedria who was lying on the floor bed. "To forge a weapon."

Pendra clicked his tongue, checking Dedria over thoroughly. "She's probably suffering from serious Mana loss, even if she didn't actually lose much. I will make her some tea, and she will need to sleep after she's done drinking." He explained, and he was gone into the small kitchen area to make the tea.

I brushed Dedria's hair out of her face, "It's going to be okay. You just need to have some rest, Dee."

Once Dedria had drank most of the tea Pendra had made, she fell into a deep sleep. I continued to sit beside her, not wanting to leave her side. Pendra walked in as the twin suns were setting, "Your Grace, you should come eat dinner." He said. "I know you are worried about her. Assign one of the soldiers to come to sit with her if you don't want her to be alone."

"I want to be here when she wakes up." I answered with a frown, looking over to Pendra. The concern was written on my face, I didn't hide it.

"She won't wake up until tomorrow at the earliest. She needs rest, Your Grace. You do not help her if you do not take care of yourself, too." Pendra insisted, and I sighed and gave a reluctant nod.

"Fine..." I couldn't help but grumble and stood, having to stretch from being in the same position for so long. I poked my head out of the room, signalling for one of the soldiers to come over to me. "Stay with her, if anything changes, please come get me." I told them firmly, and they nodded in confirmation, moving to sit beside Dedria.

I walked with Pendra to the table, sitting down with him, Bevy, Setsuna, Karne, Tianie and a few of the higher-ranked soldiers like always.

"Your Grace." The Colonel nodded, offering me a reassuring smile. "We received more transmissions from the Tower today, updates of what is going on in the world. Would you like the report?"

I nodded in response, "Go ahead." It was truthfully the last thing I wanted to hear about, I wanted to be by Dedria's side, but I knew Pendra was right. I needed to continue with my routine, to take care of myself.

The Colonel was a woman in her 40's with wrinkles around her eyes from the stress of her near 20 years of service. Her dark hair was starting to grey in spots prematurely. "The first report comes from Taranor. The Ascended Elders that Setsuna and Tianie sent reached there and Isabella Malbora did her ascension ceremony. She bonded with a Phoenix."

That got Setsuna's attention, her eyes flying over to the Colonel. "A phoenix?!" She demanded.

The Colonel nodded, "Yes, a phoenix. The ceremony lasted two days and nights." Setsuna leaned over to Karne, starting to whisper to him furiously before the Colonel shrugged and continued. My gaze stayed on them for long moments before I finally looked back to the Colonel. "A few more cities have been attacked by Nox in their search for the last shard. Hopefully, they continue to run into dead ends. Your father says the country is moving along fine, though there are some concerns about your well-being and how long you've been gone. Apparently, people are demanding their queen to return."

I pursed my lips at that, rolling them together as I thought about this. "We will go as soon as both forge weapons are complete. Us staying for them will give us the best chance of success. We need every advantage that we can get." Too many people dead. Innocent people. My heart felt heavy.

The Colonel nodded, "I know, Your Grace. I explained that to him, and he conveyed he understood as well. Unfortunately, the people demand what they demand…which is for you to return." She sounded sympathetic, but also just doing her job of being the messenger.

With a nod, I spoke, "I understand. Kayori did not say how long it will take…if Dedria's weapon takes more than a fortnight, we will leave when hers is completed. Is that fair?"

Was it a sacrifice to not have my own soul forged blade? Absolutely. I knew this, but I was getting impatient being here for so long. I could harness the Archon's ability in battle - even if only slightly. Now that I knew how to do it, I could continue to train and improve, even if I wasn't here.

The Colonel smiled, a rare sight for her. "I will do whatever you command, Your Grace."

I waved my hand dismissively, irritation bubbling but I shoved it down. "That isn't what I asked, and you know it, Colonel. Please tell me if I am being fair with my proposal."

The woman nodded and continued to smile, "Yes, Your Grace. I find it very fair."

With a nod, I turned back to my meal. "Very good." I said, glancing over to Setsuna who was still whispering with Karne. "Setsuna, you've been whispering frantically since you heard the news about Isabella. What exactly is going on and why is it significant?"

Setsuna straightened and looked at me, "Isabella Malbora bonded with a phoenix." She said plainly, still in shock over it.

"Yes…As the Colonel said. Is there something wrong with that?" I prompted, looking confused.

Tianie spoke now, "The last known Ascended that had a bond with the Phoenix was Inara, a goddess of our people. A goddess of truth, light and good fortune. Every year, at least one will attempt to bond with the Phoenix. They fail, they die during the ceremony. So…this Isabella being successful, that means something…But we do not know what. We don't know what this means for our people, we don't know why she would choose to bond with the Phoenix." As always, her voice was calm and measured as she explained something.

I looked down at my food, "…Hm. I see." I replied, "well, I hope this means good fortune for your people." I offered now, which felt was the best thing I could offer, even if it felt empty.

Setsuna nodded in response, "Whatever her intentions, we will manage as we always do."

"Thank you, as always, for explaining to me, Tianie." I added, looking over to the other woman.

Tianie just smiled in response, "It is a pleasure, Your Grace."

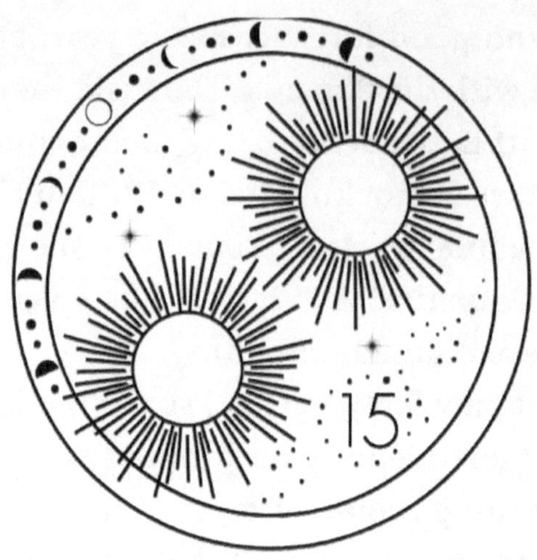

The creation of Dedria's Soul Forged weapon took 10 days and 11 nights, and she had been in her deep sleep for half of that. When she finally woke, I had cried tears of relief, even though Dedria had shoved off the concern as she always did.

Kayori walked down the mountain on the 11th day and gathered everyone around to present the weapon to Dedria.

At first, it looked like a simple blade but when Dedria took it in her hand, it shifted to a lance. Dedria grinned and spun it in a slow circle. "Amazing…" She marvelled, "thank you, Kayori."

Kayori nodded, "You are welcome." She replied and looked to me. My body went tense under her calculating, cool gaze. "It is your turn now, Johanna."

I knew how unsure I felt was visible for a moment, but I nodded. "Okay." I agreed, looking to Pendra. "You should come with us, to help get me down the mountain faster. It took us so long with Dedria."

Pendra nodded, giving a bow, "Of course, Your Grace."

Kayori shrugged, "Fine." She turned to start the hike back up to the Forge with Dedria, Pendra and I close behind. Kayori set the same ritual up silently this time, after confirming that I remembered how it had gone with Dedria.

"Remember, you need to keep your aura completely open." Kayori said as she put the final part of the protective ritual in place.

I nodded; my whole body coiled like a spring as I unleashed my whole aura. Pendra had to take a step back, so did Dedria just from how heavy it made the air feel. Kayori didn't even waiver, starting to chant in the strange ancient tongue as she reached up and grabbed the air between us.

It felt like Kayori had a grip around my throat, and I fought the overwhelming instinct to close my Aura and fight back. It was hard, not impossible, but the instinct was very strong.

But when Kayori started to cut at the air with that strange blade, cutting off part of my very being, I physically recoiled. Kayori swore at me, scolding me in different languages until I forced my feet back to my spot with the best apologetic look that I could muster.

It felt like searing hot razor blades were being shoved into my very skin and muscles, it burned and ached and stabbed all at the same time, everywhere. It felt like hours before Kayori was done, but I was sure it was only minutes, maybe even seconds. The moment it was completed, I fell to her hands and knees, gasping for breath as I closed my aura up so tightly until I was sure no one would be able to touch it ever.

Pendra and Dedria swept forward, scooping me up together and carrying me out of the maze of caves to the sun and fresh air, where Pendra shifted his form to the Drake and scooped us both up in his front paws and took off, gliding down over the treetops to the houses where he landed. The trip down the mountain this time was merely minutes, and I immediately fell asleep on the hard mat in the small bedroom I was staying in.

I did not sleep peacefully, in fact, my dreams were full of death and destruction and terror. Cities being bombed, people dying, and it was all caused by the mysterious individual that was always in shadow, carrying the reassembled Ember and resetting the world as they claimed was required for true peace.

When I finally woke, Dedria and Pendra were there, waiting quietly though the concern was written on their face.

I frowned, dread coiling inside me, "What is it?" I breathed out, barely about to speak above a whisper.

"Solaria was attacked again..." Dedria answered softly.

"What?" I jolted up to a sit, ignoring the pain lancing through me at the sudden action. "What do you mean Solaria was attacked again?!"

"Nox caught wind that you were in pursuit of the last Ember piece." Pendra frowned, looking sorrowful, "They killed 500 in their attack, and were able to kidnap one of the Generals in the Tower who knew our location."

I felt cold like ice had been poured straight into my veins. "No."

"The General gave our location...intelligence caught them on a boat off the coast of Solaria and they are heading here."

"No." I shook my head, still in denial, "How long have I been out?"

"Four days." Dedria replied, "Pendra went up to the Forge to ask about progress...Kayori says this time it is easier because she got to practice with mine. So, she thinks she will be done in the next two days."

I was doing mental math, calculating. My brain felt sluggish, slow to catch up with the frantic emotions I was feeling. "It takes 30 days for a boat to get to this island from Solaria. When was the attack?"

"The day of the Forge Ritual," Pendra answered.

"So, they will probably arrive in 25 days. We will estimate 20...we need to be off this island in five. With or without that soul forged weapon." I determined, and I was getting up to stand. My muscles ached from lying on the hard floor for four days. But I didn't have a choice. "We need to prepare." I was walking out of the room and called for the General to come over to me.

"We leave in five days. The boat needs to be stocked and provisions counted and collected. Repairs done. Fish, fruit, vegetables need to be collected. Anything Kayori and her children can spare. Compensate them with gold, I am sure they can use it to trade with." The instructions were clear, concise and I was glad my mind was catching up. My country had been attacked again; except this time, I had been Queen. I hadn't been there to stop it. If anything, my absence had been the cause of the attack. 500 more souls on my conscience. 500 more lives lost. 500 more.

The General nodded, "At once, Your Grace." She said, and she turned and barked orders out to the Soldiers that had been in the middle of training. They all stopped and moved to put their practice weapons back if they were using them before getting to work. And there was a lot of work to be done - all hands were needed to make sure they would be ready to depart in five days.

Sasori, Kayori's eldest daughter, approached me shortly after. "Your Grace," She said, giving a slight bow of her head out of respect. "Did I hear you correctly, you are leaving in...five days?”

I nodded, turning to her. Sasori was tall, taller than me, and while she was lean, she was strong. Everything about her radiated elegance and strength. To say it was unnerving at time would be a lie. I knew it was my own insecurities, to see someone so effortlessly be kind and patient and always with a smile. Someone who was well liked by everyone who interacted with her. I did my best, but I knew, probably better than most, that not everyone was fond of me. Even my own soldiers. I shook my head mentally, focusing back on Sasori who was waiting so patiently with her hands folded in front of her.

“Yes. With or without the weapon your mother is forging for me. Solaria was attacked again,” I noticed the slightest, sharp inhale from her at the news, “and we have good authority that the group responsible are on their way here.” I explained, and I hid any disappointment from my expression. Truthfully, I was disappointed in myself. Ever since I had woken up and gotten the news, I was questioning leaving Solaria, of this whole journey. We had not been able to prevent the attack in the Northern Ascended lands. We had not been able to prevent attacks all over the world. Sure, I had gotten stronger, better at controlling my Chronomancy and the Archons. But at what cost? How many lives had been lost because of my quest for revenge? Was any of it worth it?

Sasori nodded, the silence hanging in the air between us for long moments. “I will start instructing my sisters to help with your preparations.” She said finally, firmly, “you will have some more time to prepare before you face these murderers.” With that, Sasori walked away, starting to give orders to her sisters who jumped to action, eager for a change of their usual pace.

I couldn't help but admire the Kitsune's as they so easily and quickly assembled and effortlessly jumped in to help. Several were rushing off to their storage house where they stored their vegetables, grain and fruit, others were heading to the curing shack where they cured the fish and boar. They were all talking and laughing and singing as they did their tasks. I knew that they understood the gravity of the situation, that soon a group of cold blooded, ruthless murderers would be landing on their shore to hunt for the shard of Ember. It just didn't stop them from enjoying life right now.

I only hoped that they didn't pay the price for teaching and sheltering me and my friends and soldiers. Could I handle more deaths on my conscience?

For the next four days, we all rose before dawn and went to bed long after dusk, doing repairs on the boat, stocking supplies, fishing, hunting and gathering everything we could to replenish the supplies for the journey back to Solaria. And we had to plan to bring more - we would need to take the long way and travel North for seven days before turning East towards Taranor and Solaria and then travelling South along the coast until we got to one of Taranor's ports where we could then travel by land further east and then south through Taranor's capital, then Bell's Crossing, and down into Solaria to the Obsidian Tower.

The evening before the day of departure, Kayori finally emerged from the mountain trail, carrying the same shimmering sword she had presented to Dedria. She had not come back to the small village since the day of my ritual, and we all could only assume she had slept very little and had barely eaten while she had worked to finish the Soul Forge weapon.

She looked exhausted as she stepped up to me, I saw it in her gaze, in the very slight tremor in her hands that she did her best to suppress, in the weary lines in her forehead, "I present you with your Soul Forged weapon." She said, offering it out. "I am relieved I finished it before you departed."

I reached forward, slowly, and took it by the hilt. I wasn't prepared for it to feel like an extension of my arm when I held it, completely effortless. Not like any other weapon I had ever held - where I had to actively think of it being an extension of my arm. No, this…it was like my very being understood that it was part of me. It shifted form slightly, the hilt changing shape to fit my hand perfectly and the blade lengthened another five centimeters. I stepped back so I would have enough room and gave it a practice swing. I was not able to stop the smile that spread across my lips. "It's…perfect, Kayori. Thank you." I closed my eyes and focused a moment, and the sword disappeared. Just as easily, faster now even, it reappeared in my hand. I unsummoned it once again and stepped forward, embracing Kayori in a hug. "This is the best gift I have been given. Thank you."

Kayori nodded, awkwardly returning the hug. "May it strike true when it is needed, and may you never use it if there are other options available." She said, untangling herself from the embrace and sitting on the ground with a sigh. "I need tea…and food…and sleep."

Sasori saw to it at once, having some of her younger sisters get tea and food prepared for their mother before she helped her to a better spot to sit. "Of course, Mother. Come. Come." She said gently, but firmly.

Kayori got up with the help of her daughter and moved off to her small house that she stayed in alone with a silent nod of thanks.

I watched her go, contemplating those words. Would there be another option, with this group? It didn't seem possible. Would I be doing Kayori a disservice for not trying? What if I did try and just ended up being punished for it? Is that what my mother had tried in her final moments? Had she tried to reason with her attacker?

The questions piled on top of each other in my brain until it physically hurt, and I finally shoved them down and away into a dark corner of my mind. I would never be able to get the answers to most of them; I would never know what Mother had said or thought in those moments.

With a silent sigh, I turned and walked back to Pendra and Dedria, "Are you ready to leave tomorrow?" I asked.

Dedria rolled her eyes, "Oh yes, totally looking forward to boat travel again, can't wait." She said, the sarcasm was heavy.

Pendra just chuckled, shaking his head at Dedria, "It will be excellent to start heading back to Solaria, and putting all of this travelling behind us." He replied, "I miss the comforts of the Ivory Halls."

I forced a smile as I sat down, "I do miss a proper bed." I agreed, "And a hot bath would be nice. One with oils and salts." Not a lie, my body was still sore from the nights of sleeping on the hard floor, or hard ground, and the beds in the boat weren't any better. Forget about going without a proper bath.

Dedria laid down, staring at the ceiling, "A meal that doesn't include fish or hasn't been cooked over fire." She agreed wistfully, "Gods, or pastries...I miss pastries."

The three of us reminisced into the night over what we missed and what we were most looking forward too, finally falling asleep and waking up just as the first of the twin suns crested the horizon. Soldiers were already up, getting any final supplies brought over to the ship before starting the process of getting over themselves. I watched over on the beach quietly, and as the last trip before Dedria, Pendra and myself would be on, Kayori walked up to me. She looked better than she had yesterday, with a good meal and a restful sleep. She was holding a bundle wrapped in cloth, but I got cold just looking at it. "The Ember shard." I said, not having to ask. I knew.

Kayori nodded and offered it to me. "Yes." She said. "It will be up to you to keep it safe now."

I took it, though the hesitance was clear. Just touching the bundle made me feel so cold it hurt, and I quickly stashed it in the small chest at my feet. "I will keep it safe." I replied, "I know what is at stake."

Kayori nodded, grasping me by my left shoulder. "I know you do and will." She replied, watching me with an almost motherly gaze. It felt strange, to be on the receiving end of that when Kayori so often gave it to her own daughters. "Take care of yourself, Queen Johanna of Solaria, Ash Queen, Herald of the Archons. The world depends on your success…and you can not succeed if you do not put yourself first once and a while."

I pondered over that advice for only a moment, then disregarded it. "Thank you, Kayori. I will." I felt I had to tell her that, even if I didn't intend to listen, "thank you for your hospitality and graciousness while we have been here. You did not need to open your home to us…but you did. And I will never be able to truly repay you for that."

Kayori was critical as she looked me over, "As much as I am…resigned to admit, I think it is time I stop hiding and start serving the world as I was meant to. The way my father would have wanted." She patted me on the shoulder, "Thank you, for bringing my father back to me."

My aura involuntarily flickered, and the form of En-Kai appeared beside me. He spoke through me, which I was annoyed by, and he knew it, as he had on the very first day we had arrived here. "Daughter, I am sorry for the hardships you have had to endure without me. And yet, despite that, you have raised beautiful daughters, the future of our kind that will carry our values and knowledge around the world." He stepped forward to press his snout into her body, "You have strength beyond measure. Do not forget how strong you really are."

Kayori's body quivered at the touch, "Thank you…" She whispered, and the form shimmered and faded away. She reached up, pushing a tear away from her eye. I didn't bring attention to it.

Dedria stepped up then, "Johanna, it's time." She said, and the dinghy was waiting for us, Pendra already inside and the Soldier looking moderately impatient.

I startled, "Oh! Yes. Apologies. Kayori, thank you again. May Arcanis shine her light upon you." I offered, scooping up the chest that held the shard and following Dedria to the small rowboat that would bring us back to the ship.

Once there, I stared out over the rail with Pendra and Dedria on either side of me. "Time to go home, and deal with Nox once and for all." The ship didn't take long to start moving, for the beach and the island to start getting smaller.

Dedria patted me on the back, "That's the spirit." She smirked. Still, none of us moved, watching the land slowly disappear until it was completely out of sight.

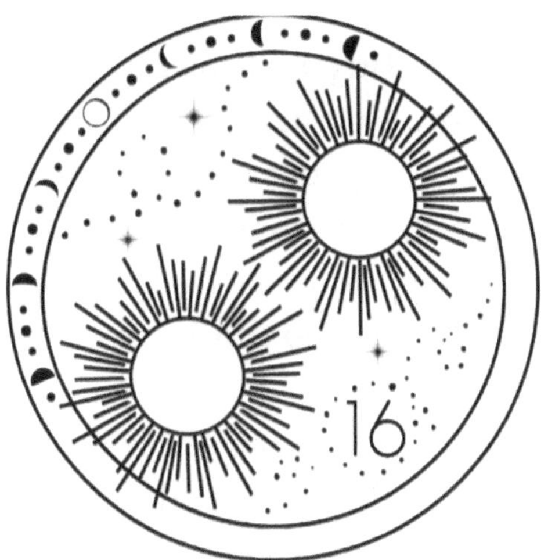

I leaned on the railing on the bow of the boat, staring out at the deep blue waves. We had been on the boat for six days, driving ourselves further north before we would finally turn west towards Taranor and then south along their coast. A waste of time but needed. The last thing any of us wanted was to run into Nox on the open ocean. Not when we had no idea what sort of weapons or skills we would be up against. The first day on the ship, Pendra had spent hours braiding my hair into box braids, and now I had it pulled up into a ponytail.

I couldn't stop thinking about Kayori's family, back on the island. I worried they would be hurt or killed. But this was Kayori, and all her daughters had proven to be incredible fighters. They would be able to defend themselves. At least, I kept telling myself that. I wasn't sure if we would know the outcome until we sent a boat there after we had made it back to Solaria. So, for now, I buried that worry deep inside my heart, making it nice and small so it would be easier to ignore for now.

Dedria moved up beside me, glancing over to me. "Thinkin' about Kayori?" She asked.

I looked at her with a tense expression, "What, I have a sign above my head broadcasting my thoughts now?"

Dedria's amusement was obvious as she smiled at me. "Not quite. You get this look on your face whenever you think of her. It's a mix of awe and fear and respect. You only ever get that look when it comes to her." laughed Dedria, patting me on the shoulder. "They'll be okay. You think Kayori is going to let Nox hurt any of her kids? Please."

I sighed, my shoulders slumping as I leaned forward more on the railing, "I hope so." I did not sound convinced though, and I knew it. I watched a small league of Leviathans - great sea serpents, splashing and playing in the waves not far off. For a moment I wished to be as carefree as they were, where the only worry they had was where their next meal would be.

Dedria reached over, flicking me hard in the ear. "Enough moping of things you can't change."

Pain stung through my head. Wincing, I reached up and held my ear and giving Dedria a glare. "What was that for?!" I protested.

"You're moping. It's boring and overdone. C'mon, let's go do something. Train or study or something other than staring at the waves for the whole day. Honestly..." Dedria rolled her eyes, hip checking me as she turned and headed to the center of the ship.

As I started to turn to follow, I spotted a small black dot that looked hazy on the horizon. It didn't fit in, and I knew something was wrong. "What is that?" I shouted to the captain.

The captain moved to the side railing, using a telescope to look towards the haze. "I don't know what to make of it, Your Grace." He said, looking over to me.

I headed over quickly, climbing the steep steps two at a time and taking the telescope when handed to me, using it to focus on the darkness. At first, I didn't know what to make of it either. It was like shadows were carrying a robed person towards us, but that wasn't right either.

It was only with a sick feeling in my stomach that I realised that it was not shadows but living dead. Necromancy, a forbidden and grossly outlawed practice of Chronomancy. "Dedria..." I called down, keeping my voice steady but cautious. Whoever this was, they were coming fast. "Captain, get this ship going as fast as possible. Use wind magic to get it moving faster, even." I warned.

Dedria used her chronomancy to appear beside me, she moved so fast even I couldn't really track her, taking the telescope and focusing on the dot. "Oh, that is super not good..." She muttered. "Like...super, super not good."

I couldn't help but pinch the bridge of my nose, "Thank you, that is very wise." I said, tone dripping in sarcasm. "What do we do about it?" I pressed. Dedria was the more experienced Chronomancer. I had to default to her.

Dedria thought, pushing her tongue into the inside of her upper lip as she contemplated, "Ppppfffft. Well, our only option is probably going to be fighting. Bonus is there is two of us, and one of them. Downfall, we have to fight what is probably a Grand Master level Chronomancer who I've never even seen before and at best we are two Journeyman so..." She shrugged with a grimace, and she actually forced a smile. It was self deprecating.

Grand Master, a term used in the guilds. A Grand Master

usually oversaw the guild, guiding curriculum and the day-to-day operations. They were the best of the best and had the highest level of mastery of their Aspect. A Master could challenge a Grand Master at any time to obtain the Grand Master title, but only if they won in a duel. Journeyman was below that and Apprentice was below that. However, a student could only obtain Apprentice status once they had shown they could do the bare basics of their aspect. All this meant was that the robed figure flying at them using Chronomancy was arguably stronger than Dedria and I combined.

I sighed, glancing to the Captain, "Anyone who isn't essential, get them down below. Have Pendra and Bevy with my chest in one of the dinghies, and if we do fail cut them loose and Pendra is to transform and fly straight to Solaria." The instructions were firm and without question, and the Captain just nodded and saluted, turning to start barking orders as sailors and soldiers started funnelling down below the ship deck.

I looked to Dedria, "Let's get ready." I said, and I slowed time, everyone around us barely moving as I dragged Dedria along to our cabin for the both of us to get into our armor. It had to be lightweight, but strong. The metal was enchanted to protect against spells and to be stronger against blades. Both of us had chest plates, shoulder guards and guards on our thighs. Otherwise, it was just enchanted leather. As we got ready, we didn't say a word. The grim reality staring us down - it was time to face Nox.

All our efforts to catch them or get ahead had failed. Now it was just the moment of countless days and nights of training, of bruises and falls and beatings all for this. It had come too soon, but not soon enough for me. Emotionally, I was as ready as I would ever be for this moment. I had been counting down the minutes since I found Mother dead with that broken blade in her chest and that fury had started boiling. But at the same time, I wished we had more time. More time to train, to practice, to prepare. Just more.

My chest plate had the Solarian Monarchy Crest, a Wyrm circling around an obsidian sword with its mouth wide open, embossed onto it, with the motto 'Forged by Obsidian, We Never Waiver' in Solarian inscribed under it. The Metal was coloured to be a dark steel grey. My hair was arranged into as tight of a bun as it could be.

Dedria's chest plate had the Heart Crest on it, which was a trio of three blood-soaked roses with thorns on the stems, but flames of fire were licking at the bottom of the stems and creeping up to the petals. The motto was inscribed in Taranorian Common under it, 'Blood Forged by Fire'. The metal on hers was coloured to be more red in tone, ominous and daring. Dedria had also pulled her hair back and up into a bun, tying it off with a piece of silk fabric.

The two of us made our way in tense silence back up to the deck, time still slowed to a crawl around us. We stood facing the black hazy dot, and I finally released my hold on time, letting things flow back to normal again.

The ship was starting to increase in speed, the Captain and his crew pushing it for all it was worth. Even then, the figure and their undead raft was gaining on us.

My stomach turned uneasily, a feeling of dread overcoming me. I contained it, locking it away. Even as Dedria cursed softly, unleashing part of her aura and harnessing it as she murmured in an ancient, nearly dead language. Dragonic, I had heard her speak it very rarely, same with Veronica, and Jessica. A small spark appeared in her hand, and suddenly her whole hand was a light in white hot flame. It was so hot that even I could feel it, and I couldn't help but ponder, just for a moment, on how Dedria could stand it.

Dedria started to bombard the figure and the dead with the balls of flame when they got within distance. It slowed them - but only slightly. I knew it wouldn't be enough.

I summoned my Crystal Forge weapon and stepped back, harnessing the power of the Archon's and Maria eagerly met the call, the ethereal armour of the fallen queen overlaying my own in a crisp light blue colour.

In a blink of the eye, faster than even I could track, the Figure was on the deck of the ship, right between Dedria and I. Dedria let the flame on her hand dissipate, and she summoned her lance.

The figure reached up and pushed the hood back, exposing their face. Her face, I realized. Pale skin, with black hair and delicate features. She had one piercing blue-grey eye, the other had a scar running through it, but the iris seemed to be intact and was blood red. Her gaze turned to me, and she smiled. She was beautiful in a terrifying and unforgiving way. The smile was not kind, no, it was cruel and caused that dread I had carefully contained to bubble again.

"You are quite a meddlesome little girl, aren't you?" She asked, and her voice was sharp, unforgiving.

"Rozalin Heart." Maria's voice rang in my head. "She should be dead! She should have died in the explosion that created Ground

Zero."

I kept my cool, though I could feel the anger of Maria building in my mind. "Wouldn't have to be if you hadn't had killed my mother and attacked my country not once but twice." I answered, proud my words didn't shake. Proud of how strong I sounded.

Rozalin Heart grinned more, though it was not one of true joy, just a deep amusement, "Oh yes, your mother. Hmm...Serena, was it? She put up a good fight, I will give her that. I gave her a chance to give me the shard of her own free will, she refused. Foolish, very foolish. I always get what I want. Maria knew that."

It felt like an ice knife had been driven into my chest, and it took everything in my power to not buckle and show weakness. Confirmation, that Rozalin Heart had killed my mother. That my mother had fought until the very end to keep the Ember Shard safe. "Not anymore." I replied tersely.

Rozalin laughed, but it was cold and mocking, "And what are you going to do to stop me, Queen?"

I clenched my jaw, my teeth grinding, and without saying a word to each other, Dedria and I charged forward.

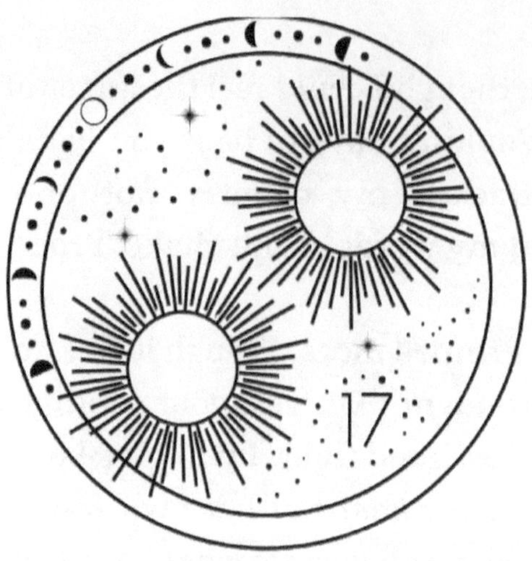

The fight lasted less than a minute, the sound of metal on metal and the blur of three Chronomancers fighting on the deck of the ship was all that the Captain and what was left of his crew on deck knew.

To Dedria and me? It was fierce, fast and brutal. We worked in perfect sync, and even if Rozalin was hundreds of years old with a Grand Master status, holding off two Chronomancers could not be an easy feat. But she sure made it look easy, her motions fluid and relaxed, and she always seemed to know where the two of us were and when we would attempt to strike. That only made me angrier, and with a feral scream I managed to disarm Rozalin. Stroke of luck, or a distraction from Dedria, I didn't know.

Rozalin only laughed, stepping back from us and toward the railing. Her gaze was dancing between Dedria and I, who stood side by side, weapons pointed at her. "Well, this was a very educational visit, if I do say so myself." She said with a wry smile, and took another step back, and another, until her back was to the railing. "I must say, you two have made impressive strides. But you still won't stop me. This world will be cleansed of corruption and imbalance." She shifted and stood up on the railing. Her movements so fluid, so effortless. Her gaze pierced right through me, "and I will start with your precious little country first and finish what I started oh-so-long ago..." She stepped back, off the railing and into the open air.

I knew immediately Rozalin's undead horde had caught her; I didn't need to look over the railing to see that. I heaved a breath, panting slightly and I sunk down to a sit. "Damnit." I hissed as I leaned my head into my hands, digging my heels into my eyes.

Dedria was panting beside me, "We have so much more work to do if we have any chance of beating her." She said, "She held us off like it was nothing."

I just barely nodded, still hiding my face, "I know."

"Maybe Mom will have something that can help us."

"How did she live?"

"...I didn't even think of that."

"Yeah, well Maria sure thought of it...let me consult with her." I got up and headed down to my quarters, the sailors and soldiers were already milling about and heading back up to the deck to resume work.

Pendra and Bevy were in my cabin, and both looked worried. "Are you okay, Your Grace?" Pendra asked, moving towards me, his Queen.

I nodded, heaving a soft sigh. "Yes, I am fine..." I replied, but I knew I did not have that usual air of confidence. "It was Rozalin Heart. I don't know how she is alive."

Bevy moved forward, slowly at first and then she practically ran the rest of the way, and wrapped her arms around me in a hug, which I returned.

"I'm sorry for scaring you." I said softly, my hand circling on her back.

"I wasn't…wasn't scared." Bevy said, looking up to me with her wide eyes, "You are very strong, yes yes, she wouldn't have beaten you." Her words had conviction to them, in her mind, it was not an opinion, but a fact.

That just prompted a smile, even weak, to spread on my lips, and I leaned down to kiss Bevy on the top of the head. "Go up to the deck with Pendra. It's safe now, okay?"

Bevy nodded, letting her go and she grabbed Pendra's hand, dragging him out of the Cabin excitedly.

I sat in the middle of the floor, closing my eyes and letting my hands rest in my lap. I took several deep breaths, in and out, in and out as I fought to clear my mind of all thoughts, as hard as that was. With a small pull from the Archons, I found herself in the black void of my mindscape again.

All four Archons stood in front of me, Maria with pursed lips, En-Kai with his tails dancing behind him, and then the two I had only met briefly, Rachael and Liang. Rachael was tall, with hair so long it went to her mid back, pale skin and bright blue eyes. Liang was shorter, and he was built stocky. I could see Yeska in his face and eyes, the same wisdom and kindness of my Godmother. My heart ached at the reminder.

"Rozalin, huh?" Rachael asked with a smirk, "that's annoying, but not something we can't deal with."

Maria scoffed at that, "Rozalin killed me." She countered, tone sharp, "She should have died in Ground Zero when I did."

Liang yawned lazily, "Except she didn't, obviously. We can't lament on the past, Maria. We need to push forward. I think it's time for Rachael to start having Johanna call her forward. She's the Master level Chronomancer. She can impart some of her knowledge and skills on Johanna."

"Finally, someone sees some sense here!" Rachael said, throwing her hands in the air. "I've been arguing with Maria about that forever."

"She is a Maracroix!" Maria spat, "And I was the one to fight Rozalin, don't forget that."

En-Kai let out a growl, "And you lost, evidently. We can not keep wasting time. Rozalin knows the skills Johanna has and will be preparing against that. You have no more information to give her."

Maria scowled, "That's fucking bullshit and you know it. I've barely shared any of my knowledge with Johanna. I still have so much more to teach her."

I stood and just watched them bicker back and forth, my own irritation growing and finally I interjected, "Stop talking about me like I'm not here." I nearly shouted, and all the Archons quieted instantly. "You're all right. Yes, Rachael needs to start helping me train. But Maria, if you've held back on me when I have successfully communed with you, that's on you. I need that knowledge and training, you were the last one to fight Rozalin Heart and until today, everyone thought she was dead. So whatever happened all those years ago, it worked well enough to keep her in hiding."

Maria did not stammer or waiver at that, though her voice was gentle when she spoke next. "I did not wish to overwhelm you. I thought we had more time."

"Clock has run out and the alarm is going off, Maria. We're out of time, we were out of time a week ago." I replied with a sharp tone, even going as far to glare at Maria. Could I help it? No. I was angry, angry things had been withheld from me.

Her ancestor sighed, "I am sorry, Johanna. I should not have let my judgment prevent me from teaching you more."

"Teaching me more? You've barely taught me anything at all." I bristled; was it cruel to say? Maybe, though the feelings of betrayal and hurt were coursing through me.

En-Kai interrupted now, "Now is not the time to fight," He rumbled, "Johanna, all your anger and betrayal you are feeling right now, it's all valid. We all feel it. I know, it is disappointing and frustrating. There's no way around that, there is no excuse for it. None of us can explain our lack of foresight and inaction, there is nothing we can do to fix that. But we can move forward and work towards a better relationship. This is new for all of us."

Rachael nodded, "Mhm, yup, like he said." She agreed.

I pinched the bridge of my nose, though I couldn't help but hear the wisdom in En-Kai's words. "Fine…" I muttered, grudgingly.

Liang nodded, "Perfect! Excellent." He clapped his hands, "We can take turns. Each of us can have two hours with Johanna a day. We can do whatever we feel will help expand her skills or knowledge in that time. From running a country to combat or whatever we feel she needs."

I gave a resigned sighed, but I nodded. "Fine, very well. That will be suitable." I replied grudgingly.

Rachael clapped her hands again, "Excellent! Now that that is settled, we should get to work." She sounded so delighted and chipper, it grated my nerves. I truthfully could not fathom why she was so happy, why she just seemed so at ease and eager to move on.

"Tomorrow. Not today." I said as I shook my head.

Maria frowned, "Let me talk to her." She said, once again like I wasn't right here, and the other Archons all looked to her, then each other before one by one, they disappeared from the vast and empty space.

I glowered at Maria, "Who says I want to talk to you?"

"Johanna, please," said Maria with a sigh, a plead in her gaze, "I was wrong. I shouldn't have held out on you. I am sorry, I can't change the past. You know that. But from this moment forward we are here for you. Whatever you need from us, our wealth of knowledge, wisdom, all of it…It's here. What I did wasn't right. You have been through so much, even since you were a little girl. We've seen all of it." She turned in the black void, and it would start to light up with memories. My memories.

The first was when I at five, maybe six. I was with the Crown's personal tutors, going through history lessons and social problems. Things that were too advanced for my age at the time, but here I was, arguing the benefit and detriment of a government paid health care system to my own mother. She was there, smiling so brightly as I spoke so passionately about the issue. Three years after this, Solaria had enacted such a thing. All I could remember though, was the feeling of love and warmth that radiated from Serena. How proud she was of me. Tears burned my eyes, but I forced myself to keep looking.

The next was when I was ten, curled in a chair, and Kira who was barely a year old was in my lap, and I was reading her a book out loud. Kira hadn't been diagnosed yet, that would happen in another six months. I remembered this, clear as day, even if the memory was silent as it played along like a bright light in the darkness. How my little sister had let me read to her, occasionally babbling and pointing at pages. My heart ached to have my sister in my arms again. Ached to have her healthy, safe.

After that, it was just my father and tutors. My mother barely there, that bright presence of Serena was gone. Attending meetings with the Lords and Ladies of the country, with diplomates of different countries, sitting silently as my father navigated trade and treaty agreements. Mother busy, furiously searching for a cure for The Rot during every waking moment.

What moments I had gotten to see Mom, conversations revolved around Kira. How I had to be gentler with Kira, more kind, more careful, quieter, softer. But it was Dad and Kira who kept me really going. Every night, after lessons, I would go to Kira's room and sit with my little sister to help her with her homework and then read to her. We had read epic novels together, finished series about groups of ragtag friends saving the world, about unlikely heroes and masterful villains, about unlikely romances and morally grey characters. We had laughed and cried and would stay up too late reading, often ending with me realizing partway through a chapter that my sister had fallen asleep against me.

I felt the strong pang of worry in my chest, missing Kira deeply and suddenly. "Do you know how she is?" I asked Maria now.

Maria shook her head, "Our influence in the world isn't strong enough to see beyond what you see. We don't know anything more than you when it comes to your family." She admitted softly.

I frowned, looking down to my hands. They were blurry, the tears still burning my eyes. "Kira was diagnosed before she turned two. I wasn't even 11 yet. Mom basically abandoned me to try and save her life." I said softly. "I didn't hate her for it. I would have done the same, you know? If I was her, and my daughter had The Rot. I'd do anything in my power to save them. I would search the ends of the earth for a cure. But it still hurts. My most formative years. When I got my period, I had to tell Pendra, not my mother. My first crush, my first dance at a gala, my first kiss. All of it. She missed all of it. And I didn't even get to tell her before she died." Towards the end my voice was choked up, fighting the urge to cry. To let all the tears fall. I hadn't cried over these things yet. I was stronger than that, I would not feel resentful to Kira.

Maria moved forward and wrapped me in a comforting hug. "I know." She said softly, "I know. I am so sorry, Johanna."

It took me a few moments to regain composure. I gave a heavy exhale, "I don't want to be that to my kids. I don't want ruling a country to stop me from being there or my children...How did you do it?"

Maria stepped back, looking deep in thought, "I'm a bad person to ask." She admitted, "My son was 5 when I died. I'd like to think I was a good mother to him, that I loved him enough and spent enough time with him. But those are probably just my thoughts, telling myself that instead of facing the guilt that I left him alone in a cruel world at only 5 years old."

I nodded; I knew that. Her son had taken the throne at 15, the youngest King. By using Ground Zero as an example, the destruction it had caused, he was able to find common ground with Taranor and stop the war. "He turned out to be a really good king." I offered, "He worked out a peace treaty with Taranor as soon as he took the throne at 15, and settled the tensions that were brewing between the Lords of Solaria."

Maria smiled at me speaking so fondly of her son. "He did turn out pretty good, didn't he? I'm glad I surrounded him with the Advisors I did. They made sure to raise him with the values and ideals I would have."

I took a deep breath, "What am I supposed to do after this is all over, Maria? What would you have done?"

"There will always be evil in the world, Johanna." Maria chuckled, "The Chonomancer Guild dissolved after the War, once the atrocities being committed there were found out. It's been hundreds of years, with Chronomancers continuing to be born and having to hide their powers or dying for not being able to control them." She reached out and cupped my cheek, tilting my face up to look at her. "I think you and your friend should reform the Guild in Solaria. Welcome Chronomancers from all over the world to a space where they can learn how to use their powers for the first time in generations, under your guidance."

I smiled at the idea, "...Yeah...Yeah, Dedria and I could do that. That could work." I agreed. I didn't have to be a Queen remembered by how I got the Throne. I could be remembered by what I created in the aftermath. The good I could do.

"You will find ways to truly make your mark on the world and make a difference. Being Queen is your bloodline, but being Ash Queen is your purpose. You will change the world, for the better." Maria said and kissed my forehead in such a motherly gesture. "Go, take the rest of the day with your friends, tomorrow we start the real work."

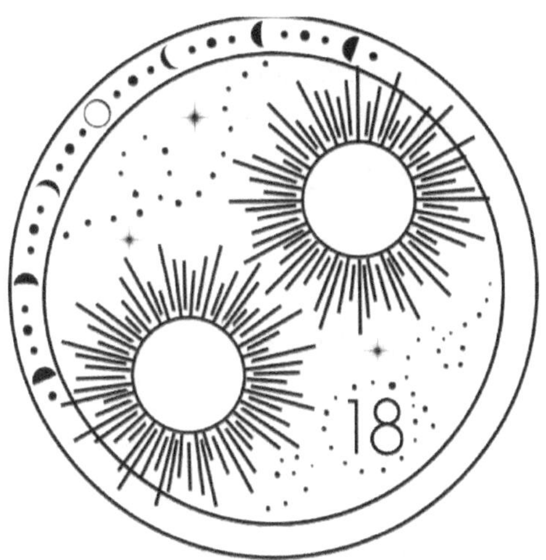

"You need to already have your second jump point created before you even get through the first one." Rachael voice rang mentally. She was running me through very complex and advanced Chronomancy techniques, notably the 'double jump', in which a Chronomancer had two tunnels created and moved from one to the other seamlessly, allowing them to move around objects more fluidly.

It was easier said than done, unfortunately. Just like everything else in Chronomancy. To create two paths at the same time took double the focus, double the mana and often led to me going straight into the object I was trying to avoid, or into the wall of the train we were now on, travelling through the Taranorian mountains towards Bells Crossing.

I threw a harmless blast of wind against the wall in frustration as I crashed into the training dummy once more, "I'm never going to get this."

Rachael sighed, "Yes you will. You just need to breathe and stop trying to focus on speed and instead focus on doing it right...speed will come with time, Johanna. Go back to your starting point."

I grumbled the words back to Rachael in a childish, mocking way, and moved back to the other side of the car, righting the training dummy as I did. "It doesn't matter if I can't even get it right to begin with." I answered, "I just can't make two separate tunnels to move through. I keep merging them and slamming into whatever object I'm trying to avoid."

"I know you are getting frustrated," The Archon acknowledged, "would you like to take a break for the day? Perhaps we can focus on something else."

I shook her head, feeling particularly stubborn today, "No. I'm going to get this." I answered firmly, staring at the training dummy. "So, first tunnel to the right…" I muttered, focusing on a point just to the right of the training dummy and channelling my mana. "And then imagine the point I can't see…and create the second path…" I charged forward, only to slam headfirst into the dummy again.

I had been at this for days, since the day after meeting Rozalin Heart on that ship. That had been nearly 17 days ago, and I still hadn't gotten it, even with practising it for several hours a day. Meanwhile, En-Kai and Liang worked with me on my diplomacy skills while also training me in various combat methods, and Maria focused solely on combat training so I could be more prepared against Rozalin.

I had picked up so many skills in the last 17 days, including learning a whole new language, but this one skill eluded me. It was infuriating, I couldn't fathom why it wasn't clicking, why I hadn't gotten it yet. It seemed so simple and straightforward on paper, to draw a line from point A to B, and another line from point B to C. So why couldn't I do it?

"Johanna, there are other things you can focus on learning with my guidance. Let's stop this for now and focus on something else. I think the more you focus on this, the more you become frustrated, and it is leading to you failing more." Rachael said after several moments of tense silence, "Perhaps we can get Dedria and work on chronomancy combat some more."

I gave a frustrated and determined growl, getting back up and putting the dummy back in its spot. "No, I don't want to stop trying." I answered, marching back to the starting spot.

"Johanna, please..."

I blocked out Rachael's voice, gaze fixing on the point where I would step before making the turn around the dummy. I took a few deep, even breaths, channelling my mana and darting forward.

Travelling through a Chronomancy 'Time Jump' was strange, it was like taking the space that was to be travelled through and condensing it to step through it like a door or short tunnel. All the Chronomancer had to do was walk or run through to the end point. The ability to condense this space varied from mage to mage. Dedria could travel through a 10-foot space in a step, where for me it took two or three.

I hit her first point and found the 'x' that had been painted on the floor, the point at the back of the car I had been trying for nearly 10 days, almost right in front of me, the black tunnel of my Chronomancy fully formed and I darted through, hitting the 'x'.

I whooped in joy, laughing and starting to jump and dance around. "I did it!" I shouted, absolutely elated.

A double jump was much harder for another Chronomancer to

track. Where they might see the first tunnel, or starting point, they would not see the second until already travelling through it. Mastering this technique was invaluable in the future battle against Rozalin. It could mean the difference of life, or death.

Rachael pushed through the block I had put up, "You did." She praised, "Very well done. But can you do it again?"

That practically stopped me in my tracks, "You know, you are about as much fun as Maria." I shot.

"Well, that's a bit rude. I am much more fun than Maria."

Dedria came through the other end of the car now, interrupting the completely silent conversation, "Hey, we're approaching the Crossing."

Bells Crossing was a smaller independent state, governed by a single Baron and Baroness. Its lands had once belonged to Solaria, but it had been won by Taranor during the last war, and then the Duke and Duchess of the time separated from Taranor and declared itself its own country. It consisted of the smaller trade town that spanned across 1600 metre canyon, using 5 giant stone and metal enchanted pillars that were 150 metres wide to keep it aloft. On either end it had a bridge that could be lifted to prevent Taranor or Solaria entry.

Approaching the Crossing meant an end of the line with the train we were on. We would have to gain passage through the Crossing and then board the waiting train on the other side of the canyon so we could finish the final leg of our trip to the Obsidian Tower.

I knew Pendra would try to insist they stay with the Duke and Duchess, but that was the last thing I wanted to do. I wanted to get back home, to my family, and get the last part of the Ember into the Ivory Halls where it could be safe, away from the hands of Rozalin Heart.

I nodded and headed to Dedria, "I did it." I announced with a half relieved, half proud smile.

"You did? Damn. I bet Pendra forty gold you wouldn't get it until after we got back to the tower." Dedria replied, and laughed at the look of absolute betrayal I was sure was painted on my face. "What?! It's not like I've had a lot of other things going on for this trip!"

I huffed a breath of air, "I hate you." I grumbled, marching past her through the cars towards the front of the train. Along the way, the soldiers of Solaria were getting ready for departure, packing and arranging, each would give a bow as I passed and greeted me with 'Your Grace'.

Finally, I got to the car that Pendra and Bevy were in, "How far away are we?"

"About twenty minutes," Pendra replied. "The trains in Taranor are significantly slower. We really do have to try and get them on board with the Solarian engines."

I rolled my eyes, "They don't want to pay for it. They will continue with their inferior technology. It isn't our problem." I replied, "Just be glad they let us use a train at all. If we had to go by horse and wagon it would have taken us five times as long."

"If I never have to ride in a horse and cart again, it will be too soon." Pendra retorted, his long tail flicking around him in irritation at the mere idea of it. "The Duke and Duchess will be there to receive us. You are positive you do not wish to rest for the night here, Your Grace?"

I shook my head, "We are more vulnerable travelling. We need to get back to the Halls as soon as possible. That's the safest place for us right now." My tone was firm, no room for argument.

Pendra just gave a sad sigh, he had looked forward to a more comfortable bed and a hot bath, but he understood my reasoning and would not argue about it. Still, I could see he was disappointed. He had also wanted us to detour to the Capital and see the Grand Archmage and the Archmage Council, but I had put a halt to that. We didn't have time for Political posturing anymore. We had to do it in Lethiarum, because we wouldn't have been able to move through the underground Mountain Pass without the King. But that was months ago now. I wanted to go home.

I patted him on the shoulder, "I know you're disappointed. Once this is all over, we will visit the Baron and Baroness properly. But for now, we need to push on. Our journey is almost over."

Time seemed to crawl as slow as the Train as we approached the station and slowed to a halt. Finally, the brakes fully engaged and the movement we had all become accustomed to stopped. I led the procession off, stepping down the stairs onto the platform and casually looking around. The station was quiet, it looked like the Baron and Baroness had cleared it of civilians to ensure I would be safe. They were at the end of the platform, talking quietly among themselves.

Baron Tetbald had deeply tanned skin and stood at 2 metres tall, his black hair was cut short. I remembered on the day of his wedding he had been lean and fierce and could swing a sword as well as the best of them. But the years of a more relaxed, peaceful lifestyle had taken its toll and he had put on some weight, especially around his middle.

The Baroness however was as radiant as the last time I had seen her, with porcelain skin and blonde hair with bright blue eyes. As I approached though, I noticed the Baroness was with child. She still had some time to go, but the bump was there.

I gave a small nod of my head as I reached them, "Your Grace," I greeted the Baron with a polite, but feigned, smile.

"Ah! Your Royal Highness!" The Baron exclaimed, his voice carrying, and he took me by the hand, giving a bow and kissing the back of my hand. "My, how you have grown!"

I kept that polite smile pasted on my face, "Yes, indeed." I said, trying not to sound stiff, turning to the Baroness. "Congratulations are in order. I am sorry, you must have alerted my Mother of your news, and it wasn't brought to my attention. When are you expecting to be due?"

"Another two months, Your Royal Highness." The Baroness replied, her voice softer and more demure.

"Two months! So soon," I replied, and made a mental note to scold Pendra for forgetting to warn me of this. "May Arcanis shine on you and the babe during the delivery." I offered the traditional blessing of Arcanis.

That got the Baroness to smile, and I knew that news of my Ash Queen status had spread. "Thank you very much, Your Royal Highness."

Baron Tetbald held his arm out to his wife, and when she took it, he offered the other to me, I had a moment of reluctance before I did the same. "You are sure you can not stay the night, Your Grace?" He asked.

"I can not, I am afraid. I have been away from home for too long and seek the warmth of my own bed and comforts of the Halls." I answered, and once again my tone conveyed successfully that there was no room for argument.

Baron Tetbald nodded, "Very well. We will cross with you to the other side as is customary. I do hope you will visit. Your mother was due to visit us, before her unfortunate death. Though I can't imagine your Halls can be so comfortable? All the way on top of the tower, and so dark!"

I bit down on my tongue to prevent myself from saying anything crass, "Once the perpetrators who attacked the Halls and the other countries have been apprehended, I plan on doing a proper visit of the Crossing and Taranor. I promise to keep you well informed when that time comes."

He clicked his tongue, "Such an unfortunate thing. Have you discovered what the cause of it was in your journey?" He inquired, and I glanced up to him with natural suspicion.

"We have some leads, but nothing concrete, unfortunately." I replied, and I felt his arm tighten against his side.

"Is that so? You have found nothing at all? So many days away from home and you are returning without so much as a single concrete lead? That isn't like a Maracroix at all."

My heart started beating a little harder, "Well it was not all to waste. It's just time to return to the Tower and compare what we've found to what they have discovered." I was doing a quick assessment of the situation. Pendra and Bevy were travelling with the Ember shard in Bevy's bag, and they knew what to do in the worst case. Fly back to the Tower together to safety and leave Dedria and I behind with the Soldiers to fight our way out. Getting the Ember shard to safety was paramount. "Why are you asking, Lord Tetbald?"

"I am just curious what the new Queen of Solaria has learned, that's all. It can be such a dangerous world out there, you know. So, it's surprising to me you haven't learned anything at all." He replied, and he sounded so nonchalant over it.

Dedria coughed behind us; we were halfway through the Crossing now. "I think Her Royal Highness would rather not talk about our trip. It's been so long and has taken so much out of us." She increased her pace until she was side by side with me, but her gait was one of pure leisure with an air of arrogance.

Tetbald glanced over to Dedria, "...Sorry, I didn't catch your name..."

"Lady Dedria Heart." She answered without missing a beat, giving him a catty grin. "We are just seeking to return to the Halls as quickly as we can. Surely you understand if you've been away from the comforts of your warm bed for more than a night. Though, that probably isn't a problem for you, Lord Tetbald? By the look of it, you spend too much time sitting around now."

He sputtered, "H-How dare you!" He exclaimed.

"More like how dare you, Lord? Speaking as you have been to Queen Johanna. Not even an apology out of you for so blasé bringing up the death of her mother. I remember when your father passed, you mourned for twelve months before you even left the Crossing. And yet Queen Johanna here left after five months, seeking vengeance for those that had a hand in her mother's death and you practically mock her for not finding anything. Shame on you, Lord Tetbald. I thought you had more class than that." Dedria shot back, her blue eyes turning on him with an intense gaze. "Trust me when I say that this display will be getting back to my mother. See, she really, really hates anyone who disrespects the Maracroix family. The late Queen Serena was her best friend, and Queen Johanna is practically her daughter. So your next words better be begging for forgiveness."

Dedria had him cornered, whatever force that was causing Tetbald to dig into what we had found was not as powerful as a threat by a Heart. Heart Industries in Taranor, the company that Veronica owned, was one of the biggest exporters to Solaria, and all of those goods had to pass right through the Crossing as it was the most cost-effective. The other option was sending the goods by ship which easily quadrupled the travel time since there was no safe way through the mountains that lay on either side of the deep canyon. The Crossing was the quickest, fastest and safest way.

But a slight to Veronica Heart? She was petty enough, and wealthy enough, to take the slower, more expensive route if it meant shunning those that dared insult her. The Crossing got to tax all those goods, still a fraction of the cost of the longer journey, so Heart Industries was a huge income source for the small country.

Tetbald started to backtrack, "I just meant, er. I'm sorry, Your Royal Highness." He stammered out. It was almost comical to see a man of his stature stumbling over his words the way he was.

Dedria scoffed, "That is a piss poor attempt at an apology, Lord Tetbald. Try again."

He pursed his lips, "...My apologies for being so disrespectful to you and your mother's memory, Your Royal Highness."

I felt the tension melt from me at Dedria stepping in and handling it. "Apology accepted, my Lord. I appreciate you seeing the sense of it."

Dedria smiled and had me take her arm, pulling me far enough away from Tetbald I had to remove my hand from his arm. "Perfect. Now that that nasty business is over with, how has your pregnancy been so far, Lady Bells?" She asked with a perfectly polite smile.

"I have been managing. I suffered from much sickness and fatigue in the beginning." The Lady replied with a relieved smile, "it's all over with now and I am feeling a little more like myself, though I grow bigger every day and am not able to do all the things I am used to."

"Oh, I'm sure a lady such as yourself has so many things to do," Dedria replied, giving me a subtle wink. We were approaching the second bridge now, the thick timber and metal bridge was wide enough for six horse carts to cross side by side, and along each edge were small vendors selling goods and trinkets. Some from the Crossing, some from Taranor, some from Solaria.

I could feel all eyes on us, soft murmurs and whispers filling the air as we crossed the bridge, the air alive with voices but none of them loud enough to hear. I pressed forward, and my foot finally touched the hardened path on the other side.

I was home, the Obsidian Tower was only 3 days from here with the faster Solarian trains. We were so close.

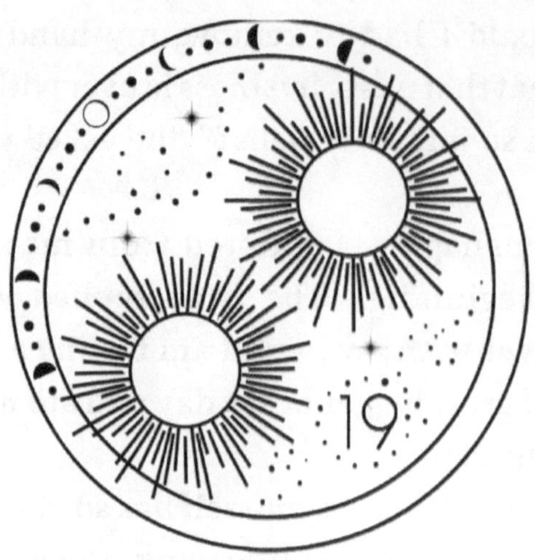

My lips released a relieved sigh as Dedria, Pendra, Bevy and I stepped into the mechanical lift that would bring us up to the Ivory Halls. I hadn't allowed my father or sister to meet me at the train station, it was just too risky right now. Not when the vision of Rozalin riding that mass of corpses in the sea still plagued my dreams.

Pendra's tail swished against the metal floor, his scales making an audible sound from it. Not unlike the rustling of metal scales brushing beside each other, "I am very relieved to be back in Solaria, I must admit Your Grace."

I nodded, "I am as well," I admitted softly. "Bevy, you will meet my father and my sister soon. I promise they are very nice." I added softly, looking over to the young girl.

Bevy jolted up, she was leaning against the railing and staring out the glass of the lift at the scene below. "Sorry, sorry, I wasn't listing, nope, nope, nope. Was looking down below! Those are like wagons but aren't horse powered! What are they powered by? How are they moving? How do they know where to go?"

I couldn't help but chuckle at all her questions, "Those are vehicles. They are steam and mana powered, like our trains.

They have one person who drives them around." I explained, "I was saying you will meet my father and sister soon."

"Oh, yes yes yes! Dowager King Simon and and and Princess Kira! Yes, I am very excited to meet them yes. The Princess is close to my age, yes, yes?"

"She is, she's a year or two younger than you."

"Do you think she will like me?" As Bevy asked it, her smile faded, and she looked worried. She was so open with her expressions, it reminded me so much of Kira, who was the same.

Still, Bevy's sudden vulnerability took me back a moment, and I gave a soft, reassuring smile, "I promise you that she will like you." I said, crouching down to be more eye level with Bevy. "You have nothing to worry about in that front, okay?"

Bevy brightened and she smiled again, "Okay! And and and I get to see the library, right? You, you promised me!"

"Yes, you get to see the library, and you will have tutors and instructors who will teach you whatever you like." I promised, straightening to a stand again and ruffling Bevy's hair gently. I took the girl's hand; the lift was slowing as we got closer to the entrance to the Ivory Halls.

The lift shuddered and creaked as it reached the top, the metal doors being pushed open from the outside by two Elite guards who took a deep bow as I stepped out first, with Bevy by my side. It had been refreshing to see the familiar uniform, the helms that hid most of their features. They hadn't been with us on the journey, mostly because I had enough soldiers already, and as much as I hated to admit it, their presence hadn't saved my mother.

On the other side was Simon and Kira, waiting quietly though they both smiled wide, and Kira ran forward. She no longer needed her cane, by the looks of it. Relief struck me hard, making it almost hard to breath. The tell-tale black veins of the Rot were fading and looked more like fading bruising, pale purple and yellows. She wrapped her arms around my waist in a hug. "I missed you! I bet you saw so many cool things. You will tell me all about them, right? Did you beat the bad guys? That's why you're home, right? You beat them! Oh! Is this Bevy?! Papa told me about her! Hello! My name is Kira, just Kira. You don't have to use Princess. It's a bit stuffy if you ask me, right? Oh, I'm so excited you're home Johanna! Look! Look! I'm doing so much better! Momma's research is working! And Tyne has been so, so great. She visits me three times a day and makes sure I drink all the stinky tea but I'm feeling so much better now, and I can run and jump, and Papa is even letting me learn how to ride horses and practice with the combat instructors and it's just so so so great! You've missed so much!"

My brows lifted as I took it all in, and I slid my hand from Bevy's to put both hands on Kira's shoulders, "Breathe. Slow down." I said with a chuckle, "I know you are very excited for me to be home, but we will have plenty of time to catch up, okay? I'm glad you're feeling better." I leaned down to kiss Kira on the head. "How about you show Bevy around the halls and show her her room before bringing her to the library, okay? Can you do that for me?"

Kira nodded, grabbing Bevy by the hand. "Of course! C'mon!" She said, and she was hauling Bevy off. I could already hear them talking and laughing.

I glanced back to Pendra, "Follow them." I instructed, and he nodded and headed off after them with long strides.

Simon moved forward with a relieved smile and took me in a warm hug. "Welcome home, my dear." He murmured into my ear. I didn't let myself sag under the warmth of his hug, the relief evident in his voice. I was just as glad to be home. "There is a lot we have to catch up on together, let's head to your office and you can fill me in on yours, and I will fill you in on what has been going on here over hot tea and coffee and snacks, hm?"

Dedria gave a relieved sigh from behind me, "Oh thank Arcanis, I can not wait for fresh, good food and coffee." There was absolutely nothing in her tone that suggested she wasn't going to be there - and I was glad, because I wanted her there. Despite a few rough patches in the journey, I couldn't imagine Dedria not beside me anymore. Couldn't think of not having her opinion.

That earned smiles from Father and I, and the three of us headed through the Halls towards my office. "Thank you for taking such good care of my daughter, Dedria." Simon said.

Dedria shrugged nonchalantly, "Well it's not like she gave me much of a choice. She gets into so much trouble you know." Her words were teasing, but fond.

Simon grinned at that and laughed, "Tell me about it. Did she ever tell you about how she snuck out of the Halls when she was nine and went to the Royal Stables and got into the Nightmare's stall?"

"I am going to ask the Archons to smite both of you." I said, shaking my head at them both. "And for what it is worth, Father, I did not sneak out, I merely asked the Elite to bring me and them obeyed."

"From my recollection, the Elite said you gave them a note from me instructing him to bring you and if they did not, I would have their head for treason. Excellently forged, by the way. But fake all the same. Really, their head for not bringing you to the stables? So dramatic."

I was still proud of that note, even if I wouldn't admit it. Still, I countered with a faux glare, "I was nine!"

"You knew better."

"And? I was still nine. I wanted to go visit the stables, Kira had just been born and you and Mother were busy with her and I was bored in the Halls. I didn't have much of a choice."

Simon laughed and pulled me up against his side in a squeeze, his lips brushing me on the forehead. "I'm sorry we didn't pay as much attention to you back then." He said now, sincere and sad.

I just shrugged, looking away. "It happened; we can't change it now." I said finally.

"Okay," Dedria interjected, sensing my tension, "I am not here for emotional apologies between the two of you. If you don't mind, how about we get to the matters at hand?"

I was relieved at her changing the subject, so I just nodded, "I think that's fair."

Between the two of us, Dedria and I recounted everything of importance that had happened since my last major radio communication back in Lethiarum until we arrived in Solaria. He said nothing, as I spoke about the Archons, about Karne, the Ember shards, the trip to Kayori, the Soul Forge weapon. His brows had wrinkled as we spoke about Rozalin on the ship. Dedria took perhaps too much joy recounting Tetbald's bullshit in the Crossing, especially him putting him in his place.

Simon sat quietly, listening and mulling over it as he drank some coffee. "Rozalin Heart, you are sure?" He didn't quite believe us, and we could both tell.

I nodded, "Positive. Maria is positive as well."

"…Troubling…she has been missing for nearly a thousand years. Where has she been all this time?" Simon questioned. It wasn't like Dedria, and I hadn't thought about that endlessly.

"Not a clue." I admitted honestly. It wasn't like Dedria, and I hadn't thought about that endlessly, and we still didn't have the answer to that question. "All we know is that she has a group of Chronomancers with her, and she's seemingly proficient in Necromancy."

Simon's upper lip lifted at that, a look of pure disgust, "Nasty, dirty, unholy magic. If she uses magic like that she can not be helped or saved from her path."

Dedria choked out a laugh, "You thought she could be helped or saved?!"

"It is Johanna's duty as the Ash Queen to try and bring peace and light to those corrupted." Simon said now, obviously confused at Dedria's laughter.

"No offense, Uncle Simon, but the most merciful thing we can do for Rozalin Heart is kill her. Maria Maracroix failed, Johanna will not. No matter her 'duty' as the Ash Queen. Her first duty, first and foremost, is to keep Solaria safe. That means killing Rozalin." Dedria retorted.

I lifted my hand before my father could speak, "Do not talk about me like I am not here, and I do not get a word in on what my duty is." I said, tone sharp and unforgiving. "At the end of the day, I will do what I must to protect Solaria and the World. But Rozalin Heart killed Mother, and I also think justice should be served for that."

Simon pursed his lips, "Justice changes depending on the

viewer. You see it as justice, but Rozalin would not..."

"Since when are you on Rozalin's side?!" Dedria snapped, visibly agitated. "Serena was your wife!"

"I know that. I loved her for longer than you have been alive!" Simon snapped, "I am just trying to ensure my daughter does not slide down a slippery slope in which she cannot return from, while you are all too happy to push her down it."

"Enough!" My voice cut through them arguing, and my tone was furious. "I will decide Rozalin's fate, as is my right as Queen of Solaria and as the Ash Queen of Arcanis. There will be no more discussion or arguing over this. Now please, Father, enlighten us on what we missed here while we were away. Please." My voice was still tense, and I hoped the look on my face expressed how exactly I felt about them arguing over this - angry.

Simon and Dedria went quiet as I spoke, and both had the sense to look ashamed. They glanced at each other sheepishly and mumbled apologies to me and each other.

"Obviously there is development with the cure to The Rot. Tyne is continually trying to make more concentrated versions of it that can be given in a medication form of it, but she has been unsuccessful thus far. She has shared her concerns about it being a treatment for the symptoms, but not a cure for the disease itself. So even though Kira is improving, she is worried that if we stop the treatment she will regress. So it's a matter of...quite frankly, just tests and experiments." Simon explained, his tone had changed from being angry and frustrated to the calm, measured voice that I was used to when it came to him.

"Good. We will continue supporting Tyne however we can.

Finding a cure for this is paramount." I determined, finally taking a seat and pouring myself some coffee, adding sugar and cream to it. I had a feeling I would need the extra boost in the coming hours.

"Of course, Your Grace." answered Simon with a tense nod. "We have not heard much of Nox, I suspect because they were hunting you. Hmm…The fodder crops we use to feed the livestock went through a blight; we suspect something that was introduced during the latest Nox attack. So, we had to do a cull to get rid of the livestock we could not feed properly. We are using ongoing freezing enchantments and spells maintained by the power of Ground Zero. Frustrating, as it will affect our yield in the next three to five years, but it is something we will deal with. If needed, we will have to import livestock from Taranor or the southern States."

I nodded, finding some paper and an ink and quill and was making notes at my desk. "Worse things could have happened; it could have hit our fresh fruit and vegetable stocks."

He nodded in agreement, "Castian arrived back yesterday, he has been a very busy man. He was delighted and requested an audience with you as soon as you arrived. I told him that that was up to you, and if you did want to give him an audience he would be informed."

I made a face, not seeking to give audience to everyone that had asked while I had been gone, but Castian had been looking into the Age of Dragons, it's possible some of his discoveries could aid with the oncoming conflict. That's what I reasoned. At this point, I was desperate for any help, even if it was in ancient artifacts that probably wouldn't help me at all. "Very well." I looked to the Elite that was inside the room at the door, "please have a courier find Castian...err." I paused, having to think hard to recall his last name. "Wesner, yes. Have a courier find Castian Wesner for an Audience with me in three hours." I said, and the Elite bowed and left the room to do just that. "Gives me some time to have a hot bath and get changed into something more...queenly." I said, standing up and shoving a scone in my mouth in a very un-ladylike way. "Dedria, I want you there as well." I added, and Dedria just nodded. We both knew why, and that went unspoken between us.

"Naturally." She replied with a grin.

I left the office now and headed to my quarters, my servants already waiting for me and immediately got to work filling the tub with water and warming it, adding salts and oils and scents to make it smell wonderful and relaxing. One servant helped me out of my travel clothes - lighter version of my regular armour, taking them away to be cleaned. I knew they smelled and that I was rank as well, I had been travelling in them for far too long without a proper bath.

I sank into the warm waters with a relieved sigh, leaning my head back against the edge as all three servants got to work undoing the braids Pendra had put in my hair on the ship. They worked quickly and efficiently, and most importantly, silently.

Though, after travelling for so long, always surrounded by noise, the silence got unnerving. I had grown used to Soldiers shouting and talking and laughing, of sailors working, of the noise of the trains. The silence now felt so unnatural.

"How have things been in the Halls?" I asked finally, breaking the silence.

The servants looked startled, and they all nervously glanced at each other.

"...Very good, Your Grace." One answered finally. She had been around the longest, her name was Elizabeth. Her voice was quiet, but I could tell she was not being entirely truthful.

"You can tell me the truth. Please. If things have not been going well, I need to know." I pressed, gently.

Elizabeth hesitated before she spoke next, "Your father has been...lashing out more. I fear the stress and sadness has caught up with him."

I reflected on that, how he had been so quick to fight Dedria on my role. How he was ready to decide my responsibilities for me. "Yes, I agree." I said finally, "I am back now, that will no longer happen. It won't be tolerated; he can not be treating any of the servants poorly. You serve the country by serving me and my family. It is of the utmost importance that you are treated with respect and kindness."

The servant's cheeks tinged pink, and she gave a slight smile at that, "Thank you, Your Grace." She offered. "We are done unbraiding your hair. Please sit up so we may wet it and wash it now."

I did as asked, and the servants used bowls to pour water over my head and hair before using various products to cleanse the dirt, sweat and grime of the journey. Once they were done with that, they stepped away so I could clean my own body, a boundary I had since I was old enough to do so. I called them back in when I was ready to get out - that was a requirement. A past queen, pregnant at the time, had fallen when getting out of the tub herself and had died from hitting her head on the floor. After that, no royal was allowed to leave a tub without assistance.

They helped dry me and then tended to my hair, adding moisture back in with more products, defining the tight curls and making sure they would stay. "Would you like your hair in braids again, Your Grace?" Elizabeth asked.

I shook my head very slightly, "We do not have time for that right now. Just refine the coils as best you can and add the adornments."

The three nodded in unison and got to work, and before long my hair was complete. Elizabeth stepped back, "I pulled your three favourite gowns for you to wear, Your Grace."

I considered for a moment, "The blue velvet, I think." I always felt beautiful in the velvet, and comfortable.

Again, the three of them helped me into the undergarments and gown. It was heavier, being velvet, but it was eye-catching and the feeling of like I belonged as Queen settled over my skin.

By the end of it, I only had ten minutes before I was due to meet Castian in the Throne Room. I did not rush, but my pace was not slow by any means. Dedria caught up with me just as I reached the lift, and the two of us travelled down to the Throne Room floor in comfortable silence.

I walked into the Throne Room from the back entrance, Dedria just behind me and to my right. Castian was already there, with three large crates opened with dried straw bursting out of them, and one exceptionally large one, taller than I was tall and was as wide as four of me abreast, which was closed.

Castian gave a deep bow, "Your Grace," He said softly, "Thank you for seeing me on such short notice. Welcome home."

I took my seat on the familiar throne, "Rise." I said, "What did you bring home to Solaria from your travels?"

Castian smiled and it reached his eyes, they danced in the light, and he was so eager to share. He was handsome like this, so bright with joy. "Amazing things!" He answered, "Books, in Dragonic unfortunately...Dead language, but it is possible we may find someone who will be able to translate them. Jewelry, more exquisite than anything I have ever laid eyes on, gems as large as your fist. Weapons, still razor sharp and perfectly honed. But none of it compares to this!" As he spoke, he moved from open crate to open crate, holding up matching items with each one he named.

Then he moved to the last crate, still closed, and he snapped his fingers and three assistants moved forward from the side, and with his help they undid the straps holding the sides of the crate together, the top already gone.

As the sides fell and hit the floor with a loud thump that reverberated through the whole room, the straw inside fell away and revealed a blood red egg.

A dragon egg.

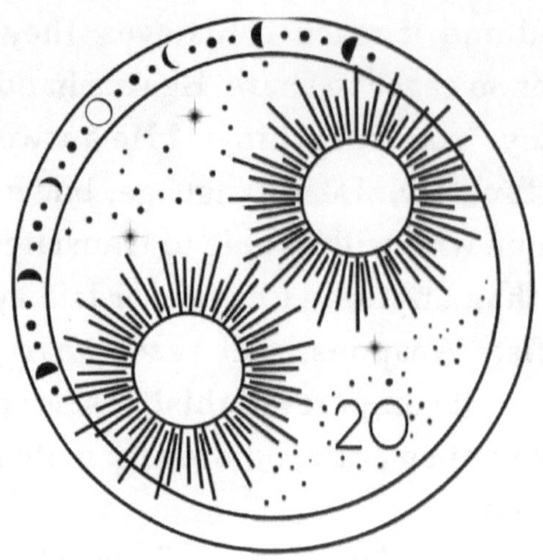

"Is it real?" I asked, and before even I had really registered, I was on my feet and walking forward.

"Of course, Your Grace! And even more, it is still alive! Whatever is in this egg has been dormant since the Age of Dragons!" Castian exclaimed, with that same brilliant, excited smile. "It is not a fossil; I am sure of it." I hadn't even had a chance to ask, "We checked it for aura and mana signatures the moment we found it, and it has an aura. Small...but it is there."

I laid my palm on the egg, it was warm. It was ever so slightly textured, and it reminded me of the overlapping scales of a real snake. Smooth to the touch, but the slightest ridges could be felt. It had looked like nearly one solid colour from the Throne, but from here it had small gradients, the outside of each scale was darker than the centre, the colours bleeding together. "It's beautiful..." I murmured, and I looked to Castian, "we must try and hatch it. Dedria, you can read Dragonic right? Like your mother?"

Dedria startled from her spot, she had been entranced by the egg as well, as was every Elite in the room. "Sorry? Oh, yes. I can."

I nodded, "You and one of Castian's assistants will work together to read through the tomes, see if there are any answers for incubation." I said firmly now. "If there is a living dragon in here, it deserves the best chance to hatch."

Dedria wrinkled her face up; reading was not something she enjoyed. "Of course, Johanna." She replied.

Castian was already over to one of the smaller crates, digging through the books. He produced one that looked to be bound in Wyvern leather, the pages aged parchment and probably very brittle. "When I looked through this one, it seemed to have schematics for something, but I could not work out what." He said, "Perhaps this will help. Please, Lady Heart, wear gloves." He produced fine cotton gloves out of his jacket pocket, handing them to her. Dedria nodded, taking the gloves and sliding them on before carefully starting to go through the book.

Castian turned his attention back to me. I was circling the egg carefully, running my hand along it. "I do hope Your Royal Highness is pleased?"

I looked at him and nodded, "I am." I replied, "very much so. And I am very impressed, a Dragon Egg..." I clicked my tongue, my mind barely able to keep up with everything I was feeling and thinking right now. "If there is one, it is possible there is more."

Castian grinned, "Just my thoughts, Your Grace!" He exclaimed excitedly while clapping his hands together.

"Then you will see if those books, with the help of Dedria deciphering them, have any more locations for possible ruins like the one you found in the Southern Mountains. And you will search all of them for more eggs." I replied, losing myself in thought again.

Dragon eggs. Dragons! Dead for many millennia, thought to be completely extinct. The Dragon Wars had been a race war - the dragons had fought each other until none had remained. They had been the most powerful species alive. They had been so smart, so technically gifted when it came to crafting. We saw evidence of that with Lethiarum still standing, its bones having been built by Dragons.

But now I stood in front of one, even unhatched, my hand on one that was warm, and I could feel the life pulsing inside of it. It was weak, feeble. But possibly, just possibly, they could be made strong again. They could hatch.

Perhaps I could bring the Dragons back. Any country that dared try to think about war with Solaria in the future would surely reconsider. Their lifetimes were also thought to be impossibly long, maybe even longer than a Chronomancer.

Provided I could win the dragon inside this egg to my side. Provided they didn't hate me and all people for the extinction of their kind. But maybe I could help them see sense, see that I was trying to revive their species from quite literally nothing. Perhaps...perhaps. Not getting hopes up though, maybe this dragon would never hatch. Maybe that is why it didn't hatch during the time of Dragons. Maybe that is why it was left in ruins, to rot and die.

I wouldn't know until the dragon inside hatched. If it ever did.

Castian had been talking while I had been deep in thought, and I tuned back into what he was saying. "...Who knows what other marvels other ruins would have! If this egg can be dormant for as long as it has, maybe a real Dragon could be dormant too?"

"Let's not get ahead of ourselves..." I replied, shaking my head.

Rich of me to say, given everything I was still considering. Hoping for.

Castian nodded, "Of course, Your Grace. Silly, foolish dreams of mine, of course."

Dedria clicked her tongue, "I found something...schematics for an incubation...hm. Don't know this word. I think the closest would be an underground cave. It says they used hot springs below a constructed cave, it kept it warm and the humidity high." She said, looking over to us. "It must be hot, though. They supplemented the heat of the cave with...eternal Dragon Fire below each egg. Yeah, I don't think you want that."

I kept my hand on the Egg, something inside me was preventing me from pulling away from it. "We must use heat lamps for some of the agriculture. They are enchanted to withstand high heat, and we could potentially hook up a shard from Ground Zero to it, that would provide more than enough power to keep Dragon Fire going."

"Johanna, that's incredibly dangerous. If you fail, you could cause irreparable damage to the Tower and Halls." Dedria's gaze was steel on mine, and I met it with my own determination.

"It is worth a shot."

"I disagree."

"It isn't your call, Dedria." I reminded, tone getting sharp. I looked to the elites, "Go down to agriculture, obtain four of the largest heat lamps we have. Procure four stabilised shards from Ground Zero. And bring one of the engineers up here." I instructed, and one of them bowed and left without question.

Castian watched all this, absolutely elated. "Brilliant, Your Grace!" He clapped, "Absolutely brilliant! But where will we get Dragon Fire? Such a spell is incredibly rare, it requires immense power…"

Dedria pursed her lips, "Me." She replied, and shot a glare at me that only a best friend could.

"O-oh! Lady Heart! Well, I must say, this is nice and tidy." Castian laughed, "Should we move the Egg, Your Grace?"

I contemplated and nodded, "Yes. We will move it to one of the rooms three floors up." I replied. It would be safer up there, and further away from Nox. Nox couldn't hear about this, if they did…they would probably try and steal the Egg. My heart ached at the idea of it being in their hands.

Castian nodded, and with his assistants they unanimously cast a spell strong enough to pick up the egg from the straw. Just one of them would not be able to move it, it had to be all four.

I nodded, "Come." I said, and without waiting, I headed out the back entrance to the lift. We all fit in the lift, barely. It shuddered, creaked and groaned as it started to rise up, and made a bit of a sickening jolt downwards before it corrected itself and continued up the three floors. My stomach was still righting itself as I led them through the maze of halls to the correct room, it was mostly empty, save for a few oil paintings that were covered. Elites had appeared and with more direction were removing the paints and moving them to a different room.

"We will need heat proof material to cradle it and keep it upright." I said, "something that will retain temperature."

Castian glanced around, "Why not the very obsidian the tower is made from? Does the tower not keep pieces in case of repairs to the outside?"

I clicked my tongue but nodded, looking to another Elite. "Have a stonemason bring up a piece large enough to hold the

Egg. We will need it carved out here to cradle it properly." Once again, the Elite nodded and disappeared.

Over the next several hours, the slab of obsidian arrived, and the stone mason expertly carved out a large enough divot to perfectly cradle the egg, though he had no idea what it was for, just given directions. While he was doing that, I oversaw an Engineer fit the heat lamps with the shard from Ground Zero. The Egg had been moved to a different room while this was going on, I would take no risks of word of this egg getting out beyond those that already knew about it.

Once the Engineer had given instructions on how to light the lamps, they left, followed quickly by the stonemason. And then it was just Dedria, two Elites, Castian and his three assistants, and me. Castian and his team carefully moved the egg into the obsidian slab, and Castian dismissed them.

I looked at Dedria and gave a slight nod.

Dedria sighed audibly, her disapproval of this still clear, but she channelled her aura, the air getting thicker around them as the flame formed in her hand. One after another, she pushed the flame into the heat lamps, the crystal giving a dull blue glow as it activated and started to power the flame. The room started getting warmer with just one lamp being lit, and after the third it was like being outside in the desert during mid day. The fourth made it sweltering.

I frowned, "Should have thought about that..." I muttered, glancing at one of the Elites. I was about to speak, but the egg seemed to vibrate and suddenly all the heat was being absorbed by it. The room returned to its cooler, livable state. "Oh, that is a relief..."

Dedria just nodded, "Uh Huh. Can I go to bed now? It's the

middle of the night. I am exhausted."

I just nodded, "Go." I murmured, "I'm going to stay here, for now. All of you leave."

Castian hesitated, watching me with a slightly concerned look in his eye. "Your Grace, you should go rest. Today has been a long day, not including your travels."

I glanced towards him, and I dismissed his concern with a shake of my head. "I appreciate your concern, Mister Wesner, but it's misplaced. I am fine." I insisted when he hesitated, and he sighed softly and left.

Once the room was completely empty save for me, I took a seat beside the egg, putting my hand on it again. It was warmer now, but not hot enough to burn. "I hope you can hear me..." I started softly. My words were hesitant, not sure what to say. "Maybe I'm crazy for talking to you...the Archons would probably say I am. Everyone else would too. A lot has happened since you've been warm like this. My name is Johanna Maracroix. I'm Queen of a country called Solaria. Dragon's...don't exist anymore. Or we thought they didn't, until we found you." I leaned my forehead against the shell, "I don't know what I'm expecting. The world is in danger, and I'm hoping you hatch in time to help..."

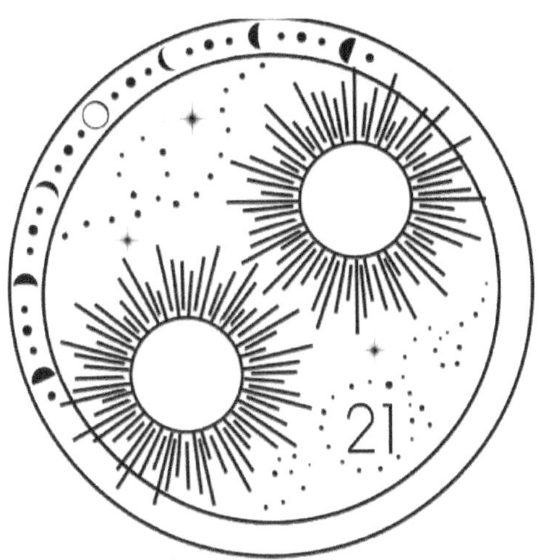

T he next day, I woke in the room with the egg absolutely famished. I rubbed the sleep from my eyes as I wondered when I had dozed off. Slowly stretching out the kinks and sore spots with a wince before trudging my way back up to my quarters to change into training attire and meet Dedria in the training hall before breakfast.

Dedria was already in the training hall, and she arched her brow. "What took you so long?" She asked.

I shrugged, "Slept in." I replied nonchalantly. It wasn't a total lie.

Dedria didn't look like she believed it, but she also didn't question me further, just grabbing two of the practice weapons and tossing one of them over. "Let's do this then."

I caught it, and the two of us got to work. I worked on summoning different Archon aspects and using their powers and knowledge, and Dedria worked on defending against them as I learned from them. It was not always the most challenging for either, but it was all we had. It was also routine and predictable, and we both generally left our sessions having learned something new.

"How are we going to beat Rozalin?" Dedria questioned as she lifted her weapon to block a strike.

I took a step back, pursing my lips together. "I don't know." I admitted, unease coiling inside me, "It felt like every time we got close on the boat, she was able to see the attack, even if it was coming from behind her. Right? I'm not imagining that?"

"No, you're not." Said Dedria, who shook her head and pushed forward with a series of attacks.

I gritted teeth as I blocked and parried, even if some of Dedria's attacks made my arms ache. "That's a relief."

"Still doesn't tell us how to deal with it."

"No. Maybe I can probe Maria about it. Give me a moment?"

I paused, prompting Dedria to step back respectfully and go to get some water.

"Maria?" I asked mentally, reaching out to the Archon. "Maria? Maybe you can help us."

Maria answered after a few long moments of silence, "Help you with what?"

"Dedria and I were talking about Rozalin, and how we can defeat her...And it feels like she was able to see us and our attacks, no matter where we were positioned around her. Even if one of us was behind her, she knew..." I explained, hesitating slightly.

Maria retracted a moment, and my skin tingled all over as the Archon prodded my memory, pulling forward the fight on the boat. "Strange, her one eye is red. It wasn't red during our fight."

"What do you think it could mean?"

"I don't know...I will talk with the others." And that feeling of Maria being close was gone again.

I looked back up and over to Dedria, "She said Rozalin had a red eye, and it was strange, but she didn't know what it meant."

Dedria shrugged, "Well alright then. I'm done for the morning, you?"

"Agreed, I still have a lot to catch up on being back."

Dedria nodded, putting both the practice weapons back and looping her arm through mine. Side by side we went up to the dining room, where Bevy, Simon and Kira were already eating. Kira waved excitedly, "Morning!"

"Good morning." Dedria and I said in unison, and we smirked to each other, sitting down and starting to dig in.

"What did Castian find?" Simon inquired now, looking up to us. He hadn't been present for anything with Castian the day before.

"Books, some weapons, some art and sculptures." I explained, not revealing the Dragon egg to him. I wanted to keep that from him for now. I didn't want to deal with his probing questions, or managing the aftermath if it didn't hatch. "Dedria can read Dragonic, so hopefully the books will be enlightening and can tell us more about the Age and Wars."

Dedria wrinkled her nose, "I'm seriously stuck with translating duty?" She pouted.

"Unless you know of someone else who can read Dragonic and would be willing to do it that isn't your mother or sister." I countered with a grin.

Kira piped up, "Can I learn?!" She asked excitedly, "Will you teach me, Dedria? Please please please?"

"...Sure, I can try." Dedria said, but she gave me a pleading look, begging for me to interrupt and get her out of that.

I just shrugged, sipping at some coffee and nibbling at the food I had on my plate. "I have Open Court today, don't I?" I asked

Father now.

He nodded in response, "Yes. Do you want me to hold Open Court instead for you?" He offered, "I imagine it being on your agenda on your first full day back is not appealing."

I shook my head, finishing my cup of coffee before speaking, "No, I will do it. They need to see me, know I am here and okay."

I got up and nodded to everyone, heading to my quarters to bathe and change into a gown for Court. My servants helping me every step of the way just like the day before. I ended up in a red silk gown and a metal under bust corset that alluded to armor, a symbol of power and strength.

Just over an hour later, I sat on the throne, lifting a hand to motion for the Elites to open the doors and start the day.

The day droned on, most issues were small and inconsequential, but I knew they mattered to the citizens standing in front of me.

That was the case at least until a mother and son approached, their clothes, while clean and not torn, were of simple cream and black linen and oversized. I couldn't help but wonder if those were the nicest clothes they owned. I knew there were citizens in Solaria that didn't have much, but sometimes I forgot that some didn't even have properly fitting clothes.

My dress felt suffocating as I observed the pair.

They both bowed, and the mother spoke, her voice trembling with nerves. "Your Grace, thank you for seeing us. My name is Donatella, and this is my son, Nevyn. My husband died in the attack that also killed the Late Queen Serena, may Arcanis shine on her."

I felt a frown tug at my lips, and my brows furrowed together,

"I see. I am very sorry for your loss, both of you. How can the Throne help you today?"

Donatella wavered; her bottom lip quivered as she composed herself. "Is it true Your Grace is a Chronomancer?"

"Yes, I am."

"Nevyn has been showing signs that he too is a Chronomancer, Your Grace. With my husband gone, I struggle to put food on the table and keep the roof over our head. I was hoping Nevyn would be able to get a job when he turns 17 in two months, but no job will hire him if he does not have control of his abilities…and he has no one to teach him."

I knew what Donatella was asking without her saying it. For me to take her son in, to teach him. "I understand your plight, Donatella. I do. However, if I take your son in, then every budding Chronomancer across the country and then the world will also seek me out for the same, and I am not presently able to do that." Not right now, but soon. Soon.

Donatella sniffed and nodded, ready to turn and leave. Nevyn stepped forward however, and when he spoke, his voice sharp and full of youthful indigence. He was probably only a few years younger than me. "Who cares? You have enough to house and feed thousands I bet!" His mother looked mortified and went to speak but I lifted my hand to silence them both.

I took an even breath before speaking, "You are angry, rightfully so. It isn't fair- your father was torn from you, like my mother was torn from me. Shortly after, you came into your powers, and you have no one to guide you. No Guild to join, no master to seek out except for your Queen who isn't even a Master. The only difference between us, Nevyn, is that I sit upon this throne, and you do not. Your anger, all of it, is justified and

I understand it, far more than you probably know." I was sympathetic to him, it wasn't fair. I was lucky, I had Dedria, and Veronica, to guide me, I had the ability to seek out tutors and the time to learn. He did not, his mother probably worked multiple jobs and long hours to ensure he stayed fed.

"How many siblings do you have, and how old are they if you have any?" I asked now, gaze flicking between him and Donatella, who still looked mortified, mouth open in shock.

"Three. They are fourteen, twelve and six."

"And do they each have their own room?"

"No. We all share a room; mother has her own."

I looked towards the scribe who was making notes, "Which Diplomat unit has enough room for them? So, they can each have their own room."

The Scribe stammered at being asked a question, "Uh, well, Unit 39 does, Your Grace."

"Very well." I turned to Donatella and Nevyn, "You will bring back 3 Elites to your home. They will assist you in packing and moving your things to Diplomat Unit 39, until the Throne has obtained a permanent residence for you." I mentally ran through the stats of each unit before continuing, "From my recollection, it has 5 bedrooms. Enough for all of you. You will be clothed, fed and housed. A small price to pay for your Husbands sacrifice. If, and when, a Chronomancy Guild is opened or I can teach Nevyn what he needs to know of his powers, he will be accepted without application."

Donatella almost collapsed, having to grip her sons arm to prevent herself from doing anything truly embarrassing. She dropped to her knees in a deep bow, "Thank you, Your Grace!

Thank you!" She said and started to sob.

I nodded, feeling uncomfortable at her display of gratitude. Was it that big of a deal? Looking to the Scribe I spoke, "I also want every family who lost a family member from either Nox Attack to be checked in on. Ensure they have food, clothing and shelter and adequate funds to keep it that way."

Nevyn bowed at the waist, then pulled his mother to a stand. "Thank you, Your Grace." He said, but his voice still had a bit of bitterness to it.

"That's enough for now." I said to the Elites at the door, "I need a break. We will resume in two hours."

The Elites nodded, closing the doors and stepping outside.

"Your Grace, that is a great expense to the Throne." The Scribe stammered now, hesitant to even speak up about it.

I shook my head and shot him a disapproving look, "No, it's not. They lost family, it is the least the Throne can do to ensure they are taken care of. It is our responsibility to care for our most impoverished, it is the least we can do." I got up, heading out of the room through the back and up to the dining area where lunch would be waiting for me.

I didn't even get a chance to sit down before Maria's voice sounded in my head, "We believe we have narrowed down what that Red Eye of hers was."

"Oh?" I answered mentally, sitting down with a sigh and grabbing some coffee. I normally preferred tea, but my whole body was exhausted.

"Yes, we think it is an ancient magical relic called a Demon Eye. Combined with her Chronomancy abilities, it allows her to track and predict the movements of those around her. She probably lost that eye in the explosion we created, and she tracked that down."

"Great, so she can see what I'm going to do before I do it? That's how she knew Dedria was going to attack even if she couldn't see her."

"Correct."

"So, what do we do about it?"

"We don't know yet."

"Well, what do you know?"

"Well, it was made in the Age of Dragons, but after the Dragon Wars and their extinction it was lost to time. Ancient writings described it as a Demon Eye because of it's red colouring, and how it was crafted from the soul of a Demon of Hel."

I couldn't help but roll my eyes, "Myths. Hel doesn't exist."

"Even if you believe such, it is an incredibly powerful artifact, and you will not be able to beat Rozalin while she has it." Maria answered.

"Maybe some of the tomes recovered from the Dragon Ruins will have some answers. I'll ask Dedria to start going through them for that."

"Excellent idea Johanna." Maria sounded proud, and then her presence faded away.

I released a quiet sigh, my appetite lost so I finished my coffee and wandered the halls, finding myself back in the room with the Dragon Egg.

"Hello again." I said, moving over and laying a hand on the shell. "You wouldn't happen to know what the Demon Eye is, huh? Probably a stupid question, you were probably created after it was created. Still, if you knew that would be quite something…though none of it matters unless you hatch."

The egg seemed to vibrate gently against my hand for a few seconds before it went still again, and I smiled. Whoever was inside could hear me, which was reassuring. "Well, maybe we will find out together soon." I offered, and then I left the room, heading back to the Throne Room.

One of the scribes entered the room, "Your Grace." She said, "Sir Delain is here, and he is requesting an audience with you."

I ignored the coiling tension in my body. I couldn't place if it was excitement, or dread, "Very well. Bring him in, and everyone leave." Everyone did not include the Elites stationed in the room - but the other scribes and servants left as Delain walked in.

Somehow, he looked older, more mature, though he still had that roguish grin when he saw me. He bowed, "Your Grace." He said.

"Sir Delain. What can I do for you today?" I answered, and I knew my face soften at the sight of him.

"I seek permission to court you."

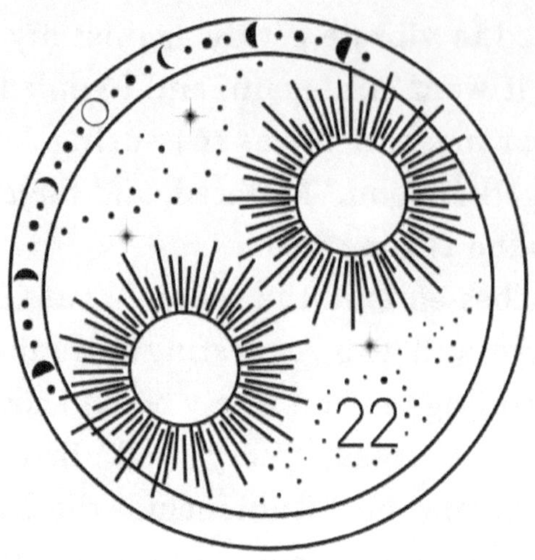

22

That coiled tension got worse, my lips pursing together and jaw tightened. "Elites, out." I commanded in a bark, and even though all ten of them looked to each other, they all obeyed and filed out of the Throne Room. Only once they were gone would I get up and approach Delain. "You what?" My voice was sharp, and full of disbelief. We had talked about this. I had made myself clear!

"I seek permission to court you." Delain repeated, calm in the wake of my oncoming fury. His brown gaze never left me, never faltered.

"Delain, we talked about this at my ascension. I can't..." I started to pace back and forth five feet in front of him, though my gaze never left him. I had to move, had to get the energy out.

He tried to take a step forward, but stopped when I lifted a hand to stop him. "Johanna, come on. You and I both know if your mother hadn't died..."

I flinched at the mention of Mother, of the time before, "And that was before. Before all this...before Nox and the Ember and..." My hand slowly dropped to my side. My voice wasn't strong no. It was weak, and I hated it.

He moved forward and took my hand in his, it felt so small compared to him. He brought it up to his lips, placing a kiss on the back of mine. "Queen Johanna, I don't promise to be the right one for you, I don't promise to fix all your worries and aches. But I know you. I know your favourite type of cake, how you like your tea, I know your favourite colour, and that you like fall best because of the storms, and that cactus flowers are your favourite flower because how can something so beautiful come from something that hurts everything around it. I know you prefer rubies to emeralds, and sapphires above both. I know you like the feeling of velvet over satin or silk. I know your favourite dish, your favourite book, and how you've read it at least a dozen times since you were twelve. I know so much about you and you know so much about me. Please, let me try to ease your burden. Let me in." He wasn't begging, not really. But his voice was soft, reassuring.

As he spoke, he slowly pulled me against him. A small part of me marvelled at how solid he was, how strong. One of his hands cupped my face, his callused thumb brushing along my skin. He smelled like the middle of summer, of the suns heat on the sands and the breeze that brought the promise of rain. He always smelled like that, and it made my heart ache.

I closed my eyes and shook my head weakly, "I can't..." I whispered.

"You can," He said softly as he leaned his forehead down against mine. He was so close, so impossibly close. He tilted my face up to meet his, his lips brushing against mine in a feather light kiss. Just a shadow of what he felt had burned between us for years. What I had felt, too.

Goosebumps crawled along my skin, and with a show of great

will power I stepped away. Even if I wanted to remain in his arms, to kiss him and embrace that urge to accept love, I couldn't, not here, not now. "If someone catches us like that…"

He looked disappointed for a split second but had the sense to hide it. "I know." He answered, "Please. Please just accept my courting request. Please, Johanna, have some faith in us…"

I had to turn away and took a shaky inhale, "Fine…fine, yes." I answered, "You. You can court me." I didn't have to look at him to see the smile on his face, I heard it in his voice it when he spoke next.

"I will do everything in my power to make sure you are happy, Johanna. I will."

I nodded numbly, still not looking at him, "Leave me Delain, please." I said softly, and I heard his foot fall receding out of the hall. As the door opened and then closed, I walked back to the Throne and took a seat. My mind was racing, my emotions a jumbled mess inside of me. I covered my face with my hands, trying to compose myself.

I sniffled a little and brushed a few unexpected tears off of my cheeks. I wanted Delain, and had wanted him for some years, but not under these circumstances. Not while I was Queen, not when Nox was running around. I had dreamed of my courting to be when I was a Princess, full of balls and galas and parties, of walks through the Tower with watching Elites always close by. Of hidden jokes and laughter, of peace and joy and happiness while I fell hopelessly and relentlessly in love.

That was just another dream I had to mourn. Another reality that would never be. And Delain knew me from before, before everything changed. Would he still have that same affection for me now? Once he knew who I was now? The lengths I would go to for revenge? He said he knew me, and that was true. He knew my favourite things - though that was not the same as knowing my soul. Could he still love me now, with my soul so consumed by anger?

I shook my head, I had to believe he could. So far, he was the only one that had wanted to court me, through all of this, he was the only one that had expressed interest, and not once but twice. So I had to try, because there was a time, not that long ago, where I had wanted him, too.

I reached over and rang a bell, letting the Elites and Scribes know they could enter. "Let's continue." I said, once they had all filed back in.

Later that day I would be sitting in the room with the Dragon Egg, I spent what seemed to be every spare moment here. I was reading silently through various reports and taxation records, things I had missed while away, things I needed to catch up on. The boring reports however were not pulling my thoughts away from Delain, of his warmth and his hand on my face. His lips brushing against mine.

En-Kai sounded in my mind, which startled me out of my trance. "Johanna. Liang and I have been speaking of the Eye."

"Okay," I replied, putting the papers down on the ground so I could focus on them instead. I waited a few quiet moments, before prompting, "What of it?"

"We both agree that it is something we have both witnessed in our times. So, we concur it is something created during the Age.

From our limited experience with it, it seems to take hold of a...host, for lack of a better term, who is driven to madness." Liang answered now, "It was an artefact within my father's treasury, and he tried multiple times to use it and failed. However, my uncle was able to take it, and that is when the first division of the Empire happened."

I knew the history of the Trussam Empire, so it was easy to recall the details, "Right. He slaughtered the western lords of the Empire and seized the land and people for himself, right?"

"Yes, well done remembering. It was only when his wife poisoned him some thirty springs after that for him to die, and the Empire was rejoined as one. Otherwise, I am quite sure he would have lived much longer."

"Great, so all this tells us it existed before Rozalin was even born, and that...the one guy we suspect used it had to be poisoned for him to die. I will be sure to try and infiltrate Nox and have Rozalin poisoned." My mental tone was dripping with sarcasm and bitterness, this didn't help me at all. It got us nowhere.

"I know you are frustrated, Johanna, but this is something. It tells us that Rozalin is weak, she is not thinking clearly and will do anything to get her way. That means she has weaknesses. We can exploit those." Reasoned En-Kai, "We can try and plant false information, send them on the wrong trail..."

"That won't do anything if we don't know what she's looking for." I scowled, "We are grasping at straws, trying to find any advantage but it's impossible with the fragments of information we have right now."

Liang sighed, "Let us discuss more between ourselves and we will see if there is anything else we know. Maybe Rachael has some ideas for us too." He offered, and the presence of the two Archons faded from my mind.

The frustration I felt was palatable in the air around me as I grabbed the reports and records, piling all the papers together and getting up to leave the room. Maybe Dedria had found something in the books. At this point, anything else was more helpful than what the Archons had given me.

I found Dedria in the expansive library, my best friend slowly dredging through the various Dragon books that Castian had brought back. "Hey." I greeted, taking a seat across from her.

Dedria looked up from what she was translating onto some new paper, "Just so you know, I hate you."

Laughter bubbled in my chest, "Noted, do you want a break?"

"Need is more like." replied Dedria, getting up from the table and joining me in leaving the Library and heading up to my office for lunch and privacy.

Once we got there, Dedria got a servant bringing them freshly brewed tea, sandwiches and pastries. "So how was your morning?"

I sat down, sighing a bit. "Court was boring, mostly. Except a kid who's father died in the first attack, him and his mom showed up. He's probably 16. And he's a Chronomancer. His Mom apparently can barely afford to keep their roof over their heads and food on the table, and since he's a Chronomancer he can't get a job. Not if he can't control his powers."

Dedria frowned, "That sucks." She said softly, "I can't imagine what that family is going through."

I nodded solemnly. I couldn't stop thinking about that kid, and how angry he was, "I can, sort of...only difference is I'm a Queen and I have a best friend who's a Chronomancer." I looked down to my tea and took a sip before continuing. "I put them in one of the apartments that is meant for delegates from other countries. Make sure they're provided for...and am doing the same for any other family who lost someone that day."

"You are a good person, Johanna. That's generous of you."

"I'm just doing what needs to be done..." My confusion obvious, because why wouldn't I do these things?

"Needs, maybe. But it doesn't mean you have to do it."

"Right, I suppose so."

Silence hung in the air while the two of us sipped at our tea and ate. I spoke next, speaking quietly, "then Delain showed up."

Dedria stared at me, jaw dropping in shock, "way to bury the lead, Johanna! What happened?!"

"He asked permission to court me. Formally." I answered, but it must have been obvious I was withholding information. From the way I couldn't meet Dedria's eye, and how I carefully controlled my expression.

"Okay, and? What did you say?" Dedria's gaze was intent on me, scanning for any hint, any tell.

"I...kicked the Elites and Scribes out of the room. And reminded him about my ascension ball and what I told him then, and how I couldn't do that. Not while Nox was running rampant...and then he took my hand and pulled me against him..."

Dedria's eyes grew wide, and she leaned closer, "did you kiss?!" She gasped, a grin sliding across her lips.

I knew my cheeks were warm and flushed, and I shook my head, "No...not...really. He did remind me that if my mother hadn't died, we would probably be courting and maybe even be engaged."

Dedria looked absolutely delighted, "Oh! Oh! Delain is so handsome, and smart, and kind. You two have flirted at every ball since you were like, fourteen." She giggled, "honestly, it's about time something went your way."

"...So, you think this is okay? I don't want people to think I'm not prioritizing Nox and everything just because I am accepting a suitor."

"Please, if anyone says that I will deal with them myself. You deserve to have some happiness, Johanna. You've spent every waking moment since your mom died learning how to run the country, hunting Nox, training, travelling...You taking on a suitor is for Solaria, too. Having a King could only help you; it would be someone to help with the responsibilities with the Monarchy and running the country." Dedria reasoned, leaning back in her seat with a coy grin. "Oh...If you see him shirtless do tell me everything, hm?"

"Dedria!" I gasped, covering my mouth with a hand. Not that I could stop myself imagining it. "That's so indecent!"

Dedria laughed, completely delighted, "Oh don't be so demur, Johanna. He's a catch, and you know it."

I sighed, moving my hand from covering my mouth to rub the back of my neck. My body felt like it was on fire at the idea of Delain shirtless. "Of course I think that. I have enjoyed Delain's company at every chance I have been given. His family is well respected, he is kind, and empathetic and yes, handsome. I know he would make an excellent King...But."

"You don't know if he's your king." Dedria finished but shrugged. "You don't know until you give him a chance."

"I guess so." I relented, "in those Dragon books, have you found anything about the Demon Eye yet?"

"They called it Drax's Sight." Dedria answered, "the limited stuff I've found so far is that it was created by the dragon Draxus, and it lead to the start of the Dragon wars."

I frowned, hopelessness flooding me. "So not much." I replied.

Dedria nodded in agreement, "Not much." She agreed, "but I'm still early on. I might find some more as I go on."

"Yeah, I hope so." I replied, pouring another cup of tea. "Did you want to keep your break from the books going and join me down in the labs while I check in on Tyne?"

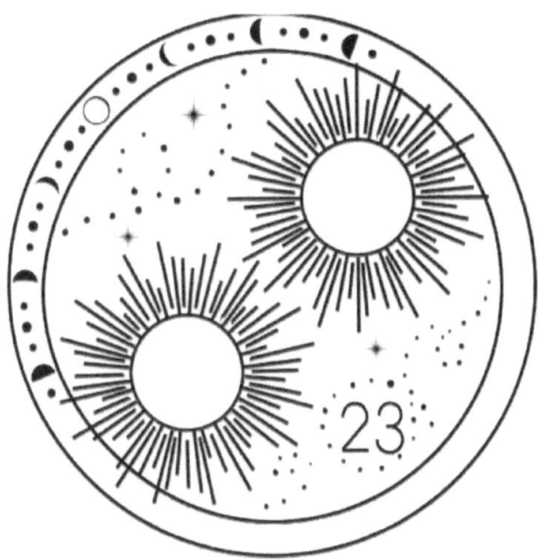

yne could be heard talking to Bevy before Dedria and I even opened the door to the laboratory. "Oh, Tyne. You've met Bevy?" I inquired as we walked in.

The scientist nodded, "Yes, Your Grace. Pendra brought her down yesterday because she expressed interest learning in medicine and wondered if she could learn under me. I agreed, it should not be a problem should Bevy not prevent my research."

"I won't!" Bevy pouted now, looking to me, her blue eyes wide and watery. Pendra had managed to tame her wild blonde hair into a neat braid. "I've been doing my best! I help clean and and and get Miss Tyne anything, anything she asks for!"

Dedria snickered from behind me while I lifted my hand to stop Bevy's rambles, "I am sure you are being very helpful, Bevy. Tyne, how are things going with the cure?"

Tyne clicked her tongue, "Troublesome. While the tea is proving to reverse the effects on the Princess, taking her off the tea only leads to the disease progressing again. None of the plants we have are old enough to provide fruit yet, and I hope those will further progress."

"Hm. And my mothers notes haven't provided any other ideas

towards it?" I asked hopefully, glancing toward Bevy who had moved away and was starting to clean some equipment.

"No, Your Grace. Everything I've been doing are just speculations your mother made. Thankfully, her speculation of the plant being a prevention for the disease has bought us an unfathomable amount of time. As long as the Princess continues drinking the tea every day, her condition improves."

"Then if she has to drink tea for the rest of her life, she will do it with a smile..." I said, and I would make sure Kira did. I'd shove it into her mouth if I had to.

"Well, I hope that one day soon I will find a cure." Tyne offered a confident smile, "for now, yes, she will be drinking the tea for the foreseeable future."

She then turned to pick up a clipboard, "I do have some interesting enhancements the agriculture department has proposed, would you like to go over them now?"

I nodded, "Very well." I replied, glancing to Dedria. "We don't have anywhere to be, right?"

Dedria rolled her eyes, "Nope, the world isn't depending on us to save it at all." She answered sarcastically, moving through the laboratory now to look at all the different and strange equipment. Even I couldn't place what most of it was, truthfully, forget about knowing how to use it.

Tyne glanced between us, brow arched curiously but she shrugged it off, "Anyways. As it stands right now, we currently produce more food than the city is currently consuming. Which is excellent, it allows us to export the remaining to Taranor and to the other city locations within the country. However, our projected population in the next forty years will exceed what we can produce at max capacity, not accounting for any blight, herd losses or weak crop yields. Currently each floor is 7 metres tall, split into two levels, and each level has six garden beds that stretch length wise along wall to wall.

"However, if we were to move to vertical gardening like proposed here," She would pass a chart and illustration, "We could condense our crops ten-fold. Say one square metre right now can hold...10 lettuce plants. If we instead switched to these vertical gardens, we could grow nearly 100 plants in the same space. And we would be able to more densely pack these beds in, because we would not need as much room to move between them like we do the garden beds since we would be able to access it from all sides. If we add rotating gears, we would be able to pack them even more densely since we would be able to turn them to get access to the side needed."

I looked over the chart and illustration, "Very interesting concept." I replied, "How would they be watered?"

"We would run pipes top and bottom of each pillar, interconnecting all the pillars together to the same water source as they do now. Water could be recycled into the system."

"Why wouldn't we expand outward?" I questioned now.

"Too expensive, too much time and resources. Refurbishing existing structures will be cheaper and faster than the time-consuming process of making the floors larger. Doing this would also allow us to upgrade and add easier maintenance hatches to make upgrades and repairs in the future."

I was grateful Tyne was so in touch with all of this. It really made everything so much easier for me. She was always able to answer questions in a way that made the most sense to me and I always felt confident with authorizing changes. Before my

Mother had died, I had been liaising with Tyne for several months and authorizing some things on behalf of the Throne, taking that burden from my parents.

"Hmm. Let's trial it. Half of basement floor 15 can be converted to this model. Let's see how our yield goes before we start transitioning the rest."

Tyne grinned, "Thank you, Your Grace! I will let the teams know immediately."

I offered her a smile I hoped looked genuine, "Thank you for having teams foresee the problem. Now we get a chance to get ahead of the issue and will be able to export even more to our other cities and even Taranor."

Dedria made a gagging sound in the corner, "Do you have to be so polite and official all the time?" She asked me teasingly.

"Do you have to be so grating and critical?" I asked, giving her a glare, "just because you were raised without good manners does not mean I have to partake in the same."

Dedria laughed and shook her head gently, "You don't need to have a shining Queen at every moment, Johanna."

With a clear of her throat, Tyne interrupted the banter, "Sorry, Your Grace, if we can continue?"

"Yes, yes, of course." I turned back to her, "Sorry, Tyne."

Tyne and I spent the next two hours discussing further research and improvements that had been waiting for my approval. Tyne glanced towards Bevy, "Get me the Ground Zero Crystal, please."

There was a silence that filled the space as Bevy reached out and it looked like she grabbed something, but the Ground Zero Crystal that was inside of a glass tube lifted from the countertop and moved to Tyne while Bevy didn't move from her spot looking into a microscope.

The three of us all looked between each other, not sure how to process that. Finally, it was me who spoke. "Bevy?"

"Huh? Yes yes?" Bevy asked, finally pulling away from the microscope. "Oh, I didn't get the crystal. I'm sorry."

It was in Tyne's hands, but it seemed Bevy had clued into the fact that she hadn't gotten up to grab it and bring it physically to her mentor.

"That's the thing, Bevy...you did." I said gently, motioning to Tyne who was holding the tube.

Confusion crossed Bevy's face, "What? No, no. I didn't get up. I..."

Tiang's voice echoed in my mind, "She's a telepath." But when I reached out to talk to him more, he was gone.

"Hmm...Bevy, do you ever find yourself able to hear other people, even when they may not be speaking?" I prompted gently.

Bevy tilted her head, "Well, I have lots of voices in my head, yes yes. Voices that sound like you and Dedria and Pendra and sometimes the servants and Tyne..." She trailed off, frowning a little. Taking in my expression of measured calm, the expression on Dedria's face of clear shock, on Tyne's calculating gaze. "That's not normal, is it?"

I shook my head, moving up to her and crouching to get more on her level, "No...Generally not." I replied, "Bevy, have you ever heard of a Telepath?"

The younger girl giggled, "Well, yeah, but they're just myths!" She replied.

"I don't think so. They are very rare, yes, but not myths. You moved that object to Tyne without getting up…You occasionally hear our thoughts. And now that I think about it, I have never sensed an aura from you…I assumed that meant you were a Mute, but it is clear I am incorrect on that. Telepaths do not have auras, as they do not use Mana…" I clicked my tongue as my thoughts raced. "I do not know how we will go about training you to use your powers, but we will find a way. I promise you that."

I knew I couldn't ask other countries for their Telepaths. Most kept any telepath a closely guarded secret, if the telepath made themselves known at all. Though even considering that, maybe Yeska could advise me on what to do. I just wanted Bevy to have the best chance of succeeding and being in control of her powers. A telepath that was out of control was even more dangerous than a Chronomancer. They could stop hearts with a look, break necks with a flick of their wrist. Move objects hundreds or thousands of kilograms like it was a sheet of paper.

Bevy shrugged, "I know you'll take care of me!" She said with a bright, reassuring smile.

I had to smile at that, it was barely there and gentle, but it was there all the same. "Alright, I have to go send a letter. Tyne, we are done right?"

"Yes, Your Grace." Replied the scientist, turning to start her work again.

Dedria and I headed out in silence, but as soon as we were in the lift heading back up to the Ivory Halls, Dedria let out a low whistle. "Damn, telepath? What are the odds that you picked out the only Telepath slave in that entire place."

With a sage nod, I remunerated on this, "It's unreal." I agreed,

"But she's my responsibility."

"How are you going to manage a Telepath, Delain, a Dragon Egg, and Nox? On top of being Queen of a Country?"

"You know, you don't have to point all that out."

"Am I your best friend if I don't?"

"I think if you keep reminding me of these things then you won't be my best friend."

"Fine...I will stop reminding you." From her tone though, I didn't think she would.

As the doors opened in the Halls, I ended up almost nose to nose with Delain.

"And this is my cue to leave." Dedria said and she quickly left as I glared daggers into the back of her head.

"Hello, Delain. Have you settled into your room all right?" I asked finally.

A charming smile crossed his lips as he bowed, "Hello, Your Grace. I was hoping I could join you for afternoon tea?"

"I already had tea with Dedria earlier." I replied, glad I wasn't lying. I still wasn't sure I was ready for being courted. To emotionally tackle the four months of silence I had gotten from Delain after Mother had died.

"Ah, shame. Lady Dedria and you spend a lot of time together, don't you?"

"Well, she is my best friend, and she's helping me train as a Chronomancer."

"And that's the only reason?" Delain asked, glancing down to me now as he offered his arm. "Let me walk you back to your office, Your Grace."

I visibly bristled at the first question, "What is that supposed to mean, Delain? Are you implying that Dedria and I are...what, lovers?"

"I don't know. Are you? There is no shame if you are...disappointing for me for sure though."

"No, Delain, we are not lovers." I nearly spat the words out, angry that he even asked that. Angry that he thought that was appropriate. I had accepted his courting, hadn't I? Had let him live in the Halls?

He just smiled at my tone, and that made me angrier, "Sorry if it was offensive, Your Grace, But you do understand how I may have reached that inquiry?"

"No, frankly, I do not. Yes, I spend lots of time with Dedria. I value her knowledge and opinions and think that she makes me a better Queen." I replied, voice tense. "I will have you know that she encouraged me to give this courtship a chance. But now I am reconsidering that..."

He still was smiling, and I had half a mind to slap it off his face, "Then perhaps I owe her a thank you."

"Oh, I am sure she would love to rub that in my face," I grumbled, shaking my head a bit.

We had reached my office by now, "Well this is you." Delain said, letting me have my arm back. "Will I see you during dinner?"

"I always try to have dinner with my father and sister, yes." I replied, "you will also meet Bevy."

He looked curious at that, but didn't ask, hoping instead that I would clarify. I didn't however, all I did was turn and open the office door and step inside, closing it behind me and leaning against it with a bit of a relieved sigh.

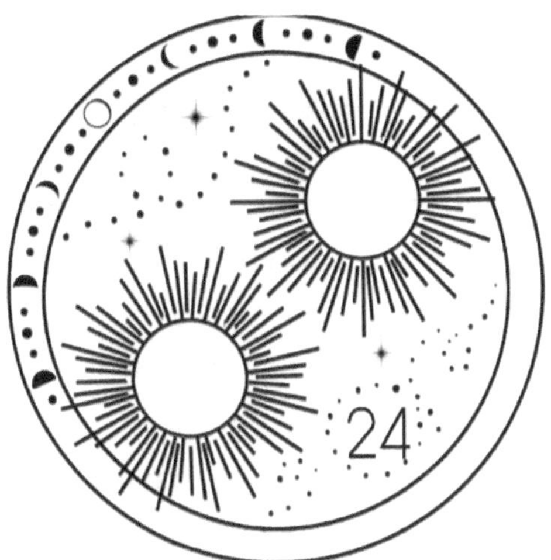

Days passed mostly quietly, a letter had been sent to Yeska asking about any possible telepaths that could help with Bevy, and I had successfully managed to avoid Delain for the most part with the exception of dinners each night. I was still simmering with displeasure over him not listening to me, but he was probably right. We couldn't wait forever, could we?

After dinner each night, I sat with the Dragon Egg and either read to it or quietly went over the country's reports.

Today though, he intercepted me on my way to my office, "Your Grace. You are looking radiant as ever."

I pasted on a smile, "Delain, good morning. How can I help you? I was just on my way to my office..."

"I was hoping you would humor me and join me for a walk around the lower levels?" He asked now with that charming smile. A year ago, it would have made me weak in the knees, would have made my stomach flip and my heart to pound. Now? I wasn't getting that. I was getting dread instead.

"I don't know, I have a lot to do and..." I faltered at seeing the look on his face. Even if I was trying to steel myself and focus on everything else, I had to do, I remembered what Dedria had told me, and even my own father. I remembered all the dances Delain and I had shared, with whispered secrets and jokes. "I suppose me taking a break from it this morning will be fine, though. And it will do some good for the people to see me out and about."

Delain grinned even more, if that was at all possible, and he offered his arm to me. "Thank you, Your Grace."

I nodded and took his arm, the two of us turning away from my office and heading back towards the lift that would bring us down to the lower levels. "How have you been settling into the Halls?" I asked once we were inside the lift, taking a measured step away from him even though there were four Elites standing in each corner.

"Quite well, Your Grace. I marvel every day how beautiful the Halls are and how lucky I am to be allowed to stay within them." Delain replied, looking down towards me. "Are you enjoying being back home?"

I nodded, "I am, I missed my family and my country while I was gone." I did not sound disingenuous, quite the opposite. I had ached to be back in Solaria for most of the trip, anxious to return even if my journey was to get stronger to fight Nox. To fight Rozalin.

"Well, I know the people are happy to have you back as well. You being out of the country, there was some moderate unrest while you were away. The King Dowager handled it gracefully, as he always does, but there was still that unease."

My lips turned down slightly at that - Father hadn't told me about any sort of unrest. In fact, no one had. They had all insisted everything was fine - what else had happened that was being hidden from me? Still, I brushed that off, feigning like I had known that. "It's been an uneasy period. It is understandable that the people would have some worry of their new Queen leaving the country after an attack like we faced. However, if I hadn't had left, we wouldn't be close to stopping the people that attacked us and killed my mother."

We were not that close - we still couldn't find a way to stop the Demon Eye and had no idea when or where Nox was planning to strike next. Dedria and I spent most of the afternoons going through texts and old tomes, using our Chronomancy so we could spend as much time as possible on it without any true time passing at all. All that effort had come up short so far, though that didn't stop us. There were thousands and thousands of books in the Ivory Halls library and even in storage, and we were determined to go through every single one if it meant there was an answer buried there.

"Your determination is admirable, Your Grace. Solaria is lucky to have you." Delain said as the lift slowed to a halt and the doors opened. We had decided on floor 10 of the north most portion of the tower. It held one of the main shopping districts. I took his arm again and we stepped out, joined by another 6 elites that carefully spread around us.

The lower levels of the towers were zigzagging, slightly slanted streets that curved in an oval going up and up and up. Shops and homes piled on each other to the ceiling of that floor. Alleys and side streets existed, though flat, where more homes and shops or amenities were found. Truthfully, it was a maze. The ceiling was enchanted to have the sky from outside, and lights made it feel bright enough.

As we walked through the bustling street, citizens pointed us out and whispered to each other, bowing or curtsying as we passed. I slowed as they approached a bakery that smelled divine, of fresh bread and stewed fruit and sugar. I pulled Delain in, the Elites quickly adjusting their formation and moving in with us.

I approached the counter, "Good Morning." I greeted. Behind the counter was an older woman of shorter stature and round, her hair was graying, and her face wrinkled but I could tell that some of the wrinkles were from years of laughter.

The woman gave a curtsy, "Your Grace!" She said, her voice wavering, "It is an absolute pleasure for you to come to my humble shop today!" She was brushing off the flour from her apron, eyes wide.

Delain smiled, "It smells amazing in here," He replied, "Reminds me of the kitchens at home."

"Thank you, Sir! I can not dare compare myself to the esteemed cooks that have served under either of you, but I do try my best."

"My sister loves anything with jam in it, especially gooey so it's extra messy." I said, "Do you have anything like that?"

"Of course, Your Grace! Absolutely!" The woman answered, and she quickly grabbed a woven basket lined with fabric, starting to delicately take things off of the lined shelves behind her and laying them into the basket. "Is there anything you would like, Your Grace? Sir Delain?"

I spoke before Delain, as was expected since I had been addressed first. "I like a good scone to have with my afternoon coffee, and my friend Lady Dedria Heart enjoys cookies." As I spoke, the woman shuffled around and added more things to the basket.

"Do you have anything savory? Particularly something with a bit of spice to it?" Asked Delain, that charming smile on his lips. Still nothing, I got nothing from it.

"Yes, of course Sir Delain. Absolutely." She nodded, and when the basket was almost overflowing she put it on the counter.

"How much?" I asked, and one of the Elites was pulling out a coin purse.

"Oh, no! I would never dream of charging Your Royal Highness for my goods." The old woman said, looking appalled at the idea.

"You provided us with goods, even if I am Queen it is only right I pay for them. I do not have my head so high in the clouds that I think otherwise, good Ma'am." I was flummoxed, the Crown always paid for goods. We paid for the food in the halls, the clothing we wore, the furniture and art and books we used. We never took anything from our people for free, as least, that's what I thought. Sure, when I had been younger and exploring the lower levels I got free things, but I had been younger then. I had never thought about it.

"Oh! No, I would never suggest! Your Grace, please!" The woman looked mortified now that she may have offended me.

Delain couldn't help but laugh, patting me on the arm. "What Her Grace is trying to say is that after her journeys she has recognized the importance of paying others for their goods and services, and she would feel wretched to take free goods from one of her own people." He explained, "that being said, may I pay for them instead? Would that make you feel better?" When the woman nodded, he pulled out his own coin purse and pulled out fifteen gold. "Is this enough for us disturbing your morning?"

The woman stammered, "That is far to much, Sir Delain!"

"I think it is just enough." He said, stepping forward and taking her hand, placing the coins in her hand and closing her fingers around them. "Thank you for your baked goods, they look delicious. I can't wait to have mine for Lunch today." He said, picking up the basket and letting me take his arm again.

The two of them left, and I stared ahead, unable to look up to Delain. "You were very good at that…" My voice was soft, part of embarrassment and part to make sure no one could hear us.

"Good at what?" He asked, looking down to me, confusion painting his features.

"Good at talking to her, I made her feel terrible, and you just swooped in and made her feel better."

"Hmm…I can see how it might look like that." He conceded, "she wasn't as afraid to insult me. Asking her Queen for money for her items, that's taboo. Most provide services and goods to the Monarchy for free, it's a privilege and they get bragging rights over it. So, you asking to pay was almost like telling her that she couldn't tell others that you had been in her shop and tried her goods."

We got things for free from our citizens? And they only got bragging rights? My stomach turned at that. We had to do better for our people. "I had no idea." I admitted, shame filling me and causing my cheeks to heat.

"And why would you? It is never a situation you have been in before. Don't worry yourself over it, now you know for next time." He winked to me, "It does smell very good though."

"Yeah, it does." I agreed, still not glancing up to him. I felt so discouraged, I had all but insulted one of my citizens when I had just wanted to pay her for her goods. It was hard not to feel foolish and embarrassed over it. "Thank you." I added after a minute of silence.

He smiled, "You are very welcome, Your Grace." He replied with a nod of his head.

As we kept walking through the district, I spotted a few things I wanted for Bevy or Kira and arranged with one of the Elites to have one of the couriers from the Tower come fetch the items. A few books, a dress for Bevy in a pale blue, a new game using dice, some earrings for Kira. I had Delain pay for all of it, and once we were back in the lift, I got the coin pouch from the Elite and count out coins to pay Delain back, holding them out to him.

"You don't have to pay me back, Your Grace. It was my pleasure to pay for everything on our morning walk together." He said, but at the insistent look I wore he took them from me and put them in his pouch. "Thank you." He added.

Once the lift reached the Ivory Halls and the doors started to open, a General was waiting outside. "Your Grace!" He said, voice booming as he saluted me. "I request your presence immediately."

I couldn't help the startled look cross my face, "Whatever for?" I asked, "Is something going on?" I added hastily.

"Indeed, your Grace. But it is best we talk about it in the Communication Centre." He replied, folding his hands behind his back.

I just nodded, stepping away from Delain, "Very well, let's go." I replied, and we were off, both of us walking quickly towards the Communication Hall.

The large room was a flurry of activity as always, people moving from desk to desk, talking quickly and quietly and then hurrying from place to place, reports being filled out and radio feeds being monitored. Before Mother had died, I had taken every chance to sneak into this area and just watch the people. There were always people in this room - the activity never stopped. Even now, even if I was anxious and worried about why I was here, I enjoyed the energy. It always made the air feel alive.

"Why am I here, General?" I inquired as I took in the scene.

"Perhaps we should do this in one of our meeting rooms, Your Grace." The General offered, nodding towards one of the doors.

I followed him into the room, concern bleeding into my expression. "Why are we having to discuss this in private, General?"

The General coughed, grabbed a folder with a transcript and passing it to me. "We received radio communication from the Southern Reaches. The Ascension lands. From the Alpha Setsuna of the Plains...She claims that Isabella Malbora has travelled to the Southern Reaches and has every intention of attacking Lethiarum to free the slaves there. Setsuna is requesting that you fulfill the promise you made her on your journey together."

I froze, my blood running cold as I scanned over the radio transcripts. "Did she say she's available to talk to me?" I finally asked.

"No, Your Grace. It was a very short conversation, from my understanding. It is also very late there; she is probably asleep now." The General explained calmly, though he could tell I was tense. "Would you like us to send a communication to them in 8 hours and get you if she responds?"

I barely nodded, "Yes, yes that sounds good. I'd like to talk to her, thank you." I replied, putting the transcript down on the table. "Is that all, General?"

"Yes, Your Grace!" He saluted, and I turned to leave. I wove through the halls, lost in my own thoughts. Some deep-seated part of me wished I could be there. Wished I could help, even if I knew it wasn't my place. I wanted to help right the wrongs in the world, but I had my own battles at home to deal with, first.

Part of me felt betrayed - I had promised Solaria's help to them, but after Nox was dealt with. After I had avenged my mother. It was too soon for it to happen now.

I shook my head forcefully and found myself taking familiar steps up to the roof of the Tower. I silently moved to the railing, leaning against it. "It isn't up to my schedule. Being angry at them for not following my schedule isn't reasonable. They need to do what is best for them and their people." I muttered, rationalizing with myself. I shouldn't feel the anger that was brewing inside of me over this.

I thought of the king there, trapped in his bed, sick with Rot. I thought of all the people that lived in that country, who might not own slaves and frown on the laws there. Those people might get hurt in the process. If I warned the king ahead of time, told him to free all slaves before hand, could I save those people from getting hurt?

All the machines down that were spread on the outskirts of the tower down below, which looked like tiny, minuscule toys from all the way up here. They were loading and unloading trains, preparing goods for shipment, even assembling things. I just watched, feeling conflicted and confused.

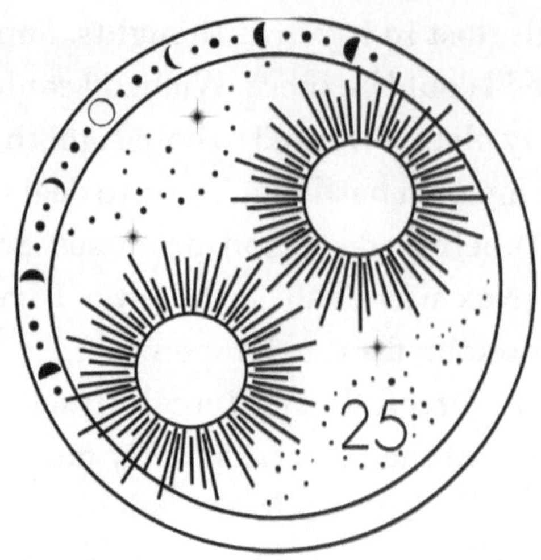

I woke the next morning, restless and tired from a bad night sleep. I still felt off from the events of the previous day. I crawled out of bed, letting my handmaids and Pendra get me ready for the day. I had more open court today, as well as all the other duties, but I honestly wanted to sit in my room and contemplate the paths ahead of me.

I sat quietly as Pendra tended to my hair and the handmaidens handled my nails and skin. I felt the pull of the Archons drawing me in, and I eagerly responded.

Pulled into the empty space where they stood was still dizzying, though I recovered quickly this time. "Thank Arcanis…I need your input and wisdom."

En-Kai nodded, moving to brush up against me. Even if this space wasn't real, just the power of intense mana and meditation, where no other beings could exist, it felt real all the same. His fur impossibly soft, soothing. "Yes. We have felt your unrest over what is happening."

I brushed my fingers through his thick, soft fur and sat down with a heavy sigh, "I don't know how to proceed. Sending support is nonnegotiable. I know that. Setsuna, Tianie…I made my vows, I will not go back on it."

I watched as all of them moved so they were all sitting close to me in a circle. Maria to my left, En-Kai to my right, and then Rachael and Liang finished the circle. "They are undoubtedly expecting your support, in any way you can spare it. Do you know the status of the army?" Maria reasoned with a nod.

"The timing is…not exceptional." Liang cut in, irritation in his tone. "You promised the help of Solaria after Nox was defeated. You have not done that yet; how can they expect your support when you have so much left unfinished?"

"Still, how much help will an army be against Nox? How many soldiers will help in that final fight?" Rachael countered as she cast a disapproving look to Liang. She shifted back a few feet so she could stretch her legs out in front of her and lean back on her hands. "It might come down to you and Dedria against Rozalin. And in that case…well. It doesn't matter how many soldiers you have at your back; they won't be able to fight her."

"Even if that is how it turns out, there is the rest of Nox to consider." En-Kai rumbled, his tails coiling together into one great mass. "Other Chronomancers, who may not simply stand aside and watch Rozalin be struck down."

It was comforting in so many ways to watch them talk through all my own worries, even if I knew they wouldn't stop me. To see some of the greatest warriors and leaders in all of history to feel those things too? Nothing could have been more reassuring. "Setsuna and Tianie are my friends…and we could use the Ascended as allies."

"If they win." Liang pointed out sensibly, "If they fail, we lose the troops and supplies we sent."

En-Kai rumbled a growl at that, his irritation so clear even I could feel it, "They will not lose. If Isabella Malbora has bonded with the Phoenix spirit, she is the next incarnation of Inara. She is going to bring the biggest boon of prosperity that the Ascended people have seen since before I was even alive."

"Back up, who is Inara?" Rachael asked with a grin, and she sat up. The delight in her eyes at a change of conversation was clear as anything - she obviously had been bored with the war talk.

The great Kitsune had a smirk tugging on his lips, his face expressive despite his form. "Inara is one of the first four gods the Ascended and Kitsune worship. The four are the Phoenix, the Chimera, the Giant Land Tortoise and the Serpent. Inara, Lanielle, Resonance and Corsis. The Four Pillars of our people. Inara, prosperity and rebirth, Lanielle, ever changing and adapting, Resonance, wisdom and growth, and Corsis, determination and fortitude. Before Arcanis, before Osian, there was Inara, Lanielle, Resonance and Corsis. They shaped the continents and created the magic that thrums in every living being, they pulled the Spirit Realm and linked it with our own, allowing the Ascended to bond. Lanielle even created Kitsune's, blessing us with our many tails and two forms. Then the Dragon Wars happened, and three of the four went into hiding and were never seen again. Inara died, protecting the Ascended during the Wars.

"Isabella bonding with the Phoenix, the only Phoenix spirit in the realms, that means Inara's spirit has found another worthy of it. Worthy to bear the burden of bringing prosperity and rebirth to the Ascended and the Kitsune's. They will not lose." He spoke the last four words with such finality, there was no room to doubt him.

As En-Kai spoke, in the space between us, he formed visions of each when he spoke of them, bringing them to life. Inara, tall and beautiful, hair red and orange and yellow like fire itself. Lanielle, a shorter woman with 3 tails, one had the head of a serpent, the other the tail of a dragon, the third a fox. Resonance, a mammoth of a man with broad shoulders and the meanest look about him. Corsis, tall and lithe, dark skin and patches of deep green scales on his neck, arms and chest.

We sat quietly as we listened, this was all new to us. I couldn't keep my eyes from the illusion, "But En-Kai, you are an Archon of Arcanis, how can you believe in other gods?" Maria asked, watching him intently.

En-Kai chuckled, "There are more than two Gods, child. Arcanis and Osian do not have physical forms…The Four Pillars of the Ascended do. I believe out there, Lanielle, Resonance and Corsis walk free, having forgotten the burden of serving their people. Perhaps Inara's return will make them remember. Or maybe I am wrong, and they are lost to the ages."

I pinched the bridge of my nose, unable to help myself. "So, you're basically telling me if I don't support the Ascended now, I'm going against one of their gods? That's one way to enter their bad books." I knew I sounded exasperated and frustrated.

They all laughed at that, and En-Kai nodded, "Yes, when you put it so bluntly."

"Great. Super…" I muttered, my tone bleeding sarcasm. "I still can't go against Setsuna, and this whole…Inara thing," I waved my hand around in a dramatic way toward the current vision of the Phoenix hanging in the air in front of me, "makes it obvious I can't go against her…so I guess we send help. But what sort of help?"

It dawned on me then, that they were just humouring me. That there had only ever been one path forward - supporting my ally and friend.

"Soldiers, supplies." Maria offered. "I am sure your general will know the numbers better in terms of offering support."

I clicked my tongue, contemplating a moment. "Very well. Guess I have a meeting with him." I said, and the void in my mind, full of the Archons, faded away as U regained conscious thought in my body. Pendra was just finishing with my hair, and I wondered what sort of expression I had on my face while speaking to the Archons. I made a mental note to ask him later.

Once he was done, I rose to a stand, "I have one meeting to handle before court opens." I told them, "please inform everyone that I may be a little late, depending on how long it takes."

Pendra bowed, "Of course, Your Grace." He said, and he turned and left.

I took a deep breath before heading off, out of my room and down to the floor I had visited too often as of late to the Military Operations Centre. The room, as always, was a hive of activity. I spotted the general, speaking to a young woman in soldier fatigues. They didn't hide the concern on either of their faces well. My footsteps were sure and confident as I approached, and immediately both the General and Soldier were bowing. "At ease." I said, giving a slight motion of my hand for them to straighten.

"Your Grace, what brings you down here today?" The General asked, offering a slight smile that did not reach his eyes. I wondered what the soldier had been telling him before I approached, what had caused him to look so concerned. I would get a report on it later, I was sure. But a nagging part of me wanted to know now.

"I am here to discuss Setsuna of the Plain's request of us." I said, "but I need to understand where our army stands, how our supply caches are."

He nodded, "Of course." He replied, perfectly stone faced. He motioned towards one of the meeting rooms, and this time, I lead the way into it. Once the door was shut behind him, the enchantments sealing all sound inside, he spoke. "We have thirty thousand soldiers. Half of those are on reserve - working other jobs but should the call come, they will report. Our supply caches are fully stocked, with a thirty percent overflow, ready for any war that Nox brings us."

I nodded and paced the room as I thought. Thirty thousand, more than I had originally anticipated. When was the last time I had gone over the numbers? Never, probably. Father had probably gone over them last, after Mother had died. I hadn't touched anything regarding the military since taking the throne. "We send five thousand." I determined finally. "Of non-active duty. And we send that additional thirty percent of supplies. Everything that can be spared. Weapons, food, armor."

The General watched me intently, critically, "You are sure of this, Your Grace? Entering a war against Lethiarum. Even if it is with the Ascended..." His face didn't betray his doubts of the young Queen standing before him, but I felt it in his question.

I pursed my lips, "The King of Lethiarum allows slaves in his borders. Thousands - thousands of Ascended are within his country, held as slaves. Nothing more than property. Forget about all the non-Ascended. Infants and children, held in chains, ripped from their parents, siblings. Left to be owned by monsters." My words grew heated, and the air around me rippled from my aura. "I am not here to seek your counsel, General. I am here to issue an order after learning where we stand. Now do it." I had moved to the door and opened it with a considerable amount of force before I stalked out of the room and away. Everyone in front of me cleared the way - and I suspected it was not just because I was their Queen, but because the air around me had grown heavy under my Aura reacting to the anger bubbling in me.

I made my way swiftly through the halls and lifts back to the back entrance of the Throne Room. Dedria stood to my right and just behind, in her honoured spot, and Pendra further in the corner to my left, closer to the scribe who was writing everything down.

Eventually, I heard my stomach growl in empty protest, and I was sure it was loud enough that Dedria heard it as well. I lifted my hand up before the next petitioner entered, "We need to break for lunch." I said, and the doors closed. I got up, Pendra leading the way to the back area, and then to another room after that which had a table, chairs and had places set for us. Hot tea and food already there, and I thanked Arcanis for it as I sat down and grabbed one of the sandwiches. I took a bite and couldn't help the slight moan of contentment from slipping between my lips. It was so good, just what I needed.

Dedria and Pendra exchanged looks and giggled, "You should have let us know an hour ago that you were hungry, Johanna." Dedria snickered.

"I didn't notice until my stomach made that sound." I admitted sheepishly once I had swallowed.

"I am pretty sure everyone in the whole Tower heard that." Dedria laughed, before grabbing one of the sandwiches for herself and starting to eat.

We ate in silence, devouring the food in front of us eagerly. Only when we had turned to the tea and our hunger was sated did I speak again. "I am sending five thousand soldiers and as many supplies that we can spare to Setsuna." I said, lifting my gaze to meet Dedria's.

Dedria didn't frown, as I suspected she would, instead she smiled. "I was wondering when you would see the sense."

"Oh please..." I loosed a huff as I shot Dedria a glare. "It must be nice to have so many opinions and not be in charge of anything."

Dedria laughed, "All I'm saying, is you hummed and hawed over it for far too long. You know there was only one way to answer her calling in that promise. Anything else was you making excuses to not fulfill your half."

I grumbled, sipping at my tea. "Even so, it was not an easy thing to decide."

"No, sending soldiers out to die is never easy. It should never be easy. If it becomes easy, then something is wrong." Dedria nodded, stirring some sugar into her fresh cup of tea she had poured. "I know you want to be there with them. I do. I know you want nothing more in the whole world than to be on those front lines with your soldiers and cutting down those slavers and their ilk. I know that is what is eating at you, what made it such a hard choice. Because you need to be here. Because of Nox. But you can not always be on the front lines. Sometimes the best thing is you being here, at home, fighting to make sure those Soldiers have a home to come back to."

I contemplated the sense in that, the silence hung in the air between us. "When did you start being so wise?" I asked finally, and Dedria shot over a rueful smile.

"Since my best friend became the Ash Queen."

"If only all of their wisdom somehow made me so wise." I sighed, and I stared into my cup of tea.

"It comes with time, Johan. It does. You will get there." Dedria replied, and she tipped back the rest of her tea, swallowing it in one gulp before she got up and grabbed my arm, tugging me up with her. "Come on, let's get back to it."

The rest of the day was a blur, and the scribe noted as the doors finally shut that it was the busiest petition to date, with over two hundred people. Thankfully, most of the requests had been small and inconsequential. Easy things for me to fix, and I was glad for it.

"I need a break from people for a bit...I'll be up for dinner in a couple of hours." I told Pendra and Dedria, "If everyone gets hungry before me, don't wait."

Pendra frowned, worry etched on his features, "You never miss dinner with your Father and the Princess, Your Grace."

"Nothing is wrong, Pendra. I just...need a break from all the noise. If they want to eat with me, send someone to get me. I'll be where I usually am."

Dedria just hooked her arm with Pendra's, "You heard your Queen. Come on." She tugged him away, even if he shot a worried glance over his shoulder.

I went to the room with the Dragon Egg, sitting with my back against it, laying a book in my lap. "I'm sending troops to help Setsuna. And supplies, everything we can spare. I only hope Nox doesn't attack with an army..." I heaved a sigh, before opening the book to a marked page. It was a novel, of great sacrifice and love. Silence settled over me for a moment as I lost myself to my own worries. I shook my head and started to read aloud.

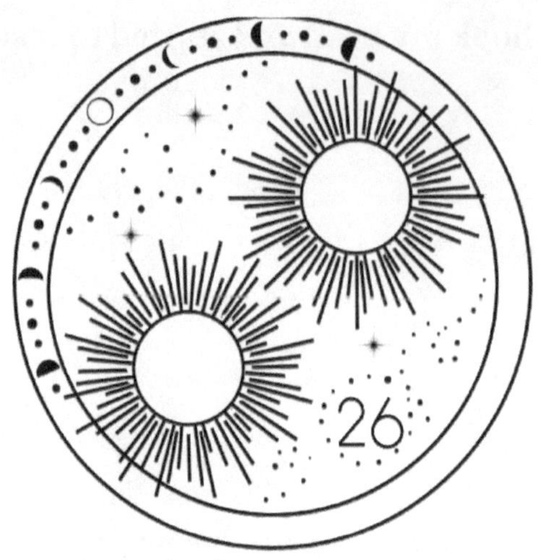

F

eeling something before hearing it was never a good thing, and when I felt a force that pushed my body away from the egg and even cracked the wooden door to the room. I panicked, channeling Chronomancy and forcing myself through the tunnel on hands and knees and sliding to a stop just short of the wall. I scrambled around, staring at the egg - or, what was left of it. The shell was in scattered pieces all over the room, and where the egg was a wyrmling. It couldn't be bigger than a very large dog, or a very small horse, depending on how you looked at it.

Its scales were black and red, with golden eyes that were trained on...on me. Its wings were small, maybe a little deformed, but they were being stretched out slowly.

I swallowed, a lump in my throat, "Hello. My name is Johanna Maracroix, I'm the Queen of a Country named Solaria." I was shocked at how my voice didn't come out in a croak.

A voice sounded in my head, deep and masculine, and it sounded amused, "I know who you are, Johanna. I heard your voice every day since the warmth came."

That made my cheeks go warm, and I stumbled over my next

words, "R-Right. You heard me! That's...that's great. What...what is your name?"

"My name..." The wyrmling seemed to think, "Barloc...Yes. My name is Barloc."

"Okay. Barloc." I nodded as I got up and straightened my clothes. "It's...nice to finally talk to you."

Barloc stepped forward, circling around me and sniffing at different parts of me. Up close his scales were closely locked together, and they looked smooth but the spikes on his back and down his tail were razor sharp, even as a wyrmling. "Thank you for waking me from my slumber. I've been waiting for a reason to wake up." He thrummed, the air around him vibrating.

"Uhm, you're welcome?" I said, staying completely still. Barloc picked up that I was tense, and he nudged me in the thigh with his snout.

"Would you be more comfortable if I took a more familiar form?" He inquired, moving to stand in front of me again. His head tilted to the side, like a curious dog.

"Familiar...form?" I asked, looking confused and then before my very eyes, his form shifted and rippled into a man. Over 2 metres tall, with dark skin and the same golden-yellow eyes. He had a long tail, with the same pattern as his usual scales, as well as two horns coming up from his temple and pointing back behind his head. He was handsome, almost annoyingly so. His shoulders were broad, and despite him having just hatched, he was well muscled. Everything about him reeked of pure power.

And he was also completely naked.

I instantly covered my mouth, and then my eyes. "Oh! Arcanis above." I yelped, backing up into the wall. Oh gods, he had been naked. My heart was pounding, and the smallest voice in the back of my conscious wanted to look again. To touch him. Was he as solid as he had looked?

Barloc laughed, and it felt like a warm hug. Or maybe that was the tail wrapping around my waist and picking me up. "Do I make you nervous, Johanna?" He asked with a wide grin. "I can feel your heartbeat through my tail."

"I am not nervous. Just, shocked. That's all." I hastily replied, shaking my head but not removing my hands.

"You smell nervous." He grinned as his tail pulled me towards him. "Your aura is very powerful. My memories do not tell me of humans with such power…"

"Memories? But you were in an egg. How do you remember?" I asked, frowning even if he couldn't see it behind my hand.

Barloc chuckled at that, his tail shifted on my body to the point where I became acutely aware of the tip resting right against the underside of my left breast. Warmth pooled between my legs, which was completely asinine because it wasn't like I had ever been touched that way before. "Genetic memories…I gained memories of my parents when I was laid. But I could not access them until I had hatched…"

I tried to shift in his grip and bit down on the corner of my lower lip. The tip of his tail as casually, sensually, brushing back and forth on my shirt idly. "That…You know, that's not the weirdest thing I've heard recently so I'm just going to trust you…"

He finally put me down, but he didn't move back from me, his hand lifted, taking me by the chin and tilting my face up, his thumb brushed along my lower lip until my teeth let go of it. "Better." He said, and I could hear the smile on his voice, "I am starving. Can we continue to talk over food?"

My heart had practically risen into my throat, "F-Food? Su...sure. Yeah, we can get food." I nodded, but when I tried to get the door to open but it was lodged firmly shut because of the damage to it.

Barloc gently moved me aside with his tail, stepping forward and with barely any visible effort at all, he managed to get the door open, though it was clear it wouldn't close again. He stepped back, allowing me to get in front of him and lead the way. Though I paused when we were in the hallway.

"You should probably...shift back to your normal form. You are...naked."

Barloc laughed, and it made my heart flutter uncomfortably fast, but he nodded and shifted back to his normal form. His wings didn't look as deformed and squished now.

I started to lead the way again, going through the maze of halls and stairs and lifts until we got to the big kitchens. All the servants and chefs froze as I stepped in and the dragon wyrmling followed.

"Hello, everyone. U-Uh. Look, it's complicated, but the Hall's newest honoured guest is very hungry. Can you bring us- him, food in the dining hall?" I asked, trying not to sound as nervous as I felt.

As quickly as the servants and chefs had all stopped, they all sprung into action. I looked over to Barloc, "Come on." I said as I left the kitchens and plodded with soft steps down the hall to the dining room. "Do...you have any questions for me?"

He tilted his head to me, and his voice sounded in my mind again, "I feel like if anyone has questions, it will be you having questions for me, Queen Johanna." He sounded amused and curious.

I flushed at that, my hands smoothing over the skirt of my dress nervously. "W-Well yes, I have questions. But I don't know where to start, really."

He watched me intently with that golden gaze, but he was curious, not malicious. "So, start with the first one that comes to your mind."

My mind was a flurry, a sandstorm racing through the desert unstoppable, thinking of all the questions I could ask him, and his chuckle sounded in my mind. "We have the rest of our lives to talk to each other, Johanna Maracroix. You do not have to ask me everything right now."

"Can you...can you hear my thoughts?" I asked alou.

He just shook his head in response, though he seemed amused that I wondered that. He didn't offer me anything else, and I wondered if he could just read me that easily. That unnerved me, more than anything.

"How long ago were you laid?" I tried.

His voice slipped back into my mind, "Hmm, I don't know. I was warm...and then it got very cold, and I slept. And then I was warm again, and I heard your voice, talking to me..."

"How did you not die?" I asked and I leaned towards him, curious and a bit afraid.

He thought about that for half a minute before he responded. "While in an egg, a dragon can go into a hibernating state and development halts. However, if it happens too early, they will die if they are not brought to a heat source again quickly enough. I was almost ready to hatch, when it got cold. It being cold told me it wasn't safe for me out in the world, so I slept until it was. That is what brought me to you."

"Do you think it's possible there are other dragon eggs, asleep like you were?"

"Hmm…It is possible, if they were in a similar developmental state as I was. But without checking the old hatching caves and temples, it's impossible to say."

"…Would you be able to give us the locations of those places, if…if needed?"

"I can probably point them out on a map, if that is something you want, yes."

"Is that something you want, though?" I suddenly felt the need to make sure he was doing what he wanted, too.

"Hmm…I can not answer that yet." His gaze flicked towards a door hidden in the wall that led directly to the kitchens, moments before servants started carrying in a few trays loaded with different food and placing them down on the table in front of Barloc.

He looked back to me, "This will not be enough…I will need more than this. Much more." He sounded, but he already had his snout in the bowls and plates, devouring all the food in front of him at a scary pace.

I choked on saliva in shock, "More…he'll need more." I said, tone a little frantic. The servants nodded and rushed back to the kitchen to oblige.

Barloc had the plates cleaned in minutes, and he sat back. Had he already increased in size, I wondered. He looked bigger than he had when he had hatched - but that wasn't possible, was it?

"How fast are you going to grow?" I found myself asking. My body felt strange, this whole experience felt unreal.

His lips pulled back from his teeth in a toothy grin, "I expect I will double in size every week for the first two months, and then afterward I will double in size every three or four months until reaching nearly my adult size in two years...However Dragons do not stop growing. An Ancient Dragon is so big it can block the suns, but it can take hundreds or a thousand years to reach that size."

I had to process that information before I spoke again. "A thousand years? How old do Dragons get?"

"Theoretically, five to ten thousand years. Depending on the breeding. I am a War Bred dragon...My body and mind is built for war and fighting. Scholars are smaller and sleeker in nature, but they are better apt for languages and teaching. There are blacksmiths and farmers and various other specialty breeds, but they all are variations of War and Scholars. The exception being Couriers - they are quite small, even at adult size, and are suited to speed and agility."

"I had no idea Dragons had so many different variations." I admitted.

He showed that toothy smile again, "How would you, Queen of Solaria? Dragons have not roamed these lands in thousands of years, from my limited knowledge of this time. Our knowledge and history were lost to the sands of time. But thanks to you, we may wander again."

Just as I was about to speak again, the servants returned with more platters loaded with even more food, and they quickly cleared away the old dishes and platters and placing down the new ones.

Barloc scanned it and nodded, eagerly digging in again. "Tell them thank you, this food is divine. Tradition for Wyrmling's says we must kill an animal as our first meal. I am glad to not have to do that."

I paused, my lips curving into a smile, and looked to the

servants. "He says thank you, the food is very good." I told them, and they flittered and whispered to each other excitedly before they rushed back to the kitchen.

He devoured everything in front of him once more before he spoke in my mind, the warmth of it seeping through my very core. "That is much better." All said, he had just eaten enough food that normally would have fed 10 grown men, and Barloc still had glint of hunger in his eye. "I will need more soon...but I do not feel like I will go crazed now. Is there another place we can talk, more private perhaps?"

"More private?" I asked, swallowing. I couldn't help the vision of him in his human form, fully naked in front of me. How muscled he had been, how handsome, and that damned tail brushing against my breast. My cheeks heated from the thought.

Barlock chuckled, as if reading my mind. "Is that a problem?"

"Nope." I croaked, standing up and adjusting my skirt. "We can go to my quarters, and I can have Pendra take your...your other forms measurements so we can get you some proper clothes."

"Who is Pendra?" He sounded suspicious, dangerous, which sent a chill down my spine.

I looked down to him as I forced myself to start walking, "He's my personal assistant. He...does everything I need to make sure I don't lose my head through the day."

He nodded at that, his shoulder brushing up against my hip. "Very well. I suppose I can abide by your clothing society. In Dragon society we did not wear clothes in our shifted form. We had no need of them..."

"So...everyone was just naked?" I asked, feeling my face grow hot again.

He gave me a toothy smile, "Of course. When we are in our true forms we are 'naked' as you say...why would we force ourselves to wear unnatural things in a different form? We did wear clothing, armor, when meeting with Humans and the lesser races. But when interacting with each other, never."

"I am pretty sure that breaks several Solarian laws..." I mumbled, so flushed that even my neck and chest felt hot.

His chest rumbled in a laugh that vibrated the very air around us, "So, no chance I will see the Queen of Solaria without clothing anytime soon, then?"

I stumbled, catching myself on a wall as a cough of shock escaped me. I hadn't expected that and completely lost all my composure. "P-Pardon!?"

He laughed again, watching me intently, "Forgive me, that was inappropriate. It has been such a long time since I've spoken to others, and of all my memories...none of the human women were as beautiful as you."

I managed to compose myself, barely, folding my hands in front of me and steeling my face, "Well I am one of many. You will find beautiful beings across the world."

Barloc watched me intently, those gold eyes sharp and like he didn't approve of my deflection, but thankfully he didn't push me further and changed the subject. "You are a very strong mage. A...Chronomancer, you called yourself, correct?"

I heaved a mental sigh of relief at the change of conversation, "Yes. I can...control time, to a point."

Barloc nodded in understanding, "Hm, we called them something different in our tongue...but their Order was full of nobility, bravery and justice."

"What? That...shouldn't be possible. The first Chronomancer

on record was Victoria Heart." I stammered. If he was telling the truth, that changed so much when it came to the Chronomancer history.

"I am quite sure. Though Draxel hunted them to near extinction. It could be that the ones that were left, if any, went into hiding and the powers went dormant until this...Victoria Heart was born." He explained, watching me curiously. In this form I couldn't gleam what he was thinking. His expressions were more limited.

I opened the door to my suite, where Pendra was organizing and tidying. "Pendra," I greeted, stepping in and then I stepped aside for Barloc.

Pendra turned towards us, about to speak but no words came out. Stunned to silence from the dragon in front of him, I wagered. Not that I could blame him.

"Pendra, this is Barloc. Barloc, this is Pendra. He is a summoned servant, bound to the crown." I explained calmly.

Barloc tilted his head, and now I was sure he had grown even on the walk to the room. Those gold-yellow eyes scanned Pendra intently, but his lips pulled back from his maw in a smile. "Greetings, Pendra." I knew his voice sounded in both our minds from the uncharacteristic shocked expression on Pendra's face.

Pendra recovered gracefully, and he bowed to Barloc. "Hello, Barloc. It is an honor to meet you." He said, looking to me. "How may I be of assistance, Your Grace?"

"Barloc can shift form into something more like you, but he will need custom clothes to be made. Can you please take his measurements and have our tailors start making clothes of his status?" I explained, andoffered a kind but pleading smile to Pendra.

Pendra nodded, and he moved quickly, pulling out the pedestal that I stood on to have my own measurements taken, as well as a privacy screen and setting it up. "Barloc, if you do not mind, if you come back here and stand on this in your shifted form, I will take your measurements at once."

The dragon complied, and within thirty minutes it was all said and done and Barloc was back into his true form, lounging on the cool tiled floor. His gaze was on me, where I was sitting at my desk filing through reports quietly. We remained like this for several hours, me going through the reports and my work quietly while he drifted in and out of sleep, occasionally being brought huge platters of food which he devoured.

Suddenly his voice sounded in my head, "What are you working on?"

I startled, turning towards him, "I don't know if I will ever get used to that." I noted. I still wasn't used to the Archons doing it.

He gave a grin at that, showing those sharp teeth, "Apologies. I'm just curious as to what has your attention, is all." He offered.

I looked back to the reports, "Mostly financial reports...some crime reports, taxation changes. Necessary to keep the country running but that doesn't mean it isn't boring."

That laugh, deep from his chest, sounded again. It warmed me to my core, and I couldn't understand that. "From what you told me while I was still in my egg, you handle it admirably." He explained, but he motioned to my bed. "You should rest, however. It is late."

My gaze shifted to the clock on my wall, and a frown crossed my face, "Arcanis above, is that truly the time? Sorry, yes. I can get Pendra to bring you to a suite for you."

His head tilted, "I suppose me asking to sleep in your room is also inappropriate, for human standards. Very well." He nodded, and stood, stretching out his body and wings.

I watched him, still overwhelmed with how fast he was growing and just his mere existence. "Yes, very inappropriate." I agreed, getting up and going to the door. "Please have Pendra come and bring Barloc to his suite for the night." I told the guard outside of the door. The guard merely nodded and quickly left to locate my assistant.

When Pendra returned, Barloc left with a simple 'good night, Queen Johanna', and then it was quiet again. I heaved a sigh, getting changed into a night gown and crawling into bed, staring at the ceiling. I had spent the whole day in my room because I didn't want to answer all the questions about Barloc, from Dedria or Father or Delain or Kira.

I found myself climbing out of bed, bare feet silently crossing the floor to the door. The Guards were gone now - they had only been stationed outside my door because of the Dragon in the room. Though I seriously doubted they would be able to do anything, if Barloc had chosen to attack me.

The halls were still and silent, everyone in their rooms and asleep, so I was able to get to Dedria's room without being seen. A quick double 'rap rap' on the door, and I slipped in. Dedria looked at me from her bed, confused and half asleep.

"You better have a good reason for this," she grumbled, yawning as she sat up. "I was almost asleep."

I hurried over to the bed, crawling in beside Dedria and sitting against the headboard with me. "The egg hatched this morning."

"Hold on, what? It hatched? It hatched and you didn't tell me! I thought you were locked up in your room because you weren't feeling well or something. Do you know how many questions I had to deflect from Delain?" Dedria feigned anger well, but I knew she wasn't angry or upset. I could tell by the slight curl on the edges of Dedria's mouth.

"He hatched. Scared the daylights out of me, too. I spent the whole day with him in my room because I didn't want to deal with the questions. I'm sorry." I leaned into Dedria, a smile on my lips as well.

Dedria huffed, pushing on my shoulder playfully. "That's such crap. You just didn't want to share them. Wait, did you say him?"

"I did." A blush was creeping across my cheeks, and I could feel it. I only hoped the low light of the room prevented her from seeing it.

I could feel her eyes scanning me intently, "Why are you blushing? Oh gods, you do not have the hots for a dragon, do you? Delain will be crushed. Cast aside for an overgrown fire breathing lizard."

"Dedria!" I gaped, jaw dropping as I stared at my friend. "That was rude. Barloc is kind, and he doesn't just have a dragon form - he has a human form, too!   And he's...he's incredibly handsome, when he's in it!"

"Which was how often today?" Dedria asked, eyes lightening in delight at how flustered I was right now.

I looked away, swallowing. "Well, only once...for about five minutes. But that's because he was naked, and..."

Dedria cackled in delight, bumping her shoulder up against mine, "Oh, I get it. Her Royal Highness has never seen a man naked before."

I grumbled, pushing back against Dedria, "I couldn't sleep, in my room alone. Can I stay with you tonight?" I asked, casting a glance to her.

"Always." Dedria answered, sliding back down the bed and under the covers and I sunk down as well. Within what felt like moments, the two of us were fast asleep, holding hands under the covers for comfort.

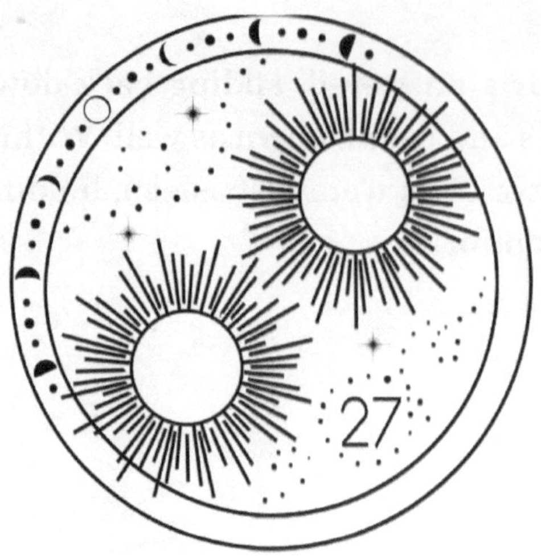

I woke before Dedria and the rest of the Ivory Halls and snuck back to my room before anyone discovered us. Even if we hadn't done anything indecent, I knew whispers and rumors could slip out and that could be a public relations nightmare for the monarchy. It was better this way, even if it meant waking before dawn.

I changed and got my hair ready myself, quietly and meticulously putting each fine metal strand into the mass of curls on my head. It was therapeutic in a way, to do it myself instead of having anyone else do it for me. I dressed in a lighter weight linen blouse and a pair of cotton pants. I would change later, into one of the formal dresses, but I wanted coffee and breakfast in my office first before I put on the rest of the mask I had to wear.

I slid on a pair of silk slippers, suitable for walking the halls and in my office before heading quietly to the kitchen where I asked them to bring me coffee and a light breakfast there. I thanked them with a smile and nod before I was on my way again, unlocking the enchantments to my office with a subtle wave of my hand in front of the handle and walking in.

My coffee and breakfast hadn't even arrived yet when an Elite knocked on the door. "Your Royal Highness." They said, bowing deeply at the waist. "There is someone demanding your audience at the gates."

I looked up, their mask obscured their face, and it was enchanted to mask their voice too. They sounded neither man nor woman, but it kept their identity and family safe. Being an Elite Guard was the ultimate sacrifice in Solaria, but also the highest honour. "And why should I give them an audience?" I asked.

"They claim to be from Nox." The elite's words sent chills down my spine, the hair on the back of my neck standing up.

I unconsciously ground my teeth together, but I nodded. "Go wake Dedria. Tell her. I will go get changed. I want 30 Elites to escort this person from the Gates to the Throne Room." I said firmly. "And put the mana suppressor cuffs on them."

Very rare, very expensive hand cuffs. The enchantment was so difficult to do that only two enchanters in the entire world knew how to do it, but the enchantment completely suppressed the aura and mana output of whoever wore such an enchantment. They were only used for the most offensive, dangerous criminals.

Such as someone who worked for Nox.

I sat in the Throne Room an hour later, in my armour with my Soul Forged blade in its sheath on my hip. Dedria stood a little behind me to the right, also in her full armor with her own blade. Pendra stood behind me to the left, his tail flicking around behind him in irritation. 30 Elites stood in the halls, 15 on either side, lining the walls. Delain was off to the left side of the raised platform where I sat on the throne, he had insisted on being here. We had argued about it for five minutes, until I realized that there was no convincing him of otherwise and had shouted 'fine' at him and stormed off.

I would apologize for my temper later. Maybe.

Beside Delain, in a perfectly cut and tailored suit, stood Barloc. He was taller than Delain by a full head, which felt obscene to me since Delain was already tall - taller than I was at least. He was standing there totally relaxed, his gold gaze scanning over the Elites occasionally, but I found mostly his gaze stayed on me. Every time I glanced over towards him, his eyes met mine. I was doing my best to ignore it, ignore him watching her, judging me.

The doors opened, and more Elites filed in, surrounding a figure in the centre of them. I tried to catch a glimpse of who it was, what they looked like, but I couldn't until the procession was at the base of the steps and the Elites in front moved aside with military precision.

It was a man, with black hair and pale skin and startling green eyes. He was as tall as Delain, maybe a little taller, and he stood tall and straight, shoulders back. He was looking around, and his gaze landed curiously on Barloc, but he didn't linger it there, turning it back to me. He was unsmiling, and the look in his eyes reminded me of the General. Calculating, perceptive and completely and utterly unforgiving. His clothes were worn, and his pants were torn in a few places. Like he didn't have any other clothes to wear.

"You asked for my audience." I broke the silence. "Why?"

The man's gaze watched me intently, but he couldn't see anything but a confident, cold exterior. I made sure of that, even if the very air around me thrummed with power, with the need to unleash fire on this man and burn him to ash right there.

"My name is Salem Ortega, I am a Chronomancer who previously aligned with Nox." His voice was calculated and calm, it didn't hold any arrogance to it. "Rozalin Heart and I were in the Chronomancy Guild together, before Ground Zero was created by her and the late Queen Maria. I joined her cause because of what that guild did to me. I wanted to watch the world burn for the atrocities there. After the final conflict between Solaria and Taranor, Rozalin and I put ourselves into a chronomancy stasis - preserving our minds and bodies at the age we were at, healing any wounds and injuries, and set ourselves to wake 10 years ago."

So that explained why Rozalin was still alive - she must have escaped the blast of Ground Zero and put herself in this stasis.

He continued, not pausing as I processed this information. "However, I woke alone. Rozalin had already risen from the slumber 10 years before I did. And the Rozalin I found was not the one I had fallen in love with, before the sleep. She was crazed, determined to burn the world order down. Yet I continued to follow her, because she was still the woman I loved, the scars still fading from what the Guild had done to me. What they had forced me to do. We created Nox, together. A new Chronomancy Guild, to train young Chronomancers about their powers, to rip the world order down and build it anew. But that is not what happened. The same crimes committed against me, against Rozalin, she started to commit against them. I fought her on it, but she didn't relent. And then the search for the

Ember started. The attacks on the cities, on the people. I could see the cycle starting all over again - a power hungry leader, using Chronomancers to destroy lives no matter the cost. So I left."

I bit the inside of my cheek, leaning forward so my elbows rested on my knees. "Say I believe you. Why do you come to me, Salem Ortega?"

"Because I heard about what you offered that young Chronomancer and his family. A chance to learn his powers, so he may live a normal life. Be a productive member of society." Salem watched me, his green eyes darkening with suspicion. "Or are you just like Rozalin, and seek to use him as a weapon as well?"

I lifted my top lip in a silent snarl at the suggestion, "Excuse me?!" I hissed, "How dare you align me with her? She is a monster. She has killed thousands. She killed my mother." I was shaking with fury, and my aura reacted, making the air around me ripple.

Whatever reaction he had been looking for, he didn't let on. "I know all too well the things Rozalin has done to this country. I am sorry about your Mother - I tried to stop her." He sounded sincere, and he reached down, still manacled at the wrists, and lifted the hem of his shirt up his body. He was well muscled, though I noticed the fresh scar, wrinkled and pink just below his bottom ribs on his right side. It had to be longer than my hand, and I wondered how he survived such a wound. "I paid for it and barely escaped with my life."

My gaze darkened, eyes narrowing slightly as I watched him intently. "So what? I offer a young Chronomancer a chance to learn and thrive. Why does that lead to you coming here, to me?"

He watched me, those green eyes intense and calculating as he took me in. I knew he was looking for any trace of a lie, any sort of deception. I knew he wouldn't find it. "I want to help. To teach them. To make sure they can have what I didn't."

Dedria spoke up from behind me, her voice cool and confident. "And how are we supposed to trust you? How do we know you aren't here to spy for Rozalin?"

"I do not blame you for thinking that." He sai, voice calm and it almost had a hint of apology to it, "but I am done with Rozalin, and Nox. I have been done with them since they attacked Solaria the first time and stole the Ember shard from here. I have been lost, without a purpose, for months. You can lock me in a cell, keep these manacles on me, whatever makes you sleep better at night. I would not blame you for any of it. All I ask is that you give me a chance to prove myself - let me try and earn your trust."

I glanced back to Dedria, a silent question hanging between us before Dedria inclined her head slightly and I looked back to Salem. "Why does she want the Ember? What is she going to do with it? And what of the Eye?"

"She seeks to open a rift to Hel." He said, "to allow the Demon Lords through to destroy the world before locking them up with it once more and letting a new world order form, with her at the top...the Eye she got through a bargain with a demon, who helped her find it when it was supposed to be lost to eternity." He explained, "a bargain that will allow one of the Demon Lords to remain here and have her as his wife and Queen."

The silence that filled the room was palatable as we all digested this knowledge, and it was Dedria who broke the silence, "Well that is significantly worse than we thought it would be."

Salem chuckled, though it was dry and humorless, "she is determined to watch the world burn. No matter the cost. I know you do not trust me yet, but I hope with time that will change, Your Royal Highness."

"We will see how much of the information you just offered us is true." I retorted, leaning back on the throne. "What did the Chronomancy Guild do to you, that started to lead you on the path you were on?"

His face darkened from the memories that flooded through his mind, his hands curling into fists as his gaze dropped to his feet. "They beat me, made me kill everything from kittens and puppies to orphans to my very siblings. And then they made me bring them all back to have me kill them again." He ground his teeth together, "over and over again, until I no longer questioned when they pointed me in a direction and told me to kill. I slumbered for 600 years, but my mind was not fully silent. I had a lot of time to…process my trauma."

Once again, the silence hung in the air, the weight of his confession was almost suffocating. "I am sorry." I whispered, "we knew the Guild was corrupt…but not to that extent."

Salem shrugged, and I could tell he was trying to not be bothered by it and failing. His gaze lifted back up to me, where I read it on his face, plain as day, that he did not blame me. I knew he had no reason to, but something about it felt open, honest. "That is why I need to know if you will keep your word. If you meant it, when you said you would teach them to control. Not teach them to be weapons."

"No, I have no interest in turning them into weapons. If, if Dedria and I form another Chronomancy Guild here, we will seek to teach them control and mastery. So they may forge their own path in the world. Combat is useful, as it is to every student of any magical discipline, but it will not be forced." I explained, my voice was still soft. I was still mulling over what Salem had revealed of his past, and it weighed heavily on my heart. I hadn't put much thought into the guild, honestly. What sort of structure we would have, but I knew what I said was the truth. If a student of mine didn't want to fight, I would never force them.

Salem nodded, and he lowered himself onto one knee, bowing down, "then I pledge myself to you, Queen Johanna. Give me a chance to prove myself, to help teach the students in the new guild to have a life I will never have, and you have my loyalty."

Dedria scoffed, "And what is your condition, Salem Ortega?" I asked, voice sharp.

I raised my hand, "Dedria…" I said softly, giving her a look that told her to remain silent. Dedria looked back to me, pursing her lips unhappily.

Salem lifted his head, looking at me, and then Dedria. "Not a condition, just that I ask you hear me if I tell you that you are following the wrong path if I sense that."

"I have no intention of following the wrong path, but very well. I will heed your words, if you earn my trust to have the spot you so yearn for." I said, and I waved my hand. "Dismissed. The Elites will bring you to your cell."

Once he was gone, and the throne room was empty outside of Dedria, Pendra, Delain, Barloc and I, we all looked around to each other. Pendra spoke first, voice indignant, "I would not trust that man as far as I could throw him."

I couldn't help but laugh at that, "Well, I don't trust him either. But he deserves…he deserves a chance to prove himself, does he not? After all he has suffered, everything that was taken from him, don't we owe him that?"

Barloc's deep voice rumbled out, "Not everyone does deserve that chance. You would not offer such a thing to this Rozalin, would you?"

"I agree with the Dragon." Delain said, shifting up the steps to stand closer to me. "We don't know him; we don't know his motivations." I couldn't help but notice Barloc's intense stare at how close Delain was to me now, and I tucked that question in the back of my mind for when I was alone with Barloc later.

"Obviously I wouldn't offer such a thing to Rozalin. But Salem isn't her, and if he is telling the truth, about him trying to stop her from killing my mom, then he deserves a chance. I didn't sense a lie on him, did any of you?"

"Maybe he's just a good actor," Dedria huffed, "He's been alive longer than any of us - maybe except Barloc but he slept for how long of that?"

Barloc shook his head dismissively at that fact, "He didn't smell like he was lying. Though he did smell nervous, that's probably because he was expecting you to execute him. Which I would still consider." His voice was deep and gravelly, and I got the sense that it was because this Dragon was feeling protective over me. I had to push that to the back of my mind, I had to contemplate that later, along with the intense gaze from earlier. Maybe with Dedria over a glass or three of wine.

I huffed, my voice sharp, "Enough. I am not executing him. He is going to get a chance to earn my trust, and it will not be easy. But if he is telling the truth - about Hel and the Eye and the Demon Lords, we have a bigger problem on our hands. I thought she was going to attack the world with the Ember, but if she plans on opening a gate to Hel and let demon armies through, then this is bad. Really bad."

"That puts it mildly…" Dedria muttered, rolling her eyes. "We need to find out where she is and try and intercept her. Maybe he knows."

Barloc shook his head, "He said he hasn't been around Nox since the first attack on Solaria. He probably has no better idea of where they are than we do. That will be a dead end - if he's telling the truth." His tail swished behind him on the tiles, deep in thought. "But perhaps he can track them, he knows their auras, their habits, if anyone can track them, it would probably be him."

I sighed, leaning back into the throne and running my hand down my face in frustration, "I will think about it." I said, suddenly getting up. "But for now, I am starving and haven't had any coffee. So, I am going to go do that before I discuss this anymore and possibly make a decision that I will regret." I quickly headed off, conscious of both Delain and Barloc's eyes on my back.

Dedria easily caught up with me, matching my strides. "For what it's worth, you…giving this Salem a chance, it proves you aren't like Rozalin. Rozalin probably would have executed him on sight. You're better than her." She frowned, "but we better not let it get out that you are offering redemption to a member of Nox, not unless you want a civil war on your hands." She slung her arm over my shoulder, pulling me into a side hug.

"Hm, thank you for that, that wasn't something I had considered at all." I replied, sarcasm dripping. My body was tense, though at the friendly touch I did relax slightly. "Do you know why Barloc was there?"

Dedria shook her head, "No, though I suspect he had heard

Delain mention it to your father in the hall on the way down." She paused and cast a curious look at me. "Why?"

I felt myself wanting to frown, but I bit it back. "It's just...strange. For him to be present for something like that, don't you think? Delain...sure. Delain is courting me, he wants to be present to show me his support, how he can be strong and wise in these situations. But Barloc? Why does he care? He's a Dragon - he has no allegiance to Solaria..."

"No allegiance?" Dedria barked a laugh, grinning wildly, "Johanna, you are the sole reason his egg was found, and he was able to hatch. If you had not found him, he would have slept for eternity." She shook her head, that smile still present, but it had morphed to one of disbelief at my clueless expression. "He owes his life to you. I have barely spoken to him, but I suspect that if you asked him to kill for you, he would, and he wouldn't hesitate."

I felt warm from my cheeks to my chest at that, and Dedria's words struck true even if I didn't want to believe it. "Well, fine. Maybe that's the case. But I told him he does not need to stay here - or...anything." I winced as Dedria bumped my ribs with an elbow. "Okay, okay...noted. He wouldn't leave."

"Now that *that* has been discussed." Dedria huffed, "can we discuss the obvious tension in the room between the two of them while you're present? Because I am pretty sure if someone breathed wrong in your direction, they would be scrambling over each other to defend your honor." She laughed, obviously delighted over this.

I groaned, giving Dedria a critical look as we finally reached my office and sunk into our usual spots. "I don't want to think about that. Not in the present."

"Why, because you can't fathom two incredibly handsome men - even if one is a Dragon, wanting you?" Dedria's gaze felt cold on my skin, and I couldn't fathom why.

"Dedria, it's not like I have a hall full of suitors." I countered, bristling. "And I know very damn well why, because my Mother was murdered and within weeks of my ascension to the throne, I left the country to try and find the culprits. But we've been back for nearly a month, and Delain is the only one who has asked."

Dedria pinched the bridge of her nose before she reached back and brushed her braid over her shoulder, starting to undo the tight ribbon that held it before combing her fingers through the braid, loosening and freeing her hair. "Arcanis above. Johanna, Delain has staked a claim on you since you were 16. He was the only one you had more than two dances with at any gala or ball or wedding. And you have been more than accepting of it, don't be dense and pretend otherwise. If your mother hadn't have died, we would be planning your wedding right now, you and I both know that. We've talked about that. But when your mom died…You pushed him away. You pushed us all away. You shut down. But that claim he put on you didn't just disappear. Everyone respected it, waiting with bated breath for him to decide you were ready for him to ask to court you…Because the only person that knows you better than him is me. And I told him you were ready."

The words settled over me like a thick veil, and my heart ached. My brown eyes shifted from where I was stirring my coffee to Dedria, "What do you mean you told him?" I asked now, voice barely a whisper. I couldn't stop a sour taste from forming in my mouth, and I washed it down with a sip of coffee, even if it was a bit more bitter than I usually took it.

"We've been in contact…since your Mom died. He sent a letter to me after it happened, asking if I had heard from you, how you were. Because every single one he sent to you had gone unanswered. And I had to tell him that all my communication with you had gone unanswered as well. We have kept in touch since, though most of our conversations have revolved around you." Dedria replied, and she sounded so matter of fact, so unapologetic. So like herself and it made that sour taste in my mouth intensify. But this time it wasn't from feeling betrayed by Dedria, but by someone who I thought would never keep those things from me.

"I didn't get any letters from him. Or you. Or anyone." My voice was still soft, but it had grown sharper, and I didn't miss the frown that spread on Dedria's face, the furrow of her eyebrows in concern.

I carefully placed my coffee cup down, rising to a stand, each movement with a purpose and I had to still my whole body from shaking with rage. My feet moved before I fully thought, and I was out of my office, moving down the hall. My gaze caught sight of Delain, and not far behind him Barloc. From the shared shocked expression that morphed into concern, I knew what my own face was betraying. "I do not want to talk to either of you." I said, tone clipped and sharp as a dagger as I stalked past them.

But not so far past them, because just at the end of the hall lay my father's office, and I threw the door open with no regard for what he was doing or even caring if the door would survive my fury.

Simon was at his desk, pouring over documents and memos and what looked to be reports from the General, and his gaze flew up to the doorway in alarm. "Johanna?" He asked, his tone that pacifying calm he was so good at, even if his shock was laced through it.

Except now, my gaze was practically red as I glared at him, and it took everything I had to suppress my aura, to stop from shouting, to keep myself from shaking in pure fury. "Can you tell me why, Father, that all the letters my friends sent me in the months after Mother died somehow did not make it to me?" Simon's eyes widened, and I felt a deep and terrifying amount of satisfaction at his shock and how he couldn't even answer me. "You thought I wouldn't find out? With two of them in these very halls? You thought they would never mention it, how I failed to respond to all their communications in those months following Mom's death? That they would just assume I was so wracked with grief that I wouldn't even be able to respond to them reaching out?"

He swallowed and opened his mouth to talk but I cut him off. "I don't want to hear it. I don't want or need to hear whatever excuses you have for it. I am so...so inexplicably angry and betrayed by you. I needed my friends, Father. I needed their comfort, their words and their thoughts. I thought I was totally alone, without a single explanation. I thought they had just decided to give me time, space. Things I did not need or want. Not that you *kept them from me.*" My voice dropped and I hissed the last four words. I had to take a few deep breaths, and I pushed my shoulders back, lifting my chin. "From this moment, you are relieved of your duties as King Consort. You will be given an apartment to live in in the lower levels of the halls, one that will fit your position. But your services are no longer required."

I didn't give him a chance to speak, I simply turned heel and breezed past Delain and Barloc, who hadn't moved from their spots but were both looking dumb founded, past the guards who stood unblinking and unmoving, past Dedria whose jaw had dropped in shock from where she had stepped out into the hall to watch. I went right into my office, shut the door behind me - gently, I had enough sense of that. When the latch clicked and I had locked it, I finally let the tears fall. I sagged against the wooden door, sinking to the floor and letting out a ragged sob.

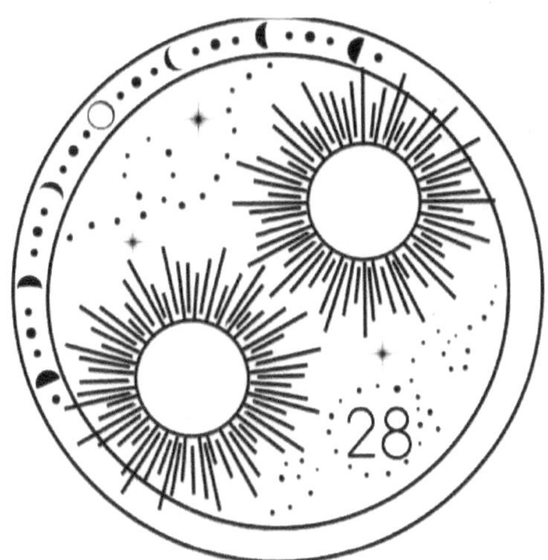

I didn't know how long I sat there, against the door of my locked office. I was glad for the soundproofing enchantments, glad that no one on the other side could hear me crying. When I finally rose to a stand, I had to suppress the urge to throw things, to destroy everything around me. I bit back the sour taste in the back of my throat, swallowed down the pulsing anger and took a handful of deep breaths. Just as I felt I had a handle on it, there was a knock on the door that startled me.

I knew I couldn't hide the puffiness around my eyes, or the redness there. I wouldn't be able to hide that from anyone on the other side - I wouldn't be able to hide the weakness I was sure it showed. I contemplated not answering, not until an achingly familiar voice came from the other side.

"Johanna...I know you're in there. Let me in, please." Delain said, and it sounded like he was leaning against the door, pushing his head into the part of the door where it met the frame. The idea of him standing there like that almost made me weak in the knees. My bottom lip quivered again as I froze with indecision, and, perhaps against my better judgment, I stepped forward, slowly opening the door.

He swept in, shutting the door behind him quickly and quietly with his foot as his arms slid around me and pulled me into a fierce hug. Her eyes closed, and it took everything inside of me to not break again. His smell had never changed - he smelled like the desert after the rains hit. Of damp sand and flourishing flora. My arms wrapped around his waist, holding him as tight to me as he held me to him. He was so solid, so strong. So here.

"I didn't know you hadn't gotten my letters." He whispered, "If I had known that I would have shown up...I would have come, Johanna. I should have come. I shouldn't have just...waited for you to come to me. I am so sorry." His voice sounded thick, full of regret and pain.

My shoulders shook as I fought back tears, and I violently shook my head against his broad chest, "Don't. Don't apologize. It's not your fault. It's...he betrayed me. He walled...he walled me off." My voice cracked, and I was failing. Failing at hiding the sadness of being alone for those torturous four months, surrounded by nothing else but responsibility and the overwhelming anger and bitterness and sense of vengeance. I had lost myself completely in those four months, and it was only during the trip with Dedria, then being back home with her, that I had started to find myself again.

His grip tightened around me, his lips pressing against the top of my head in the mass of curls. He didn't have anything to say to that, and I got the marked impression Delain wasn't happy about what Father had done either. Minutes ticked by as we just held each other in complete silence. He finally broke it, "It's...what he did was wrong. Terribly, inexplicably wrong. I will never, ever dispute that. And I am furious with him too, trust me...I had a very nasty few words to share with him that I am not proud of, Johanna." He said, and his lips pressed on my temple now. "But he doesn't control you anymore. He stopped being able to do that when you became Queen. You will never be cut off from those that matter to you ever again. You will never be cut off from me ever again. I won't allow it. I would rip apart the world before I allowed that to happen again."

Somehow, we ended up on the couch, side by side at first but somewhere in his speech he pulled me into his lap to face him. His hands were warm on my hips, and he stared up at me. When had he ever stared up at me? I was always shorter than him, even in heeled shoes. I lost myself in his gaze.

Swallowing hard, my gaze flicking between his lips to his eyes and then down his body. My hands were resting on his chest, and Archons above did he ever feel strong. Had he always been this muscled, this strong before? I remembered thinking about it, in the Throne room when we had almost kissed. It was more obvious now, somehow. My cheeks felt hot, "Delain..."

He tugged me closer, "Johanna, please just...listen to me, okay? You don't answer to anyone anymore. Not your father, not those pretentious old men who call themselves your advisers. You make the rules. You. We don't have to adhere to the rules anymore. I love you. I have loved you for years. And I have waited for you for long enough - we have waited for each other for long enough. We don't have to wait anymore." His voice was deep and had a tinge of desperation to it.

I scanned his face, breath hitching. I hadn't had anyone outside of my family and Dedria tell me that they loved me. And for some reason, maybe a very foolish reason, I hadn't expected it from Delain, while I straddled his lap, eyes puffy and red from crying. I opened my mouth to speak, but I didn't get a chance. His hands lifted from my hips, gliding along my sides, his touch searingly hot. Up over my shoulders to my face where he cupped my cheeks and pulled me in for a kiss.

It started tender, my breath hitching in my throat again. All my thoughts scattered to the wind at his lips on mine. We broke apart for a split second, and I reached up, cupping one of his cheeks, the other fisting his soft linen shirt as I leaned back in. Those tender movements turned feverish and frantic, I was wholly inexperienced against Delain's sure and confident movements. One hand went back to my hip, trying to tug me even closer to him though I was sure that wasn't possible. His other hand was on the back of my neck, warm and the calluses rough, making sure I couldn't escape backward and away from him.

Teeth clashed, tongues brushed against each other, and he caught my bottom lip between his teeth, eliciting a soft gasp. I felt his growing hardness below, and I flushed at the realization. Then his mouth was moving along my jaw, his hand that had been on my neck reaching up to my hair and gently guiding me so he could kiss along that sensitive skin, even nipping with his teeth. I let a strangled moan loose, and his grip on me tightened.

"Archons, Johanna." He hissed, "Do you have any idea how long I've waited for this?" He sounded frustrated, but maybe that was just the fact that his pants were so uncomfortably tight.

I couldn't help but laugh, light and breathy and for this moment, it felt like the missing piece had slotted back into place. "About as long as I have, probably." I answered, and I smiled at him. This was probably a mistake, but it sure didn't feel like one.

Delain just stared at me, in wonder and amazement, "You are

so beautiful when you smile." He said softly, "you haven't been smiling enough lately."

My brows furrowed together at that, the smile fading, "I don't know about that." I countered, feeling self-conscious.

"I do," He sounded confident, and he leaned in again, catching my lips with his again. His hand tugged at my hip, making sure I became even more aware of what was in his pants. "Marry me." I opened her mouth to respond, but he didn't give me a chance. "I know, I know…bad guys to catch, world to save, but after all of that is done, marry me. Johanna, I am yours. I will forever be *yours*."

I swallowed, unease rippling through and over me. "Delain, I don't know how this conflict is going to go. Of course…Of course I want to be victorious. But if I'm not." The anxiety was clear in my voice, the slight waiver to my words.

"You will be victorious. Failure is not an option for you, it never has been. You will succeed, because you won't accept anything less." He countered, not wanting to hear what else I had to say, and his faith in me made me lean back, eyes wide.

"Delain." I breathed, my teeth biting my bottom lip as I took him in. Hair slightly tousled, shirt wrinkled, lips red from kissing. "If I fail…I need someone I trust to be here for my sister. To help her navigate all of this. Someone who will take care of her and make sure she will stay true to who she is."

"Don't be foolish, that won't be needed." He shook his head. Disbelief radiated from him, and it made my heart ache. "You will not fail."

"Delain." I said his name sharper now, and I sprung out of his lap. Breaking that grip of his was easier than I thought, though maybe he hadn't been holding me that tightly after all. "Listen to me. Gods, please just listen to me." My voice broke, and my eyes started to water. Still emotional, after finding out what my father had done. "I need you to be there for my sister. To make sure she stays good. Make sure she knows that being true to herself is more important than anything else. I didn't want to have this conversation with you yet, not now. Not like this." I gestured between us, "But if Dedria and I don't succeed, I need someone here that I can trust with Kira."

He stared at me, and I knew neither of us were sure how we had even gotten to this point. I could tell he was wondering how I decided now was the time to have this conversation, when he had been begging me to marry him moments earlier. Why was I asking him to take care of Kira? The answer should have been obvious to him, he should know that besides Dedria, I trusted him the most. I trusted that if I died, he would do exactly what I asked of him. "Don't make me stay here while you go out and risk your life again…" He whispered, shaking his head. "Don't ask that of me."

"You can't come with me when we find Rozalin. You have to stay here." I said, voice just as soft, shaking my head in disbelief. "Why would you think you'd be able to come with me?"

"Gods, Johanna! Why wouldn't I be able to come with you?! I'm courting you, and you expect me - me, who is begging you to marry me, to let you go out there and face an unknown evil and risk your life while I stay here?" His anger burst then, and he launched to a stand, towering over me. His face was twisted in betrayal and anger, "How could you ask that of me?!"

I took a step back, mostly out of shock at how angry he was, that quiver on my bottom lip disappearing as I steeled myself. He saw it, those tears drying, and the sorrow replaced by a cold exterior. "I am not asking anything; I am commanding that of you. As your Queen." I said, and I turned, moving to the door and opening it. "If you may leave now." I added, and the sharpness in my voice cut him deeper than the command.

His upper lip lifted in distaste, but for whom he didn't know. "As you command, Your Royal Highness." He hissed, stomping out of the room, and I shut the door behind him silently.

Once he was gone, I heaved a sigh, leaning back on the door and counting the seconds as they passed. Gods, what had just happened? I had just been trying to be practical - that I might not survive the encounter with Rozalin. I had been planning on asking him to be an adviser to Kira, there was no one I trusted more besides maybe Dedria. But him asking me to marry him was too much. Too much too fast, and he had just doubled down on acting like everything would be okay. It had burned me, had made me not feel heard. That had been infuriating, absolutely infuriating, and it was a trend with Delain I wasn't enjoying.

Another knock on the door knocked me out of my train of thought, and I stepped away from the door and yanked it open, "Delain, damn it, I do-" I cut myself off, staring not at Delain who stood in front of the door, but Barloc.

Was Arcanis and Osian mocking me? What sort of cruel thing was this?

He stood there calmly, his long tail swishing along the tiles idly. "Sorry to interrupt. I just wanted to ask if you are okay." He said, that deep rumble of concern in his voice washing over me, and it practically reignited the fire Delain had lit earlier. There was a glint of danger in Barloc's gaze - he had heard the name I had said as the door opened and had seemed to make a mental note of Delain being on my metaphorical shit list right now.

"Yes, I'm fine." I said, tone polite but forced. "Sorry, I thought you were someone else." I did my best to school my features into the cool indifference and calm that I had spent my whole life practicing.

A smirk crossed his lips, telling me that I had failed hiding anything. "Evidently." he replied, and the corners of his eyes wrinkled with that smirk. "My wings have finished settling and the bones have firmed. I believe I can fly now." He added, obviously wanting to distract me from my spiral. "Would you do me the honor of witnessing my first flight?"

I didn't hesitate, "Yes." I answered, stepping out of my office. He took a step back to accommodate the move, and then another, giving me more space. "Yes, I would like that very much." A much-needed distraction and something no one alive had ever seen - a dragon in flight! I would be the first to see it, in this new Era of dragons returning. My heart started pounding at the mere thought of it, and my face flushed with excitement. "The top of the tower. It will be safer there." I added as I turned, shutting and locking the door behind me. I moved quickly, knowing that every one of Barloc's steps was two or even three of mine. As predicted, he kept up easily. I felt his gaze on me, searing my skin, one with unasked questions, but he was respectful in keeping them to himself.

He didn't remain totally quiet, however. "I heard what you said to your father. Though I am pretty sure most of the Halls did." His lips curved into a smirk once more, though his next words were softer, "I am sorry you were alone in those months. I...I remember the time when the heat stopped - when." He paused and grimaced. "When my caretakers and parents died. I didn't know what was going on then - I inherited knowledge and memories from my parents from the time before I was laid, but not after. So, I waited, and waited, and waited for the heat to come back. And it didn't." He glanced over at me; his voice was thick with sorrow and my heart ached for him. "Not until *you*. Not until you had Castian go looking and when he brought me back and the heat returned and I heard your voice, I knew so much time had passed. That all the Dragons were gone. And the only thing that made it bearable was you."

I clasped my hands in front of me as I walked, and we walked in silence down two more halls before I found any response to that. "Thank you, Barloc." I whispered, and even though my whole being hurt for him, knowing he knew what I had felt those months, it eased some of my pain. "I am sorry you lost all your Kin. If I could go back and make it never happen - even if it meant the destruction of everything I knew, I would. A whole race effectively wiped from the earth...all their knowledge and history gone. That is a tragedy. It is."

He smiled at me, even if it was one of those sad, sorrowful ones. "Thank you, Johanna." He continued, "I believe that you would, if that was something remotely possible."

I reached out and touched his hand, just with the tips of my fingers, and it was only a graze, but his gaze darted down to where it happened. "If I survive Rozalin and her madness, we will find the other Dragons. You will usher in a whole new era of Dragons." I promised.

"And I will do everything in my power to make sure you defeat Rozalin." He agreed, "I have been talking with Dedria and...Tyne, is it? About the Eye that Rozalin has. We are prototyping a few armour options that will protect you both against its methods." His smile had shifted to one of sorrow to one of determination, and fuck if I didn't respect that.

"You know of it?" I inquired, my eyes widening in wonder. We were climbing the steps to the top of the tower now, and he was behind me as wee climbed.

"I do." He replied with a firm nod that I couldn't see, "It is not so simple as it being crafted by demons…though a demon did have a hand in its creation. Only because Draxel killed that demon and ripped its eye from its skull, harnessing otherworldly powers to create it." He explained, and he sounded bitter. "It was with that eye that Draxel was able to bring down my Kin. I am sure of it."

I slowed to open the door, stepping outside and holding the door open for him as he stepped out after me. I watched him carefully, and I saw that cold, steely determination in his eye. He wanted to defeat Rozalin as much as I did, because Rozalin was in possession of something that had brought an end to his expected future. I understood that all too well. "Then I will not stop you." I said, fingers brushing against his hand again as I turned and looked around the empty space. "The Enchantment to protect from the winds goes up about forty feet." I explained.

He moved towards the center of the wide-open space, and I averted her gaze when he started to pull his clothes off. "Some warning would be nice." I said, voice strangled. All I was met with was the rumbling laugh, and I felt his aura pulse as he changed back to his true form. Only then did I look back over to him.

He was larger than a horse now, maybe nearly as large as one of the mechanical machines that loaded and unloaded the train cars. He spread his wings out, stretching them wide before he tucked them in. He lowered his body slightly, and then with a power I knew was only possessed by Dragons, he launched into the air and unfurled his wings, beating them hard as he gained altitude.

He broke through the barrier with no issue, and he flew higher and higher. A smile spread on my face, and my hands cupped together on my chest as I watched, my heart swelling with awe. I stood, watching and smiling so hard my cheeks started to hurt as he flew and soared. I knew all those on the ground thought Barloc was nothing more than a bird, and for some reason that made me laugh. He dove and spun and played in the winds, and a thunderous roar emitted from him, but it didn't scare me. Instead, I laughed some more and felt tears prick at the edges of my eyes.

I was openly crying when he landed some thirty minutes later, and the moment he saw my tears he was in front of her in his shifted form, one hand on my cheek and concern written on his features. I didn't even notice or care that he was naked.

"Johanna, what is wrong, My Queen?" he asked, gaze scanning mine as one of his thumbs brushed away the tears.

I shook my head, laughing again, "Nothing...nothing is wrong." I said, taking a deep breath. "Watching you fly - it was the most beautiful thing I've ever seen, is all."

Barloc tilted his head, concern morphing to curiosity and amusement. "Is it now?"

"Absolutely, unbelievably so." I nodded, hands resting on his broad chest. He was taller, wider, stronger than Delain was. "I don't think anything will ever compare to what I just witnessed."

That golden gaze never tore from mine, but I felt the thrum of approval come from his chest with my entire being. "I do not know your customs and things, but it is my understanding that Sir Delain is…courting you? What does that mean?" He asked now, and his voice was rougher than before. It made warmth swirl low in my belly.

I didn't move from him, just entranced. "He wants me to marry him…Courting is us telling the world he seeks for my hand and us getting to know one another before then."

A deep growl emitted from him, which confused me. But it shouldn't, should it? I had seen how he had looked at me during the audience with Salem. "And if I sought to have you as mine? Would I need to…court you as well?"

I swallowed hard and nodded, "Yes, that is the…expected order." I replied, "I…I humored him, with his Courting request. I have known Delain most of my life, and before my mother died, everyone expected us to court and get married. Though now, things have changed so much, and I can barely focus on it right now. There is-"

He cut me off, "There is so much else to worry about." He finished for me, and he nodded. "Then I will withhold my own Courting request until Rozalin and her ilk are defeated." He stepped back from me finally and went to retrieve his clothes. His gaze had been one of determination and want. The air felt so cold without him.

I was stunned, having not expected that at all. He was respecting my wishes. More than that, he understood my reasoning. My mind was reeling, and I turned towards him just as he pulled his shirt on. "Barloc?"

He looked over to me, wordlessly waiting for me to continue but indicating I had his full attention.

"Thank you."

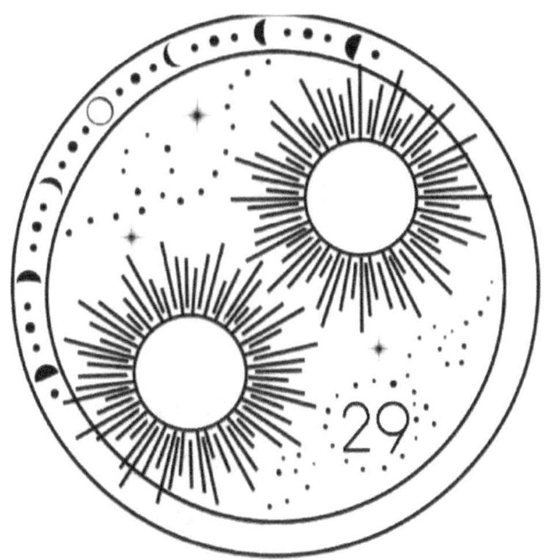

I didn't see Delain for several days, thankfully. It seemed we were both avoiding each other, and I wasn't bothered by that in the slightest. Instead, I spent every waking moment training with Dedria, checking in with Tyne and Bevy, holding Court and then Dedria, Tyne, Barloc and I spent whatever was left of the day finessing various prototypes Barloc had come up with to defend against the Eye.

It was late, the suns had set, and all the enchanted lights were on in the library. The four of us were the only ones there - the Librarians had gone, and I had dismissed my guards over an hour ago. Barloc was standing, and he was leaning down over me, Dedria just to his left and Tyne was on the other side of the table.

"The eye sees things before they happen." He explained, his hands were in his pants pockets, but I felt the heat of his body even if he wasn't touching me. "Sort of, at least. Even a Chronomancer can't trick it. It can tell which direction you are going to move before you step, how you will swing your weapon or move to defend. Perhaps our failing with our designs is because we aren't looking at this from a logical point of view."

He clicked his tongue, looking around and he straightened, pacing back and forth. He closed his eyes, tilting his head back. "If you are fighting someone, what cues do you look for when it comes to deciding how you attack?"

Dedria and I glanced at each other before I answered, "Their face, usually. Most people look towards what they are going to do next."

"Exactly." Barloc grinned in response, opening his eyes and looking down to me now. Every time his gaze was on me, I ended up warm all over. "But what if you couldn't see their face, or even their eyes? What if you could only see yourself?"

Dedria laughed at the concept, "Well, I'd be trying to destroy that as quickly as possible, it'd be unnerving."

He slowed to a stop, turning towards us. "So, if that would work on you, why wouldn't it work on Rozalin and the Eye?"

Tyne froze, and she was digging through the files spread out on the desk. "Ah!" She snapped her fingers, pointing at Barloc. "Brilliant! Yes," She laughed, an odd sound coming from the Greenseer. "Here. Queen Serena was spearheading the development of these for the Solarian Elite Guards, and eventually the armies." She ripped one of the papers out of the folder, laying it out in front of me. "We hadn't even built the prototype yet before she passed. But look." She tapped the paper with a renewed energy, her gaze alight with excitement.

The paper had various schematics for a heavily enchanted helm, and the front was labelled as being reflective like a mirror. It had notes, in Serena's writing, and I felt my heart pulse with an aching pain I had buried months ago. "Mom was designing this?"

Tyne nodded, "She was." She replied, and her voice had

softened. "We had all the parts ready…it's a one-way mirror, so the wearer can see through it with perfect clarity, but it's heavily enchanted. So heavily enchanted even Dragon's Fire can't break it - that's the theory, at least. Light weight, too. I can have the teams assemble it immediately and get them started on production for the rest. With your blessing, Your Grace."

One of my hands had dropped to my lap, and it clenched into a fist, my nails digging into my palm until it hurt. "Yes." I said, looking up from the sheet to Tyne. "Yes, please."

Tyne quickly collected the papers, bowing deeply at the waist before she was gone, rushing out of the library with a purpose.

Silence filled the air, Barloc and Dedria just watching me take several deep breaths. "Well," I said, looking to them, "we have a direction now, right? Perhaps we should go to bed, it's…" I glanced at the old clock, "Archons, it's nearly 2am."

Barloc nodded to Dedria, "I can escort the Queen back to her room," He offered, but from his tone it wasn't an offer but a statement. Dedria hesitated, but with pursed lips she got up and nodded.

Dedria snapped something in Dragonic, eyes narrowed on Barloc in pure suspicion.

Barloc's chest rumbled with a deep laugh, "Very well, Shadow of the Ash Queen." He agreed in common, offering his arm to me.

"I hate when you talk about me in a different language like I'm not right here…" I grumbled to Dedria, getting up from my seat and taking Barloc's arm. Dedria was already half-way gone, and she flipped us a crass gesture in response.

Barloc chuckled again, "She cares about you a lot," he looked down to me as we started to walk. "I admire her dedication to you. If only everyone in the world had someone as half dedicated to them as Dedria Heart is dedicated to you."

"Why do you say that?" I asked, looking up to him with a curious gaze.

"It would be a better place," He offered, "to know you always have someone who will go to war for you? With you? Who is loyal, but is also not afraid to criticize? That is a friendship almost everyone deserves, don't you think? And you have it with her, and you're still so young."

"I suppose," I gaze was unfocused, distracted. "Do you think my Mom knew? With the design of the helms? Do...do you think she knew about Rozalin, and the Eye, and all of it?"

Silence filled the air as Barloc contemplated. I only asked him because he was unbiased - he didn't know my mother. He still barely knew me. So if anyone felt they could speak freely about this, I truly felt it could be him.

"I think it is possible your Mother suspected it and found the solution before anyone else. I believe she was frighteningly intelligent - if you and all her research with this Rot disease is any indication. She found a possible cure for it when no one else had, and I think that's incredible. So, for her to know about Rozalin and the Eye? I don't find that hard to believe. I think that ultimately, you need to decide what you want to believe when it comes to this. But, for what it's worth? Perhaps her designing this helm - it was a gift for you. To finish what she knew she would never be able to finish."

His words settled over me in a numbing blanket. We were almost to my room when I spoke again, my voice very soft. "I didn't know her that well. When Kira got sick...she focused all on that. I mean, she ran the country, too. But when it came to spending time with me, teaching me. She stopped. And I understood. We didn't know if the medications and things were going to work with Kira, we didn't know how much time we had left with her. So, I don't blame Mom for spending every moment she could with her. I did the same. But there's this…tiny kernel of resentment inside of me. Resentment that she didn't spend even a little bit of time with me, that she thought that I'd always be around, and didn't even consider that she might not be around too."

Barloc slowed as we reached the door, and he watched me intently, absorbing what I was saying. "Nothing I say will make that feeling go away or make it better." He said, and his voice grew intense with his next words, "Johanna. When I came to your office the other day, after you had gotten angry at your father…and you opened the door and had been snapping Delain's name." He pursed his lips, and I recognized that same dangerous look to him. "I wanted to rip him in half. He had upset you, and my first instinct was to tear him apart."

I froze, eyes growing wide. "I…I don't know what to say to that," I admitted, feeling my cheeks go hot.

Barloc stepped closer to me, "I don't want to wait until after you fight Rozalin. Even if I think you'll be successful…even if I know you will. I don't want to wait for you. I know that's scary and you're not ready for that. And I will respect it. I will also respect it if you do not want me, and you want Delain instead. Even if I won't like that. But don't make the same mistake as your Mom did, thinking that others will be around when you might not be around."

I visibly winced, leaning back into my door. "Point made." I managed out, looking up to him. "Could it just be that I'm afraid? My Mom left this giant hole in the world when she died. It hit so many…and I don't want to leave a similar void."

He stepped closer to me, not touching but close enough for me to feel the heat radiating from him. His voice dropped an octave, "Johanna Maracroix, when your soul leaves this world, it will be felt across all the lands and seas. There will not be a being alive who won't feel it."

His words seared through me straight to my heart and I swallowed hard. "I don't know about that." I whispered.

He chuffed at that, shaking his head, "I do." He reached past me, opening the door and he let me step back into the room, staying in the doorway. "What will it be, My Queen?"

I stared at him, "We shouldn't…" I murmured as I took another step back.

"Not what I asked." He replied, stepping in now, just enough to close the door behind him. "What do you want?"

I knew exactly what he looked like under those clothes, muscled and broad and perfect. I didn't even have to imagine it, it flashed in my mind vividly and I felt the flush intensify. "I barely know you." I tried now.

He smirked, that golden gaze on mine with an intensity I had never seen from anyone before. I took another step back as he spoke again, "Not what I asked." He didn't move from his spot, but his presence took up so much of the room.

Swallowing, I took another step back. I knew where everything in my room was, but I still squeaked when my left thigh bumped against one of the small tables. "You can't just be attracted to me because…because I was the one that had a hand in you being found and hatching." I said, eyes wide. "You have barely met anyone!"

His smirk turned into a full grin, but it didn't seem to reach his eyes. "I don't need to meet anyone else, when my soul is tethered to yours. No one else matters to me, Johanna." There was a slight growl to his voice, and he stepped forward, only once, but it caused me to take several more steps back.

"Barloc, that's foolish. You surely don't mean that." I pressed, hands reaching back behind me until I found the edge of my bed. I took comfort in something solid behind me, because the whole room seemed to be moving because of this conversation. Or maybe it was the lack of sleep.

"You take me for a liar, Johanna?" he asked, stepping forward again. I had nowhere else to go, and he knew it. "You don't, even I know that. I knew from the moment I heard your voice; I felt your hand on my egg. That the Fates had kept me hidden and sleeping until you were ready for me. I was meant for no one else but you, Johanna Maracroix. My entire being belongs to you, and no one else. No one else will ever compare to you."

My breath hitched in my throat, and I stared up at him. I was completely and utterly speechless, I didn't have words. That frustrated the Hel out of me.

"Dragons call the connection a Compatible Link...the Spirit Ascended and Kitsunes call it Soul Mates. It is incredibly rare for Dragons to find it, especially so soon after hatching. But the Fates smiled on me, making sure that the one that hatched me would be my Compatible. I could never be with another if you live. Never." He stepped forward again, those long legs covering the ground to me effortlessly and easily. He was so close to me, and I was breathing hard, staring up at him. "Johanna Maracroix, you may die in the coming battles. Do not make the same mistake your Mother did. Do not put living aside on your quest for revenge. Live, as she would want to see you live."

His hand reached up and cupped my cheek, that damn smirk on his face again. I swallowed hard, bottom lip quivering just ever so slightly. "I don't know how." I murmured.

"Then let me show you." Barloc rumbled, and he tilted my head up more before he leaned down and caught my lips with his.

Where Delain's kiss had felt right, this kiss felt like a fire would burn me apart. There was nothing slow or gentle about it, Barloc's lips claiming my own, his tongue sweeping into my mouth and tangling with mine. His hand left my cheek, trailing down my body to land on my rear as he leaned down over me, laying me down on the bed. "Do you like these clothes?" he asked, his voice so deep and full of want.

I shook my head, though I didn't know why. I did like these clothes. I didn't get a chance to correct myself, because Barloc shredded them with a spell, leaving me in my underwear and bra. I closed my eyes, not wanting to see the look on his face as he saw me bare before him.

A thrum vibrated the air around him, one of pure feral approval as he leaned down, kissing along my jaw, down my neck to my chest. His hand cupped one of my breasts, and his teeth peeled the fabric away. I gasped as his mouth closed over my nipple, eyes popping open. His mouth was so warm, and everywhere his lips touched left a trail of heat and desperation for more. My hands were fisting the blanket below me, unsure of what to do with them.

I felt the smile on his lips as his tongue ran along the sensitive nub, and he switched sides, doing the same thing before he trailed further down my body, kneeling on the floor in front of me. His lips and teeth nipped at my hips, then my thighs, avoiding that heat of want building between my legs. I had heard some of the servants' murmur about these sorts of acts, long ago when I was younger and didn't understand it. Those indecent stories and how the servants had giggled and blushed over it flashed in my mind, and I opened my mouth to protest.

I didn't get a chance; his hands had reached up to pull my panties down my legs and he discarded them to the side. He leaned back in, spreading my thighs with his strong hands. That tongue spread my lower lips, and the growl that emerged from him rattled my bones and masked the strangled moan that slipped from me.

He teased and explored me, taking his time, that golden gaze flicking up to my face as he unravelled me. His teeth grazed against the bundle of nerves, and I had to bite my lip to suppress a loud moan and I flushed down to my chest. I felt one corner of his mouth lift in a smirk as he ran his tongue along that spo, swirling over it over and over again. Arcanis above, he was so good at this. He knew exactly where to touch, how firmly to grab my hips to keep me still. He would guide my legs up over his shoulders, letting me tug at his body with them desperately. Fuck, I had never thought pleasure like this was possible.

I had never felt so weightless, my hands curled in the blanket, my voice filling the room until I heard nothing else. My muscles grew more and more tense, legs quivering against his strong hands. I didn't process pleading with him, begging for more and more. His tongue started to flick across that bud, faster and faster. I cried out, hips bucking against his strong grasp as he forced me through my orgasm and past it, vision going dark as the intense pleasure rolled over and through me. I had to push him away with my feet when it became too much, panting hard.

He licked his lips, leaning back on his feet as he watched me, that smirk still on his face. "Absolute perfection…" He rumbled out in deep pleasure.

He moved up beside me, laying on his side and pulling me into him. He brushed his fingers through my hair gently, and he pressed a kiss to my forehead. "Sleep, my Queen." He murmured.

Even though I was acutely aware of his hardened length pressed against my hip, I fell into a deep sleep easily, so utterly exhausted from the past weeks and months.

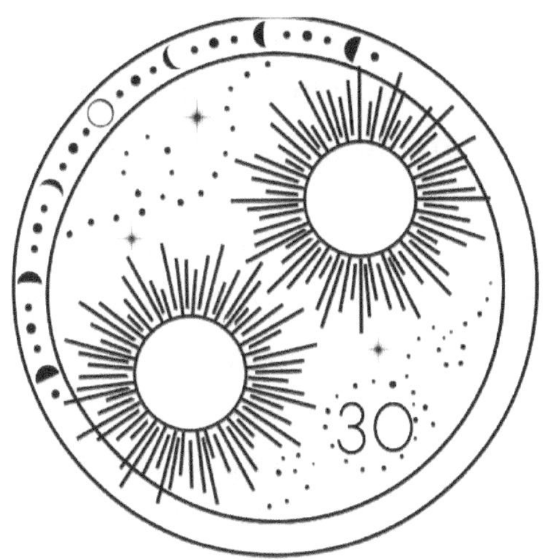

I woke to the sound of a banging fist on my door, and my eyes fluttered open. At first, I was thoroughly confused by the warm body beside me. No, not beside me, practically under me. I was not in Dedria's room; I was in mine. Then the memories of the previous night flooded back, and a flush rose to my cheek as I looked up and spotted Barloc's face. I was practically wrapped around him, my legs tangled with his, an arm slung over his abdomen.

Even in the darkness, I could see he was awake, and he had a sleepy grin on his face. "I'll shift." He said with a stifled yawn, and he did me the favour of peeling himself away, moving off of the bed and changing into his natural form, curling up on one of the plush rugs and hiding his face under a wing. His breathing slowed and deepened, and to anyone else he seemed asleep. Not me, though, I knew he was awake.

I crawled out of the bed and flicked on a few of the enchanted lamps, pulling a robe over my body as I went to the door and opened it. On the other side stood the General, and he looked just as tired as I was. "General." I greeted him, my voice still heavy with sleep, and he bowed to me. "What is it?"

"We have received a message from Lethiarum, Your Highness." He said, and he held out the folded paper. "Received over the radio twenty minutes ago...broad casted to every country."

I took it with a frown, glancing down to it, scanning the contents quickly and then up to him. "Thank you." I said, and I shut the door in his face. I barely heard his grunt of displeasure at being cut out of me reading it fully. As I turned back towards the inside of my room, Barloc had untangled himself and was watching me in his Dragon form. Even in that form, I saw the curiosity on his features. Quietly, I walked over to one of the couches and sat down, unfolding the paper and reading what was inside.

This is Isabella Malbora, broad casting from the country known as Lethiarum. Today at 18:23, King Ravan surrendered his country to the Spirit Ascended for the crimes committed against their people. Crimes of Slavery, Kidnapping, Rape and Murder. He will be executed for these crimes, with no trial, in three days at noon. Setsuna of the Plains will assume control of the country immediately, and Lethiarum will formally join the Ascended Lands. Any previous allies of Lethiarum who move to stand with the previous King will be considered enemies and we will react accordingly to any threats as acts of war. We thank Queen Johanna of Solaria for the aid of 5000 soldiers and equipment, as many on both sides of this battle would have died without their assistance. We mark Solaria as the first official ally of the United Republic of the Ascended, and hope many join them in the coming days as a stand against the horrific practices that Lethiarum and its people participated in.

I covered my mouth with one of my hands, reading it over

several times. My heart thudded so loud in my chest I heard it, and I closed my eyes. I heard the click of Barloc's talons on the floor before his head pressed against my side. No words, just a reassuring presence as I processed the news.

I didn't know how long I sat there, but the small clock on the desk read somewhere around 6 in the morning. "Barloc?" I said softly, looking down to his dragonic face.

He shifted back to his humanoid form, sitting on the couch beside me. "Yes, My Queen?" he asked, cupping my cheek to angle my face up to his. The fact that he was completely naked, again, didn't escape my notice, and it made me feel hot all over as I remembered what he had done only hours ago.

"How did we only sleep three hours?"

He laughed, deep and full as he scooped me up like I was nothing more than a doll, carrying me back to my bed and lying me down. "Sleep, My Queen." He said as he laid beside me, his lips against my temple.

Even though it felt impossible, with the news of Lethiarum and the knowledge of the blood that had been shed there, I fell into a troubled, restless sleep. A sleep full of nightmares and death.

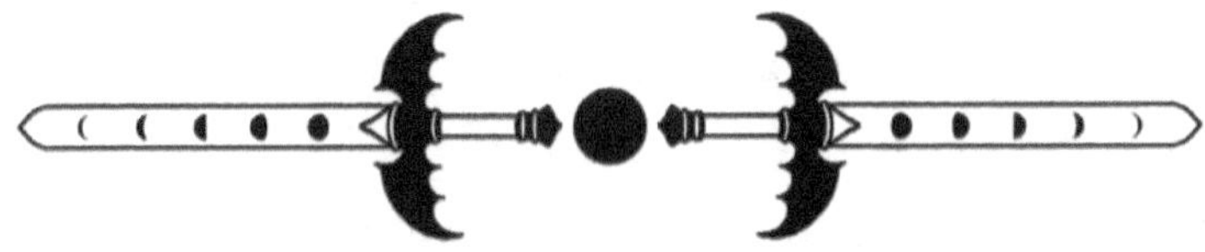

Barloc didn't allow anyone to disturb me, and I woke impossibly late. The clock read three in the afternoon when I finally woke, somehow, I felt more tired than I had before reading that letter, but for me to sleep until three in the afternoon?! I had missed all of my training, Court, meetings with different Lords and Ladies of Solaria. I scrambled out of bed, almost face planting into the floor when my legs got tangled in the top sheet and duvet. A warm pair of arms wrapped around me, pulling me into that warm broad chest. "Careful." Barloc's voice murmured into the shell of my ear, full of amusement. "I had Pendra clear your entire day and tell everyone you were sick."

I went hot with anger, spinning towards him and bringing a fist against his chest. "You had no right!" I snapped, glaring at him.

He didn't let me go, and that arrogant smirk crossed his face. "No, perhaps not. But you kept crying and screaming in your sleep and weren't resting properly. So, I told Pendra to do it. He didn't listen to me at first. I had to strong arm him into it before he eventually agreed."

I bristled at that, and I lifted my arm to hit him again. He caught my wrist with his hand, and he tilted his head, "Now, my Queen, I advise you stop hitting me because you're upset unless you would like me to hit you back." His tone was deep and gravelly and wholly suggestive, it made my heart quicken and my knees go weak.

"Let me go." I said, yanking my wrist from his grip and getting off his lap, stalking several feet away. "I slept a whole day away; I don't have the luxury of doing that!"

"Unfortunately for you, you cannot save the world when you are so exhausted you are falling asleep standing up. You need to rest and take care of yourself, and it has become very apparent to me that you are not doing that. So, I am being forced to make sure you do." Barloc countered and damn him if he wasn't right. I would be useless if I didn't sleep properly.

"You still don't get to decide that for me." I snapped, turning on him.

He crossed his arms over that chest, not moving from his spot on the bed. "I don't see anyone else doing it. Unless you would like me to step aside for Delain." The way he said Delain's name made the hair on the back of my neck stand on end. I knew suddenly there was nothing Barloc would hate more than Delain caring for me.

"I would rather neither of you, quite frankly." I answered sharply, crossing my own arms now. "I am perfectly capable of taking care of myself."

"That is debatable." He scoffed, and he scanned me up and down like a predator. "I think you are doing quite a terrible job at it, quite honestly. So, it seems we are at an impasse."

I lifted the corner of my lips in a sneer, "It seems so."

The silence built between us, and he broke first. "I asked for a few reports to be delivered regarding that Salem fellow as well. They are on your desk."

"Why would you do that?" I pressed, not moving and remaining perfectly still.

"Because I recall he wanted to defeat Rozalin as well and offered to train you. And you said it was up to him to earn your trust. So, according to the reports, that is exactly what he has been trying to do for the past two days." He explained, and he watched me so intently I felt bare.

Or maybe, I realized, it was because I was practically naked. Perhaps his gaze wasn't heated with aggression to make sure I cared for myself, but from want. My heart fluttered remembering the pleasure he had given me last night. I unconsciously bit my bottom lip as I watched him, wondering what other pleasures he could give me. A knowing smile spread on his face, his golden eyes practically sparkling, practically begging me to go to him.

With a flush I instead went to my closet and dressing space, pulling on a pair of leggings and a sweater before emerging and going to my desk. I picked up the reports, stopping to stick my head out to the hall to ask the two Guards to please ask the kitchen staff to make me some tea and food and bring it to Barloc and I. I settled back into the couch, all under Barloc's ever watchful gaze, and flipped open the reports while pointedly ignoring him. I had to ignore him, because I could still feel how it had felt to sit on his lap when he had pulled me back in towards him before I had fallen asleep again. How hot his body had been, pressed against my back and thighs. And the unmistakable hardness that had been there, too.

It seemed, in the very short time Salem Ortega had been held in the dungeons of Solaria, that he had been nothing but compliant and willing. He had no complaints over how he was treated; he did not grimace or growl or protest. Any question asked of him regarding Rozalin Heart and Nox had been answered without hesitation and to the fullest extent of his knowledge.

I scanned through each question and answer, carefully catalogued and recorded. He provided exact geographical locations of bases Nox had operated from. Names of Chronomancers that had joined the cause, and where each of them had been from. But any questions about him had remained unanswered, and all he ever said was that was something I would have to ask him.

Grudgingly I rose to a stand, the food and tea had been

delivered nearly an hour ago and I had eaten my fill. Barloc had eaten the rest. I glanced to him, he was sitting in one of the chairs reading one of my many books, "I can't hope that you will stay here?"

His scoff was answer enough, and I merely rolled my eyes, collecting the reports and leaving without another word. I made my way down the halls to the various lifts that brought us to the bottom most level of the tower, to the fourth quadrant that held cell after cell, barely illuminated by the enchanted lights. Pockets of darkness lingered in each cell, and even if the bodies of the occupants were held in shadow, I could still spot their eyes piercing, following me. A few hissed or sneered at the sight of me, but none dared say a thing.

I was sure it was because of Barloc's hulking form following just behind me, of those fire gold eyes meeting each gaze that dared even breathe wrong in my direction. For now, I ignored it, gliding through the corridors until I was brought to one block of cells that were more illuminated than the rest, with larger beds, a desk, even afforded paper and charcoal and books on request. Salem had been given some luxury since he had turned himself in, but I knew he still wore the restrictors that would block his magic.

Most of these cells were empty, thankfully, and I counted each door they passed. Fifty-six before we got to the one with Salem Ortega inside.

He was sitting on his bed, his back against the wall, a book in his lap. His gaze lifted to me the moment I came into view.

"Your Highness. I did not expect your presence today." He said, and he moved off the bed with a grace that could only be earned from the many centuries he had been alive. It was absolutely unnerving, how smooth each of his movements were, how purposeful. The only being I had seen with such grace had been Kayori.

"I've been reading through your answers." I said, and I lifted the file of reports. "I couldn't help but notice every question about you was only answered with me having to ask you."

Salem gave a slight nod, and his gaze flicked to Barloc though it was so quick I almost missed it. I had a feeling I only saw it because he allowed me to see it. "Because you deserve to hear it coming from me, not written on a page."

"Very well." I lifted a hand, and two guards carried over a table, and another carried over a chair for me to sit on. "Let's talk."

Salem's lips barely lifted in a smirk, and he pulled the chair that sat at his desk over in front of the bars of the cell, sitting down across from me. "Then ask away."

I watched him carefully, "Tell me about the Chronomancer Guild."

He tensed and went very still, enough for me to see it. It was like he had stopped breathing from ho still he was. "The Guild was nothing more than a way for Taranor to train killers to further their own agenda." His tone was crisp and cold.

"How long had you been a part of it, before everything happened?"

"Long enough." He was content to leave it at that, but from my silence, he lifted a lip in a silent snarl and continued. "My powers manifested when I was 14. Young, especially for a Chronomancer. I was sent there by my parents shortly after it happened. By some fate of the gods, my three siblings were also Chronomancers, and they followed within three years after I was there."

That satisfied me, and I gave a slight nod. I was writing these answers down. "What was it like there? How were lessons structured?"

"Do not tell me you plan to follow the original when it comes to building your own Guild." His gaze narrowed, and that piercing gaze flicked to Barloc who let out a low growl.

"I don't know what I plan to follow, as I don't know what would be suitable yet. Which is why I'm seeking to know what it was like originally." My tone was dismissive and uncaring for his judgment. I had no actual intention to follow in the original Chronomancy Guild's footsteps, if Salem's stories were true. Still, I needed to know how to not do things.

Salem relented, "It was...unforgiving. Mistakes meant being beaten. Anything less than perfection, anything less than the utmost control over the powers we had was considered failure. We all had to learn jumping, to learn double, triple or quadruple jumps. To slow and increase time, even in the smallest of spaces. We all had to learn necromancy. Often times we had to kill something - someone and bring them back. Over and over again."

I involuntarily shuddered at that, Necromancy, a horrible practice. To harness the soul of a being, any being, and to bring it back to a mortal form. It was unnatural. Even Osian, the God of Death, scowled upon it. "Was there...typical guild structures?"

He shook his head, "I believe you mean apprentice, journeyman, master. No, there was no such thing. Either you were the student, or the teacher. Or...as I preferred to say, a survivor or the abuser. Not everyone survived." His gaze was hard as the very rock that held the Obsidian Tower together, and just as cold.

"It doesn't mean much, but I'm sorry." I whispered, and I knew he believed me. That I was sorry for what had happened to him, even if I had no part in it.

"I appreciate that anyway."

"What else happened in those halls?"

"Rozalin had a sister, Beth. They were close as anything...but where Rozalin was a fighter, one that would burn the world, Beth was gentle and wanted peace. Beth didn't survive. That's what broke her, I think. Finding her sister dead. She was the equivalent of a master by then, she could have used Necromancy to bring Beth back...if only for a little while. But she couldn't...no. She didn't want to. She buried Beth off of the Guild grounds and went on a rampage. She killed twenty of the teachers and admin staff before she was stopped. Though they didn't kill her. No, they took her away. Next time I saw her she was...she wasn't the same. It was like they had taken the very essence that made Rozalin...Rozalin and removed it and left a blood thirsty killing machine. They could point, and she would kill anything in her way.

"After that, she started training me. I started seeing glimpses of her from before, and I held out hope that she was still in there. I kept with it, trying to bring her back, make her remember. I tried to resist the necromancy lessons, doing the bare minimum. One day I walked into the training hall for our session. She wasn't there...one of the other Masters was. And so were all of my siblings. Except they were in chains. The Master told me that I had to choose. To accept my powers, or to leave my parents totally childless. And then they killed them. All three of my siblings, in one motion. My two brothers and sister." His voice, Arcanis, it sounded dead.

Silence hung between us, the weight of it heavy. I worried my bottom lip, feeling the weight of what had been said weigh on me. "Salem…"

He pressed on, like a soldier going to war, recollecting all of these memories. "I don't remember bringing them back, but I did. In my anguished state, I…I tethered their souls to me. I can bring them back whenever. Wherever. Their souls will never be at peace for as long as I live. I can't undo it. Because I have no idea how I did it in the first place."

I had to put the fountain pen down, staring at him, tears forming in my eyes. I couldn't help it. I would have done the same with Kira, in his position. With my mother. "Salem."

He looked up to me finally, having looked down to his hands part way through. His gaze was a mix of sorrow, deep and unending, and a spark of something I knew all too well - determination. "That's why I have to be sure you're different…that's why I have to have a hand in this Guild you're forming, if you'll have me. I was 19 when my siblings were slaughtered, and I bound them to me. After that happened, I became just like Rozalin. The last part of me was broken. They had shown me if I didn't fall in line, they would take everything from me. And they didn't even hesitate. Three other Chronomancers, all powerful in their own right, gone. To send me a message. It took me hundreds of years in a stasis state to rebuild myself, to repair what they had broken. So, when I heard, you were going to teach other Chronomancers? That you were going to offer them an opportunity to learn? You understand why I had to come here, don't you? To protect them? Rozalin is repeating history, and I can't stop her - but you? You can. If you let me train you, you can. You can stop it. Stop her. Stop the cycle where I failed."

I just nodded, "Okay." I said, and I lifted my hand for the guards again. "Please release Salem Ortega from his cell." I said, voice barely a whisper but they had no issues hearing. Barloc's growl emerged from behind me, and he stepped up behind me, bending down to whisper into my ear. His warm breath cascading down my cheek and neck.

"Is this wise? He could be fooling you..."

Salem's gaze snapped to Barloc, "I am not fooling anyone. She can keep me in chains and with these inhibitors on me for all I care. She doesn't even have to let me out of this cell unless she's ready to train with me. If there is one thing, I have learned about Her Grace is that she will do nothing unless she wants to."

Barloc let out a snarl, lip lifting in a feral way as he straightened to his full height. "I did not ask you."

"You are both exhausting." I cut in, before Salem could reply. "Barloc, yes, I am quite sure. No, I will not allow him to walk without the inhibitors on. But, for now, he can be removed from the cell and put in more...hospitable lodgings under guard until tomorrow when we will train." My tone was one of exhaustion, of being tired of everyone always questioning me. At least Salem had stood up for me, which admittedly was perplexing since I had him in a fucking cell right now.

Barloc scanned my face, but he relented and nodded, "Apologies, my Queen."

I rose to a stand, brushing invisible lint and dust off my sweater. "You're not sorry, but I don't expect you to be. Do it again, however, and I will give you a reason to be." I smirked as I sauntered past him, giving him a wink as I did.

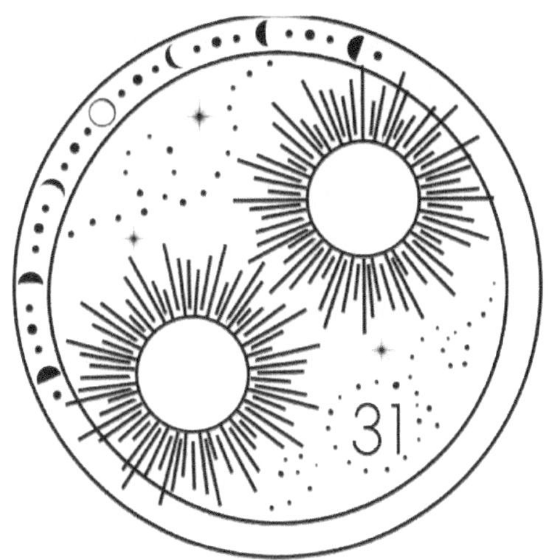

s I walked into the training hall three days later - that was the soonest Salem agreed to start training me, though he had watched me and Dedria train. He had said, with no uncertainty, that watching how I trained and moved and fought was the only way he could see what I needed to learn if I wanted to beat Rozalin. While irritating, I understood the logic to what he was saying and had agreed.

As I strode into the room, Salem was already there, holding a practice stick in each hand. He stood with that same unnatural stillness he always had, watching my every move even if his gaze never shifted from my face. I felt small in front of him. Not like I felt small compared to Barloc, where he towered over me, but small as in Salem was centuries older, with multiple lifetimes of experience and horrors behind him. I held myself taller, pushing my shoulders back and lifting my head higher.

"Good morning, Salem." I greeted.

Salem nodded in greeting, which was about as much respect as I figured I'd get from him. "As I mentioned...we will start with training just you in the mornings, and then I will train Miss Heart in the afternoons for the next few days, and then you will train together against me." He tossed me the stick, which I caught easily. "Your goal for this morning is to hit me with that."

I blinked at him, adjusting my grip on one end of the stick. "I just have to...hit you, with this?" I asked, properly confused.

He didn't even bother saying anything, he just nodded in confirmation. That made me more irritated than anything else. I darted forward, aiming the stick for his side, and he moved aside fluidly, avoiding it with a wide margin.

I kept going, always on the offensive and Salem on the defensive. No matter how hard I tried, I was never able to land a hit. By the time the three hours was up, I was drenched in sweat and frustrated beyond belief. I had even used Chronomancy, using what skills I had mastered to try and hit him, and I had still failed. More infuriatingly, he hadn't even broken a fucking sweat.

"I don't understand, Dedria and I were able to land a few hits on Rozalin - we disarmed her! But if she's anything like you, we shouldn't have been able to do that." I panted, dropping the stick as I stumbled over to the side counter that had a sink and glasses, getting myself a glass and practically drowning myself as I drank all of it.

"She let you hit her." Salem said solemnly, approaching me with ease so he was only a few feet away verse across the hall. "To boost your confidence, only to obliterate you in the final confrontation."

I couldn't help the dread that sunk into my gut. "She would let us hit her?" My disbelief was thick in my voice, and I hated that I didn't mask it in front of him.

He nodded, "Yes. Rozalin was an exceptional fighter. One of the best, only Chronomancers, and the Late Queen Maria could stand against her."

I worried my bottom lip, refilling my glass and drinking it more slowly this time. "What if I had Maria's skill while being a Chronomancer?"

"I suspect you would stand a better chance then." He didn't look confused, that mask holding, but there was a very slight confused note in his voice.

I put the cup down, a new flood of determination filling me, striding past him and picking up the stick and turning back to him. "Then let's try again."

Salem turned as I had walked past him, "Your Majesty, I don't want to push you."

That feeling of dread ebbed away to the burn of irritation, "I didn't ask." I said, sharper than I intended. Nothing I could do about that now.

He sighed but relented, striding to take his defensive stance in the middle of the room. I saw now that he had a similar stance to Rozalin, with an air of ease and confidence that hung in the air around him.

I practically prowled to a space ten feet from him. Taking a few deep breaths, I centred my mind, and dug through my pool of mana before finding that little kernel that unlocked the power of the Archons. Mentally I brushed up against it, and felt it open to me.

"Hello dear." Maria's voice sounded in my head, and I couldn't help but smile as Maria's power flowed through and around me, that ethereal armor forming as I looked to Salem. His face betrayed nothing; all he did was give a subtle nod to tell me he was ready.

I charged forward with a renewed energy, my mind flooded

with the knowledge of Maria's training, and Salem managed to only dodge twice before I caught him in the thigh with the stick hard enough to bruise. I couldn't help but let out a whoop as I stepped back from him with a smile and let the connection with Maria fade.

Salem scanned me, "I knew you were the Ash Queen, but seeing it is different." He admitted, "I believe, if you keep that connection during your final conflict with Rozalin, then you will probably stand a chance...but our focus still needs to be training you, and your mind. Not having Maria's knowledge help you. And you being able to hit her won't mean anything if she puts Dedria down."

That cold feeling of dread bloomed again, "I won't let her take Dedria from me too." I bit out, my expression and gaze hardening.

"No, I suspect you will try very hard to make that true. I suspect Dedria is far more advanced in Chronomancy than you are - she has been in her powers longer and comes from the Heart family. That being said, Rozalin has always been a weapon first and a person second. All her training has centred around killing others, that is not the case for the two of you. Your combined weaknesses far outweigh hers - it will be my job to minimize those weaknesses as much as possible, while showing you all of hers."

I watched him intently as he speaks, recalling one thing he had told me back in that Throne room. "And you are sure you can have such a direct hand in killing her? You love her."

He pursed his lips, looking down to the floor before he looked back up at me, a fire burned in his eyes. "I loved the woman she was - not the woman she now is. The woman I loved died a long time ago."

I couldn't help the frown that crossed my features, "I am sorry, Salem." I said softly.

He just nodded, "Yeah. So am I."

An uncomfortable silence filled the air between us, and I sighed softly, putting my practice stick back in the basket where the others were. "Would you like to join my Court for lunch?" I offered suddenly, turning back to look at him.

"I appreciate the offer, Your Majesty, but I think it would be best if I don't. I don't think many in your Court are fond of me. Normally that wouldn't bother me, but I think for now it's important I keep my distance. At least for now." Salem moved forward as he spoke, returning the stick he was holding before he sauntered from the hall.

I firmly tamped down the disappointment, sauntering out of the hall and taking a quick stop for a hot bath in my room since I was sticky with sweat from the training session, changing into a deep teal gown before I went to the dining hall. I heard the members of my court - my friends, before I got to the door. Dedria and Delain arguing about something foolish, Bevy and Kira giggling to each other, Barloc talking to Tyne who must have been pulled away from my lab by Bevy. I knew too in the many floors below me, all the citizens of Solaria were bustling, eating lunch or shopping or working or learning. It wasn't just about Mother anymore, defeating Rozalin. It was about my country, all the other countries, my unlikely friends across the seas. About Yeska and her empire, about the Ascended and their newfound freedom from Slavery, about Kayori and her many daughters.

The weight of it all pressed down on me suddenly, and I had to put a hand on the wall beside me to keep upright. It was stifling, but inhaling deeply, I straightened and strode into the dining hall with a smile pasted on my face. I knew Dedria saw some of the stress in my gaze - Dedria knew me better than anyone. I was grateful when she didn't say anything, only slid over on the bench to make room beside her. "Come on, the chefs wanted to make some of the Ascended cuisine from when Setsuna and Tianie were here. I guess they spent the past few months sourcing all the spices. It's so good, it's like I'm back there with them." Dedria grinned.

I sat on the bench, sandwiched between Dedria and Kira. I didn't think, in that moment, there was anywhere I would rather be. I noticed Kira sipping at a cup of purple hued water and suspected that was the Burnberry Bloom tea. "I can't wait." I offered and reached forward to start dishing up a plate I had been passed by Tyne who sat across from me. As promised, the food was excellent. Maybe not as good as when we had traveled with Setsuna, but food always seemed to taste better when eaten under the open sky. That, and Tianie and Setsuna had years of experience cooking that food, verse the chefs that were just taking translated, written instruction on how to cook various dishes.

Still, we all ate our fill, and we were all deeply content after. So content that we barely even spoke. Dedria broke the silence first, "I shouldn't have eaten so much...training with Salem is going to suck."

Laughter blossomed from me, unable to help myself. "Yeah, the whole task for the day is hitting him with one of the practice sticks. Not even a sword, a stick."

Dedria pretended to gag, "Arcanis above, I can't imagine a

worse Hel."

"Well, that's it. I wasn't able to do it without channeling Maria." I smirked. I looked forward to seeing Dedria struggle too, honestly. Not that I would ever admit that to her.

That caused my friend to groan and lean her head on my shoulder, "This better be worth it." She grumbled, staying that way for a few long moments before she peeled herself away from me and off the bench, leaving the room with a grunt.

Kira glanced to Bevy, then Tyne, "Can Bevy stay and play with me this afternoon?" She pleaded.

Tyne gave a slight shrug, "I do not see the harm in that, do you, Your Grace?" She asked, looking to me.

I shook my head in response, "No, I don't. Though it won't be all playing - you have lessons with your tutors, Kira. Bevy can attend them with you."

The two girls grinned to each other and fast as lightning they scrambled off the benches and out of the room with squeals and giggles.

Not wanting to be left alone with Barloc or Delain, I quickly turned, slipping off the bench and nodded to the men, leaving the room without another word. I had to get to the throne room to hold Court anyways.

My feeling of dread never eased fully, even as the day progressed. I was about to call for the end of the petitioners when Castian walked in. "Mister Wesner." I said, scanning him over.

As he approached the dais, I noticed how dusty he was, like he hadn't had time to get ready to be in front of me. That wasn't right, he was always in his best clothes when here. He was breathing hard, too, like he had just been running. His face was a mix of worry and anxiety.

"What is wrong, Castian?" I asked, that feeling of dread tightening in my stomach, ready to explode.

He looked up to me, "My team and I were going through the desert to a ruins location we read about in one of the books we found. About 200 kilometers from here. But as we got close, we felt dozens of auras, so we got as close as we dared. The ruins had been uncovered. Nox is here, Your Royal Highness."

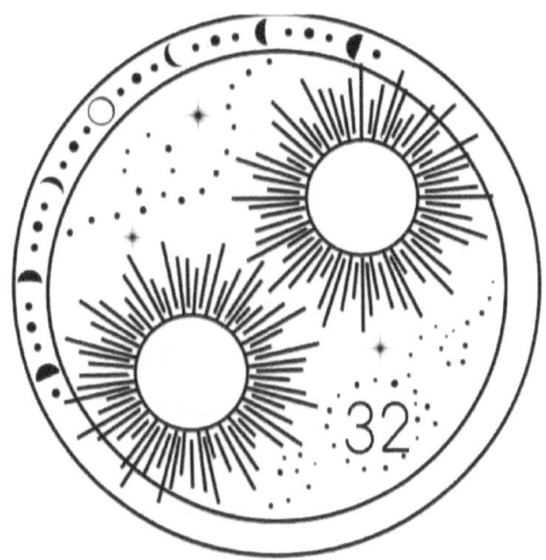

I didn't hear anything else Castian might have said, the roaring in my head drowned everything else out. I barely remembered rising to a stand and striding away from the throne, heading straight to the training hall where Salem and Dedria were supposed to be, barking to one of the guards to fetch Tyne and the prototype helms at once. Instructing another to get the General of my armies.

The roaring in my head didn't stop until I walked into the training halls and saw Salem and Dedria sparring actively. But as soon as I walked in, they stopped and turned to me.

My face must have betrayed me, because they both dropped their practice blades and waited for me to speak.

"Nox is here." I managed to get out. "In Solaria...at a ruins in the desert."

Dedria glanced to Salem, "We're going to need your help."

Salem simply nodded, a rueful smile spreading on his lips, "Get me armor and a blade, and my will is yours."

"Let's go." I breathed, and the power of the Archons stirred inside of me as I turned heel and walked, not ran, to the lifts that would bring us down to the armory. "Get Barloc." I told another Guard.

I didn't know why, but I wanted, no, needed Barloc there, with me on that battlefield. Maybe it was the knowledge of what Dragon fire could do, or that he had promised me that he was with me, always. Maybe it was just my mind doing the math, and any extra brute force would be needed against even the smallest force of Chronomancers. Because no matter how many trained soldiers I brought, they were outnumbered and outmanned.

I knew the odds were never in my favour since she learned about Nox, but odds weren't something I believed in anyways. Not in this case, it was always going to come down to determination - and compared to Rozalin, I had way more to loose. I was, and would, always fight harder. I had so many to save. So many relying on me.

Failure was never an option.

Barloc joined us wordlessly at the doors to the armoury, as did the General.

I grabbed my armor, the burnished metal with the sigil, the snake coiled around a sword mouth open, of the Monarchy on it. I put it on wordlessly, not needing help as Dedria started to get into her own. "Find Salem armour and a weapon. I need half the fighters Yeska sent. And ten of the all terrain vehicles. Barloc, you'll be in the air. You can breathe fire, right?" He answered me with a rumbling laugh of confirmation.

I turned to the General, "There is a chance I do not return from this." I spoke plainly and evenly. "Even if I don't, I will bring Rozalin Heart down. That is not in question. Keep my sister safe. She is the future of this country if I fall. Do not, under any circumstances, General, fail her."

He saluted me, "Of course, your Grace." He barked an order to another soldier in the room who dashed off. Probably to get those soldiers from the Trussam Empire, and to get the vehicles ready.

Just ten, Tyne sprinted in, carrying two helms with a perfectly mirrored surface. She was panting, and sweat was on her brow. "I...Your Grace." She said, holding out one of the helms.

I took it and slid it on. I could see everything, there were no blind spots. I slid it off, "Thank you, Tyne." I stepped forward and put a hand on her shoulder. "Keep my sister safe, you can find the cure for her illness. When it is found, the cure will be free to all who need it, Solarian or not. Be sure that happens. Keep being brilliant, Tyne." Words unspoken, the knowledge that I may never see her again hanging in the air.

Tyne's bottom lip quivered, her face flooded with emotion, but she nodded and bowed. "It has been an honor, My Queen."

It was Salem who broke the tentative silence, "We should go."

Dedria, Barloc, Salem and I all looked between each other, and we wordlessly left the room. Tense silence hung between us as we wound through the halls to the main lift that would lower us down to the ground.

As we stepped off, the immediate area around had been cleared and soldiers in uniform were rushing around, relaying commands in calm but hurried tones. I was grateful that none stopped to salute or wish me well. My group was directed to one of the armored vehicles, and Salem, Dedria and I climbed in.

Barloc stood on the ground, and in a flash of blinding light he was in his true dragon form, and he took to the air, flying up above the massive walls into the open air with a roar that absolutely made Soldiers and the Citizens pause.

Within ten minutes, the vehicles were rolling out of the massive gates of Solaria, directions obtained by Castian.

I finally broke the silence, watching the dunes roll past them. "Whatever happens, we must kill Rozalin. No matter what - she must die."

Dedria smirked cockily, but it didn't reach her eyes, "Yeah, well we won't be dying with her. That isn't an option. You're going to grow old with me, bitch. You don't have a choice on that, alright?"

I just reached over, gripping one of Dedria's hands as the silence filled the space again. The only sounds were the tires rolling over the ground, the engines powered by shards of Ground Zero.

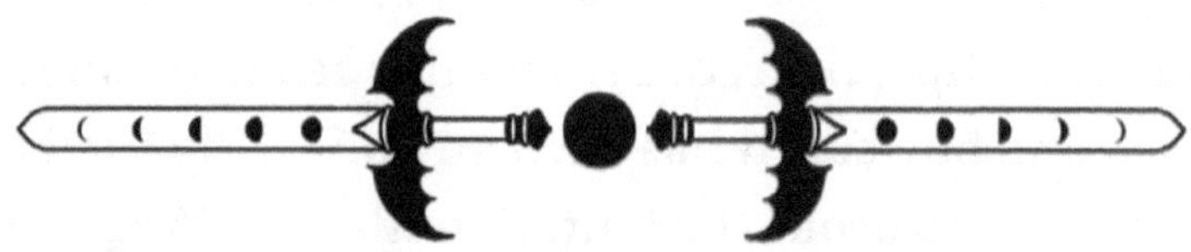

We felt it first, the pulse of Rozalin's dark aura as we closed in on the distance. Barloc flew far above us, looking like a bird from this distance. The vehicles slowed and stopped; the soldiers all grim as they climbed out of the vehicles. Even though the warriors from the Trussam Empire were renown for being some of the best in the world, who knew how they would stand against Chronomancers.

I looked to them as they took formation, "I know you are here on order of your Empress. The Trussam and Maracroix family have stood side by side for generations, and you being here, so far from your families and home and comforts that you know means more than you know. I know I am asking you to walk into a fight you may not walk from, one that I may not walk away from, but beating Rozalin and Nox is something the world depends on. She seeks to destroy everything you know and love, from Solaria to Taranor to your very own Empire. She won't stop, not unless we stop her. If you fall today, you will have done so knowing that your friends and family are safe. You will be remembered for generations as the last guard against Rozalin Heart."

Despite my best efforts, my speech felt hollow. Still, I summoned the Soul Forge blade, grateful for the weight and balance of it. "Salem, Dedria and I will go in first. You will follow - and Barloc will follow that with his fire."

All two hundred and fifty of them hit their sword to shield in confirmation, and I turned to Salem and Dedria. "Let's go." I breathed, and the three of us turned and climbed the dune, cresting it to see the Ruins that had been cleared, and the unnatural darkness that clung to it despite the Suns that still hung in the air.

Salem spun his blade in his hand and let loose his aura. It felt thick on my skin, and made me impossibly cold despite the heat, and he triggered a spell that brought forward three ethereal figures. His siblings, I realized. I was not filled with horror at the sight, but I couldn't place what I did feel. Sadness? Anger? A mix of both? He glanced to me and nodded before he disappeared from the top of the dune. I tracked him to the outskirts of the ruins, and the only way I knew he was doing what he had promised was the many auras that filled the area started to blink out of existence. One after another, auras disappeared.

Dedria shrugged, and she launched down the dune with me following behind her, the two of us darting to the left most side.

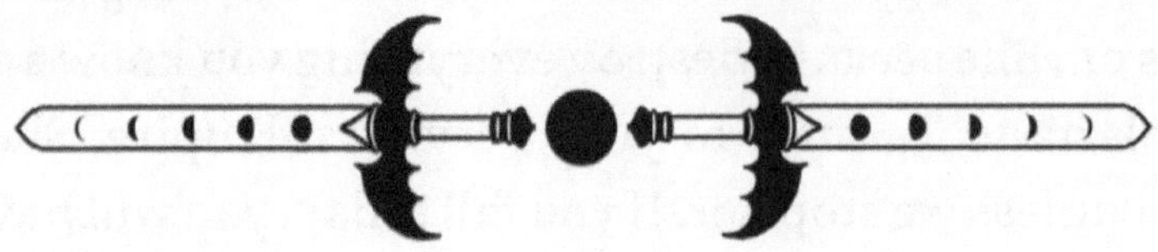

Finding Rozalin was quicker than I thought it would be, the heat of Dragon Fire burning hot behind me, the sounds of the fighting loomed around me. It was getting louder now, more shouts of alarm, of swords clashing, sometimes the wail of death. I blocked it out, I had to. I had lost Dedria at one point, separated by a few members of Nox. Dedria had shouted for me to keep going, and I had. Though being away from her, it was tearing something apart inside of me.

Rozalin Heart sat in one of the largest buildings in the ruins, the Ember in the centre of a circle of ancient script drawn in blood. As I stepped into the space, Rozalin smirked. "Took you long enough to find me, Ash Queen. But you are too late...the Lords of Hel will walk this plane again and will destroy the systems that destroyed me." She looked back to me and rose to a stand. Her eyes were sunken, her face gaunt. She looked frailer than before, her veins on her arms black. The clothes she wore were dirty, torn. She almost looked like the corpses she could rise from the ground.

I slipped the helm down my face, "No, not if I have anything to do with it." I murmured, harnessing Maria's powers and charging forward. Rozalin caught my blade with her own, the shriek of metal filling the space. Despite how she looked, she was still fast. Really fucking fast.

Rozalin grinned at me, but it was cruel and hateful. "Not likely. It's already started, Ash Queen. You can't stop this."

Maria's voice didn't appear in my head, it didn't need to. I just knew how to move, and I could tell the Helm was working, too, because I managed to catch Rozalin on her left thigh with my sword. Thank fucking Arcanis for that. These helms were all possibility, we were never going to get a chance to field test them until this moment. Maria's knowledge flooded through me, and I knew then that Rozalin's left side was her most vulnerable.

However, I couldn't ignore the growing power at the center of the room with the Ember and that strange script. Whatever was going to happen, it would be soon. I needed to move faster.

I caught Rozalin's blade with my own as Rozalin made a swing for my head. Gritting my teeth, I shoved back, spinning my blade to try and disarm Rozalin.

Frustratingly, Rozalin kept hold of her blade, using the momentum to try for an upswing at my chest. I leapt back, the shriek of sword on armour filling the space before snarling to myself before I lunged forward again. We kept like this, this what felt like endless back and forth. Exchanging blow for blow.

I didn't know how much time had passed, the only way to track each passing moment was from the clash of the swords, though the power building from the Ember was making my head ache. Finally, I managed to cut through Rozalin's Achilles tendon which forced Rozalin down to her knees.

Rozalin's grin was still that savage one she had at the start of this, and I lifted the helm to look her in the eye properly. "Go ahead, Ash Queen. Cut my head off, succeed where your ancestor failed...but know that you didn't save the world. It's happening...The world is going to change." She laughed, it was awful, filling my throat with bile.

Still, I didn't hesitate, driving my sword through Rozalin's smile in a scream of brutality.

[355]

The Ember flickered, and I realized too late that Rozalin must have been feeding it mana through the whole fight - and killing Rozalin only triggered it.

I spun on the ball of my foot, charging out of the building and shouting for Salem, for Dedria, for the Soldiers to get out. I barely made it fifteen meters before the explosion.

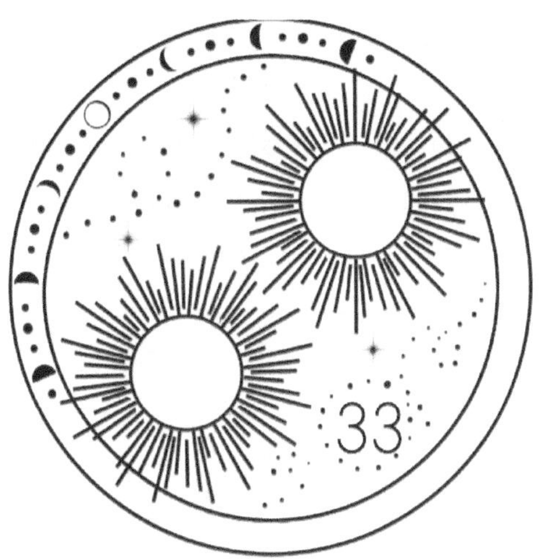

My ears were ringing, and I felt hot sand under me. My vision was blurred as I tried to open my eyes, forcing myself up to look around. "Dedria?" I called, "Salem? Barloc?" Or I thought I was speaking, my tongue felt like it was saying the words, but I couldn't hear myself. My head felt like it was going to explode, and I couldn't hear a damn thing except the ringing.

I rubbed my eyes, trying to clear my vision. A dark shadow passed over me, and the ground shook. Barloc, that had to be Barloc landing beside me. My vision cleared just enough to make out the blurry shape of the Dragon. Relief flooded my veins, he was alive. He was safe. But I still needed to find Dedria, and Salem. I tried to stand but felt I couldn't. I couldn't gain purchase on the sand, too weak, too unstable. Fuck.

Barloc's snout nudged me back down, and it was only through his telepathy that I heard his voice. "Stay sitting. That explosion threw you two hundred meters. I had to catch you with magic. It's a miracle you're alive. I'll find Dedria and Salem."

I nodded, or I thought I nodded. His shadow slipped away from me, and I stayed sitting. The bone deep ache sunk in, and my vision slowly started to clear. I zoned out, staring up at the blue sky.

A hand grabbed mine, and I looked over. Dedria, it was Dedria. I started to sob, lunging at Dedria and hugging her so fiercely I was sure I might break a bone or two on both of us. I still couldn't hear a damn thing; the ringing was still present. We sat like that, holding onto each other, both relieved that the other was alive.

Barloc returned with Salem some time later, and most of the soldiers. By that time, the ringing was gone, but there was an unease settled over all of us. Finally, Dedria and I pulled apart, looking toward the ruins.

That was when I saw it. Five stories tall, and just as wide. A swirling, black and purple mass. Dedria broke the silence first, "What the fuck is that?"

Barloc shifted back to his humanoid form, not caring about his nudity. "That...is a portal. To another realm."

Dread filled my stomach, and I wanted to vomit, and I looked to Dedria. "I failed." I whispered.

My best friend just shook her head, "No, you didn't."

We remained there, staring at the portal until the suns started to fall in the sky. I finally looked to the Soldiers, "A group of you, return to Solaria. Tell them what is here...and that we need to set up a containment area."

Ten of them nodded and turned, heading to the vehicles to do just that.

I looked back to the portal, and my gut tightened as a figure walked through.

Acknowledgement

I absolutely would not have been able to write this book without the endless encouragement of my husband. My biggest cheerleader and supporter, when I told him I was finally going to write this book, he asked when it'd be done for him to read it.

I also absolutely would not have been able to finish this book without my friends turned test readers - from pointing out larger flaws, to tiny errors, this wouldn't have become the book you are all reading today.

And as I said in the beginning, dear reader, this book wouldn't be here if not for the possibility of you. This story has been something living within me for over a decade, and finally being able to put it to paper, with the hopes that it would find those that need Johanna and her journey the most was what fueled me in those dark moments of writers block. Don't worry - her story isn't over yet. If anything, it's only just begun.

About The Author

Jolene C. Pitts
Jolene lives in British Columbia, Canada, with her husband, son and many pets. Between spending time with her family, writing and working her full-time job, she consumes books at near breakneck speeds. She also enjoys playing a variety of video games, and rewatching some of her favorite shows for the millionth time.

You can find Jolene C. Pitts on Instagram & Threads (jolenecpitts_author).
or at
https://www.jolenecpitts.com/